Evan

spencer mclean

This is a work of fiction. Names, characters, places, and incidents either are the product of the author's imagination or are used fictitiously. Any resemblance to actual events, locales, organizations, or persons, living or dead, is entirely coincidental and beyond the intent of either the author or the publisher.

EVAN. Copyright © 2010 by Spencer McLean All rights reserved. Self-published via CreateSpace.com. No part of this book may be used or reproduced in any manner whatsoever without the express written permission of the author except in the case of brief quotations embodied in critical articles and reviews. For information contact mail@spencermclean.com or visit the author's website at www.spencermclean.com.

Cover design by Chris Stewart

ISBN: 1456483242
ISBN-13: 9781456483241

LCCN:

For Those Who Are Fearlessly Themselves

ACKNOWLEDGMENTS

First, to the strong women in my life who have made me who I am: Blanche, Carolyn, Helen, Leanne, without your guidance and example, this novel would not have been possible.

To Sandie McLean, who gave me my name and my life. Without your love, perseverance and sacrifice, I would not have a future.

To Amy, my dearest friend, for being critic, editor, cheerleader, and faithful intellectual companion. Without you, very little would be possible.

To Chris for the cover and to Jamie for the feedback, without you this book would be a shadow of itself.

And finally, thank you to all the Carters and the Johnnys of the world, people unafraid to speak their minds no matter the consequences. Without you, we would not be free.

PROLOGUE

The world is rain.

Thick sheets of it tumble mercilessly from a blackened sky, lashing at the runner as he plunges down a confusion of rubbled streets, crooked alleys, and forgotten passages. Twice now he's spent breath he cannot afford, on prayers to a god he cannot feel, for just a moment's reprieve from the water filling his filthy boots and pouring into his stinging eyes. Nothing... on and on it comes. And through it, with the grace of a wolf and the will of the wind, the Demon still hunts him, blacker even than this alien sky.

Its boot falls are thunder in the Runner's ears, drowning out the suffering of his hammering heart. Has he gained any ground? Desperate to know, he pivots right, hard, peeking over his good shoulder before diving down another abandoned alley. Closer now! It gains on him, a shadow grown larger and darker since last he risked a look. Is there no escape, no refuge, anywhere within this maze of blemished brick? If he could only stop, think, plan... but demons give no quarter.

A sharp pain in his side explodes into a crippling stitch as the Runner is forced to vault a figure prone across the end of another alley. One more of the city's many homeless... he has no time to sneer.

His death is the Demon's purpose. It had made that perfectly clear during their one and only encounter, a lucky glimpse of its dark silhouette reflected against a shop window blurred by rain. Providence had warned him an instant before the Demon's gloved hand had risen, a gun clutched in its leathered grip.

How had it identified him? The Runner had sensed no danger, to himself or the mission, when he'd stopped to admire a collection of forgotten figurines piteously clustered under grimy glass. The family of miniatures had struck a familiar cord: the caring mother, the strong father, and the blessed infant given into their care. But why, he had wondered, were the sacred three huddled on some forsaken mountainside and not in the barn as scripture told?

Bullets dispatched from the Demon's matte-black weapon had put an end to his musings, smashing through the closed storefront, the exploding shells disintegrating the neglected icons in a storm of fragmented fire.

He had run a good city block and thanked his god for sparing his life before realizing he'd been hit. Now, each frantic stride is a painful reminder of the bullet that, in grazing his left shoulder, has reduced his arm to a throbbing ruin. An inch the other way and the exploding shell would have... God forbid. Three shots fired back at the storefront; none since. Intelligence put their standard firearm at 15 rounds. Twelve more without reloading... The grim math powers him into another intersection. Left this time, to something like daylight!

The rusting dumpster had been blindly and thoughtlessly tucked just inside the alley entrance. As he turns sharply into the corridor of his salvation, his wounded limb leads the way, smashing into the corner of the overfilled bin. His momentum spins him free, but the damage is done. Nuclear agony detonates inside his wound, mushrooming out to turn his knees to water and his skull inside out. And now he cannot see, alley and sky and that sliver of daylight blurring out behind the fragmented light rioting behind his eyes. How much blood did he leave on that damned thing? How much is he losing now?

The dumpster could have been excellent cover for an ambush, but he's staggered a good 30 feet beyond that now and it isn't in him to return. A lidless crate must do. Its contents long since plundered, the wooden contraption is now a catchment for rainwater. He shudders into a crouch behind it, tucking his healthy right shoulder into the scummy alley wall and leaving his throbbing left exposed. But he has no choice. He can't outrun his hunter now. Nothing for him but to face this head on and put his life into God's light.

From the slender sheath on his left leg, the Runner's only weapon finds his right palm. But the ten inch blade that gleams in the downpour offers only a moment's solace. Somewhere along the way, he messed up, revealed himself, his intent. But how, where?! He's only been here a day and most of that he squandered locating the damned warehouse, only to find the workers within ignorant of the harbingers sent before him. That at least explained the silence upon his arrival. The enemy had been busy.

Had the Demon spotted him at the warehouse? No. If it had grasped the significance of the warehouse, it would be rubble and he'd be buried beneath it. So it does not know everything. In disgust, he shoves away his flash of satisfaction. He is the only harbinger left alive on this side of the divide. And here he is, all his faith crammed into this length of meager steel, bright to his eye in the sullen night.

Poor as his prospects may be, one thing is in his favor. The sizable dumpster he careened into halves, the ten-foot gap through which the Demon must come to press its attack. But against him is the blood. He looks down to find it burping from his skinless left shoulder. Made inky by night, the crimson river bathes his left arm, running in rivulets from his hand to the filthy ground beneath. He has only seconds to make a move, up to the dumpster, or stay here and hope the Demon is careless.

No more boot falls... no more pursuit... silence but for the rain splashing off grimy concrete. Will it mistake him for a bum? The puddles he's forged have turned him into a thing of filth. Will it...

There!

The Runner flinches as a rock shoots past the dumpster, slicing the storm in a flight that carries it over his head and into a noisy landing beyond his wooden bulwark. If the throw seeks to provoke him into giving away his position, then the Demon knows him not at all.

Stillness.

Another hurled stone, another miss, cracking off a spray-painted logo tagging the alley's far wall.

Focus. Ignore the shoulder. Be ready.

Boom! Boom, boom!

The gun transforms the night, warping the downpour with light and thunder. The Runner bites back a startled cry as the wall three feet above his head dissolves into a shower of pulverized brick. The second bullet streaks past his wounded shoulder, missing him by ten inches as it pierces the alley's heart, detonating behind him. Somewhere in the cacophony, a fire burns as the third bullet rearranges the far wall into a mess of obliterated paint and stone. Covering fire? Hoping to get lucky?

Even alert to the ploy, the Runner nearly misses the Thing flying for him. It seems smaller now, little more than a shapeless blur in this soupy, nocturnal chaos, but then the devil can take many forms. The crate had failed to keep the hound from scenting his blood. No options now, no retreat.

One-armed, he meets the charge head-on, which is more honor than it had given him, his blade cutting the rain as it flashes for that shadow's throat. But the Demon is faster, an iron hand clamping down on his wrist, arresting his attack. Soaked, they grapple, straining for dominance as the rain beats down on them, washing away his sins. As he drives his knee up at the Demon's groin, he has a second to wonder why a bullet isn't already ripping through him, exploding him in two; another second to wonder if...

Crack!

For a timeless moment, the world is incandescent. He's falling even as he registers the sound of his face breaking under a blow from the pistol's unyielding chrome. His knife clatters into the night as he's slammed into the ground with a whoosh of escaping breath. His mind screams at his body to respond, but he's so slow. So slow!

Not much of a fight. The Runner's shuddering body heaves for oxygen as his knife is kicked down the alley by boots that step near him. Dimly, through the blood and the light, he makes out the outline of his enemy crouched nearby. A gloved hand rakes back a cloth hood to reveal short ebon hair soaked in spite of the hood. A woman with murderous green eyes that burn from a pale face awash in rain and shadow. Her damp leather coat clings to solid shoulders. She is tall, for her kind. But the rest is lost to his tortured sight that throbs with the beat of his panicked pulse.

Oblivion...

She must have kicked him; he can't remember. The alley's pavement is now his universe, his bloodied mouth awash in a puddle of filth. Another cough... feeling his body curl up on itself. No, he will keep his dignity.

"How many've you be here?" The smoky voice would have authored chills down his spine if her heavy boot wasn't already crushing it. His mind screams at his tired body; fight! But all he can manage is to curl his bloody hand into an impotent fist, trapped at his side.

"How many?!" Impatient, the boot lifts from his tortured back to smash another kick into his aching ribs, flipping him back into the world. Hate blazes down at him, his tormentor's tensed features blocking out the foreign sky. "If you don't talk..."

"Then what," he croaks out a laugh. "You'll kill me?"

"Fine," the Demon snarls, resolved. "Send one... send a hundred. They all'll be like you, dead'n forgotten." Her face is a fearsome thing, lips drawn back, white teeth gleaming. "It be no trouble to me."

The figurines return to him, exploding in a hail of sacrilegious gunfire. He should have known in that moment the Demon had him, everything following on her inevitable triumph. Well, his body may be hers, but he still owned the mission; priorities shifting in him, resolving a new objective. Just a seed of doubt... that's all he needs, the right words, to plant them in her, to watch them mature and broadcast the perfume of fear. For the next harbinger...

Her hand is on him, scavenging. His murderer will find very little. Long have they planned for this, long have they trained, to come to this city of monoliths, with naught that could jeopardize their mission. He'd laugh were his battered body capable. As it is, his embarrassingly feeble attempts to fend her off, to roll away, only engenders in her the same cool contempt the victorious cat holds for the crippled mouse.

When the bitch finishes pocketing her trinkets, he knows the time left to him has been all but spent. Her calloused hands ascend to his neck, her thick fingers encircling him, her thumbs almost delicately poised upon his unguarded throat. She is so close, he sees her eyes knife him, searching in him for withheld truths; he smells the meat on her breath, a meal that will not be her last; and he tastes her sweat, the bitterness sharp as it drips onto his tongue. How the knife, which had left a long, white scar just under her left eye, missed blinding her... but then the devil does claim the lion's share of luck. He will give her nothing.

"Alright, sipio. When you in Hell, you tell them." She squeezes his throat, each finger a band of steel. He is not her first.

Now then... no second chances.

"We will find her," he whispers. "Others will come." Her grip loosens. "If all that stands between us and she is you." His bloodied lips manage to smile. "God rest her soul."

Scowling, she releases him and uncurls to her full height, immune to the storm raging around them. It's the grace born of repetition that allows her to slip the gun from her coat and to fix the maw of its muzzle upon him in one fluid movement. Yes, he knows it well, awareness yielding to instinct born of competence.

"I be giving you one last chance now." But she knows he will not submit.

He sees in her eyes not only the fear of failure, which causes her to look away from him, but the memory of killings past. His brothers... he mourns them even as his swelling pride grants him a moment's peace from pain. They had been strong to the end. They had given her nothing.

"Just one," he smiles. "Just one..."

The Demon snarls.

Da, quaesumus Dominus, ut in hora mortis nostrae Sacramentis refecti et culpis omnibus expiati, in sinum misericordiae tuae laeti suscipi mereamur. Per Christum Dominum nostrum. Amen.

This being not his first brush with death, the ancient prayer, the prayer of his youth and later of his training, comes quickly to him, beseeching of the divine to preserve his soul. The God has blessed him with children, bestowed him a body worthy of defending the Enclave, and seen him through this critical mission. To be good with God, as the mortal life ended, he'd have given anything.

In earlier times, the leaders had to ask for volunteers. Not now. He and his kind had been proud to step forward, proud to be selected, proud to go. The mission had to be completed, a pathway opened to a future under an authentic sky, a future for his children and their children. Fear had never once touched him, not during the selection, not during the training, not even during the coming. This is everything. God would agree.

The Demon's gun coughs twice. His body bounces as the first shot fires into his chest, the second exploding through his throat. Her face is awash in his field of view; it fractures into countless glittering stars as numbness takes him. He had given her nothing; this was his last, hopeful thought on this earth.

***

It's their eyes.

How she recognizes them, the pits of zealous fire that burn away all the softness meant to temper the human soul. Well, they are out now, extinguished by her second shot which took her kill high up, under his chin, and kept on churning until there was nothing left to destroy. The Law could still fingerprint him for an I.D., but they won't care enough to try. This Warren hasn't seen an honest cop in 20 years and this nameless, paperless, and friendless man won't be the one who ends that streak.

Through the leather of her glove, Morgan can still feel the killing heat radiating from her gun. She looks at it, her Old Faithful, then at the lifeless body sprawled in filth just beyond her scuffed boots. "That be the last one," she vows in a voice trembling with a rage she had refused to let him see. "That be more than enough."

No witnesses, none dumb enough to show themselves anyway, she stoops, seizes the dead man by his jacket and drags him behind the crate he thought would save him. "Stupid sipio," she sneers. "Now it's your grave, the rats your pallbearers."

There will be more. His kind has never lied. They kill, without conscience, without remorse, but no, they never lie. Strange the places one finds truth in the world. Five minutes, she figures, for the Warren's dwellers to descend upon the body and strip away their share. By then, Morgan has quit the alley and is well into retracing her steps out of this maze-like hellhole. Under normal conditions, flight from a place where people pull down street signs for firewood is frustrating. With the rain sheeting off her leather coat, drooling down the back of her neck, and generally reducing visibility to a few miserable feet in any direction... this city...

Fifteen minutes later, she rejoins civilization; stepping out onto a street she recognizes... shops instead of shuttered buildings. By now, Morgan can't stop shivering. She's worked for kings and dictators, watching horrible crimes executed in places without futures. And one stinking scrot, with his zealot's eyes, does in her nerves? It's just the rain, she tells herself, the rain and what she's going to do to her contact the next time she gets her hands on him.

On her way out, she comes abreast of the storefront that started all of this. What in the pawnshop had so caught the dead man's eye? Her boots crunch over shattered glass as she comes to stand in the very spot she shot at not an hour ago, staring in as he had at a place neglected by time and the cruelties of urbanization. What of value the urchins of the Warren hadn't already stolen her shells tore apart, leaving only smoke and debris. Or...

Reaching around broken glass, Morgan plucks a singed figurine from the corner of the ruined display. An infant in his cradle, the Infant... the rest of his family lost to darkness and her destruction. For a moment, she considers rescuing the piece, but no. Better to leave it, in the middle of the display, upright and waiting for the worthy.

Not far from the shop, her ride waits for her, pitched up behind another of the Warren's overstuffed dumpsters. A flotilla of trash spills freely past her boots which squelch through the muck with each stride towards freedom. With a last look round, she stows her gun and tells her bike, "It's Morgan." A soft beep announces the bike's recognition of her voice pattern. The powerful alarm disengages, allowing her to glide her hands over leather and chrome, checking her two-wheeled steed for tampering, finding none.

The moment the light went out of that zealot's eyes, he became her sixteenth on this job. Sixteen in six weeks... their instincts speak to training second to none, training that has bestowed upon them toughness equal to their unwillingness to talk. Venomous snakes in a concrete jungle and nothing but those eyes to distinguish them, eyes that follow her even in dreams.

Stop!

Whenever she mounts her bike and thumbs the engine to life, nothing else ever matters. Obligations, expectations, necessities... they all tumble off her like broken chains, leaving only solitude, the monogamy of her and lady midnight. She kicks up the stand, kills the brake and fires herself into the dark.

Content to be thoughtless, she rides from the City's colorless slums and into the welcoming embrace of its million prismatic lights. They wash over her as she gracefully weaves into omnipresent traffic. It is known the world over as a city of perpetual motion, a creature of commerce that crawled out of the ocean bay that birthed it, only to sprawl across the land for leagues in every direction. But it isn't motion or commerce that appear on the postcards dispatched to the homelands of its amazed visitors; it's the monolithic towers that stretch so high that, from the City's heart only a sliver of sky remains to the human eye. Those towers are intimidating to anyone who hasn't matured in the long shadows they cast upon the world and its globalized trade.

A foreigner, Morgan is among the awed. Her home is far north of here, where all this rain would be accumulating into drifts of snow and where darkness has become something of a fetish. Ten million people crammed into 30 square leagues... she could find enough work here to last her a lifetime... and yet this is only her second visit. She has no plans to return.

The intersection's blue stop-light affords her a chance to take in the towers surrounding her. Downtown, where the City's commercial districts slope towards the bay, every building visible to the unaided eye is at least 50 stories. Their superstructures are legislated Conplast, a ruddy gray material that, in more pleasant conditions, grants the towers a kind of imposing uniformity. Tonight, under this darkened sky, gripped by this ominous downpour, they look like nothing less than bloody fingers thrust forth from the grave. Effective against bomb strikes and earthquakes, they said of Conplast. Less harmful to the environment they said. Nonsense, all of it, it is an excuse to demolish the old and develop atop the still steaming ruins. The beast of capitalism must be fed after all.

For all of that though, the seamless, authoritarian structures are worthy of respect. Flying into the City, her mortal mind had struggled to cope with the scale of it. The plane's belly had skimmed over untold towers - each Conplast rooftop, be it peak or dome, festooned by solar panels, swaths of black amidst patterned lights. Morgan remembers thinking the sun's light would be mostly absorbed by the monoliths, leaving only the dregs to splash upon the streets below. And she was right, but she had not counted on the million streetlamps stepping into the void, more than happy to bestow their artificial light on this industrial paradise. Rather appropriate, in the end.

Morgan is alerted to the light turning in her favor by the scrot behind her leaning obnoxiously on his horn. A glance over her shoulder finds a carefree man in his fancy, carefree car. She smiles, feeling the comforting curve of her gun pressed close. Just another mindless drone on another self-important mission to nowhere. She turns back and gives her steed its head, blasting through the intersection and away from the temptation to make him her second of the evening. Life, she decides, is so much better when reduced to the blur of rain light at 90 LPH.

Since arriving, she's been laying her head in a rented room on the fifth floor of a nondescript apartment building slouched down in Northwest. The manager, a drab man in his sixties, sporting one of the weakest chins Morgan had ever seen, had let her pay in cash. She didn't tell him that it was only this increasingly rare virtue that sealed the deal. It certainly hadn't been the stench of cat piss in the elevator, or the hallway's 20-year-old carpet in a hue that reminded her of vomit. She has her key out, as she approaches her door. Her elderly neighbor has made cabbage, again and a pity she'd scorched it, again.

The door yields to key and hand, but before Morgan can take a step, it hits her. Instinct honed across years of living on the edge puts Old Faithful in her left hand. The gun is an aging but venerated model, Estrian, made from composite plastic assembled from a dozen discrete pieces, which individually have never made a skyport scan so much as blink. The newer members of her trade favor less reliable Disposables, the throw away weapons that make it harder for the authorities to work up a history. But when there's someone waiting for you, in your own room, someone careful enough to lock the door behind them, a gun's dependability trumps its traceability every single time.

The door's cheap wood reverberates as her boot rudely kicks it the rest of the way open. The sad little kitchenette light is on, the living room light too. She smells rain; the sliding glass door, which grants access to her tiny deck, is wide open, having permitted more than the wet night to cross its threshold. She enters, gun up and ready.

Morgan has done little to deliver this place from its life as a dingy apartment. She's ignored the pleas of the blank white walls to be adorned, appreciating the irony of the suggestion that no soul lives here. No carpet to speak of, aged hardwood in its place. She likes that each step on the warped floorboards is audible to the attentive ear. The unused kitchenette is to her left as she enters, messy bedroom to the right. Ahead, the living room: battered leather couch, glass-topped coffee table, a bulky video box sentenced to confinement in the corner. Nowhere to hide...

Her left heel closes the front door just as the toilet flushes. Three steps take her through the kitchenette and she puts her shoulder into the wall just beyond the bathroom door. Her gun is poised to strike. An adventurous vagrant? A bored thief? A careless killer... she takes a breath, holds it, as the door opens inward, the light is off, the figure beyond motionless. Strike or be struck, she brings her weapon to bear.

"Morgan." The voice is male, cultured, and calm. Her contact.

"You should be waiting in the hall." Snarling, she stuffs the gun back into her jacket and spins away, stomping into the kitchen. Two long fingers tug open the cooler door to find: cheese surrendering to mold, half a sandwich she'd made a couple of days ago and hadn't finished, and mustard. She pulls a bottle of Roots from the bottom shelf.

"I'll take one." She hears him settle in the living room.

Morgan twists the cap free, and tosses it down onto the counter. "Scrot," she spits, loud enough for him to hear.

By the time she's fortified herself with a long pull from the bottle and grudgingly followed his wet footprints, her guest has adopted a comfortable lean next to the ancient video box, his hand resting on its dusty lid. There is no denying the man's appeal: brown hair left unfashionably long, intense hazel eyes which know the answer before the question is asked, the hard line of a mouth on business. He's taken the liberty of drying his ugly yellow raincoat over the back of a nearby wooden chair. With the coat gone, he is left in a hooded sweatshirt of anonymous gray, worn jeans of a faded blue and black rain boots. Those eyes... she's careful not to meet them.

"I'll give you a minute to calm down." He watches her coolly, not a speck of tension in him. He's the only man she's ever met who owns more confidence than she.

With a grunt and a breath, she sets gun and drink on the coffee table before pulling off her wet leather coat and draping it over the arm of her couch. She shuts the sliding glass door against the night and pointedly locks it before it hits her. He scaled up from outside?! Eager for another pull, she fetches her bottle and collapses onto her couch, her gun hand rubbing at tired eyes. Her hood is damp against the back of her sweaty neck.

"If you think you be getting an apology from me, think again." She contemplates the random disorder of the bubbles flitting through the dark liquid in her bottle. "Got me out there, flying half-blind, no names, no goals... out there on your say so. My man, he comes to me and tells me everything be changing, that it's never mattered more than now. Then he goes away and he sends me his little notes, so's I can do his dirty work for him."

She glances up and finds him infuriatingly unmoved. It rekindles her earlier fury. "On your word I do this; on your word I kill! Necessary, you say; protected, you say... I do not have a name! I do not have a face! Even for you, for us, this be a hard ask."

He nods.

"Dying on your word!" She remembers the Zealot's taunts. "One wrong call; follow the wrong rat... game over. History only goes so far."

She watches him study her. They've never exchanged names, never had to, too many years, too many deeds, things too deep for trivialities. So long as his money flowed... but no, that's not what's kept them together all these years. That's not why she came to this place to kill for him. Faith demands more than a fat wallet.

Outside, thunder cracks, then a smear of distant lightning as rain pelts futilely against sealed glass.

"Speak! You fell into my world, remember?"

"It's a fine line we walk." Her contact reaches into his pocket, pulls free a photograph. "Interfere too much and we violate every rule we hold dear. Interfere too little..."

He approaches, sets the snap on the coffee table. One glimpse makes Morgan trade her precious bottle for the vivid image.

The face is captivating: wavy brown hair down to a pale neck, licking cutely at a furrowed brow; gray eyes that hold both the cold of a winter's breeze and the expressiveness of an artist's subject, a mouth that knows how to smile but does it rarely; white skin darkened by some eastern ancestry, but definitely Eurowan. Young too, early twenties. But even in that short time, life has left its mark. Those eyes know how to cry and hate every tear.

"This is her." She'd bluffed it with her kill in the alley, claiming ownership of the girl in hopes of extracting information from a man with nothing left to lose. Truth is she has been as much a pawn in this game as the sixteen who've fallen to her hand. Until now...

The Contact nods, crouches, the better to look her in the eye. "We're close enough now."

"To what?"

"We're close enough now. It's time you know the rest."

Morgan lays the photograph on her knee as she goes for her drink. Soon, she'll need the good stuff. The solitary bottle in the cooler's freezer, but that's for later, when the enormity of it has rammed home. For now, a quivering spike of exhilaration rips through her as she realizes the time for stalking, for waiting, is over. She stares into those hazel eyes which gleam now, with nothing less than her future.

"Finally." Her kill fades into the night, replaced now by destiny, by purpose.

It is the king of purposes.

DAY ONE

1

The Iguana is hopping.

For the bartender, Wednesday nights are always chaotic, but tonight takes the cake. A youthful crowd of screaming supporters, some in blue and others red, are glued to an important football match slogging its bloody way into overtime. Which is why the folks who turn up every Wednesday for *The Executioner* find themselves crankily squeezed into just one corner of the Collins Street bar. A few ill-considered insults and she can well imagine the two throngs rumbling in paradise.

Paradise... ha! But that's how the owner would have his patrons think of it. It's been three years since flush with too much inherited cash for anyone to spend wisely, he had bought the Iguana and transformed it from a drab but respectable establishment into an equatorial wonderland. Why? Because he'd convinced himself that, in the world's wettest metropolis, people would flock from the city over for a slice of tropical nirvana. Yeah, like his customers don't resent the illusion of comfort every time they step back out into the ceaseless rains...

Of course, he'd tapped her to carry out his so-called vision: to mount the animatronic lizards, to select the lush vistas on the living wallpaper, and to cobble together a menu that fit with such exotic locales. Bizarre as it all is though she's growing a little fond of the result. Sure, the two lizard-like gargoyles on the bar are a little much, and she had been forced to withdraw the stuffed iguanas from the center of each table when they became, as often as not, footballs, but the three perpetually active video screens, mounted behind and above the bar, made up for the silliness.

Now these treasures the owner had gotten right. Straight from the 'if you show it, they will come' handbook, he had footed the expansive bill for each of the six-foot-wide, "top of the line" projectors, insisting they display diversity in programming. "Paradise is a place for all comers," he'd said in his clipped Eurowan.

So, while the young men watch their bruising sport, and the young women *The Executioner*, only a handful heed the third screen's 24/7 news feed, currently regurgitating the now days-old footage of the fifty Afjan refugees illegally washing ashore. The authorities had collared every last one and, after politely supplying them with clean blankets and warm food, just as politely informed them that they would be returning to the hellhole from which they had narrowly escaped. With the promise of night's pleasures thick in the air, who but maybe Johnny wanted to chase their shot with a swig of immigration.

A young man, his forehead proudly bearing his team's navy blue logo, something resembling a taloned bird, orders drinks for himself and his three smiling friends. She eyeballs his I.D., overlooks its dubious origins, and serves him his four greenish drinks. Even she can take this skinny boy; his ribs, bare of fat and muscle, are visible through a t-shirt soaked with rain. He needs a jacket in weather like this.

"Molly!" Johnny appears from behind the grateful blue. Twenty-five, a handsome face in spite of delicate features, abundant curls of blond hair spilling equally over brow and nape, intelligent, clear, blue eyes that any girl could fall into on any day of any week.

"Johnny," she blushes, even after all this time. "What'll it be tonight?"

"Rayburn Light for Carter and Zia. The real stuff for me and Evan. Francis, well, who knows, right?" How much trouble has his smile caused? A lot, she wagers.

"Coffee for Francis." She nods, heating under her black tank top. "It'll be over in a minute."

"That's my girl."

He winks and gives way to another face, asking for another drink. It is the continuation of an endless, demanding crush. But thinking about Johnny, well... the monotony of it ceases to matter.

They are always here. Over the years, their numbers have fluctuated with the arrivals and the departures of intimates. But for as long as the bartender has worked this joint, the friends have claimed the same circular table against the western wall. The five pull up their chairs, buy their drinks and talk, paying little heed to the chaos around them.

Carter is Johnny's best friend, though how the two keep from killing each other nobody knows. Johnny, with his crazy politics and endless provocations, is the polar opposite to Carter who is as solid as the day is long, with chocolate brown eyes that glow with humor and warmth. The foreman of a construction crew, his face and arms bear the evidence, the former deeply tanned, and the latter as thick through as she's seen on any man outside a dirty magazine. He does the rugged ranger so well: the worn jeans, the flowing white shirt, an ever-present cap covering brown hair as straight as straw.

Fire and ice, the two of them, which is probably why their debates have become legend here. Technology, humanity, government... they agree on nothing, and do so loudly and often. In the pool she and some of the other regulars have going, she's laid $5 on immigration being tonight's bone of contention. No way can Johnny resist that footage.

Of Zia and Francis, Molly knows considerably less. Both are quiet, Zia for the love of books, one of which she always has to hand; Francis for reasons more obscure. Both are close with Evan, but while Zia has clearly emerged from the death-throes of punk with black tattoos and magenta hair, it's impossible for Molly to imagine any man more straight-laced than Francis. Even here, the man manages to be aristocratic: his face clean-shaven, his brown hair always coiffed, his clothes permanently stuck on business casual. If Zia's ever worn business casual, it was in another life.

And then there's Evan. A momentary quieting of the chaos allows the bartender to pour and serve the table's drinks. Legends of the bar deserve the personal touch.

Quiet Evan, never raising her voice in anger, never causing a fuss. She's somehow unobtrusive in an old navy pea coat forever slung about modest shoulders; battered and patched black jeans sheathing long, athletic legs; and worn but fashionable boots that look like they've walked her a thousand leagues. However unassuming she may wish to be, her face stands out. Vitality persists in these gray-blue eyes, enlivening a gaunt aspect edged in hard emotions. No, she'll never grace the covers of magazines, but there's character in her strong cheekbones and her solid nose. But it's her mouth Molly will remember. Above a stubborn chin, its firm line will not yield an inch; a defense against future disappointments.

"Enjoy guys." She sets down the drinks and, for a brief moment, meets Evan's cool gaze. In her line of work, you learn to read people, sort the ones who relinquish their troubles from the ones who bottle them up. It's the bottlers you worry for. The bartender looks away. "Y'all need anything, shout."

"Will do, thanks Molly." Johnny warms her with that winning smile before they toast their glasses.

Carter is still enjoying that first pull of a cold beer when Johnny rounds on him, mischief lighting his eyes. "You got it coming to you tonight, boy, all thanks to our beloved free press. They love their sensationalism and I love them for it. Might I offer you a refugee? We have plenty in stock. Sure, they're starving, desperate, and have had the last ounce of hope crushed out of them, thanks to our heartless government, but you can get a good deal while it lasts, two souls for the price of one."

Evan groans, Zia laughs, and Carter rolls his eyes. The bartender smiles as she ambles back to her bar, $25 the richer. Johnny's like the rain; you can always count on him.

***

"That's hilarious, Johnny. You're hilarious, because you're so right. I am the devil. I hate the poor and I sure as hell don't want them living in my streets, eating my food, and soaking up my tax dollars. You've got me nailed in one. And now, instead of strangling you, I'm going to drink my beer and pretend you didn't just dump me in with the scum of the earth."

Evan nurses her drink as she sizes up the crowd. Packed house tonight... and wow, that black-haired boy at the bar is cute, but he'll get nowhere trying it on with Molly. Evan's come here three or four nights a week for...five years now? Not once has she seen Molly play favorites despite many, quality efforts to sway her. Idly, her forefinger traces a thoughtful design on the side of her glass.

"Make light of it all you like." Johnny leans forward, intent now. "But you *do* support this government, a government which, by the way, is intent on maintaining our superpower privileges at any cost, yeah, even if the rest of the world burns. But hey, the moment we need cheap labor, the moment we need something from them, it's perfectly fine to cut a deal then. But we don't need that right now, so up go the walls, zero immigration... suck on that, you poor, unlucky bastards." Johnny is warming to his theme in lieu of his drink.

Carter shrugs. "Y'can't save everyone, Johnny. You can try, but you're gonna fail. You can only affect your own little corner of this thing we call life, man. We got more'n enough people to feed, clothe, and shelter. It ain't on me to fix what others have broken in places I've never seen. Call me selfish, but I didn't put none of your poor bastards on that boat, Johnny. I didn't shove guns into their hands when they were little kids. I didn't tell'm to fight in my wars. And I definitely wasn't the genius who told'm coming here was their meal ticket. So, does it suck for me, when my government has to turn these people away? Hell yes. But man... you can walk outside this bar, right now, and find some homeless guy, high on heaven only knows, rooting through the garbage because he might find a potato curl." The foreman took a pull from his beer. "You don't invite people to live in your house with you when your roof's leaking like a sieve, Johnny. Not unless you hate them."

"Oh man, you are so completely wrong," Johnny groans. "First of all, you're saying that we shouldn't be charitable to the rest of the world until we've fixed every single problem that ails our country? That's impossible. Not even a benevolent government, which ours is definitely not, can reach everyone. And so on that basis, we should just forget all the other sufferers on the planet?"

"No, I'm sayin' that you gotta get your house in order before..."

"Hold on. And secondly, and this is the bigger issue, we *cannot* continue to say that we're lucky to live here, that others aren't, and that that's just the way it is. You cannot *dismiss* those fifty shattered people because you and I can't figure out a way to feed the homeless! I'm tired of this unending... sense of entitlement! I'm tired of people telling me I should just feel lucky to have been born here! I get it, I'm grateful, but it's sooo easy to fall into this idea that, well, you won the cosmic lottery, to be born where you were, and everyone who didn't win, and was born somewhere else, can just suck it up. That's not good enough. We aren't the ones chewing on tree bark for breakfast and wondering when the next warlord'll come along to tell us that we have a choice, fight for him or discover what it feels like to get chopped into 50,000 pieces! We have a responsibility to them; we have a responsibility to the world, to extend to them some of the fruits of our success. We've got to live in a world where *everyone* has a little hope to leave the darkness of chaos and enter into the light of civilization. If we won't offer them hope, if we don't keep that flame lit, well... who will?"

Johnny's raised voice has drawn the attention of onlookers who stare at him, at Carter, awaiting the big man's punch. It wouldn't take more than that to put skinny Johnny on the floor.

"We could go'n for hours. It ain't in me tonight. So I'll say this," Carter growls. "Just because we got it good don't give us the right to go tellin' other people what to do, how to live their lives. We made it as a nation; we succeeded. They will too and not because we're yellin' instructions down at 'em from our high horse. And, anyway, far as my country goes... it's perfectly fine to want your country to preserve just a bit of its tradition, Johnny. We got history here, cultural history, the history of our people. It's okay to want that to stay the way it's been, Johnny. You may think otherwise, and I bet you do, but it's okay to want things to stay the same. It ain't so bad, you know."

"Cultural history, our history, tradition... treading awfully close to racism there."

"And scene..." Francis steps in as Carter's face heralds storm clouds. "Evan, how was your day?"

"Fine, Francis. Thanks for asking," she plays along. "My pimp gave me the night off and I thought I'd try to stay off the 'Dust long enough to have a beer with my pals. But I must have sat down at the wrong table. Cuz I don't know any of you, no way."

Evan's comical squint at the unfamiliar faces before her brought laughter. But she knows them, every one of them: Carter's swarthy reliability, Johnny's pale intensity, Francis' smooth stillness, and Zia's tanned wisdom. Her family, warts and squabbles and all.

"I always knew she was a 'Dust whore." Johnny tries to grin.

"Hey, what did you call me?!"

And just like that, back, on safe ground. It really has been five years since they became regulars here. Time wasn't flying - it had reached the speed of light. She'd met Carter first. They'd come to this very bar for drinks, each having brought a friend for, what, support? She can't remember. She'd brought Zia, and Carter had brought Johnny, and now here they are, years on, sitting at the same table, drinking the same drinks, trying to make sense of an increasingly senseless world. Maybe that's why her two friends find themselves on ever-thinning ice.

Evan considers Johnny. The man's passion, hell, the sheer force of his being, pulls on you like gravity. He can make converts of perfect strangers, effortlessly drawing them down into the depths of his world. But these are the few, the ones ready for his wisdom, or in need of some guidance, some purpose. Does he see how his passion repels the rest? How it hardens their hearts against him? Few, if any, manage the in-between, the stable orbit.

Is this polarization the fate of people like Johnny, people who make demands of the world around them? Does the act of striving, yearning for change inevitably alter the focus of the debate, from the man's issues to the man himself? That slow but steady transition from "We must fix this," to "I must fix this and if you're against me I'm going to convince you why you're wrong..." Is this why Carter is so admired, because he has no expectations of the world, of life, but that a few friends walk with him and permit him, from time to time, to lay his comforting arm protectively about their shoulders?

Which is the better road? It seems to her that Johnny's is difficult, lonely, and virtuous, while Carter's is easy, comfortable, and empty. No, empty is too harsh. Ordinary... yes, ordinary. But is ordinary so bad? Loneliness is a bitter thing...

In her introspection, Evan had missed Johnny's apology to Carter and the conversation's turn from the world's woe to *The Executioner*. Blinking out of her reverie, she glances over at the RealLife TV screen to find the show in its final segment, wherein the audience votes for who should get the ax and by what means.

The cast is paraded before the cameras, to air their grudges, and to plead for sympathy from twenty million people they'll never meet. Their interviews drip with spite for their fellow contestants which, of course, is what makes it such good viewing!

"I'm going with Shaza." Zia closes her thick book, hiding its white Bio-pulp pages full of perfect black type. Evan peeks at the cover, "Truth: A Rumination on Objective Reality". A little light reading for a Wednesday night. Zia flashes a challenging smile at them. "I got $5. Anyone want my action?"

"Of course you like Shaza to get the chop," Johnny snorts. "She has the personality of bacon grease."

Carter scoffs.

"What?"

"Oh, I'm just wonderin' if that little bit of character assassination there wouldn't have just a little something to do with your weakness for blondes."

"Shaza isn't blonde! Look at all that nasty black hair! How could you miss that?"

"My point exactly," Carter grins.

"So because I like blondes, every other woman who... oh, forget it. I have $5 on Dougray. The guy makes my skin crawl."

Carter laughs. "That's because he wears fur and you're a tree-lover. I have $5 on Gordon. I swear he's my uncle."

"I thought you liked your uncle." Evan blinks at him.

"He liked his uncle," Johnny smirks. "Massive past tense. Underscore it. Highlight it in big-ass neon. See, Uncle can't help him anymore... Uncle already gave him a 'start in the business.' And hey," he says, leveling a finger at Carter. "Don't you make me out to be one of these citizens-against-everything-except-puppies types. I'll have your ass up on slander charges faster than you can say 'meat-eater through and through.'"

"Evan, so help me. The guy calls me every day and it's always the same. 'Young man, how you doin' over there? Got your own crew now, huh? Why, I can remember you was just this little squeak of a thing, no taller'n your old man's knee. And when you growed, I was first to givin' you a shot. Your father was a goodly man...'"

They laugh.

"I've never met the man," Evan smiles. "But that sounds about right. My sympathies."

"Hey, off-topic!" Zia stands. "Francis, Ev, you in? They're gonna call it in like a minute here."

Judging from the cheers and groans, the football match is still in doubt. But when Evan turns to look at the RLTV screen, she finds near to every eye in the bar already there, slates in hand, firing off last second votes. Hard to blame them. Last she checked, people don't die in sports.

"I'm content." Francis hides his smile behind a sip of coffee. "Besides, gambling is a sin."

"Ha! Right," Johnny laughs. "Perfect. A puritan at the table."

"I'm with Francis. Y'all disgust me." Turning back to the table, Evan goes for her wallet. "Wagering on a glorified game show... honestly, I'm ashamed to know any of you misfits." Her hand adds an aging $5 bill atop the wrinkled three already present. "Give me Frank. He's got a ferret face that even his mother couldn't love."

"The votes have been tallied." The program's pale-faced host reserves his best solemn hush for these pronouncements. The nervous contestants mill around behind him in an otherwise bucolic campground full of trees and picnic tables. With a creepy cowl enshrouding his face, the show's bleak headsman looms next to the host, ready to pass sentence.

To preserve the theater of the thing, the host is handed an envelope which his white-gloved hands tear open, extracting a slip of paper with the will of the people scribbled upon it. He nods gravely as he learns who is to die. "Frank, you have been judged..."

Evan smiles as a ragged cheer goes up from those in the bar who'd bet on ferret face, little eddies of happiness amidst a sea of disappointed groans. With an exaggerated sweep of the hand, she claims the $20 from the center of the table.

"Y'guys should know better than to go against me. I thought we'd established that I alone can see the future."

On the screen, with the executioner in menacing pursuit, a blubbering Frank makes a desperate run for it. If he can just get to the treeline! But a panicked vault over a picnic table in his way turns disastrous when his middle-aged legs fail to provide the necessary lift. *Oohs* of sympathy from the bar as Frank's foot catches the table's leading edge, spilling him painfully forward. From there, it's a quick and graceless tumble to the ground, where the hooded headsman snares his squealing prey and drags him into the trees meant to be his salvation.

"Frank," the host concludes grimly, "scored 73 percent of the popular vote. Your preferred method of execution? Hanging." A pregnant pause as the camera stays on his dour expression, inviting the audience to imagine the execution the show does not air. "Next time on *The Executioner*..."

As everyone reclaims their seats, Johnny's eyes twinkle with mischief. "I read somewhere... they've been trying to track down some of the contestants, you know, see what it was like to be on the show?"

"Oh god," Carter mutters.

"Haven't found a single one of them." Johnny grins through the groans. "I know, I know; they probably don't do it, but you never know."

"Yeah, c'mon," Zia agrees. "They give the victims $250,000, or something, tell them to stay out of the way for six months so the show can get creepy press, that's all."

"You all know it's coming. We will eventually cave to the drama and we'll have these losers signing up, knowing they've got nothing to lose if they do get whacked. So, the deal becomes, 'you pay my family X and I'll give it a go,' and we'll eat it up. It's like public executions back in the old days."

"There's no way that'll happen. That's completely foul, man," Carter shakes his head in disgust. "It's harmless fun. Don't take tele-show melodrama and roll it into your fall-of-society nonsense."

"You say that now..."

"Maybe, Johnny. Maybe it will all just fall apart. Maybe we'll all wind up slaves to the man, scrabbling in the dirt for the last few potato curls. But that day, it ain't today." Evan stands and, with her winnings, pays for the next round of drinks. "Ran a delivery up into Wakefield the other day. Guess who answered the door?"

"Frank," Francis smiles.

"Ferret Face in the flesh." Evan grins at Johnny. "So, my friend, your fears are for tomorrow." Evan tucks her chair into the table. "I gotta check in. Doing a double tonight."

"I told you. You're gonna burn out," Zia sing-songs at her. "Money ain't everything, Ev."

"No, not everything, but it is my rent. Back in a minute."

Evan navigates the crowd, pitching up at the bar before Molly just as overhead, the final whistle blows on the marathon football match. Painted blue fists pump the air in triumph as she goes into her pea coat's inner pocket for her computer. Money isn't everything... she drops her battered and bulky slate on the bar, powering it on with an impatient flick of her thumb. Her model is so old, they don't even make it anymore! And she's not one of those people who needs a new everything, she's not, but she's tired of having to jockey around, everywhere she goes, to get the best wireless signal which, here, happens to be in front of the gargoyles.

Johnny is forever complaining about the government robbing its citizens of their liberties; but whichever government ignored the threats of the giant telecoms to create the Cloud should have statues put up in their honor.

Ten years now, they've had blanket wireless, long enough that Evan can't remember how anyone functioned before its inception. The Cloud, a network of 1,000 signal amplifiers distributed throughout the country which provide blanket, wireless access to the 'Net. Anywhere, at any time, for any duration... for free. Why? Because it costs the taxpayers a pittance to upkeep the mainframe and the signal amps, and, well, isn't everyone better off if access to the 'Net is universal? It's so self-evident, she wonders how the telecoms fought against it for so long; giant dinosaurs, as yet unaware of their own obsolescence.

"No signal." The characters slur across the blurry screen. "You piece of..." Evan lightly bangs the slate against the bar-top.

"You two not getting along?" Molly asks. "If so, you don't take it out on my counter, hear? It never did nothin' to you."

Evan looks up to find the bartender smiling at her, muscles rippling under a stretched, black tank top. Evan feels frustration replaced by something far more pleasant.

"Your thing's beeping," Molly points out.

Yes, she's finally online! Evan grins and taps the touchscreen for her employer's site and, before it can ask for her I.D., she's got her thumb pressed to the scanner at the base of the slate. "Identity confirmed," which plunges her into her work account where the run-sheet waits for her. Six packages, four central-depot pickups and two residence-to-residence exchanges. She can do this in two hours without the daytime traffic to slow her.

"Off to work. Thanks, Molly."

"For what? I'm just standin' here bein' happy there was no fight tonight."

"A fight? On your watch? No way. No one is that stupid." Evan smiles. "See you 'round."

"Oh, I know. The world just wouldn't be the same if you didn't."

As Evan returns to her table, she feels eyes on her. Molly? She looks back over her shoulder, but the bartender is calling someone a cab. Her friends then, but no, they aren't looking her way either. Unnerved, she keeps walking, eyes scanning the thinning crowd: a girl writing her slate's number on a napkin and slipping it to the boy next to her, a table of blues taunting a table of reds, a guy doing the drunken stagger to the bathroom...

There, by the door... Evan can't pull much more than the silhouette of a figure from the shadows. Whoever it is prefers the dark, even down to their wardrobe. She tries for an impression of the face, but the figure is already gone, out into the rain.

Ohhh, come on. It's nothing. And it's not like the Collins Street bar has any special lease on normal.

"What'd I miss? Johnny, you solve world hunger while I was gone?" She returns to their laughter.

"Don't tease, bitch. I *will* solve that pesky problem. And you will *all* bow before me and call me lord. Maybe, just maybe, I'll mention a few of you in my acceptance speech."

"Oh yeah? What award are you accepting?"

"Master of the Universe, naturally."

"Oh, of course, master. How could I have possibly... I insult you with my ignorance. Please forgive this lowly pawn of yours her mistake."

Her friends laugh.

"Alright, catch y'all on the other side."

2

By the time Evan pushes into the rowdy street, the rain has abated. It is a few hours from midnight, which is supposedly a time of rest, but the blues, who've taken their triumph to the street, show no sign of going home. Any excuse to party... Buttoning her pea coat, she sidesteps a handful of drunken celebrants and reaches her bike with a minimum of molestation.

Not content with whooping from the sidewalks, the carousers spill aimlessly into the roadway, eliciting angry honks from annoyed motorists. But, save for a handful of partiers who laughingly slam their hands down on the hoods of the offending cars, the loose cluster of jerseyed fans pay the drivers no heed. Windows are rolled down and heated threats exchanged. She is best gone from this scene before the unamused police mistake her blue pea coat for a symbol of support.

The Yager 20-06, with its carbon-fiber frame, puncture-proof tires, and patented drive system, is a bicyclist's wet dream of performance and practicality. The front stem, upon which the straight handlebars are mounted, permits the rider to telescope the front bars up and down: up for functional use, down for maximum velocity. The bike comes accessorized with a computer that, in addition to providing the rider a real-time map of the area, tracks speed, distance traveled, and current and future weather conditions. All this, plus a phone, is contained behind the monitor which peers out from the center of the handlebars. Downhill, on a good night, she's faster than the wind.

Evan looks up as she unchains and mounts her familiar machine. The rain has scrubbed the sky of smog, allowing a million stars, glittering like polished gems, to shine their grace upon her. She cherishes nights like these, nights of simple beauty. In minutes, she'll be in the city's thundering heart, where the natural is, as ever, eclipsed by the artificial. Is that Juno? Bright enough... the moon is coming up, gravid and glorious in waxing gibbous.

"Scrot!"

Evan blinks and looks around, just in time to see a red throw a punch at a blue. Oh right, time to go. She flexes her thighs and she's gone.

She'd pursued the humanities in her year of college, but it had been that one astronomy elective that had truly fired her imagination. Memories... she smiles, recalling how, as a child, she had believed the supernatural inhabited the moon. Adulthood's monotony had dispelled that fantasy, as well as the wider magic of the child's world, a time when reality is malleable, its boundaries undefined. That class had reminded her of those younger nights. Strange, she muses, how kids long for the respect and the responsibilities of grown-ups while grown-ups long for a taste of those early, enchanting days. The universe's idea of a joke?

Even at this hour, her city throbs. Sleek cars cut past, forcing her to concentrate. Pretty boys and prettier girls crowd the sidewalks, coming and going from clubs, theaters and restaurants that, on a nightly basis, entertain the masses. The downtown core, with its behemoth skyscrapers, its Mulcibic clock tower, and its central square, provides a constant backdrop, a theater for ten million dreams. The wealth, just to live here, is incalculable.

The central depot is one of the last non-Conplast buildings in the Core. Squat and dirty, it has stubbornly withstood numerous attempts to have it demolished, though, god only knows why. "Angel Couriers," a neon sign blazes out at passersby while, beneath the foot-high lettering, a holographic angel, with wings thrice the size of her body, flies to her destination with a precious package clutched to her breast. Evan takes the service alley, hopping off her bike and leaving it at the loading dock in back.

Same day delivery; that's the precious mission statement. But it's pay, not pride that has a dozen of her fellow riders bagging deliveries in the middle of the night. The warehouse's cavernous interior is cluttered by a chaotic array of packages eager to go out while others wait forlornly to be returned to their senders. For each of the few riders she recognizes, Evan has a smile. For those she does not recognize... an uncomfortable nod. Bernard, her fantastically rotund boss, she outright avoids, letting her palmed slate guide her to her deliveries. Chuck them in her rucksack, make sure it's zipped up tight, and she's out of there without looking back. She's back on her bike in less than two minutes.

Her load secured behind her, Evan thrusts herself into the night, just in time for the rain to kick back up. The storm drains, already laboring to relocate the earlier deluge into the city's labyrinthine underground, find this development troublesome. The fashion plates, running for cover, agree. The rider smiles and tastes the sky as she hears the first distant peals of thunder. It's going to be a long, wet night.

Humping it through a busy intersection, Evan noshes on an apple as she dives deeper into the business district. In succession, she passes a clothing franchise, an office supply and a Worldcomp outlet. She spots a few customers coming and going from the first two, but it's the ubiquitous tech chain that pulls a crowd. Through the substantial front window, she's sucked into the store's vast display, slates, holos, satnavs and everything between. Communication on a grand scale...

Compared to the new models, her slate might as well be an abacus. They not only sported improved voice recognition, they're capable of projecting a functional keyboard onto any flat surface. No spills, no worn-out keys... suddenly saving to pay her rent doesn't seem so important.

"Move along," she tells herself. "That's a good girl."

Her faultless universal location system guides her through two more intersections before pitching her up at Stewart Tower, a true hulk at 63 stories. The white-marbled lobby is bigger than the

Iguana. Evan flashes her badge at the decaying night guard whose last criminal collar had been 20 years ago.

"Name..." he drones.

Evan consults her slate. "Uh, Jason Levy."

"Twelfth floor." The balding guard buzzes her through.

Evan leans her bike against the lobby wall and lobs her apple core in the trash before storming the stairwell. She's pleased Levy isn't any higher up. She'd be forced to take the elevator and that she cannot manage without breaking out into a cold sweat. Memories of nightmares... trapped in a steel cage, its cables cut, plummeting, plummeting... deathtraps, the lot of them.

By the time she punches out into the 12th floor, she's panting. An industrial hallway, white walls, beige carpet underfoot. She raps at 1284b which, as the door swings inward, reveals itself as a plush, well-appointed conference room dripping in sleek leather.

It is unoccupied but for the creep who opens the door: forty, graying at the temples, blotchy skin. His hunched shoulders give the impression of a bizarrely narrow body not at all helped by a pinched and pale face.

"Mr. Jason Levy?" Evan inquires.

He nods, passing a spasming hand over a sweaty face. Strung out? Hungover? Afflicted with an illness curable by the blood of virgins... she does not know and is afraid to care. "I'm Levy."

"Primo." Evan kneels, unshoulders her rucksack and fetches his package.

"You were careful," Levy whispers.

"Huh?" Evan rises, package in hand.

"You were careful!"

In her hand, the package jerks!

"Uh..." Evan stares at the squirming thing, roughly the size of two boxes of chocolate stacked atop one another. She'd missed the 'handle with care' warning labels plastered upon dull-brown wrapping. "What the hell?"

Again it quivers, this time nearly jumping from her hand. Levy snatches it before she can hurl the thing out the nearest window.

"Careful! Were you careful?!" Levy's glassy eyes intensify as he clutches the agitated package in both clammy hands. "They told me that you people were careful! Careful! This was to be kept at 18 degrees. Did you keep it at 18 degrees?!"

"Uh, yeah, of course. We're...the best," Evan looks everywhere but at that writhing thing. "Angel Couriers ..." But the slogan slips away from her. What the Hell is... no. She does not want to know. Nervously, she returns the zipped rucksack to her back and grabs the thumb-imprinter. "Umm, 18 degrees, yeah..."

Levy angrily thumbs the device, identifying himself as the package's receiver, as well as recording the date and time of its delivery. With a hand that bore visible veins, in even this crappy light, Levy snatches the biodegradable receipt that pops out of the unit. "You disgust me..."

"Pleasure doing..." The conference room door is slammed in her face, the booming echo not hiding Levy's frantic footfalls which carry him to a date with whatever sick thing he'd ordered.

"What, no tip?" She huffs. "Scrot..."

Trudging down the twelve flights, Evan retrieves her bike from the wall of the spotless lobby. The security guard hasn't moved so much as an eyelash.

"Mr. Levy's a perv," she warns him. "Watch your ass." And she's out of there.

As she powers away, Evan realizes her right hand is compulsively scrubbing at her denimed thigh. It had been the unwitting victim, the hand that had gripped Levy's undulating delight. Sometimes, this job is just too weird.

And sometimes, it makes her laugh. It's after eleven bells and she's racked up four of her six deliveries. Wet and motivated by the nearness of her bed, she had turned to the fifth, a pickup from an opulent residence where an elegant gentleman, fresh-faced despite the hour, had surreptitiously greeted her. Anxiously, he handed over her delivery and its destination, a ten minute jolt to a nondescript, unguarded apartment building up in northwest. She had rolled right in, parked her bike against the lobby's mailboxes and loped to the third floor where, after knocking at 203, she had occupied herself by staring at the package in question. A shake, just to be sure...

She's done a million of these runs. A husband with a thing on the side sends his mistress an 'I'm sorry I can't see you tonight, honey' gift. The girl always accepts, though their reactions range from spitting fury to inconsolable sobbing. One lupa had actually spat in her face which, Evan decided, lent new meaning to 'shooting the messenger'. Truth is, the sobbers are worse; the girls who can't hold off, break down in private, preferring instead what little solace Evan's shoulder can offer. The absolute worst!

The wood-paneled door swings inward and a man, just out of the shower, fills her view. Twenty, brown hair curling past his damp shoulders, towel about the trimmest of waists. Damn...

"Uh, package for, umm, 'my darling Cleeves.'" The gentleman's words... "An engagement, unexpected, he said. He apologizes."

"I'm Danny Cleeves," the man nods, accepting the gift and then the thumb-imprinter. His muscled chest glistens as he takes his receipt, handing back the device. "What?" He's staring at whatever her face is doing. And just what is her face doing?! "You've never made a drop to a guy's boyfriend before?" A tiger's temper stirring in those pretty green eyes...

"Uh, no, it's not that," Evan flails. "You could. I'm just... he's just so... old."

"What can I say," wickedness in his smile, "The little green pill works miracles south of the line."

"*Oookay* then, have a nice night." Evan doesn't linger for a tip. The boy could be Areus himself... that is an image she does not need.

But for all of the insanity, there's sweetness too. Her final delivery comes from a night-blind father in his mid-fifties who pays her to deliver a present to the sheltered porch of his newlywed daughter. He wants it there for her to find when she leaves for work in the morning. Touched, she smiles at the sweet man, does the song and dance with the thumb-imprinter and executes his wishes without incident, coming off the porch with a few minutes to midnight.

Her apartment building is a dirty bricked affair set marginally back from a painfully busy street in Carson. Balconies jut out from the apartments like badly-angled teeth in the world's most malformed jaw while, below, a few battered planters line the unswept walkway to the building's front door. No attempt to plant anything in them; just hard-packed dirt without the capacity to nourish.

It had taken three nights for her to regret her choice to engage the one-bedroom on the third floor. Her little patch of home is sandwiched between a wannabe thrash-metal star on one side and a perpetually combative couple on the other. The former she had dubbed Boomboom; the latter, the Bickersons. Over the years, both had lived down to her expectations.

When the moon is full and the stars are aligned, the strains of the latest Gnroar album from Boomboom's harmonizes with the happy sounds of smashing glass from the Bickersons. If her parents could see her now.

Evan hefts her bike's fiber frame and jogs up the poorly carpeted stairs. For the meager rent she pays, it's unfair to expect perfection. Yet one headlong plunge down these crappy stairs is all that's between her and a broken neck. That she cannot afford.

Not that she'd take the elevator, even if it had been operational. And it's not. Her building's super, a man who saw to his own amusements before the needs of his tenants, had framed the elevator's door with yellow crime scene tape. She gives him credit. Unlike most of his funnies, that one's worth a giggle.

Unlocking the door to her apartment, proud 313, Evan nudges it open a foot, reaches 'round the leading edge and tugs a rag from the inside doorknob. This she puts to working free the worst of the grime on her tires before she trundles the bike inside and locks the door behind her.

Her keys land on her kitchenette's countertop as she maneuvers the Yager into its place of honor right next to the front door. She'd done what she could with her apartment. The hunter-green carpet had been kept relatively clean and so had the darkly toned kitchen with its black Simuloi countertops and its off-white tiled flooring. She'd repainted the walls white after repeated pleas to her super to enliven their shabby state went unanswered. Her living room possessed a couch covered in black cloth, a wall unit done in a cheap but faultless dark wood, two mismatched lamps on two mismatched stands bracketing the couch, and two retro speakers the size of small cabinets tucked into the room's dusty corners. It's a little slice of control in a world that seems beyond her will.

Only three bits of art on the walls; three framed photographs all clustered above her wall unit. The first is her immediate family in happier days: her swarthy father behind her, her blonde mother beside her, and her eight-year-old self in the center possessively clutching a chocolate cone. A festival, she remembers, though which one escapes her.

The central photo is of her at her year-12 graduation: the cap, the formal clothes. She's forever frozen in a shy wave to the camera, a nervous smile flickering. The last photo she'd found in a box of her parents' old wedding things, framed, glassed, and covered over with dust. Her mother is in a breezy blue summer dress, dad in a traditional dark suit. Post ceremony? The way they look at each other; how their faces shine.

She's cheered to look at them; there's no sadness here. This is innocence on parade, faces unmarred by loss and grief. Her friends are now her family, but she wants to remember, needs to remember, even if it hastens the coming of loneliness.

She showers then, watching two shifts worth of grime and sweat circle the drain. It feels so good just to stand here, under the heavy, hot spray, feeling it needle her tired skin. She closes her eyes and turns her face into that jet, letting its heat transfuse her, the whole of her. Only when the water runs cold does she step out and dry off, retiring onto her small balcony from which she absorbs one last look at the night's sky. It's still raining, but no matter. She's home now and, even though the clouds obscure them, she can feel the stars.

Evan calls up something lulling, quiet, on the stereo. Surrendering to sleep without song is always a struggle. It hadn't been 'til one of the funerals that the memory returned to her, her mother's voice lulling her younger self to sleep; unconditional love in a purer time.

How can the mind forget so much of what's so important? Photographs recall every last detail. But her memory? It doles out only fragments, a jumble of pieces that never quite fit. She wants those memories, those early times, so much. But even though now is when she needs them most, they remain lost, dismissed. Bested by a photograph...

Human superiority is a joke.

Her bedroom is spartan: a wicker chair whose service is limited to bearing her dirty clothes, a chest of drawers suffering under the weight of too many tops and a clean-sheeted bed with a colorful green duvet slung over it. Rarely had it all seemed so inviting.

There are nights, she muses, when life seems meaningless, when reflecting upon the day makes her feel as if nothing of consequence has occurred. Another day, another dollar, another beer... is it wrong to accept that not every day can have meaning? But if that day has no meaning, then what contribution has she made to the greater whole, that intangible, almost infinite force of life beyond her window?

Is it enough to be alive?

Evan switches off the floor lamp next to her bed and slides under the fluffy duvet. Finally, her eyes can close. Meaning, she decides, can keep.

DAY TWO

3

"This shit tastes like shit."

If she had a credit for every time her bunkmate had offered his enlightened opinion on the quality of the mess hall slop, she wouldn't have to be a windrider.

"It's one thing if it's just bad; bad I expect. I've gotten used to bad, but this is... this is a new level."

There are levels of bad now? Gruel is gruel. Their lunchtime restorative, a protein-heavy goo, is too bland, too much like nothing, to be offensive. It's energy, calories, in a world where calories are the difference between living and dying.

"If you don't want yours..."

Troy doesn't look up. "It ain't that bad."

The mess seats 200, 200 sweaty workers too tired or too preoccupied to be loud. Do they wonder, as she does, if this will be their last shift, or are they, like Troy, numb to that now? The heavy clack of spoons striking bowls, searching for that last gram...

Occasionally, an inspector will come out from the core to hear their gripes: the pay, the food, and whatever else occurs to them. A company man, in his company boots and his company watch, guilt-selling them on the mission, on their sacrifice for the collective. "We can't do any of this without you, without your amazing efforts."

"You've all seen the potential," he had told them the last time he'd been out this way. Pretty boy with his perfect, pretty hair. "You know how what we're doing is going to change everything. You've seen it. What we need from you all is the dedication you've been giving us. We need exactly that."

"Look, it's no secret there's been discontent, which is why we've instituted these honesty sessions, so people can talk, vent, you know, get things out on the table. We just don't want another Section 24 on our hands. No one wants that."

Of course not. Organized protests damage productivity in a time vital to the collective good. Not that lost productivity had stopped the authorities from sentencing the ringleaders to hard time in the uranium mine, according to rumor anyway. "Just tell us what you need," says the company man. "We'll get it to you."

Tonguing gruel from her teeth - it calcifies if you let it sit for too long - she gets up, puts her bowl in the recycler and, without a word to Troy, pushes out into the hallway to loading. Colorful flyers on the bare walls, godly reminders to stay strong in the struggle, to report sinful activity, to obey the laws put in place by the Continuous Council. Funny, in her father's day, it was called the Emergency Council.

No flyer is going to tell this windrider what she can and cannot do with her private time.

Loading is a cavernous, chaotic room strewn with benches and bodies. Riders come and go, anonymous in visors opaque against ultraviolet light. The new suits come to them from the shop, bright yellow, the better to spot your partner out in the Yonder, but it takes only a couple trips for the sandstorms to eat down to the bare metal skin. Gray then, dull, with only a hint of yellow under the arms and between the legs, where exposure is minimal.

Though the suits are maintained by red-eyed technicians who rely on a host of tools and tricks to keep things functional, it's the robo-techs that do most of the lifesaving. Tireless, they identify errors in filtration, in applied patches, in suit integrity until, cleared, the windrider steps into the lock, waits for the inner door to seal, and then punches out into the beyond.

As she's suited, tested, patched, and put through the lock, she's wondering just how Yonder came to be the name for this deserted expanse of gray-brown sand that stretches out to the end of the world. Sometimes the sandstorms are so strong, they gray out the sky, but even under calm conditions the sun struggles to penetrate. What must she look like from up there?

The habitat is behind her now, a patched dome, some 200 feet across, that clings to the lee-side of a hill which has saved them a thousand storms over. Winds down out of the north spend their fury against it in a war of erosion they will inevitably win. But by then, no one will be left to care.

Other than the Project, wind is about all they have left. There are hopes for other sources; "We're on target for another uranium strike," declare the company men, but in this world you don't get lucky twice. So it's wind cradles, helium balloons attached to small wheels that, when spun by the wind, generate electricity. The faster the wheels spin, the more electricity comes humming down the tethers connecting the balloons to the anchor sites arrayed around the dome. A thousand feet up, most of them, where the winds are fierce, but stop short of tearing the cradles apart. Each windrider is assigned their own patch of 500 cradles: check them for damage, patching up any signs of wear; prevent them from tangling with each other, a fate liable to bring your whole patch down on your head; and keep a watchful eye out for the next storm, each of which is capable of putting you six feet under. That's when the real pay comes, when it storms. While everyone is battening down the hatches and finding safe harbor, you're out here, in a sandstorm, knowing everything is riding on you winching those cradles down out of the worst of it. Upwards of 160 miles-per-hour on the ground, worse a thousand feet up, where the cradles would be easily torn to shreds if left unattended. And all this while you know your life rides on Fate's roll of the dice.

It's the best they know how to get done what they need to get done. And it keeps you good with the priests, which never hurts.

Of her cradles, only three need repair. She's able to winch each one down and apply the necessary patches before releasing them. Quite a sight, her gray boots digging into brown-black earth as she gazes up at a cluster of hundreds of red windwheel balloons spinning in a wind she instinctively braces herself against. It's the first thing that comes to a windrider, knowing how to set your feet, how to ride the gusts, how to surrender. She watches all those tethers strain south, amazed so few of them snap. Yeah, snap, loosing their cradles to go rocketing off into nowhere, into nothing. A nothing of their own creation...

The only blip comes at the end of her shift, a yellow recall. She winches her patch down to quarter mast and gets down on hands and knees, digging them into the earth, to ride out the blizzard of sand and debris that buffets her, envelopes her, thunders in her ears. When her shift ends, she can barely hear the bell. She has to crawl back, blind, to the lock and, throw herself inside to safety. Another day...

Troy's at the mess table again, for dinner.

"This shit tastes like shit."

She just can't, not again. She hands him her bowl of gruel and walks out, leaving his confusion and gratitude in her wake.

Her room is military chic, ten by fifteen feet of living space into which two people have to cram their worldly possessions, not to mention beds and dressers. After a long, hot, thought-obliterating shower in the block toilets, she sits on her bed, army green, and keys up her photos, needing to see Garry, needing to remind herself. She forgets his face otherwise, the strength of his jaw, the heat in his eyes. Where's her big brother now? Her brother who believed? Her brother who bought in?

"Oh, you're kidding me," she whispers as the request pops up on her screen. She obeys; what else can she do?

The priest is waiting for her in his rooms, calling her in on her first knock. A richer space than hers in every way: carpets, drapes, religious texts.

"This isn't necessary," she tries to tell him. "I'm on board. Wouldn't be working like I do if I wasn't."

But the priest just smiles at her, beckoning her to sit with him, to drink his tea, to be soothed by the stillness he tries to affect. "I know. You are an excellent worker; I looked at your records. Which is how I know that's the fifth time in the last three days you've looked at those pictures, those same pictures mind."

She bites back her anger, her violation, in an attempt to stay calm. All she wants to do is...

"He is blessed. He is in the company of God. He is in our Maker's hands. He is in our Maker's light. Surely you do not ask more of God than that."

"No," she whispers. "I'm...honored...that he was Selected." If she looks at him, meets his knowing eyes, she's certain she'll kill him.

"When the Great Tragedy struck us, we had a choice, child. We could fight on in some vain hope that matters would turn in our favor; we could relent, capitulate, cower, and wait to die; we could make good of our situation; or we could embark upon a bold plan, a plan that would restore to us all that we had lost. Our forefathers had that choice, child, and they chose boldly. They meant for us to continue the work they began in darkness, and there have been few families who have done more in that effort than yours. Your father was a great man, a hero."

And dead to her since she was six, so obsessed with trying to build the very thing that this 'priest' deifies that he has never had time for her.

"And now your brother. We ought to honor them both, as they should be honored. We should not mourn them, child."

She memorizes the pattern of his fancy carpet.

"One wonders why you chose a different path, equal in honor but lacking in... Well, I suppose that is not a matter for discussion now. We are so close now, so close. Have some tea with me, yes? And then we shall pray for him, for them. Next to God's love, your pictures are dust."

Perhaps they are dust, but they mean more to her than these empty words, these exhausted notions of a grand design. 'Have faith,' they demand. But how? How is she meant to have faith, in the science that destroyed them or the God that failed them in their darkest hour? Have they honored you, Garry, or are you just another fool? Just another believer... just another goddamned victim.

When the priest finally releases her, she goes straight back to her room and her pictures. It is the only defiance she can muster. Tomorrow, she will continue as she has, having no choice but to contribute to an endgame that has killed so many and changed so much. She stretches out on her bed and is asleep hours before curfew.

With a shudder, Evan awakens in a sweat-soaked bed, in her room, in her body. What the...! What was that? Her night-darkened room is silent but for her panting breaths.

She rises to change into a dry t-shirt. But as she returns to bed, to the dry side of the bed, a feeling pursues her, a dislocation, as though she does not quite belong here. Or is it that she does not precisely know what here is? Morning will restore order to the world, so she closes her eyes, but sleep is an hour in the coming.

4

The street is quiet at 4 a.m.

For hours, Morgan has silently observed the five-story apartment building from an alley across the way: third floor, second window from the left, number 313. She's been all around this block, searching for the best vantage of the room and its points of access. Yes, not withstanding the rats, this'll do just fine.

Around midnight, her target had rolled home. Morgan had been perfectly positioned for a good look: the patched pea coat; the slick bike; and, thanks to a streetlight's glow, the flash of an intense face. Oh, but her photograph had not done the girl even marginal justice.

Just after midnight, the light from 313 had gone out. Sensible habits... another hallmark of the lonely. What's she like? Who does she like? Is her life contained in that bar of hers? "Eye on the ball, Morgan," she tells herself softly.

If the pattern holds, another hound with zealous eyes will soon take up the hunt. For all their skill and determination, their tactics are basic. Each one makes their first order of business the procurement of a weapon, in a country with some of the most restrictive gun laws on the planet. Buying a gun here, legally mind, necessitates a two week waiting period. A couple calls back home, to some tech-savvy connections, had given her a line straight into the Bureau of Firearms in which new permits came armed with handy little photos. And for the ones who decided to play it dirty, well... This isn't her turf, but she knows how to get information. Put it about that she's willing to pay top dollar to track down some creepy-looking terrorists and watch the tips roll in. Even criminals have civic pride.

It's the zealots who cannot wait the two weeks that Morgan worries over most. These are the ones willing to improvise, to try, to throw out the rules the others seem to be following. Drag the girl into an alley and snap her neck, hit her with a car on her way to work, break into her home and put an end to her in her sleep. When seeming thousands hunt one, what need have they of strategy, of protocol? Just once do they have to be better than her, faster than her, luckier than her... just once... and it's all over.

In her line, you have to be lucky to be alive. Skill just isn't enough to escape retirement which, for most, is a permanent vacation in a bullet-riddled ditch. While she's avoided that much, Hyro had been a close call. Her left knee had been blown up by a shot straight through the joint, front entry, rear exit and her kneecap in-between. Two months confined to a bed in the district care center, under a false name, as doctors patched in tissue and steel. And the damn thing hasn't been the same since.

He'd come to her then, in that bed, when she'd been wondering if she was slowing down. "I have a job for you," he'd said with a smile towards the bulky Rehabber that had swallowed her knee whole. For a device meant to accelerate her healing, the damn thing had sure made her itch in places she couldn't scratch. "It's about a girl you're to protect." And suddenly the care center hadn't seemed so bad.

She's never had it in her to protect things. She's eight years old, slouched with the other neighborhood kids before a precinct cop who's taken it upon himself to teach those street kids a little something about the good life. The cop labors under the delusion that having them plant flowers all over their concrete jungle will motivate them to care for the place. They can plant a million of those little yellow blossoms, but their violent world is still there, unable to be tamed by any magnitude of floral veneer.

Fully aware of its ineffectiveness, little Morgan plants little yellow flowers and finds that all but a few die out quick. The cop tries to explain, to convince her it's the soil. But all she sees is the death her touch brings. Isn't that what her mother's been telling her all along, how she's a cancer, a killer of joy and how her father...

Ancient history. She is what she is and nothing is going to change that.

Which, of course, made her contact's demands of her all the more galling. She had been lying in that bed, wondering if she'd walk again and he's telling her to throw aside their tidy little arrangement in favor of protection. Leave behind a nice, profitable career for... this? An interminable vigil for a girl who...

No! She can't think about what he'd told her in her apartment while the oblivious rain battered at the window. Just another job... that's all this is.

Under gloom's cover, Morgan had installed cameras that covered all available approaches to the building in which her target now sleeps. She'd tied the feeds into her slate, which is set to alert her at the first sign of movement. Until then, she has nuts to shell and eat, a wet crate to sit on, and a photograph to keep her warm.

Those gray eyes are captivating, so marked by pain and peevishness. Fidelity to the job keeps her here, but this face makes the wait bearable. The girl is so young, so hard, yet has no idea what hardness is. Morgan smiles.

A shadow flickers. Morgan jerks her head up and checks her watch as her slate softly beeps a warning. An hour wasted in her thoughts. Angry, she silences the computer, slips it into her jacket and is up and out of that alley.

Resident, visitor, or better? He's already inside: black leather jacket, closely cropped hair, male, maybe 5' 10". Morgan's back skims the weathered wall of patterned stone next to the front door as she watches her new target scan the names along the lobby's row of tarnished mailboxes. Giving himself a curt nod, he slips soundlessly into the stairwell. Not a resident then. A visitor? She can't take the chance.

Growling, Morgan runs round the side of the building and pushes through a fire door she'd prepared for just this eventuality. Pack foam stuffed in the lock to jam it up... works every time.

Rubbery, brown carpet underfoot. She hurries into the lobby, rips open the stairwell door next to the disabled elevator, and peeks up to spy the third floor exit swinging closed. Damn!

Hands out for balance, she leaps up the loosely-carpeted stairs three and four at a time. Twelve seconds to reach the third floor; two more to fish Old Faithful from her jacket. Fourteen seconds for him to work on the girl's door... she'd have done it in ten. Cycling three quick breaths, she holds the fourth and slams into the hallway, wrist cocked, elbow flexed, gun tracking. The door to 313 yawns open.

She's down the hallway in a sprint. Her shoulder catching the wood of the closing door and slamming it the rest of the way open and into something, the bike! It's toppling to the floor, but there's no time for that.

A shadow spins and comes for her. She has time to kick the door closed before a shoulder crashes into her chest. The world goes white as her lungs explosively empty. And now it's her back on fire as she's hurled against the unforgiving doorjamb. She does not hear her gun thump to the carpet.

A hand whips up at her, a stray skein of moonlight catching the edge of the ten-inch blade as it slices for her throat. Time slows as she feels, reflected in that light, her futures, and then her mind screams a warning and her forearm shoots forward, smashing into his wrist and deflecting his attack high and wide. The blade's greedy point stabs the wood of the closed door two inches above her head, sending splinters raining down. A breath...

And then he's yanking the knife free, launching a second strike, but she's ready this time, seizing his attacking wrist and holding him prisoner long enough to bring her knee up into his groin. Her prey cries out, doubling up on his agony. And then, snarling, she's moving, using his captive wrist to spin him round so she can seize the back of his coat and drive him headfirst into the kitchen wall. She can barely breathe, but feeling his knees go wobbly under the impact tells her they are now on equal terms.

In the precious seconds before this dazed bull straightens up, she's wrapped her left arm around his thick neck, contracting it viciously. He flails at the steel choking the life from him, but her leather sleeve blunts his rage. He'll have to do better than that.

Her prey staggers ahead and into the kitchen, searching for salvation. He tries driving her into the counter, the oven, the cooler, reducing them to grunting animals. The world is crashing down around them as her shoulder knocks a toaster flying. He's going to break her back if he keeps this up. She tangles her boots with his, tripping them to the tiled floor, and they're rolling into the living room, grappling for control. Where is his damn knife?

Breaking her chokehold, her prey gasps for precious air even as he hurls an elbow into her, catching her sweet and pitching her back onto a couch. Fucking scrot! Bellowing, he follows her, spilling the furniture and returning them to the floor. Magazines fly as she lands atop him. She wastes no time, shattering his nose with a savage strike from her forearm, but now his fist is pounding at her, driving what feel like rusted nails through her battered ribs. His blood is everywhere! She has to end this! Her stiffened thumbs drive down at his eyes.

That does it. Her kill tries to curl up around this fresh agony, but her bloody hands are already around his throat, squeezing. His ruined eyes bulge. They had been so vividly blue - a cold to contain all of hell's pain.

They are blood and pulp now. But even so, she searches them, waiting for the moment when the light fades and his story ends.

A growl from beneath her...

And then this dying thing is somehow surging up at her, careening them into the entertainment center. Once, twice, three times his desperate fist hammers her side, water streaming from his cratered eyes and crimson from his ruined nose. Where does he get his strength, she marvels, as parts of her go numb.

Neither of them see the lights come on, hear the sounds of distress. Their worlds are reduced to this one, brutal moment of truth, of victory. His fists fall away, limp to the ground. And even through the beating he's put on her, she feels the darkness swell. She has won this fight. She watches as her hands expel his soul and blank his zealot's eyes.

Coughing, she rolls from her kill, her name and her world returning to her. Every inch of her throbs as she slowly sits up, clears her blood-blurred eyes with the back of a sweaty hand and looks up at a photograph made flesh. Fear's etched into every line of that startled face. An alarm clock, gripped in a trembling hand, is poised in attack, its cord trailing forlornly behind.

Silence between them, silence in the collision of their worlds.

Oh, honey, Morgan thinks, as she stares. *Why you?*

And then the girl comes alive, out of shock. "Don't move." The voice trembles, thick with emotion and sleep's disuse. "I'm calling the police." She inches around the skewed coffee table, stepping over broken glass and rumpled magazines. But even though her fear has her shaking, the white-knuckled grip she puts on her only weapon stays true.

"Don't," Morgan hacks something wet into her hand. "Don't." Wiping it on the jacket of the vanquished, she climbs up onto wobbly legs. The madly-spinning world forces a strategic collapse upon a nearby chair. "I'm not... gonna hurt you."

Morgan puts her head between her knees to reclaim her senses even as her hands feel out the worst of her wounds. Her chest is only bruised, thanks to her enemy's poor aim. A few inches lower and she'd have been fighting off a wild boar with broken ribs. "Hear me out." It's as if she's swallowed fire.

***

It's a war zone.

A broken body lies at the victor's booted feet. Based on his size, Evan guesses male, but between the darkness and his face, masked by so much blood, she doubts she'll ever know for sure. The fight's destroyed half her apartment! Her living room, her kitchen! Everything's in pieces. Even her precious Yager sprawls, as if broken, before her scarred front door.

In the tumult, Evan is barely aware of her state of undress. A faded gray t-shirt, her favorite for sleep, hangs stretched out and loose from her shoulders, its hem unanchored at her thighs. Nothing else between her and this... murderer. The clock radio, an antique she picked up from a trip to the flea market with Zia, is gripped so tightly in her left hand that her fingers ache.

"Shut... shut up and stay where you are." She needs the phone, the phone! But, flustered, she cannot look away from the corpse. Yes, the corpse... in her home. This can't be happening! "You killed him! In my living room, you've..." Something rises in her throat.

The killer straightens to a sitting position on Evan's chair, a trembling, bleeding hand clutching her ribs. The hard face is already swelling; one particular blow has split her lip, attracting her tongue to the wound. Not a shred of remorse in watering green eyes.

When the killer speaks, it's through gritted teeth, her pain and anger manifesting into a growl as good as any Evan would find in the wild. "I did my job! And if you're smart, you'll calm down and..."

"Calm down? Calm down?! You killed him!"

The instant the panicked shout leaves her lips, Evan flinches.

Silence.

Nothing from Boomboom, nothing from the Bickersons. But why does she care? She should be screaming for help. "I have to call the police. This has nothing to do with me..." Her jittery feet back her up against the battered wall unit, her hand sweeping across its disturbed surface for the phone that should be there. "Whatever...this... whatever this is, it has nothing..."

The killer coughs again, tries to stand, and decides instead that her cushioned purchase is good for now.

"Evan... you have to be calming down and thinking," she gets out, between labored breaths. "Not... here to be hurting you."

"You know my name." Quivering, Evan's hand closes over the phone's reassuring bulk. Savior! Her thumb punches it on as she brings it forward. Three digits... three digits and help will be on its way, deliverance from this nightmare. But she's no sooner pressed the first digit before she sees the gun.

It's a black thing, dark against the pale, shaking hand that holds it. And yet Evan has no doubt the killer's aim will be true. Green eyes drill into her, causing her heart to thunder.

"Turn off the phone, Evan," the killer hisses, a snake ready to strike if pushed. She produces a bottle of pills, long and thin, from her battered leather jacket and, while keeping the gun's fat muzzle trained on Evan's chest, she wedges the bottle against her knee and leverages off the cap. "Turn it off."

Rattled, she complies, but not on her life is she relinquishing it.

Evan's gaze drifts up from the gun's black maw to find her intruder dry swallowing two of the bottle's blue disks. The effect is immediate: a relaxing of the eyes, a softening of the mouth. When she stands, it's with an addict's ease. The bottle disappears.

She's tall, Evan realizes. Conquering green eyes, a feline's eyes, set off a purposeful face of angular, pale planes that tolerate no measure of weakness or timidity. Short black hair, matted with rain and grime, is slicked to a forehead drenched in sweat. Battered lips, speckled in blood, have pulled back to reveal white teeth in a jaw gritted against damage suffered. The body looks strong, but specifics are lost under the shroud of that black leather jacket. The pants are just as dark; some kind of soundless cloth.

"I'm going to be pointing this at the ground."

Evan manages to nod and down the gun dips, fixed now upon carpet a foot in front of her naked feet.

"Let's be starting again. My name be Morgan. I'm to be keeping you from this." The addict's boot rudely nudges her victim. "You weren't meant to be seeing this." Her jaw tight. "This complicates things."

"Ya think!?"

Evan feels drunk, breathing hard as she skirts the body and backs her way into her kitchen's meager protection. She has to be dreaming. "Listen...I don't know who you are or who's after you, or... I don't want to know, okay? You stumbled into my place, you fought with a guy. Maybe you wanted... maybe you wanted... no, it doesn't matter what you wanted. You did... I mean, you did what you needed to do. Just... that's over now. Thank you. I'm... thank you. I'm good now. It's good now."

"No." The addict sheathes her creepy gun in her jacket, careful not to touch her leather with hands splashed by enemy blood. "Not how this plays. You be in the line of fire. The job isn't done." The accent's thick; Belgravia? Working class... definitely not from around here. "I won't be leaving."

Oh god... there's a Dust whore in her house! Sure, there've been parties at Johnny's where matters got out of hand, and she did her own fair share of experimentation back in her darkest days, but this is beyond that; this is an addict probably ready to kill for her fix! "Okay," Evan bargains. "You... take care of him and, uh..." She's in her ravaged kitchen now, gingerly backing through clutter she'd have once said that only a tornado could produce. "And... I'll...we'll... figure something out."

"You'll be stupid... you'll rabbit... make me track you down. You'll be calling the Blueshirts."

The police? "No, I'll... I'll be here. I won't call anyone."

"Until I can be telling you how it is..."

"Yes. I'll be here." Thinking only of that gun, Evan turns away. There's an upended bottle of rum on the counter, just a single rotation from a long, destructive fall to the floor. She rescues it, sees it's only a quarter full, but that'll do in a pinch. Two quick turns of her wrist does for the cap. And then the bottle's slick mouth meets her twitching lips. And she's swallowing, liquid gold, the burn ripping through her chest as the cap finds the garbage. The bottle won't have need of that anymore.

Grunting in what Evan hopes is reluctant agreement, the woman in black stalks to her victim where she crouches and, with unmistakable expertise, strips him of a watch, a cash card, and a few subway tokens. A snort of disgust. "Every time..." And then, giving no consideration to her wounds, she slings the body onto her shoulder, as a friend might carry a companion too drunk to walk. It might've passed muster if not for the blood upon both of them a blind man could see.

"Stay," she warns, as Evan, bottle still in hand, scrambles to open the door. "Nothing stupid..." Then, with her burden across her back, she steps over the fallen Yager and into the hallway. Evan entertains her disbelief for one whole second before slamming the door in the nightmare's wake.

"Oh my god. Oh Savior..."

Frantically, she engages the door's defenses, security chain and deadbolt both. Neither will be an obstacle to her intruder's will, but right now, right here, she'll take comfort in even symbolic safety. Thus engaged, she falls against the door, her door, face pressed to its scarred wood.

"Oh Savior."

Not until she makes herself decent with last night's jeans and a tattered blue sweatshirt do her teeth cease clattering. Stay occupied... think!

But she can't, not with this mess. She sets about removing disaster's hand from her home. Her bike's given a thorough examination before being returned to its post. Then she's plucking toasters and cutting boards from the kitchen floor and setting them right. And last, her savaged living room where she numbly collects magazines and straightens her furniture. Her photographs! She sees them now, knocked crooked by the melee. Her memories... her memories watched a man die...

The carpet, too, has been a witness to the night's chaos. Kneeling before the wall unit, she finds smears of dirt, slivers of wood, and a splash of dark blood that gleams dully as it dries. This isn't happening. How could she have gone to sleep in peace and awakened to war?

It's as she kneels here, mesmerized by blood, that she realizes she's destroying evidence. The addict's threat notwithstanding, she can still summon the police; excuse away the delay and her meddlesome hand on grounds of shock. And isn't she in shock? But would they believe her? A flash of that strange gun and its huge muzzle...

Johnny's forever on about how corrupt the police are, how she shouldn't trust them. Should she run? Abandon her home for the unkind streets? She can't stop the flashbacks - waking in her bedroom to terrifying noises and getting up, still rattled from her earlier dream, to investigate... opening her bedroom door and coming upon them, two vicious dogs clawing for the slimmest advantage.

What if that animal finds out she's made that call?! It feels as if her head is going to explode!

A knife... all her efforts to erase the stain of this night and she'd missed it. Sleek in stillness, its finish gleams from beneath the coffee table. Ten inches from leathered hilt to lethal tip. She draws near, her hand automatically stretching out to enclose the hilt, to bring it to her eye. In search of better light, she stands and crosses to the window, watching the diffuse city lights break upon its keen edge. No markings, on hilt or steel. Her gun-toting intruder wouldn't need a knife's service. This belonged to another.

"Oh Savior..."

When her intruder returns, Evan's long since reclaimed her bottle. She cannot stand the sight of her shaking hands, her weakness. Until there is time to think, to process, the bottle will numb her, help her put off the decisions she cannot make.

The doorknob rattles, a quiet knock upon its heels. Her erstwhile rescuer... Does she want money now? Is she here to finish what she began? If she opens that door... A second, insistent knock.

No. She can't. To bring that addict back into her life? That's a straight-up invitation to the same chaos she had been lucky to escape the first time. But the addict won't just leave of her own volition, she's sure of that. Her bottle gripped defensively, she rises from the arm of her couch. "No..." The sound dies in her throat. She clears it. "No," this time with conviction to the thing beyond. "No... there's no way you're getting back in here. No. Go away!"

"Evan!" The addict's hiss cuts through the door like it's nothing. "I'll be breakin' the door down..."

"No, you won't, not after you... no, you won't..."

"Not leavin'." Annoyance yields to iron determination. "Might as well have it go easy, girl. Don't matter how you play this. Job says cover you. That's what's gonna be..."

And persistence is supposed to be a virtue? Evan's fidgety hands try their best to wring her bottle. "Prove it." She's shaking all over again. "Prove to me you're not some... prove it..."

"He wasn't the first." Frustration pours in from the hallway. "He won't be the last..."

Not the first... not the first man she's killed? 'The job says cover you.' 'He wasn't the first.' And now not even the rum can keep the fear at bay.

The crazy lupa is lying! She has to be lying! Evan flails about for somewhere to look, something to anchor her, finding only the familiar trappings of her now-blemished home. She knows what releasing that deadbolt will mean. But even so, she's up, her bottle poised to strike. "Savior, help me," she prays to no one as, with stinging eyes, she does it anyway.

"It's done," the intruder announces in a whisper as she steps inside and turns, locking the door in her wake. And now she's yanking soiled rubber gloves off of her battered hands. For having so recently killed, there's nothing but steely control in this damaged face. Morgan steps past Evan, unerringly locating the bathroom.

"What... did he want?"

"You..." Her monosyllabic guest finds soap to scrub her calloused hands, scowling as she watches a dead man's blood swirl into the sink's drain. "The why of it isn't for me to be sayin', not my part of the deal. For that, we be needing a few days." Washing a second time now. "Sorry," a grim smile. "Dropped in on you a little earlier than planned."

"Not your part of the deal...?" Evan's frozen to her spot near the door, her gaze flitting from the creature in her bathroom to the finger of alcohol left curled above her bottle's base.

"My man will tell you what you need to be knowin'."

"Your man..."

"Yep."

"No. No..." It surges through her, conviction, explanation. Evan thaws from her spot and starts for her bathroom. "You've got the wrong girl." That's what it is. That's what this is. "I'm not who you're lookin' for."

"Sorry, honey."

"No. You're crazy! You don't see..." Evan's winding up to a tempest when a photograph cuts her short. Fished from the woman's rain-slicked jacket, it's offered by a savaged hand thrust out from the bathroom. A chill tingling her skin, Evan sets aside her bottle and plucks it from those scarred fingers. It's her, all right, taken about six months ago while she shopped the Watermark. As she wanders away to find better light, her stranger removes her coat and begins an inspection of her myriad wounds.

"Where did you get this?" How can she look so oblivious? She places the time frame by her longer hair which hasn't lapped at her pea coat's collar in months. She looks happy, both hands occupied with cloth bags as, behind her, Zia peruses a colorful stall's selection of pastries dripping with butter. The harborside market is the city's largest, humming with business day and night. "Have you been following me this whole time?" Her fear rips right through the rum's numbing warmth.

Silence. And then a grunt.

"Tell me!"

Her cleaned-up intruder emerges from the bathroom. Minus the coat, she seems almost human, a black knight without her onyx armor. A hint of scarred collarbone peeks from the stretched neck of a worn Infinitas shirt stained dark with sweat and worse. Twenty minutes ago, there had been a body on her floor and now...

"No." Morgan checks the windows, drawing the cream-colored curtains once she's examined the street. "My man gave me the photo. I came later."

Her man again... "What does he know about me, about my life?! You have bad information. This is bad information. This isn't about me. No, he's wrong. He's got it wrong."

"No... no, he doesn't." Almost compassion in that voice. "He," Morgan points to the patch of blood on Evan's carpet, "wanted to kill you. He wants you dead." It isn't so much that the stranger's green eyes have softened; they're just not so hard. "No mistakes, no misunderstandings... nothing you could be changing. It be what it be."

This isn't happening. Evan feels a crazed laugh fight free of her constricted throat. She can't look at this thing before her, not for a second longer. She spins away, falling onto her resurrected couch.

Silence, feeling those eyes on her.

"I'm sorry. Being the one to say these things... not my job. I don't be having the words to..."

Evan doesn't look up, as if denying herself the sight of this phantom has the power to banish it from her apartment, from her life, to return everything to... normal?

"Well, I wouldn't like it either. You be crawlin' into that bottle. It be what I do too." Sympathy? Evan begins to look up when the voice continues, hardens. "But I have a job to do and I will do it. And, when this be over, and you're not dead? Then you can be thanking me. Until then, the rules are simple. Do not be fucking with me. That be all I need from you."

Evan straightens, a self-righteous burn better than booze bubbling out from her chest. Giving orders? Expecting obedience? The rum nourishes her anger, her insolence. "I make one call to the police and your life is hell..."

"You won't be doing tha..."

"No? No?!"

They stare at each other. And then the nightmare moves to speak.

"No 'I have orders'..." The burn gives a reckless fire to her voice. "No demands from you... no decrees from you... none of this 'I know better than you do.'" She stands, her cheeks aflame. "I am nobody's bitch. I am nobody's little lady." Defiant, she gulps the bottle's final measure, ignoring her intruder's glare. And then, when it has no more courage to give, "I'm in charge. I'm in charge of my life, not you, you freak show."

Shakily, Evan plants the empty bottle next to her salvaged lamp. A look back, to find that her best punch has failed against her intruder's stony exterior. She believes herself strong; she must to push through this. And yet, even with the alcohol's aid, she can't hold the woman's eyes for more than a few seconds at a time. Is it the knowledge that, behind them, is someone who can kill? Who has killed?

If this creature wanted her dead, Evan has little doubt she would be just that, so why is she alive? Why is she whole? Her 'man'... the body... 'The streets are not safe...' It all tumbles through her as she stares at green eyes unwavering in their cold resolve.

"Sleep on the couch." Evan breaks, looking away. "If you get cold, tough." She slides the murdered man's knife out from behind her lamp, grips it fiercely in a hand that, for this moment, is rock steady. "Come near me...?" The keen point of her blade lifts, points. There's no need to finish the threat.

Her intruder stares impassively at the weapon, not a muscle twitching.

Evan clocks the time – just after five bells. "I start work at 10." What's she doing? "You've got 4 hours. Follow me, don't follow me. Do what you want. Don't touch me, don't look at me; don't get in my way." And she's backing towards her bedroom, all too happy to slam the door on this nightmare.

But the second the door bangs shut, nerveless fingers drop the knife to the carpet, and Evan's stumbling unsteadily for her bed where she becomes a ball: knees kissing her chest, arms wrapped tight about her shins. She begins to rock back and forth, shaking.

For once, silken moonlight cannot calm her, meaning sleep, tonight, will be someone else's pleasure. So many thoughts, spinning, tumbling, each demanding absolute attention. She prides herself on control, on discipline, on hard work. It's how she's survived these last few years.

Gone now, all of it, with no consideration for how long it took to build those protective walls. Rudderless, her hand releases her knee to find the cordless she'd slipped into her sweatshirt's pouch. She has allies, friends who'll take her call, no matter the hour. Hell, Johnny's probably just getting home. But her thumb does not move; silence remains her confidante.

She's thinking of her dream as she uncoils to fetch the knife from where she'd dropped it. Priests in the windy desert... 'The job says cover you.'

She returns to bed, settles the duvet over her jean-clad legs and stares at the closed door, knife gripped tightly. That dream had terrified her, seized and held her. She'd give anything to go back to that moment, when nightmares were just nightmares.

What is she doing?

Why is this happening?

For the rest of the night, her eyes do not leave her door.

5

When her charge reemerges, it's nine bells.

It's immediately apparent to Morgan that neither of them has slept. The stims she'd taken ruled out rest for at least ten hours. On Evan, fear and shock had worked just as well, or so say the dark circles haunting the girl's eyes.

When Evan had closed her door, Morgan had gone about dressing her wounds. Emptying the meager medicine cabinet into the bathroom sink had unearthed enough to soothe her varied cuts and scrapes. According to the vanity mirror, she's a horror, her bruised and swelling face wearing all of the night's blows. There had been nothing for her aching ribs and throbbing side. The stims will have to do for those.

Forty minutes to stitch up her damage; twice that to cleanse her leather jacket of her kill's remains. A particularly stubborn blotch of blood had forced her into an anxious smoke on the girl's balcony.

Intermittent rains had cleaned the sky of smog, allowing her to watch it to give birth to a sunrise of cerulean and rose. No sign now of pregnant clouds. They had spent themselves before drifting away.

Not even the pulsing din of passing traffic could malign such clean and simple beauty.

Chaos rippled out from the epicenter of a mistake like waves on life's sea. She'd allowed the enemy within fifteen feet of her charge. Fifteen feet! Blindfolded, she could have shot the girl at fifteen feet. And now the fallout from that one mistake had got the girl's back up which would only complicate her job. "Damn it." She turns to ash her cigarette and...

Of stone the gargoyle has been hewn and on the balcony's guardrail it perches, a naked woman of twisted beauty. Glittering green eyes burn from a pretty face painted golden brown. The bare torso is likewise, muscled arms regally crossed beneath heavy breasts. Her waist births a serpent, a length of black flesh that coils about her, primed to strike. The eyes stare back, cunning.

"Fuck me." She blinks at the thing before flicking her cigarette off the balcony.

It's tempting to call the girl ungrateful. Morgan had saved her life. But, now, as she watches her bedraggled charge enter her bathroom without so much as a nod or a word, she works to suppress that resentment. The cliché may make it seem easy to walk in someone else's shoes, but she cannot conceive of how capsized Evan's world must be. And she, forbidden by her contact to tell the girl anything. "Everything in its proper time," he'd said. She'll not make things worse by giving into peevishness.

"Got breakfast." Morgan had run down to the corner store and bought a half dozen stale muffins. The contents of Evan's cooler she'd found to be as sad as her own. "You'll need the strength."

"Wow, thanks. All's forgiven. Forgive me, but I'm more interested in when I meet your pal, your buddy, the man who apparently runs your life? Do you fetch him muffins too?"

"Couple days." Morgan perches on the arm of Evan's threadbare couch, glaring at the two-inch band of light shining through the mostly-closed bathroom door. "We'll have to work on your manners first."

"Manners, huh?" Evan snorts as the shower kicks on. "That's rich, coming from you."

Morgan kills a fingernail. A war of words will serve neither of them. She tries a different approach. "We need to be talking about you moving out until this settles. They've made where you live, or our friend got lucky. Either way, we can't be chancing it."

Evan appears in the bathroom doorway, her eyes bluer for her anger. "Listen to me." Her shoulders quiver under the towel that barely maintains her modesty. "I don't even know why you're here, much less why I'm letting you be here. Maybe on the off chance you're right; I don't know. But what I said last night, about you not giving me orders? I mean it." White teeth flash as her lips pull back in the emphasis of each precious word. "I... am... not... leaving. And you try to change my mind about that, or anything else, and I am calling the police. That's it." And then there's just the plain wood of the bathroom door as Evan kicks it shut.

No one has ever been foolish enough to talk to Morgan that way. Anger rises in her, threatening to throw off the shackles of her control. Ignorant little... She kills a second nail.

Forty-five minutes later, there remains little sign of the evening's trauma on her charge. The stubborn eyes are rimmed in red, but all else hides behind an insolent composure. The gray hoodie and the wrinkled jeans have been swapped for a breezy white blouse under the ever-present pea coat, and black pants, made of the new shimmering sotton fabric, sheathe her long, athletic legs. Her I.D. hangs clipped to her collar, a retractable string keeping the plastic rectangle between her breasts. Strands of washed and combed chestnut hair are already curling. For one who's suffered a sleepless night of hardship and drinking, she looks a vision.

"I don't do muffins."

"What *do* you do?" Morgan can't help but ask even as she keeps her hands from becoming fists.

Evan fetches the last of her apples from the fridge, admiring the deep red before she stores two in her jacket, one for each pocket. "You're the peeping Tom. Oh, sorry, peeping Tina... Shouldn't you know that already?"

Scooping up her keys and retrieving her unscarred bike from its post, Evan walks out into the apartment hallway. Morgan barely has time to retrieve the muffins before she's squeezing through the closing door. Their eyes don't meet as Evan's key throws the deadbolt.

"Hey," Evan greets a strung-out boy of twenty who stands indolently before #312. Earnest confusion is etched across a colorless face, his hollow eyes deciding which of his two keys unlock the door before him. He does not look up.

"Boomboom," Evan tells her.

Dismissing the boy as the farthest thing from a threat, Morgan moves ahead to the elevator, pressing for the lobby. But Evan rolls past, not hiding her scorn.

"It's broken, remember? But, hey, give it a whirl. I'll meet you in the next life." Evan pushes through the stairwell door.

At this rate, Morgan's not going to have any nails left before the day is out.

"So, what's the deal," her charge asks as they make the sunbathed street. "You going to follow me around all day like my own little puppy?" She mounts her bike with a professional's grace.

Morgan's already jogging into the alley she'd squatted in only hours ago. From behind abandoned bins of trash, she wheels out her Roadie. Seconds later, she's aboard, its power throbbing between her thighs.

"A Roadie," Evan scoffs. "Oh, you're going to need more juice than that." With a snort, she's rocketing up the street, powerful legs carrying her into the glory of an autumn mid-morning.

Morgan trails behind, resisting the urge to open the throttle and teach this cocky whelp a lesson. An hour and sympathy has soured to enmity. Once this job is over, she's going to take a long vacation, where rain is a rumor and the only umbrellas anyone needs are garnishes for the drinks.

Killing is preferable to this...

Evan fills her rucksack at the central depot. From there, the magnificent city... It seems to Morgan they've conquered a thousand streets, but at least these keep her charge in sight. The three office towers Evan has slipped into force a separation Morgan cannot avoid. No pass, no entry, leaving her on the outside looking in at Evan who, each time, turns to look back at her from the lobby, grinning at her little victory.

Lunch is bought at a hamburger stand that Morgan actually recognizes. They are shoulder-to-shoulder in the midst of what had once been a residential street. Now, an open-air market, one of the city's five, sprawls chaotically, even frantically, across the converted road. Funny things, cities, possessing the power to change, grow, devour. A few dwellings persist, sheltered back from the road by high hedges, but most families have picked up and left, leaving their houses to be knocked down for more market space, more shops.

Her eyes scan the noonday crowd. The categorization of people comes easily to her now: rich and poor, business and aimless, threat and harmless. Is everyone so simply defined?

Evan startles her by thrusting a napkin-wrapped sandwich into her hands. "Well?" the girl tosses over her shoulder at Morgan, frozen on the streets. "You coming?"

They retire to a wrought-iron bench to eat as the colorful masses mill around dozens of stalls selling food, flowers, and an endless assortment of gear.

"You can keep up." Is that a compliment? "I'm impressed." The smirk seals it. If it's a compliment, it's backhanded.

She refuses to rise to the bait, keeping her eyes on the crowd. A mother passes, a boy with an ice-cream cone clutched close trailing behind her. Neither of them looks this way, but still she checks them for signals.

"All these people around, it's the safest place for me when it comes to you. Tell me something, which weighs more, you or that piece of shit you call a motorcycle?"

The punk's relentless. "You'll know when I know."

It's a good sandwich: heavy on the meat, slice of cold tomato, bit of onion. Morgan's second bite finds napkin. Her eyes find a businessman with his secretary, their hands clasped, their eyes locked.

"Look, it's entertaining and all, watchin' you trundle along behind me like a sad little orphan. But this is no dawn of a new day. There are two reasons I haven't called the cops, your gun and your gun. So don't be thinking that us sitting here is any kind of acceptance of whatever game you're playing."

"No?"

"No, it's not."

Morgan snorts, as her gaze falls on an old man in a needless winter coat, weathered hands where she can see them. "The job says protect. So I protect."

"You really believe it, don't you?" Incredulity from the needling voice behind her. "This 'man' of yours... you believe the craziness he's telling you. You're insane."

There's a lull in the traffic. Morgan turns, looks at the girl, watches her blink her weary eyes against a too-bright day. "Don't," a soft warning. "Just don't."

The girl ignores her. "I worked at it from so many angles last night."

Morgan grunts and returns her attention to the market. "And..."

"Well, if you believe that this, whatever this is, is real... and someone apparently trying to kill me last night *does* lend your case a smidge of credibility there... then that narrows it down. You believe it because you're unglued. You were stalking me, saw someone was trying to rob me and did for him. If it's that, then you saved my ass and the downside is that I'm having a burger with a nutter, but a well-meaning nutter."

"Is that why you haven't called the law?"

Evan rolls her eyes. "But if you believe it and you're not insane, then..."

There it is. Morgan turns back to the girl, finding eyes feverish with worry, worry quickly hidden from 'the nutter'.

"Believe what you want," Morgan shrugs. "As long as you're not dead..."

Evan flushes. "Very helpful. Thank you, G.I. Judy."

Morgan scowls and turns back to her scrutiny of the marketplace.

"C'mon, give me a last name. Give me something. Morgan what?"

"No..." she says with such emphasis that a bird intent upon their food startles into flight.

"Oh, I see. You're just Morgan. You're a vid-star. You and Duke sit down to rap together..."

"Listen to me very carefully. People... be wanting... to... kill...you." Burning, she whirls round and puts them nose to nose. A little thrill of delight ripples through her abdomen when the girl flinches back in fearful surprise. "Be getting that through your fool skull; no jokes, no funny word games. This morning went well; you didn't die and you didn't run away like a scared little girl. But you *do not* give me the back of your hand. I seen and done things that be putting you off your feed for weeks." The girl is biting her bottom lip now. Would it be quivering otherwise? Morgan feels her lips curling. "Beyond that, my man says you need your ass saved or it goes bad for us, the rest of us. And so what he be wanting is what's gonna happen. So finish your fucking sandwich and do your fucking job and I'll do mine." And with that, she launches off the bench and walks it off before her mouth goes too far.

How the ignorant can sit in such judgment... The world hangs on a knife point and she's in a market arguing with a child! Old enough to know more of the world than this but too uninformed to care. Her contact isn't blameless either. After all the years between them, to ask *this* of her is leagues from fair. She is no bodyguard. Her trigger finger itches too much for that.

When Morgan finally turns to eye her charge, the lithe creature sits quite still, quietly eating, sunlight on her short, disordered curls. And she the difference maker? Savior help them all. And her with her temper...

"I have six deliveries before seven bells." Evan's sullen voice easily crosses the 20-foot chasm between them. The final quarter of her sandwich she tosses to an eager bird. "Here." The rider lobs Morgan the remainder of her own lunch. "I go hard." Her jaw stubbornly set, emotion swallowed. "You'll need it."

"After that, I drink at the Iguana. It's a bar on Collins 1300 block. If you lose me, that's where I'll be, stalker. 'Til then, you think on this: I don't know who you are or what you are. I don't know why you're here. All you've given me is scraps. So I'm telling you this now: this... this is my life. My life... nutter." She hurries to her bike, throws herself aboard and, without looking back, is damn near full speed with a few powerful strides.

The girl has backbone. Morgan stows the sandwich as she follows Evan back into the city's heart. Both barrels and the girl is still standing, still fighting. Maybe they have a puncher's chance after all.

How do you convince someone their life is forever changed, that it no longer belongs to them? That maybe it never has? 'This is my life,' the girl says. And she, no wordsmith to persuade her otherwise. In this self-help society, surely someone has written a guide to the end of the world.

***

The sun has set on a blessedly uneventful afternoon before Evan pitches up at the Iguana. Mounted above the front door is the bar's namesake, Ian, a serpentine creature with glassy eyes that blink at the patrons who pass beneath him. As if he wasn't already sufficiently gaudy, Ian glows, garish greens and purples that mantle the nightmare waiting for her: Morgan, so anchored to the shadows next to the front door that not even an earthquake could stir her.

Chaining her Yager, Evan throws her shadow a brusque nod and does not stop for a chat as she pushes into her sanctuary. She hadn't known, until now, that she'd lost her tail in the busy blur of her day's errands. Is it cruel to feel pleasure at the sight of the woman's helpless fury? If this lupa follows her inside...

Decent crowd tonight; no football game, which caps the insanity. In its place, a rackball match, two sweat-soaked titans smashing a green ball at one another at bewildering velocities. The dark-haired guy on the left is cute, but he keeps netting the ball, much to the disapproval of the partisans in the half-full stands. The referee floats above the court, gazing sternly down at the contestants; a god displeased with two of his more embarrassing subjects.

The news Evan ignores. It's always something and the chances of it being to the good are nil. The RLTV screen has yet to kick into its nighttime slate, still running footage of *The Fun House*.

The program takes in sixteen initial contestants, strips away any means of electronic amusement, and bans them from leaving upon pains of disqualification. The screen is split into nine segments: the primary is always centermost, currently showing the main living area. The other segments are satellites of the primary, each trained on a room in the house. Even the bathroom is not sacred.

No audio plays from any of the secondary segments, allowing sound from the primary to come through clean. With the remote, you can replace the default primary feed with any of the eight satellite segments, centering the picture and activating that room's audio. It's revolutionary, an RLTV invention only a few months old: total voyeurism, total exposure, total guilty pleasure.

To be a contestant... hell, Evan would take *The Executioner* over the day she's had. She's always thought RLTV a little humiliating, the downtrodden prostituting themselves for cash, but it turns out that humiliation is better than abject chaos. A Root is waiting for her at her customary seat; it's good to have friends. "Guys," she greets the table: Johnny, Carter, Zia. Francis is just coming through the door. "Had a little excitement today." The words are out of her before she's aware of even wanting to speak them. A sip of cold beer to steady herself. A night gone sleepless and a day burned in motion have made her less than her best.

"Yeah? It wouldn't, perchance, have anything to do with the leather princess who followed you in here? And who is trying so very hard *not* to look this way?"

Johnny's teasing grin has Evan looking over at the bar. And there she is, her shadow, slouched against mahogany, gaze fixed on the sport beyond her. Savior, could she look any more out of place? The Iguana is hers, her refuge! "Yeah. Yeah, she cut me off, on her bike. Nearly put me on my head." She's lying without knowing why. Is she afraid her disorder will infect them, drag them down into this... whatever this is? "Stupid lupa needs her eyes checked."

"Oh, Evan," Johnny sighs dramatically. "Have I taught you nothing about girls?"

"Oh, this'll be good," Zia snickers.

"Keep in mind that I am a staunch supporter of feminism, okay? That the knowledge I am to impart is in no way a reflection of my beliefs."

"I don't remember Confucius being this wordy, do you?" Zia asks drily of Carter.

"Nope," the big man grins.

"Alright, alright. It's like this. A woman's flaws are relative to her attractiveness. It's true! Let's say you're walking down the street and someone slams into you because she isn't looking where she's going. You're annoyed because she's gotten you pretty good, plus, she's spilled her coffee all over you. But then you look up at her and you see these amazing eyes and this mane of golden hair..."

"Of course she's a blonde," Carter laughs.

"And you can tell that she's got a smoking body. Now how annoyed are you? I'll answer for you. Not... at... all. Suddenly, her thoughtlessness is a forgotten memory in the glory before you. But if this lovely creature is instead some aging hag, well... now you're yelling at her for staining your new jacket. And is she truly so blind? And maybe she ought to get her eyes checked!"

"And this relates to Evan's situation how?" Zia tries to bring Johnny back to the point.

"It relates to Evan's situation because, standing over at that bar looks like six feet of very dark, very intense trouble and, if you apply my formula to this situation, the fact that she nearly killed you, Evan, should mean about as much as a fart to a hurricane because wow... Did you get her name?"

"Leave off, Johnny," Evan tries not to scowl. "She's crazy. I don't even know why she's here. I'm just gonna ignore her and she's gonna go away."

"I doubt it. She's trying pretty hard not to look over here."

"And yes," Carter chimes in, "in Johnnyland? When a woman does not look at you, that is a sign of interest."

"Figures," Zia laughs.

"Oh, come on! You've got to at least let the woman apologize to you."

"No, I don't," Evan gives up on warning Johnny off. "Besides, sounds like you want her number more than I do."

"Oh, watch," Carter grins. "He's gonna look 'round, make sure Lohner isn't here, before he admits it."

"I ain't sayin' a word," Johnny laughs. "I'm very happy with who I have. But you, Evan? You're about the loneliest bird I've ever met. Hey, at the bar, in the leather jacket! Yeah." When Morgan looks over, Johnny has his finger crooked in welcome.

"Oh, hey," Carter frowns. "C'mon, Johnny. That's pushin' this too far."

"Johnny," Evan groans. Oh, please let her be smart enough to keep away.

But, after a slight hesitation, over her disgruntled shadow comes, slicing through the crowd and arriving just behind Francis' empty chair. A hand, gloved to hide its damage, rests on the chair-back, her bruised face grimacing through the introductions. Her devil's stare lingers longest on Evan, reaffirming her irritation.

Ever courteous, Carter offers Morgan his chair, standing and eying the creature with affable curiosity. She is the equal of his six-foot stature which visibly surprises him.

"It's okay, she's not staying." Evan squirms in her seat, willing Carter to sit down. "She," throwing a pointed look at her shadow, "has other people to run over."

Morgan grunts. If she's understood Evan's wishes, it only shows in the slightest quirk of her lips. Or perhaps that's her way of turning down Carter's friendly offer.

"You're finally introducing us to your biker friends," Johnny teases. And then to Morgan, "Nice coat. It suits you, but remind me to never challenge you to an arm wrestle. It hurts my chances with the ladies when I lose to a girl."

"When don't you lose to a girl?" Carter reclaims his seat.

"Ignore him," Johnny grins. "So, we didn't catch your name."

Evan senses as much as sees the predator shifting in Morgan's eyes as she stares at Johnny. Bruises on the woman's cheeks are sufficient reminders of last night's killing without witnessing that look in those eyes. What this creature can do when pushed too far... what she could do to Evan, to her friends... Finally, grudgingly, huskily, "Morgan."

"Nice. Well, we heard that you and Evan had a bit of a dust-up and I just wanted to say, on behalf of our girl, that she's not a bad sort. Gets testy sometimes, but all in all a good girl. See, she told us you maybe started all this, but we know better. A woman like you?

You're always in control. So we apologize for her and if you need a drink, if you wanna sit down..."

"Johnny," Evan snaps.

"What? I'm just playin' around."

"It's not funny," Zia backed her up. "Nice to meet you, Morgan."

"Mmmhmm." Morgan is still staring at Johnny. And to the extent that the man has ever felt mouse to another's cat, he's feeling it now. If it wasn't so creepy, Evan would be enjoying this. And yet... "You all be having a nice evening now." And the creature turns to go.

"Hey," Francis walks up, smiling, at least until he spots the newcomer. He stops, tries to maintain his cordial expression and is only partially successful.

Morgan, too, seems momentarily confused, blinking at Francis a few times before giving him a shaky nod and returning to the bar, her leathered back almost swallowed by the gathering crowd. What's that all about?

"I'm not so sure she likes me," Johnny confides quietly to Carter.

"Really. You think?"

"What a day..." Evan's groan gathers their attention. "And now... it's time to forget." Maybe, if she tries hard enough, she can drown out the world beyond this table. She lifts her glass, stained dark with drink. "To the days and nights that never end and oh, how we loathe them. Cheers..."

"Will I drink to that. It took me forever to find blankets for all my Afjan refugees." Carter grins as they all clink glasses.

"Oh, nice! That's classy." Johnny wipes foam from his lips. "Make fun of the homeless, penniless people. That'll help."

"Sorry, sorry, that was low." But there's little of regret in Carter's broad face, sweaty from a long day on the site. That's all it takes, one day, even in the fullness of autumn, for the poor boy to burn. "Couldn't help piling on. Alright, no more plight of the refugee."

"Now that would make a great song title." Johnny lifts his glass so that its flared mouth is an old-school microphone for his silent tune.

"Oh, please." Zia pulls her eyes from Morgan's retreating form to fix them on Johnny. "Ten seconds of you in a karaoke bar and they'd ban your ass."

"I didn't say I'd sing it well! But, I could put pen to paper. Remember, I do have a fragment of the great bard within me. I can see it now, bringing to tears the crowds of mesmerized fans, overwhelmed by the exultation of my words..."

"Yes, yes, descended from Sunspear. We know. You've told us 40,000 times," Carter snorts.

"It'll be 40,000 and one if you're not careful, oh lobstered one." Laughter as Johnny's leveled finger mocks his friend's sun-kissed nose.

"It's not my fault!"

"What, that you can't read the label on a bottle of sunscreen? I'm pretty sure that's your fault."

"Shut it. They said it was going to rain! This, this burn right here, this is on the weatherman, this right here..."

"Hey, okay, it's not your fault. I understand. Not your fault that you're a narrow-minded caveman either. No, we get it."

"Johnny, honestly, there are days I just can't make it through. And then I think of you and I get my second wind."

It feels good to close her eyes, to be still and absorb the affectionate banter, to roll her head back and stretch her sore neck, to forget for just a little while. She knows she's only delaying the inevitable, an ugly confrontation with a nutter willing to kill, but this pocket of solace created by the glow of the friendship surrounding her... if she could stay here, for just a little longer...

And yet doubts flutter at the edge of things, disharmonies to tranquility. She should've called the authorities. She should've locked Morgan out the moment the woman left with the body. The body... she lives a life of bodies now! Things had been hard enough before all this. And now...

But she can feel her sullen shadow watching from the bar, can imagine those hard, steady eyes drilling into her back, sweeping the bar for threats. What if it's true? What if some tiny measure of it is true? Seeing them fight, seeing someone die, awakened something inside her, something that writhes and squirms and demands without a willingness to admit to its purpose, its desires.

But what if it's not? Where did that knife come from? She knows where it is now, sheathed in her right boot. Hardly comfortable but eminently reassuring.

A hand settles on her forearm. Francis... She opens her eyes, smiles at him. Steady Francis, who's seen so much. His comforting proximity soothes the ripples of her discontent.

"You alright?" His voice is quiet, gentle.

"Yeah, it's just..." Flashes, worse now that she can see the merriment around her. That smashed face, Morgan's cruel hands extinguishing the last embers of life from those eyes... eyes that meant to kill her?

No... no. To what end? For what purpose? "It's a long story."

"Your new friend?"

Evan follows Francis' glance to the bar where, surrounded by untested youth, Morgan's stern, steely face stands out. She's uncomfortable, chained to her stool, a small glass of something dark set before her. Evan does not know how, but she's certain the drink is ceremonial.

"This... this isn't the place."

"Okay. You'll tell me when you're ready. You know I'll be here." As he's always been. "You sure you want that," nodding at her beer. "You look exhausted."

"If I don't, I'm pretty sure I'll go crazy..."

Francis' wise, hazel eyes study her now as they have ever since chance had crossed their paths in the college pub. He'd been weeks from graduation while she'd been completing her first semester. She'd crushed on him then, his mind, his ideas, his plans, only to find no lust there, just the comfort of a gentle soul. He had been there when it all had come tumbling down. He'd been there to offer his kindness. She still doesn't know why, with all the years that stand between them.

"If I need a place to crash..."

"Guest bedroom, second floor. It's always yours. You know that..."

She forces a grin. "Except when your harem's in town, right?"

"Except for when the harem's in town..."

Why? Why does he do this? Why does he help her? If she wasn't so afraid of the answer, she might have summoned the courage to ask him at some point. All she can do is joke with him. She steers to calmer waters.

"Do you know her?"

"Who?"

"The woman at the bar..."

"No. Can't say I do."

"Okay. Yeah, it just looked like maybe when you saw each other..."

"I thought she was going to steal my chair," Francis grins.

"That's your chair. No one is gonna steal that from you."

Early evening stretches into early night and Evan finds her life's longest day ending far more peacefully than it began. Her beleaguered body is finally demanding the price be paid for those numbing shots of rum. "I'm cashing out early tonight, guys. Need to rest my head."

"I knew that double shift would kick your ass." Zia smiles and drops her chair to four legs as Evan goes for her wallet. "Should've listened to me."

"Yeah, well, if I didn't have you to give me sage advice, then where would I be?"

"Uh-uh! You paid last night." Carter waves her off. "Your money's no good."

"You sure?"

"Yes, I'm sure. Go home, get some rest. It's on us."

"Her rest is on us?" Johnny's brows are innocently arched.

"No, the drinks." Carter glares.

"Oh, I thought you meant her sleep was on us."

"Well, as usual, you thought like an idiot."

"I love you too..."

Evan laughs, dropping a grateful hand to Francis' wool-clad shoulder.

"Let me walk you out."

"I'm not a wilting flower, Francis. C'mon."

"Okay, well, whatever's needed..."

"I know. Thank you, you know, for everything." Knowing she has another place to go, to hide, means everything. "I'll be fine."

And Evan's shoving out of there, weaving through the growing crowd. She doesn't look back to see if her crazy shadow follows her into the heavy air of late evening. She'll be there, hounding, tracking. The nutter is hardly going to give up now.

Oh, she's so tired. She's unchaining her bike even as her brain tries convincing her there's hardly anything wrong at all with settling down for a nap, right here, in the street. Just got to get home, forget about all this nonsense. It'll keep for tomorrow.

She leans into night's lengthening and winds her way to something like safety.

***

Evan's departure has reduced their table to four; three if Francis is to be excluded from their number. And why shouldn't he be? He's ignoring all else as he stares right through the door just now swinging shut behind their departed fifth.

"Francis," Johnny tries attracting the man's attention.

Those hazel eyes only reluctantly part from their vigil.

"It's okay, man. You can sit down."

Francis doesn't seem convinced, tense as he stands next to his forgotten chair in a bar just starting to hum with a young night's trade.

"That's not how it works, my friend. There's but one thing in this world that makes you that tired and it's doing the dirty all night long. The lady's got a plan, man. You can't pickle that action."

"Pickle that action?" Carter is incredulous. "Are you twelve?"

"What? There's nothing wrong with 'pickle her action'. It's a perfectly usable expression. And, hey, you knew what I meant, even if Frank here is still on planet Zingzaball."

"The floorboards caught your drift, Johnny. That's not my problem."

"Well, I'm sorry if my expression was too accurate for you. I merely meant to say..."

"We get it, you stupid sipio." Zia keeps her worried eyes on Francis as he reluctantly reclaims his seat. "What is it, Francis? Should we be worried?"

"What?" Francis surfaces long enough to blink his bewilderment at Zia. "No, no. It's okay."

"Well, we know one thing," Johnny smirks. "Leather Princess ran over Evan in more ways than one."

"I'm afraid to even ask," Carter groans.

"Evan got it on with a biker chick."

"I'm stunned that women actually like you." Zia's hands, once flat against the table, claw their way into fists. "I think maybe stupid sipio wasn't strong enough."

"I'm just trying to tell Frank here there isn't anything to worry about. There just isn't. We support her, right?"

"I'm with Zia," the foreman chimes in. "You're making a hell of a lot out of nothing just to please the perverted freak show going on in your head. You're judging Morgan's intentions on two things, that she's a girl and that she wears leather jackets."

"Girls and leather, unbeatable combination. I'm just saying..."

"No, you're assuming," Carter corrects him. "Beyond that, you're doing it to our friend. Maybe she was responsible for what happened between them. Maybe she feels bad. We don't know. And until we do know, we should keep our noses out of it when this could be anything. Morgan could be Evan's evil sibling; we don't know."

Francis looks up at Carter, frowning. Zia's mouth is open, ready to skewer Johnny, but before she can even speak...

"And I'm saying that your 'back-to-the-stone-age' beliefs make you shade this more innocently than it looks. You know what I'm talking about."

Carter darkens. "Just 'cuz I don't want to junk a few thousand years of human history doesn't make me biased. It doesn't make me incapable of reading people, Johnny."

"Alright, fine. You're right. I'm being a presumptuous ass. But let's say they *are* going home together, you know, to sleep together..."

"Johnny," Zia snaps.

"Wait! Assuming that, your belief system would put you in a position where, eventually, you'd be saying, to our friend, 'what you're doing is wrong and I don't want you to have the same rights as I have.' How's that any kind of fair?"

"Cuz there's a line, Johnny." Carter leans close, purposed. "It's got to be drawn somewhere. Give that kind of marriage the green light..."

"Say it," Johnny challenges his friend. "I want you to say the words."

Carter glares at him. "Fine, gay marriage. Greenlight that and then what, dogs, cats, ferrets... I don't care if you screw your goldfish. I don't want you to walk into city hall and marry the thing. A human woman's bad enough."

"See, that's what I don't get about people like you."

"People like me? Just who are people like me, Johnny?"

"Back to the stone-age types..."

"Oh right, how kind of you," Carter rolls his eyes. "Go on."

Johnny shrugs. "Conservatives then. Love is love, man. We've got wars on two continents while, at home, civil liberties are dying by the day. We've got problems in our streets, in our factories, in our schools, in our prisons. I can't figure out what of a million things to be pissed at when I lift my head in the morning. Hell, last night, you were in here arguing with me about the Afjan refugees! Remember the homeless guy you were advocating for? We've got him too. There are enough things in this world we can't fix. We don't have to add to our problems by saying to a whole group of our citizens, 'You, over there, who do that thing we over here don't like? You get to be second class citizens now.'"

"Fair enough... and you're right. I'd look at it different if it was Evan. That makes it real. And, you know, if she comes to me one day and says, 'Carter, want to come to my gay wedding?' I'm gonna say yes because she's Evan and I love her and nothing's gonna change that. But let's back up the bus on me being in the ignorant, stone-age camp; it's you liberals who haven't thought this thing through. Go ahead, open up civil unions, marriages, to the 'love is love' thing, what's stopping 18 people from all marrying one another? I know you can't be for older men trapping younger women into marriages. What's to stop some guy from basically buying a dozen wives? What's to stop him from doing any number of twisted things? I'll tell you what - tradition. Tradition matters, Johnny. It's what a lot of our freedoms, our culture, is based on. You take away tradition, you take away the foundation of how we've lived for all these centuries; well, you might as well just throw in the towel and walk away from our society as we know it because it sure as hell ain't gonna be the same after you and yours have finished opening up the door to every weirdo and his weirdo marriage. I don't even have to ask you if you're up for that, nutjob that you are."

"You'd be right then," Johnny leans forward to meet his friend. "Equality under the law and in the eyes of the people and the government matters more than tradition, Carter. Tradition is just an excuse for people not to change, for people to be afraid of what they don't know. It's weak. But more than that, traditions change. You'll change. I know, given time, I can make you see the light."

"Oh, you smug scrot," Carter snorts. "Great. Dog-lovers and polygamists... that's what you're giving me. That's just great."

"Forget Evan," Zia is staring at both men, their beers neglected in the heat of the exchange. "What about the two of you?"

Foreman and firebrand both glance at her, identical looks of stupid confusion writ large. "Help me, Francis. Aren't these two gentlemen giving off an inappropriate amount of man-love just now?"

Francis stirs himself from distraction long enough to smile.

Shock and more than a little dismay as the two friends glance at each other, then away, then back for a guilty peek.

"That's what I thought. Worry about your own problems before you both go off saving the world."

"But I love saving the world." Johnny clears his throat. "It's fun."

"The perfect amount of fun, and no more," Carter agrees.

"Idiots," Zia rolls her eyes. "My two idiots..."

DAY THREE

6

As the two men expected, the community field had been deserted for hours.

Perhaps, on its own, the night's mild rain would have spoiled an otherwise glorious starscape, but thanks to the industrial burn of the great city's countless lights, they'll never know. The ever present glow brightens the night from black to gray and puts paid to any notion of seeing sky.

The Contact came prepared. A yellow raincoat wraps his burdened shoulders, the delicate precipitation ticking off treated plastic.

They have engaged a park bench set some 20 feet back from a field quartered to accommodate multiple athletic codes. The nearest section is comprised of a diamond-shaped infield, strewn with dirt, and an absently-tended outfield, blanketed in grass. Lines of partially obliterated chalk connect four slate-colored pads set at each of the diamond's points while, beyond, only distant fencing shackles the outfield's weedy green. He'd found under the bench a bruised leather ball the size of a large stone which he now tosses, watching as the Fifth Principle returns it to his squeezing hand. The power of his frustration is fit to bust the ball at its seams.

"Your argument has no wisdom." This is not the first time these words have passed the tanned lips of the Contact's resolute companion. Wavy black hair framing an ageless face shows no sign of receding before the aggression of a prominent brow rippling with mounting temper. But that feeling hasn't spread to his icy blue eyes which radiate an intensity fit to shame the city lights beyond them.

"You're wrong. You must see it in them, in what they've built, in the knowledge they seek. Matters are not as they were before. They have grown; they will not listen this time. I feel it."

"It is not our province to grant clemency from ignorance." His companion's face grows sterner by the moment. "The consequences emanating from a changed course would devastate the whole, the scope of which you well know."

It is an old, exhausted argument, but the Contact is resolved that it will be different this time. "It may not be the customary way, hoping that we win more often than we lose, but I say to you now that these *old ways* are not enough, not for them. We have *seen* the price of failure; we *know* the cost in lives, in civilizations; yet out of fidelity to the middle road, you persist in shackling me. That *must* end, unless it is your wish to see another world burn."

His companion's imperious eyes spark. "Win more often than we lose..." The cultured voice is lethal, a blade ribboning the air between them. "You pass judgment on an event and a time that you did not witness. You pass judgment on your elder, and your better." Gravel crunches underfoot as the man takes a few steps towards the city lights. "From these I expect nothing. Nothing can be expected of those who know nothing. But you..." He turns to his pupil, implacable. "You have the knowledge! To choose not to heed it is an error I was certain you had... overcome."

Youth, inexperience... these have been held over him for so many years that the chafing anger they produce is second nature to him. All that they've seen and lost...

As he stares at his companion, the Contact wonders if age and experience are merely conceits glorified into virtues by old men who've grown calloused by time's abrasions. Buffers against guilt, excuses for inaction. He thinks of the Enclave, desperate men willing to devour anything simply to hold, to maintain, to survive. He imagines what they'll do if they make their greed a reality. To let that occur...

The Man's expression softens into stone. "I know why this time is different for you, but you cannot attach..." He is a frustrated father imparting the same old lesson to his recalcitrant son. "These are our laws, founded from consensus. They will not change for you. And if they will not change for you, they will assuredly not change for these you want so much to protect. If you attach, if you continue down this path, you will find only misery."

But the Contact has come too far to yield now. "We ask of them... We ask of her a sacrifice we are, ourselves, unwilling to make." He swallows, hard. "We say to her, this must be done and we watch from afar while she alone bears the consequences. The fault lies with us! This is what *we* allowed to be. This is what *we* failed to predict. And now *she* will pay for what *she* had no hand in creating."

"You tell me things I already know. We ask of her nothing more than we asked of those who came before, no more than we'll ask of those who are yet to be. We ask of her nothing more than we asked of you." His eyes have become the cores of stars; pitiless. "We each play our part, as it is meant to be. We have amended all that we will. Our course is clear."

"That may be, but the price! We are imposing our will, our rules, upon chaos. Even we cannot obviate every variable. That's a flaw we share." The Contact's hand sweeps towards the great spires of the night-shrouded city. "They find comfort in imposing order, in dominance over the life about them. It is folly. We know it is folly. Show me how we are different..."

The Man glowers. Beyond them, the city's countless lights reach out to the sky. As if in answer, a shimmering star resolves from the infinite beyond. Tinged in red, it shoots to Earth, seeking like a missile the earth it will never touch.

"There are ways," the Contact begins. "You know there are ways."

"No!" A single word and the Contact feels the door slam against him. "There is but one thing that flows from good intentions. Suffering. I believe in what I know to be true and I honor the decision of the collective. Your mandate is clear... execute it!"

Small droplets of rain grace the Man's tanned cheeks as he turns his back. "There is room for sympathy, but there is only one course."

And then he's departing, not once looking back as he passes their bench and purposefully crosses the distant street. He leaves the Contact alone in a park accustomed to the innocence of a child's laughter. They have made it destiny's playground...

Hollowed, he steps silently onto the diamond, his foot skimming the pad at first base. A light blooms up to meet him, adorning him in an emerald glow.

Another incursion had been inevitable. It is time's nature to advance cultures towards moments of reckoning, and, though some measure of these moments is invariably subject to chaos' unkind hand, interventions can still work. The others know this; they've known it much longer than he. When did their wisdom become nothing more than a veneer to hide their cowardice?

There is more than one path. He had come here knowing this, knowing his chances for an open play were slim, which is why he has laid the groundwork for an alternate route. But the cost... the risk... and yet he has never felt more certain of his proper course.

Bathed in gentle light, the Contact stares at the diamond's heart where a mound of dirt rests, undisturbed by the faint wind. He walks to it, the glow behind him fading, and steps up upon the mound's crest. The ball feels heavy in his hand as he looks to the crux of the diamond, the screen behind it. He is the only soul for as far as he can see; the only soul who knows what comes. Effortlessly, he fires the ball into the night, watching it tumble, spin, briefly defy the Fifth Principle.

It is up to Morgan now... Morgan, until he can return. He walks away, into the night. Yes, he knows what his course must be.

***

The indomitable cityscape goes on forever.

It's an amazing view from where Evan perches upon the roof of the metropolis' aged clock tower. The darkly-polished landmark of glass and stone is one of the city's grandest constructs, having marked time for centuries for the citizens below while enduring as a paean to the spirit of endeavor that built it, maintained it, and enjoined it with so many more towers of similar impressiveness. Fifty stories separate the scuffed bottoms of her dangling boots from the unforgiving pavement of the street so far below, yet not a hint of vertigo plagues her even though she's never been one for heights.

Her peerless pearl of a city had been built on a mild slope toward the sea. At street level, the decline is undetectable, but at this height the keen eye can easily track the endless march of ruddy Conplast buildings, their glittering peaks descending like shingles on a slanted roof. Pre-dawn's mystic glow favors those domed in golds, blues, greens, while towers crowned by elegant spires look, from her vantage, like swords of light thrust into the sky.

The city's five great town squares headquarter regions of those who live and work there. Their vast spaces clamor with shops that peddle food, clothes, sex, tech... much of it brought from the world over. The glory of globalization... a world shrunk to nothing.

Evan looks to the sea, which gleams darkly below the sleepy horizon. The light is insufficient to out more than the body's rhythmic undulations, but she can imagine it. By day, the twin waterfronts, separated by but five leagues, buzz with a hive of human activity while, beyond, an industrious flotilla of mercantiles and pleasure craft bob against a bed of endless blue-green. The vast, unknowable ocean from which all has come...

For one who's never given birth, the incongruity of how sheltered life can sprout from a mere handful of cells into a creature to rival its parent astonishes her. Life begetting life, begetting more life, until that life is complex enough to leave its own, immutable legacy. All of this before her, the cities, the roads, the fleets... these are humanity's true children, and the sea is mother to them all. If it could, what would it ask for that gift of life?

As her eyes wander back to her city, they fall upon a darkness missed in her earlier perusal. Buried deep inside that assemblage of monoliths oozes the smallest of blights, a single blemish on a Conplast canvas.

But it's growing! A spike of fear quivers within her as she watches the dot's nascent pulsations. Her eyes are trapped by its ugliness, its wrongness. And, as though her stare has formed a connection between them, a skein of taint rockets out to her. An oily scum finds her clothes no impediment, worming past to smother her in its necrotic caress.

And just like that, she's writhing, collapsing to her knees. It is as if all the world's ants are swarming across her skin. Frantically, she tries scrubbing away the crawling things, only to find nothing to dislodge. What's happening?! She is being cocooned by a foulness that has no name, a darkness that supersedes sight. Panic beats inside her skull, yet her frozen eyes remain locked upon that blight, that dark error.

Summoning all the courage left to her, the tainted one draws her shaking hands from her infected flesh and sends them scrabbling into the stone around her. The roof's grime bites her palms, yet she forces her kneeling body around until the error can no longer be seen. The ants quiet... still... disappear. Tears course her cold cheeks as she pants out her relief.

Desperate for a shower, a respite, she rises shakily.

A face! Looming before her, so close its distorted features blur black. Yelping, she trips backwards, needing room, but the face has a body stronger than hers.

The torso beneath the Man's washed out clothing appears normal, but the hands... they sport grotesque, bloated fingers twice the size they should be. And now she can feel his rapid pulse as those monstrous hands seize her forearms, effortlessly pinning them to her sides. Her eyes are compelled to rise and bear witness to the face, as distorted as the hands. Bulging, cyan eyes, spiderwebbed with red veins, undulate with an urgency that made their explosion imminent. His broken nose leaks crimson rivulets that writhe across cheeks, mouth and chin, all of which have been devastated by unseen blows.

A chill contorts her spine as she recognizes the man who had tried to kill her. She does not understand the how of her knowing, only that Morgan had done for him. Yet here he is, returned to complete his mission.

His arms effortlessly lift her from solid earth and thrust her out over the brink. And now her rootless boots flail over a chasm that, having once seemed so harmless, now petrifies with a near infinite fall.

The twisted mouth opens, gurgling out a final measure of vengeance. But before she can hear, before it means more than the whisperings of the wind, he hurls her into the night.

Backwards she spins, watching earth and sky trade places so rapidly her senses are soon a witless blur. She feels the wind, its cruel lash laying open her tainted skin and...

She tumbles into the black.

Sweat and stale air fill her nose, the fuzziness of desultory movement in her ears. She's not dead? She forces her eyes to open.

Her bunk, Troy's bed above hers, its mattress' rhythmic shifting forcing parts of it to bulge through the metal bands holding the bunk together. A girl's moans and then a pained cry from Troy.

The lives they lead leave little room for privacy, a reality which ought to be a deathblow to modesty. Not for her... for her, privacy is a precious thing, a thing hard-won. She climbs out of her cot, dresses quickly and is out of there. The happy combatants don't seem to even notice.

Out in the hall, the bandlights have been dimmed to a soft glow appropriate to nightshift. Door after closed door, slumbering souls trapped behind, waiting for the morning and the resumption of, what, more duties? More obligations? More of the same?

The mess is deserted, chipped chairs neatly stacked atop plastic tables. The hum of the dome's power throbs through the floor and into her boots as she steps to the eastern wall and calls up an image of the Yonder, tornadoes of gray sand spinning into a darkened sky.

That face... in her dream, it had been as if she knew him, as if he'd been her enemy, but she's never seen him before. And the city...

"Praise be," a man's voice, behind her, surprising her with its closeness. She comes round, elbow ready, her other hand going for the knife in her pocket. A devotee, young, his eyes blazing with the piety of the innocent. No robes of the priesthood though; in their stead, the sandy fatigues of a soldier.

"Praise be," she returns cautiously.

"I saw you come in here. Couldn't sleep?"

She grunts.

"Me neither." But not for nightmares, like her. With him, it's joy. It's writ across his ardent face. "I got it. The core, I got the posting."

"Congratulations." She turns back to the wall, to the sand, to the sky.

"The academy, Project training. I'm going to be working on the Project!" His excitement buffets her, bruises her.

The boy wants something from her, affirmation? Her mind, still sluggish with the leavings of sleep, can't work it out. He steps up next to her.

"I prayed. I prayed so hard. And now I am blessed."

"Blessed..." She should let the boy think what he will; it makes no difference to her. And yet... "Blessed how?"

The boy frowns. "To have my posting..."

"You prayed to him for a posting. You have your posting. And now you're blessed? That had nothing to do with you?"

He knows now, that she does not believe as he does. And so the eyes that once were spilling over with joy harden against her. Yes, a sinner, a non-believer... His mouth opens, a polite farewell poised on his tongue.

"You think this is blessed?" She points to the windowed wall, points at the gray-brown whirlwind, points at the world's wasteland. "Does this look like paradise to you?"

"It is a punishment," the boy murmurs. "We sinned. We were not good enough."

"If we'd prayed harder, this wouldn't have happened?"

He nods.

A wave of exhaustion washes over her, sweeping away her strength to reply, to argue. It's so futile, all of it, all of this. Oversensitive priests snoop on her 'for her own good' while sanctioning with their silence the project that threatens them all. The Council throws good souls after bad into the volcano while the windfarms that supply their power run perpetually undermanned. And this boy wants to talk about punishment from a being he's never seen, a being he's never touched, a being he's adopted to make his lot easier to accept.

All the games the devout play, to make their faith work for them... If they pray for rain and it rains, their prayers have been answered and they are blessed. But if they pray for rain and it doesn't rain, well, then they just haven't tried hard enough, or it isn't God's will, or they have been sinful; they'll try harder next time...

She wants to tell him that when his god gave him free will, implicit in that had been the right to choose not to worship, not to believe. She wants to tell him that free will isn't free will at all if his choices are coerced by the threat of divine retribution. She wants to tell him so many things, and have his face become Garry's face and have Garry hear these things, and have Garry choose a different road, and have Garry here with her now. If she could pray, she would pray for these things.

There's wetness in her eyes as the boy hesitates in the trough of her silence. But before he can move to fill it...

Red lights strobing; alarms crying out around them. "Crashdown," the automated warning system thunders through the dome. "Crashdown. Force Five imminent. Crashdown."

And she sees it, in the windowed wall the emergency systems haven't yet shut down, an intensifying of the wind which, to her eyes, seems to cower in the shadow of what comes.

"This too is a punishment?" she asks the boy.

But he's running, running from her, running from the only god that has ever walked the Yonder. The sandstone hurricane hammers into their hill with so much force, she watches the topmost layer literally ripped away and hurled down onto the sheltered dome which shudders under the impact, the weight. The wind overwhelms the soundproofing now, howling at the dome's exposed skin, its endurance an affront to its power.

"Why are you doing this to us?"

And then there's a breach and there's no more time for thinking as they huddle in their holes and wait out the will of a god they'll never understand.

Evan gasps awake. The world she knows returning to her upright in her real bed. The filtered light of late morning fights through her drawn curtains, eliciting an instinctive flinch, a hand over her watering eyes.

Three things immediately register: she is alive, she is already late for work, and there is someone in her room. Heart pounding, she swings her feet to the floor, afraid to look, to have confirmed what she already knows.

"You be falling." Morgan's whisper floats to her from her stalker's post, just inside the bedroom door. Her hands, a killer's hands, are buried in the pockets of her jacket. The same leathers as yesterday, battered but not beaten. On another, they'd look shabby; on her, they testify to her many wars. "Suiciding in your dreams?" Her lips twitch in something like a smile. "There be no pay for me if you be dying on me."

"Comforting..." Evan rises from bed, the hem of her favorite, baggy t-shirt flirting with her abraded knees. Two dreams now, two that she remembers. And she cannot decide which has left the deeper mark, her death, or that storm. Fragments now, the street flashing up to meet her, that taint on her skin... it blends in with a world of sand which terrifies her, as much for its repeat performance as for its violence. The whole mess drives her past Morgan, to her bathroom. "Just a stupid dream... and get out of my room."

In the oscillation of her bathroom's overhead light, Evan examined her reflection in the vanity's smudged mirror: tired eyes, a drawn mouth, cheeks beginning to sink inward. It will only worsen if *that* waits for her every time her head hits the pillow. That dead thing's swollen hands whose merest touch stole her will to act... none of it is real, not that zombie, not that storm.

"The kill, from the other night." Morgan's approach is a flicker of black at the mirror's edge. "That happens, specially when you be cherry."

"Cherry?"

"Virgin... your first. He be your first, right?"

"I didn't do anything to him. I didn't touch him!"

"But you saw." That better not be a smile in her voice. "You watched. I only be meaning that it passes. In time, it be going."

"Yes, well, you know it all quite well, don't you? Snuff out a life," she snaps her fingers. "Like it's nothing. Do you feel anything?!"

Evan bumps the bathroom door open a few more inches, splashing Morgan's battered likeness across the mirror. She glares at the image, this implacable face. There's no shamed flinch, no embarrassed inspection of her boots. She is remorseless, solemn.

What must she have witnessed to have grown so cold?

Her life has not been noteworthy, not prior to this mess at least. Nonetheless, it has been singularly her own, of her creation and her design. Until that man fell dead on her carpet, no one could be said to lay any claim to any part of her. And yet, in little more than a day, all that hard-won control has slipped through her nerveless fingers. How can you so quickly lose something you spent so long in building, piece by painstaking piece?

"This isn't working." Soberly, Evan opens the door the rest of the way and faces Morgan directly. But for the bathroom light, the apartment is dark, so her stalker hasn't far to go when she retreats to the safety of the shadowy living room, letting the gloom envelop her, caress her in all her impossible mystery. "I'm afraid of you. I am. It's not like... it's not like I don't know what you're capable of doing." She can't make out the woman's face now for the murk. "But that's the thing. You and me... belong to different worlds. I don't know where you're from and what it's done to you. I don't. But I know I need some space. I need some time. If you... if you want to help me, if you really believe... if you really want to help me, you have to give me some room, okay? I just can't... I can't. I close my eyes and... please."

"No." A whisper from the dark, denying, controlling.

"No, No, No!"

"You can't allow a dream to..."

"It's not the dream! It's someone... *murdered* in my apartment; it's the knife he was going to use to... it's letting *you* of all people sleep on *my* couch!" Tears of exhaustion threaten to conquer her. "Sounds like all this is old hat to you! Sounds like you got it all wired! Well, I don't! I don't know you! I don't know what's going on! I don't even know what's in my head!" Evan reaches blindly for the vanity, needing its support. "Please. I'm asking you. Please. You're making it worse. Okay? Just go."

She watches the dark figure consider it, or at least humor her by seeming to consider it. And then her shadow is moving forward, slipping into the light. And her mouth is opening to speak words. But Evan already knows the meaning of what's to be said; she sees it in those devil's eyes. Her foot lashes out, hooks the bathroom door and hammers it shut, on her, on everything that has changed without her permission.

"I can't." Resolve and regret from beyond the door. "I made him... I swore him an oath that I wouldn't..." A growl. "It wasn't meant to be this way. You were meant to... to be knowing. I swore him an oath."

"What's so goddamn..." Anguished, Evan splashes water on her face, eyes closed against the sting.

"This isn't...!

Silence; stretching out to twenty seconds, until Evan hears only the drip of water into the sink, the hum of the lights overhead.

"We be on the road, Evan." The voice is only inches away, determined to make her see reason. "We be on the road and to either side be the weeds, a quick way to be getting lost. You don't want to be lost, Evan. You don't want a detour. There are things it isn't my place to be saying to you, things you be needing to hear. You be finding those things only on the road, not in the weeds. I promise you."

Her eyes close. A facecloth infuses hot water into cheeks hollowed by too many dreams. Deep breaths, focusing breaths, subduing the panic hammering inside her head. "Okay," she whispers. "But tell me... tell me this isn't just you needing somewhere to lay your head on those cold, wet nights. Tell me this... means something."

"Means something?!" Incredulity from beyond the door. "Yes. It means something."

Evan cranks on the shower, keeping clear of the icy spray until it grudgingly warms to something tolerable by humans. That is one indignity she can't endure this morning, this afternoon. "This has got to get better," she tells herself. "It just has to." And she steps into that cleansing warmth.

It's getting on to one in the afternoon by the time Evan's ready to roll out. Bernard, her boss, had been furious when she had called him to explain her tardiness. His fat face had saturated the screen on her slate, jowls rippling as he angrily detailed all the ways in which she'd wronged him. Is his patience not endless? Is his generosity of spirit not divine? Both must be true for him to have the strength to put up with this younger, inferior generation. Up his ample ass is where she'd like to cram his generosity.

Her thumb covering her slate's microphone, Evan had taken a deep breath and let out a frustrated scream that brought Morgan bursting into the bedroom, gun out and tracking.

"My boss." Evan had almost laughed at Morgan's relief.

Bernard is too desperate for workers to fire her and they both know it. He grants her a full run. Grateful for the normality, she thanks him before ending the call. That ought to confuse him for a little while.

Apparently the cold front has passed. Fall notwithstanding, the day is hot enough to punish anyone unwise enough to linger under its cloudless heat. She opts for a pair of slate-colored jeans and a billowy, silver sotton blouse. Her pea coat she'll tie to her bike just in case.

As Evan makes for her Yager, she notices two apples, rich and red, waiting on the coffee table.

"Breakfast?" In spite of herself, she's smiling.

Morgan is at the window, looking out at the bright afternoon. A little nod...

"Thanks."

Her shadow has also made a considerate stab at removing the debris from the killing, debris Evan missed in her own efforts. Hesitating, she almost manages to thank the woman before the urge passes. She grabs up the bigger of the apples and takes it into the kitchen where, after a couple of juicy bites have been welcomed down her throat, she swallows two antiangs for the persistent headache that's been with her since she woke, the headache her shower's steam failed to cure.

Maybe she's overreacting. That her stalker refuses to abandon her despite every threat is disturbing, yes, but these dreams... And the woman promises answers, soon. If they don't come, well, she can always call Carter, Johnny, set up some kind of intervention. She can get clear of this. And Morgan's not all bad. She figured out breakfast.

"Evan..." The darkness in that single word shatters her reverie. "You can't stay here."

Morgan has clearly thought through what she means to say. The combativeness Evan's come to expect from her has yielded to something more solemn. There, a tall, black stranger framed by cream-colored curtains and those eyes... "This isn't secure. One of them already found you here." Even the accent has dropped away. "We have to go. I have to keep you safe. We have to go."

The arrogance of it... "I ask you for space and you want me to move out of my home?! Just how stupid are you?!" Evan frowns down at her half-eaten apple, having lost her appetite for it. "You ungrateful... you should feel lucky you're not locked up." Disappointed, she turns away, reaching for her bike. "Anyway," she tries to make the best of it, "you never know. They, whoever they are, might hit Boomboom instead. No more Gnroar."

Gods, but Morgan can move. One minute, the leather-clad creature is safely ensconced on the other side of the living room. The next, she's liquid shadow covering 25 feet of carpet in the time it takes Evan to flinch.

And then she's on her, a rough hand slamming into Evan's chest, throwing her back into the closed coat closet. Those cold eyes glitter. "You don't know me, but I don't ask for much." Her breath splashing across Evan's mouth, those white teeth like fangs poised to strike. "I do my job, I move on and I don't look back. No attachment... no fuss... no mess." She leans close. Afire. "You *got* to let me protect you and I *cannot* be doing that here."

The intensity of Morgan's conviction steals Evan's breath. Looking into those eyes, it's hard to think of an option other than surrender. But she knows how that story ends. Yield an inch, yield up one battle, and she's lost everything. She's conceded too much already; can't she see that?

"If me leaving, if protecting me, means so much to you, then tell me... tell me why."

Morgan grits her teeth.

"Exactly," Evan whispers. "You want me to trust you, to go on faith, when you don't trust me."

"I gave my..."

"Word, yeah. You said. Take me to him then. Take me to him and we'll get him to release you from that and you can..."

"I can't! He won't be there."

"Where?"

Silence and a wall behind those green eyes.

"Then I stay." Evan makes a conscious effort to steady her trembling hands. None of that now. "You can't just walk into someone's world, tell them virtually nothing about what may be going on and expect them to follow you. You can't do that to me. You can't do that to anyone. Look, I'm late for work as it is. Let's just..."

"Do I look like a liar?" Not a muscle has shifted in the woman's face and yet Evan feels the menace now, feels how her shadow has become a killer. Without blinking, that wall has fallen away to reveal just how willing she is to get the job done. "Do I look like a fool? You test me like I be one." Gloved hands reach for her, reach for control of her, that pale face dark with things better left in hell.

This time, the courier is quicker. Instinct drops her to a knee, and brings her fists together before her, punching out, at Morgan's stomach, even as her shadow's hand misses high. Connecting, hard! The sound of air forced from unhappy lungs and the leather-clad stalker is propelled backwards, eyes narrowed to angry slits.

Then Evan is up and pivoting in a tight space she knows so well. She finds the doorknob, twists it, jerks it. The hallway beyond, beckoning, reassuring. Grabbing her bike, she lunges out of her apartment, turning back to find her stalker standing there, frozen, hand on her stomach.

"Don't you dare," her outrage a whisper. "Don't you dare do that. Not to me." And she's out of there, not bothering to lock up, certainly not looking back.

They had been inching towards an understanding, or at least common ground. Well, that's done now, Evan decides. The gulf that had been between them has become a chasm fit to swallow the world. She hits the stairwell door hard, racing down the stairs, her bike's meager weight in her arms. Her home now feels like a prison.

***

Her plan had been sensible. Morgan would reasonably appeal to the girl's desire to stay alive. The disaster that had unfolded? Her deserved result for defying her instincts to bundle her out of there and appeal, instead, to reason. Fine! If that's how she wants it to play... Morgan slips her sleek, black slate from a zipped pocket, thumbs a number and hits send as she eyes the open door. At any cost, her man had said. She hopes the fool girl doesn't stray too far.

7

By the time Morgan makes the busy street, Evan's gone. Not a surprise. She uses her slate to locate the tracker she gummed onto the rear axle of the girl's bike, fetches her motorcycle, and cranks open the throttle to hurry off in pursuit.

Morgan has always known that the protection business is an ugly affair. One instant's inattention and your charge is dead at your feet, a bullet in her head because you missed the sniper's reflection in a window. That's why she'd always refused these jobs. How heavy, to have that on your soul...

But it turns out that this is also its allure, the challenge, the admirable vigilance. It tests her in ways killing can't.

No, it's the rest of it she loathes. It's the waiting for something bad to happen. It's handling the resentments of a girl who feels unreasonably caged, her wings cut. It's catching up to the girl who can't see the meteor about to land on her head, only to watch her dangerously weave her lithe bike in and out of traffic with unceasing grace, knowing that at any moment a car could hit her and put this all to bed. It's wondering why, in that secret part of her mind, she's asking herself why it couldn't have been someone else filling those shoes, doing what needs doing.

Evan takes a late lunch with Zia, the tattooed, magenta dye-job from the bar. Burritos. Morgan lingers some 20 feet behind, visible but not conspicuous. She doesn't want to spook the girl into another foolish flight. And anyway, from here, she's confident the distinctiveness of her enemy will reveal himself to her in this crowd of commercialites long before he's close enough to act.

They are in another of the city's markets, this one near the heart of the throbbing metropolis. Stalls of wares sprawl everywhere, littered with everything from tech to tea. Down here, in the core, the markets are the only tracts of land spared the crowding of Conplast towers which, though looming at the market's edges, seem to be thrust back by the power of the barter system. A soul can breathe here, not feeling as though a million tons of construct will crush it in the collapsing.

A multicultural crowd, mingling under a hot blue sky and partaking of all the market has to offer. They occasionally obscure her charge, necessitating a thrust closer. Alert, her eyes digest the faces nearest: a young Afjan mother with her four-year-old boy trying to walk backwards ahead of her, a poor middle-aged laborer who unsuccessfully hides a dozen bright red blotches covering his face and hands, a tragically overdressed and alcoholic busker whose palsied hands lay limply on an unplayed guitar.

Morgan goes into her pocket and spills the coins she finds there into the old man's empty beggar's cup. It had once been a proud can of tomato soup; now a donation's box for a soul on its last legs. The milky eyes do not register her small kindness, or much else for that matter. She wants to ask him the where and the how, but Evan's lunch is concluding and the girl is making for her bike. No more time for the sad souls who life broke.

How much did Evan confide? All? Magenta seems pensive as she rides her own machine past Morgan on her way out of the market. A glimpse of dark eyes troubled. No certainty there. Morgan wants to turn, to watch the purple hair disappear into the colorful crowd, make sure the friend doesn't intend to trail her, but she'll lose Evan in the effort.

Afternoon cooling into early evening and not once has the Hunter lost her prey. Markets and ministries, bars and boats... it matters not. Evan's patterns are becoming familiar. For Morgan, that signals the first stage of unwanted attachment.

They're on the docks when the call comes. Evan's delivering to a busy warehouse and its busier manager. For a measure of privacy, she's turned away from the sunburned man while he searches for a tip he does not have the chance to give. The girl's slate hides most of her reaction, brought before her face so she could see the caller while she absorbs the audio.

Even 50 feet hence, Morgan feels the shock. The body jerks straight, muscles rigid, head thrown back. With trembling hands, she fumbles with the slate as if its heft has suddenly multiplied a thousand times. She gives up on carrying that weight, letting it slip from dead fingers. Morgan can see now the ashen face, the blank eyes. It seems all of one movement when Evan whirls for her bike, mounts it, and flashes back the way she'd come, bolting past her tail in seconds.

Prepared, Morgan wheels her Roady around, chance connecting her eyes with the manager's, his hand still full of gratuity while he watches his courier depart, as though chased by hell's hounds. He shrugs, picks up the slate from the ground, and then starts to ask Morgan something, but she's already grabbed it from his hands. Gone.

She figured on having a race like this wired, but not for a second, during the frantic flight from the docks, does Morgan feel confident in her pursuit. She rides the faster machine, but inexperience with the terrain causes hesitations, losing her valuable seconds. Fatigue can't touch her charge, powerful legs cycling herself to her limits as she attacks every shortcut, no matter its recklessness.

Morgan's not so lucky. A congestion of cars blocks her view of Evan and that she simply can't tolerate. So she jumps the curb and rides the sidewalk, sending clustered pedestrians into a squawking scatter. Catching just a glint of silver from too far ahead... She leaves only screams in her wake.

They're three minutes from Evan's building when she first spies black smoke billowing into the sky. Street noise, normally so pervasive, is swallowed by the tyranny of sirens. Fire engines... And though Morgan hadn't thought it possible, Evan accelerates, no concern for her safety, her health.

Evan's street is experiencing sensory overload. Flashing lights from half a dozen vehicles batter the eyes while klaxons from just as many sirens assault the ears. A raging inferno consumes the third floor of the girl's building. A million shards of disrupted glass litter the street below while, above, fire has snaked along the majority of the third floor, ruthlessly devouring everything in its path. Out of obligation, three engines spray water at the blaze, but the battle seems hopeless.

Firemen exit the building, handing off frightened residents for treatment before they bravely return to the battlefield.

Evan invested so much in her flight that the sight of her flaming home seems to sever her puppet's strings. Legs refuse to pedal as momentum slowly dies and she begins to wobble. Breaking and clearing her own machine, Morgan runs to her charge's side, hands keeping her from a nasty fall. And there, clutched, they both watch chaos reign.

It has not been a simple fire. Nothing short of a detonation could have created that yawning crater along which consumptive flame now races. Morgan's eyes lower to a street strewn with more than glass: bits of destroyed furniture; an old, chunky video box half smashed to bits; a car draped in blackened curtains which now slide to the ground, one corner caught on the driver's side mirror. Devastation. A whiff of the smoky air confirms it, her nose filling with the cloying burn of the debris from a dozen lives.

"Get down," Morgan orders, wrestling an inert Evan to the curb as the fourth floor begins to notice the absence of the third. A monstrous groan emanates from the doomed structure as screaming EMTs try to clear the building while police hold back the pressing crowd as best they can.

And then it's coming down. The thunderous collapse ignites fresh screams as a second wave of debris, worse this time, hails the street. Instinct wraps Morgan's arms around her shivering charge as the air thickens with bits and pieces of things best not deeply considered.

For long moments, they keep silently to the curb. Evan has eyes only for her ruined apartment. In place of balcony, of wall, of sliding glass door stands immolation, the tattered remnants of a life sent to ashes. Even if Morgan had words of comfort to offer, the girl would not hear them.

All have been evacuated. The growing crowd of the curious and the refugee stare at the dead and wounded being ushered away. The dire are immediately loaded into waiting ambulances which speed away the second their payloads are aboard. The burnt, severely and otherwise, suffer to one side as blankets, water, and field treatments are supplied to them. Their care will have to wait.

The scene belongs to the lesser world, where Morgan had once watched while the bomb's ever-present threat devoured nations. Here, the first-responders will presume an explosion caused by some faulty stove is behind this mess. But this is not that. It never had been.

Shuddering to life, Evan's eyes focus; something there Morgan's never seen before. She fights free of her grip to stand on shaking legs and look up at where her window had once been. Just a pulseless hole now, the strobing lights from the engines bathing the maw in surreal red.

Morgan had been wrong. It looks as if the inferno's been mostly contained, but the victory is a hollow one for the third floor's residents. When they are finally allowed in to survey what had been theirs, it will be to find nothing more than rubble.

Morgan senses it in Evan's stillness, seconds before she makes a slow turn to face her.

A winter storm in those eyes. Their glacial glare cut with a fury that disregards explanation and goes straight for condemnation.

"Evan..."

"You..." The wounded thing leaps at her, hands out, palms smashing into Morgan's chest, sending them both stumbling onto the sidewalk. Morgan staggers, the cracking and groaning of her artificial knee causing it to all-but give way, but she has no time for that. Evan comes again, this time striking with enough force that Morgan might've gone over if not for the lamppost her back bangs into. Anger and desolation cuts across this face of stony despair. "Of course you did," her voice the bleakest whisper. "Of course you did."

And, with a graceful pivot, she swings astride the Yager. Without a single glance at the devastation, the rider crosses the street in a blink, hopping the far curb and firing away. It's something of a miracle the girl doesn't blow a tire driving over the street's detritus, but then she's due a break.

Morgan turns to the smoking building. In a moment, she'll follow her charge; but just now she is witness to the end of a chapter. Her hand finds her stims as she hobbles to her bike, thighs finding its saddle. The pill descends a dry throat as flame touches the evening sky. This is a night for caution. Only gods can know which way the sword will turn.

***

Evan stumbles into the bar.

She'd offered numb apologies to the many she'd bumbled into. A good thing that her carelessness had been taken for drunkenness, which left nothing worse than a chorus of disgruntlement in her wake. Not a word of it registers.

Friday nights at the Iguana are almost as bad as Wednesdays. The sport screen is alive and well with a football match. When doesn't violence draw a crowd? The RLTV screen is broadcasting some nonsense about survivalists. She can't focus to care. She is empty.

"Hey!" Molly's enthusiastic greeting dies quickly as Evan comes close. "Save us. Evan, what happened?!"

Evan finds her face in the mirror behind Molly. Her ravaged reflection stares back at her with dead gray eyes. A dark smudge stains her ghostly cheek; a remnant of what she has seen. Her hand lifts and, driven by a will certainly not her own, tries rubbing it away. She only makes it worse.

"I need something." Her voice belongs to another. "I need..." Her life dwindles within the mirror's dead eyes.

Many souls have come to the bartender to drown their sorrows. To them, she is the servant of peace. But as with everything in life, there is always a price. Molly hesitates.

"Please, Molly."

She will dream, long and hard on what she has seen. She will dream of three photographs...

The one with her at the festival with her parents had needed straightening after that first night of chaos. She had seen to it, as if its perfection bore on how they were honored. Now, they are gone. She'll have her opportunity to sift through the charred rubble, hoping to unearth a fragment of a memory. What is happening to her?

Soberly, Molly fetches an amber-hued bottle as Evan picks out the glass. Three shots, three memories... A golden river pours into the glass, a swirl of anesthesia.

"Slowly, alright?" The bartender tries to be stern even though her mouth is twisted in sympathy. "Strongest thing I have."

"Thanks." And down it goes, a cascade of bitterness. The burn begins in her chest, the birth of a more peaceful darkness, its fingers growing and stretching into her extremities. Tonight is not for slowly.

"That's not... slowly." Molly sighs and starts to put the bottle away, only to find Evan's hand gripping the woman's bare forearm. "Evan, come on. This isn't you. Let's get you over to your friends. Come on."

But Evan simply picks up her glass with her free hand and silently holds it out to be filled.

Molly swears but complies. "This is it. Whatever it is, it's obviously bad. I'm not gonna press, but I'm not gonna be the one who kills you, understand? Johnny!"

Out of the corner of her eye, Evan sees him look up from their table where Carter and Zia already sit. He smiles and beckons them both over.

"You like him, don't you?" To her ears, Evan's voice sounds like the sad grinding of neglected gears. "You should tell him. You never know what tomorrow'll bring." And before the startled bartender can more than blink, she shoves off.

Evan falls into her usual chair and looks up to find her three friends staring at her. Is it her frozen expression, or the glass of Adelsons in her hand? She suspects both as Zia comes half out of her chair.

"Are you all right?!"

"Yeah, Ev. You look like someone just killed your dog." Johnny blinks.

"Long story..." Taste-wise, Evan finds sipping the amber concoction is worse than gulping it down.

"Looks like it." Carter agrees from across the table. "What's goin' on?"

"It'll keep." Evan turns the glass in her hands, warming now with the drink.

How can she ever explain, to any of them? Two days ago, she's just a girl, trying to push through, to cope. Two days later... Armageddon. "I can't..." She can't meet their eyes. "I just... not tonight."

"Okay." Johnny sounds dubious, but the questions stop.

She can't believe it. She could give herself a thousand nights, to turn it over, to examine it from every angle. She still wouldn't understand the pattern behind all this. Or is there one? Is she just not capable of living a productive life? Is there a reason that she... More Adelsons down her throat, waiting for it to thaw her face, to make her feel.

They are staring at her again. How long has the table been silent? A minute? Two?

"Anyways..." Their eyes are unwilling to release her. "Where are Anna and Lohner?" If she can get them to talk of something else, the words, the sounds, the rhythm, might just blot out the fire gnawing its way through glass and wood, through photographs. "Haven't seen them around."

Nothing. Must she beg them?

"Lohner's been to see her mom," Johnny finally breaks, rescuing her. "Tests..."

"Tests for what," Zia asks as she lays a hand atop Evan's left, squeezes.

"Retinas? Who knows. Lohner's coming back tomorrow. I'm sure I'll hear all about it."

"You sound so excited," Carter snickers.

"Hey, it's the highlight of my week when my girlfriend bends my ear about her mom's medical results. Isn't that what we live for?"

"You're such a scrot," Zia laughs.

"I know, but you all love me regardless." Johnny brightens. "Oh, tomorrow. She's coming back tomorrow. Now we *must* drink to my good fortune."

"Good fortune," Evan tries to smile even though her face seems to have forgotten how. "You've never talked like that about a girl before."

"You've never slept with Lohner." Johnny's grin ignites a round of laughter. "And you won't be either."

Evan looks at him, confused. What? But Johnny is far too much the imp right now to fill her in. "Well, I'm happy for you. Good things come to those who..." There's a word here that's missing.

"Anna's been busy with her sister's wedding." And this time it's Carter who saves her. "But I'm bringing her tomorrow. Molly said they're running the Infinitas concert on the screens. Stadium's sold out."

"Sold out in 20 minutes." But that wasn't why Zia's blinking at the foreman next to her. "Anna likes Infinitas?"

"She's not the only one," Evan mumbles to her glass. But no one seems to hear her, much less see the band's t-shirt stretched across her stalker's chest. Her grip on the glass is about to break something, probably her fingers.

"Well, she doesn't like them as much as you do, Zia, but yeah."

"There are gods who aren't worshipped as hard as Zia worships those clowns," Johnny cracks. But under Zia's glare, his hands go up defensively. "Okay! Okay. I give up! Didn't mean it. A thousand apologies."

"She thinks the guy is hot." Carter's disapproving frown makes it clear he did not share his girlfriend's opinion.

"I like her more and more." Zia smiles.

Francis arrives, interrupting them, his face shimmering with sweat. "What a nightmare," groans the man Evan's been waiting for, the man who knows her best. "Don't take Boundary Road if you can help it. Standstill for leagues..."

Sympathetic groans from Carter and Johnny, the drivers at the table. And then Zia is quipping about how Francis wouldn't have these problems if he rode a bike. And then Francis' hazel eyes are on her and, as always, her thoughts are naked before his scrutiny. He frowns, concerned, but a tired shake of her head forces a nod from him. He'll keep the peace, for now.

"We were on about women and how their absence makes the heart grow so very fond." If Johnny senses the exchange, he doesn't let on. "An ode to women, you might say."

"Sounds very you..."

Life is so much simpler here. The bar is crowding, now that the cool caress of evening has broken the spell of the day. The warmth of the Adelsons has about chased every chill from her bones. She feels safe here, surrounded by the ones she loves, surrounded by the living. Here, she can forget.

Is it Morgan's fault? Her appearance in the drama brought on the storm that's overtaken her life, but what if it isn't her fault? What if she is what she says she is? Even after today, even after blaming her, shoving her, wishing her gone, Evan knows she has but to glance at the bar to find her stalker staring back. At that thought, she finds the stirrings of something almost comforting in the place of what should be gnawing horror. Tonight, she can't bring herself to care.

Silence pulls her back to find her friends all staring at her. "What?" The Adelsons is getting to her now.

"How's Zingzaball this time of year?" Johnny grins. "Breezy?"

"Sorry. I was just..."

This time, they wait her out.

"It's really okay! It'll keep, okay?!" She can't bear telling them, their sympathy, their worry, their confusion, their anger. Inside, she feels like spun glass ready to shatter with the first dissonant note. Desperate, she flails for something, anything to say. "Oh, Johnny, when's your rally? I keep forgetting..."

He hesitates, but he can't help himself. "Tuesday. We picked it for symbolism. One year since they signed the Security Act into law." Weekends get better turnouts, but I think the symbolism is more important. We can't let 'em think that this is dead, that we'll just allow this, like everything else, to pass us by, to stop bothering us."

"That's great. Proud of you. Gutsy thing to go up against the man."

But Carter can't let that by without a swing, much to Evan's relief. "You, my friend, have got to be the only person on God's green earth who thinks a country tryin' to protect its citizens from threats, serious threats, here, there, and everywhere, is pig-headed."

"Oh, great." Zia levels a finger at Evan. "Look what you've done."

"What about the thousands of people who'll show up at city hall in a couple of days, to back me up... they don't count?"

Carter's dismissive. "Brainwashed idiots. You actually got a brain which only makes it more painful."

"You wanna do this? Fine... I find it stupefying that you can be blind to the changes around you: stepped up police patrols, security cameras on every street so that you can be watched every hour of every day, microchips in garbage cans monitoring what we throw away so they can learn how best to sell us more crap... and that's not even the worst part."

"No, of course it isn't."

"The security database has been online for six months. Six months of logging every passport, every fingerprint, and every name of every person who comes and goes from our shores. Precautionary reasons, they say; protecting your safety, they say. Governments like fear, they like foreign threats? Wanna know why? Because it allows them to take away our freedoms while puffing up their own self-importance. And nowhere along the line do they get a peep out of the frightened public. My people are already getting reports of immigrants being turned away because of the slightest stain on their papers. Maybe they have an unfortunate name, or spent time in an unfortunate country, or have a cousin 47 times removed who once maybe had coffee with a terrorist. This is about control. This is about controlling who gets in and who doesn't without giving any consideration to anyone in need. And this is about controlling us, what we think, what we do. I will not sacrifice the values this country was founded on so that a handful of rich businessmen disguising themselves as our political masters can bend my country to their ends. No chance."

"Better safe than dead." Carter is a rock upon which the wave of Johnny's passion breaks. "You'n come to me with whatever. All I want is to work a decent paying job and to go home at night to a house not leveled by a suicidal scrot with 'a dozen' sticks of dynamite strapped to his chest. Is some of what they're doing excessive? Sure. But why you wouldn't take excessive over being blown into 50,000 pieces 'cuz you stepped out to the market for a chicken is beyond me. They can arrest whoever they want as long as they've done the crime. You done a crime, then you've put yourself into that world, under that light. Otherwise, you're fine. Simple's that."

Johnny growls in frustration. "That's it! Right there, that's it. It's your premise! It's your whole premise. It's totally flawed. See, you believe the government'll do right by you as long as you don't break any of their rules. That's it..." The blue eyes blaze. "The people who run our nation are out for themselves. They spend fortunes to get themselves into office because they know that's where the big deals get cut. They don't wanna miss out. They can control the game! The more they control, the more they profit. That's the bottom line, my friend. And the fact that a hardworking guy like you is willing to give unto them the power to destroy your life... They sucked you in! They got you. They sucked you in, your benevolent government..."

"Oh, Johnny." Carter sounds almost sorry for his friend. "It's not that at all."

"Then what is it?!"

"I recognize my own ignorance. You're convinced you can do better; there's no way. You can't claim to know how all of this works, the programs, the databases, the policies. Neither of us can get our arms completely around even one of these big programs, let alone all of them. You bust yourself workin' for a public interest group and worry about makin' rent. I run a construction crew and spend half my days worryin' that me or one of my guys is gonna get his head cracked open. When in there do we got time to know how Social Aid works, or why it don't. And if we can't figure out how they work, then we can't go 'round sayin' they are corrupt, can we?" A finger forestalls Johnny's interruption.

"And to that end, far as security goes, you and me don't have a clue of what kind of threats are out there, Johnny. They don't tell us because, to tell us, they'd have to show us how close to oblivion we are on a daily basis. Man, that wolf's always at the door and I don't need panic in my streets. I'm gonna trust in the grace of God and the good people who bar that door 'cuz I know they know more'n me. That's it. You look at the shadows around you and you try to find how it's tryin' to trick you, how it's tryin' to pull one over on you. I look at the shadows and I see just a shadow because, sometimes, that's all it is."

Johnny blows out a long breath and, with a shake of the head, he extends his hand. "I guess we don't know all the complexities, the truths. And you're right, about how you and me are different. You don't want to be burdened by the things you can't change. Me... I have to know. I can't just... surrender." Johnny goes for his drink and takes a long, calming pull. "Alright, fine. But I want you all to remember this, right here, right now. When Saranthium was laying siege to Trassilus and Oregar tells his pals that they're going to build the wooden horse, there was one person in Trassilus who saw how it would all play out."

Zia laughs, "Here we go."

Evan's head feels full of fog. So when she speaks, it takes her a moment to realize it her voice she's hearing. "Never read the *Milanium*." Zia and Johnny are staring at her with matching horror. "Hey, Ajirus can kiss my ass. I understood like every third word." Those swirls of Adelsons amber have set her body to humming.

"Alright, go on," Carter groans. "You won't be happy until you tell us."

"Kerrilia: daughter of the Trassilian king; brother to Palaymius, the leader of the Trassilian army; beloved by a god, Lorus, who gifted to her the ability to predict future events. And what happens when she tells her people of their demise via the gift horse?" Johnny leans forward, an orator's intensity in his face, "Nobody believes her. Not a single soul trusts her enough to question... to work it through. And for their distrust, the lot of them get ground into dust; a civilization destroyed because they put their heads in the sand, not wanting to believe in a woman who could see their future and reveal to them their folly."

"You tell it well." Zia can't contain her amusement. "But let me get something straight. Not only does this case of yours rely upon a poem written thousands of years ago, not only are you putting your supposedly erudite ass next to an accursed prophetess; not only are you telling us that you and you alone can see the future, but you are willing to state, here and now, that you are in fact a big, flaming girl. Do I have all that right?"

Carter and Francis burst out laughing as Evan fixes her hazy gaze on a disgusted Johnny.

"Alright, alright. Yep, that's it. Get it out. You're *soooo* funny, Zia. What are you laughing at?" He gives Carter's shoulder a playful punch.

"You were being an ass. And it's apparently my mission, in this life, to bring you down a few notches." Zia winks. "You're not the only one who's read a book or two, Johnny."

Johnny shakes his head, helpless. "Fine. I'll cop to the pretension, but my point holds. No one ever listens to the predictor of doom - they wanna think that it'll sort itself out. That is the truth and you all know it. So you can call it crap, but when it all falls bad, I expect every last one of you to think back to this moment and apologize to me, you know, while your worlds are caving in. I want credit, dammit."

"Alright, Kerrilia. Whatever you say," Carter snickers.

And now Zia's piling on. "No, no, no. He's definitely a Kerrie. Grow out the hair just a little bit more... give it a bit more conditioner..."

"Like he doesn't already spend half what he makes on shit for his hair."

Johnny yields, hands in the air. "Alright, alright! Tough crowd! Molly!"

The bartender glances over from her station, rag in hand.

"You love me, right?"

Molly smiles, slowly shaking her head.

"No?! I'm crushed!"

"Not your night, my friend," Carter finishes his drink. "Not your night."

Evan laughs. It's a quiet sound, tentative, as if whichever part of her that commissioned it isn't sure sound will actually emerge. They are good for her, these few, her family. Maybe it doesn't matter, in the end, that she's lost what she's lost to ashes so long as she has them. People over possessions.

If any of them had been caught in that fire...

She can still feel Morgan, behind her, like a black cloud she cannot shake. More, she feels a solidness in her gut, like cancer. It whispers to her, promising that this is far from over. She isn't aware of having moved until her hand settles on Francis' forearm, fingertips pressing into expensive sotton.

"I'm going to need a place."

Through watering eyes, she takes in the face of a man who has been there for her so many times. Is that how she knows he'd sooner die than turn her down? "A couple of days, at most, I promise."

Francis simply nods. No prying, no conditions... "Let's get you settled in before it gets too late. We're going to have to put some water into you."

Fatigue gnaws at Evan as she pays and puts her wobbly legs under her. Worried goodbyes, their faces blurring into a single mass of concern, concern she cannot accept. That thing in her gut is pulling her towards something, something dark. And if she knows anything, the less they know of it, the better. She looks back at them, just once, when she and Francis reach the door, one last glimpse of their faith, and then she's gone.

DAY FOUR

8

Evan has lapsed to sleep.

A glance over at the girl slumped next to him, as Francis pulls his seasoned, blue Pedarius into his modest driveway, confirms as much. The poor thing had been exhausted to begin with. Add to that the straight Adelsons...

Checking his disapproval, he alights from the executive car, skirts its sleek hood, and quietly opens the passenger door, stirring her with a gentle hand to the shoulder. "Come on." He's coaxing a wounded bird. "Let's get you inside."

The middle-class townhouse is kin to the dozen others lining the north side of Gibson. The street had been named after its developer who, decades earlier, had purchased undeveloped acreage and transformed it into a sleepy borough uncorrupted by the city's core architecture. A visionary of planned communities, the man had been rewarded for his shrewdness when the cost of core real estate had priced out the modern family, relocating them here to these sleepy hollows.

With Evan half asleep on his shoulder, Francis fumbles his key into the front door's sturdy lock and then puts his shoulder to the painted wood, pushing his way into a dark, hardwood foyer. Like much of the house, the decor is plain, lousy with warm, inoffensive earth-tones splashed across every surface. Detecting his entrance, the foyer walls softly glow, their chocolate light sufficient for him to orient himself and guide his incoherent pupil up cream-carpeted stairs to a second floor rife with empty rooms. Many had been converted to other uses simply out of boredom, legacies of pursuits adopted, mastered, and forgotten. He maneuvers Evan to the one room whose purpose has remained constant since he bought the place nearly ten years ago. "Here we go. Almost there."

Francis palms open the wood-paneled door, helping Evan into a room that, without the bed nestled against one wall, might have been mistaken for a study. The spotless carpet is a darker burgundy than the walls which have been done in an early cinepaint, a substance which reacts to ambient light by changing to a complementary hue and, in doing so, displaying one of a handful of pre-selected patterns. Dormant in darkness, the walls are uniform but for a doorway into a tiny bathroom and the curtained window that looks out upon the peaceful back garden.

"That stuff really went to your head."

He puts this to Evan who, stirring now, slowly breaks from his side. Haunted, her eyes worn out from more than drink, her pale face a magnet for shadows, she takes in the welcoming interior of the room as if not quite believing it.

"Shouldn't be here." Words slurred, knees unreliable, she deposits herself upon the forest green duvet thrown across a double mattress. "It's too much to..." Her hand itches at her nose and scrubs at her eyes so roughly he has to reach out and stop her.

She looks up at him, her eyes dead with drink, more of her mind elsewhere than here, with him. And so he studies her, his Evan.

Even at her worst, and he has seen her hit some monumental lows, she's attractive. She so often acts the standoffish tough; but there's a vulnerability in that face that, as much now as in those exciting, early days, draws him down into her orbit. The eyes have changed little over the years: still sea-gray, still that hint of sweetness filmed by dark pain.

"Y'always said come to you, but you don't know." Evan sprawls backwards upon the bed. "You don't know." Her hands cover her face now, palms settled over her mouth, muffling her lament. He knows those lovely palms, their callouses and their fateful lines. "I don't... I don't..."

Pulling himself from her, Francis fills a cup of cold water from the bathroom's tap. "Don't worry. We can talk about it in the morning." He projects calm as he kneels at the bedside, tugging her back into a seated position. She moans a protest, but he wraps her hand around the cup anyway. "It'll go easier if you're hydrated."

It has come to this. Worn, she stares down at the cup as if divining its purpose. And then she's downing its contents in two goes, pausing to blink up at him, at the room. Her lips form soundless words as her free hand rubs at her neck. Then, finally, "Where do I go? Francis..." She hands him back the cup, gets awkwardly to her feet and leaves him, for the bathroom. The door closes quietly behind her. Not even the lost can deny biology.

When Evan reemerges, she's steadier. Francis has retreated to the bedroom door, ready to give her the peace she deserves. That lovely, pale face flickers with a thought that the mouth opens to speak, but no words come. She turns away, embarrassed. "Night, Francis."

He lingers, hoping she might change her mind, show him the source of her silence, but her back stays to him, unflinching.

Patience, as always. "Night, Evan."

He stares as the door clicks closed. Confidantes and companions... He'd seen to it that there had been no secrets between them. And his wish had held true until now, when she shares but half truths and heavy silences. Frustrated, he makes for his room, but finds sleep difficult to obtain.

The morning dawns brightly. Francis surfaces from meditation to the warbling of joyful birds outside his bedroom window. The bedside clock glows 9:40. Squinting against the light, he rises, showers, and is downstairs frying breakfast by the time Evan's awake and moving around upstairs. He'd put out fresh towels for her; she knew where to find the rest. It's important she feel at home.

A breakfast of eggs, bacon, sausage and toast is hardly the stuff of healthy champions. But as a feast for the hungover, it will do nicely. Reading and his experiences in the world tell him as much; he's never touched alcohol.

While the cozy smells fill his tiled kitchen, Francis glances into his sun-kissed garden, reflecting upon the first time he'd truly revealed himself to her. The campus quad... She'd been so hard: combat boots, torn jeans, pink hair, and a leather biker's jacket. But even if he hadn't already known as much, her self-consciousness announced to anyone willing to see that punk was merely a stop along the way in a broader search for... something. What that was, well... He could have given her ten-thousand words and a whole semester to form them, and she couldn't have explained it. Poor soul...

Over their first beer in the campus pub, she'd told him of her father's recent death from pancreatic cancer. Twenty-five faithful years on the job site, three years shy of retirement for which he'd made so many plans, and it ends in a sterilized hospital room, his steadfast vitality reduced to skin and bone consumed by tubes. She could not hide the ache. She never could.

"I never just tell people this stuff," she told him over that cracked tabletop. "But you're different. You're different."

The death had brought forth a destructive streak, made her swift to fire upon those who, in her eyes, had failed her. Those qualities of community, passion, love, that sustained the human soul through times of strife are, for both of them, unaffordable luxuries. She is, after all, meant for greater things.

They had come together then, the older guiding the younger around the worst mistakes, but it's more accurate to say that he had tried. The impossible stubbornness of a teenager had proved difficult to overcome. Three months he'd had with her, three months to create a tether of trust with which he could lead her. Then tragedy struck anew and, with one blow, nearly ruined everything.

Evan had just turned nineteen when her zealously-fit mother suffered a lethal heart attack while jogging. He'd been with the daughter when the call came, summoning her to the hospital. He drove her, and looked on helplessly as she endured this fresh agony. This was God's plan? This was... fair?

A congenital heart defect had been the culprit. The doctors had insisted Evan undergo testing to determine if mother had passed the flaw to daughter. It had come as no comfort when the tests came back negative. She'd live a long and healthy life, this only child who had buried both parents within the span of a year. No aunts and uncles to take her in, no cousins or grandparents. The damage that aloneness had wrought had nearly put paid to everything.

He butters lightly toasted bread as he recalls the day that, not three weeks later, his charge had quit school. She could not continue in such a pointless pursuit when life, at any second, could end. He had thought of convincing her otherwise, but one look into her adamantine eyes had disabused him of that. If God, or fate, she had argued, could not find the will to care about those whose lives were shattered by the senseless deaths of their loved ones, of those dearest to them, then why should she care about them? The only wise course is to leech from life every moment of pleasure before it's her turn to fall into nothingness. She is wrong, but being wrong has never mattered to the grieving.

"You look like you're a million leagues away."

Evan's voice echos through the kitchen, startling Francis from his reflections. "Smells good. Hope you don't mind. I put my stuff in the wash."

She wears now the laundered odds and ends of things left behind during prior stays, dark blue sweatpants with fraying bottoms and a faded green top across which small fish appeared to swim. She sits at the table behind him, her fidgeting hands molesting a saltshaker as she blinks at the new day. Yes, the eyes are red and watery, her nose congested, but that her head's not in some toilet suggests she's skated from the worst of last night's excess.

"The morning-after special." Fried eggs for him; scrambled for his pupil. Yes, he remembers. "I'd say it'd fatten you up, but we both know your bike would make a liar of me."

"I still hate my thighs."

"Pah, you're a goddess." He dishes and serves breakfast, then moves to pour himself coffee, orange juice for her. One of the morning's merry birds lands on the kitchen window ledge, chirping at them as the scent of bacon fills the air.

"Someone tried to kill me last night."

Juice spills onto Francis' hand as the glass nearly meets the tiled floor. Slowly, he faces her, blinking.

"It wasn't the first time, apparently." Evan's gaze is glued to her plate, lips twitching nervously. "Happened two nights earlier and maybe before that." Solemnly, she loads eggs onto her fork and, with some measure of relief, delivers them to her mouth. "Guess three times really is the charm..."

Falling into a chair opposite, Francis examines her face. It's easy to detect the tension in the quivering mouth, the guardedness in troubled eyes, the wrinkle that will form from a brow so furrowed. Damn...

"Morgan. The one you introduced to us the other night..." His mind races.

"Mmmm?"

"Was she the one? Did she try to..."

"No." Evan's teeth worry at a corner of her toast. "But she... she was there. Showed up on my doorstep, what, Wednesday night I guess?" Her quiet laugh chills him, something of the insane swirling within. "Well, she ignored the doorstep part. Came right through. Some guy was in my place, trying to... she, uh... she took care of him."

"Evan, this is," he doesn't have to work hard to splutter. "What've the police to say?"

"Haven't told them. It was all so... It all happened..." Evan finally looks straight at him, anger and frustration coloring her pale face. "I had... I didn't know what was going on! What would I say?!" She grimaces. "Anyway, it doesn't matter now. It's just a crazy story only you'd believe."

"You should have come to me sooner." Irritation flaring, he stands and plants his hands on the table. "I'm your friend. You should have let me help you."

Those spooked eyes flash. "I'm not a baby, Francis. I can take care of myself."

Take care of herself! His mouth opens to escalate the argument, but a grunt contains the urge. He reclaims his seat, his untouched food cooling before him. "Why doesn't it matter anymore?"

"She uh... did away with the uh... evidence. Not that it would've mattered." And now she can't look at him, pinning her gaze to the safety of her plate. "Last night, someone... blew up my apartment." Anguish has swallowed her temper. "Got a call from this guy on the second floor who has a thing for me. He said, 'Are you out?' I asked him, 'Out of what?' 'There's a fire,' he said." Her lips tremble. "You wouldn't have believed it, Francis, glass and shit all over the street, fire just ripping through the building, smoke everywhere. Whatever it was took out half my floor. Morgan and me, we..." The fingers perform an agitated dance along the rim of her half-cleared plate. "We saw the floor above mine come down and..."

"Your pictures." The three framed photos had been the first things in her apartment, even trumping her bed. She glances up, eyes shimmering. "Oh, Evan... I'm sorry."

Looking away, the girl who now owns little more than the clothes in Francis' washer fights for composure. "I'm half sure I'm dreaming. This guy busts into my place and this lupa is on him out of nowhere. They're on each other like wolves and I'm standing there with my stupid clock radio, wondering whether I'm high as a kite. Then, she... and then he's lying there and she's telling me that she's... been sent to protect me, that I'm in danger. All this and then the fire..." Her hands grab at her face in frustration, trying to squeeze sense out of her skin.

"Do you think she... started... had something to do with..." A terrible calm is in him as he tries piecing it all together. So many years, so many plans... It's coming to a head now.

Evan flinches. "I blame her, but I don't think she pulled that trigger. She wants me to trust her, I can see that much." When her hands come away from her temples, they are fists. "She knew we were on thin ice. I mean that's one thing about this, Francis! I look at her and I know... It's the strangest thing. I just know... that she..."

Evan picks through her eggs with no more grace than her words. "She's always with these 'I can't tell you what the deal is,' faces and the 'we'll go talk to my man soon' crap. She knows what this is about, but there's something else too. I've seen a lot of faces, Francis. I just don't think she wants to hurt me, which is crazy considering what she did to..."

"Her man..."

"Yeah, he's this..." Her bitter laugh returns. "He's above her. I guess he knows the whys and hows. Savior, I can't even believe I'm saying all this."

Francis finds himself standing at the window, staring at his pristine garden. The way the sun brings out all the color in the world enlivens it from something drab... He feels Evan's eyes on him, but when he glances back, she is stealing from his untouched plate.

"I haven't had a good meal in days. I'm not dying on an empty stomach."

"Don't talk like that," he snaps, returning to the table. "We're going to figure this out. Is it something you saw, something they think you saw? Is it something you have that you don't know you have? If we can satisfy them..."

"You know my job," Evan snorts. "It's a blue moon when I make a normal delivery of a normal package to a normal person. It could be anything."

"But this started 48 hours ago. So, what changed?" He retakes his seat, sensing the moment's enormity.

That has the gears working as she gnaws her bacon. "No... I mean, there was Levy, but he was just pissed that I wasn't being careful. But he got his delivery. And what does it even matter? It's not like they've stopped to ask me to surrender, Francis..."

"Don't get chippy. I'm trying to help you..."

"And that's another problem. Assuming this is all actually happening and I haven't gone batshit, they aren't messing around. This is hit and run. This is 'we want you gone.' The stuff we care about, valuing life and honor and all that? They don't care... Johnny, Zia, you, Carter, anyone... If they're doing this to me, what... c-can't carry that, Francis, not after..." The specter of her buried family darkens her face.

"Let us worry about us," he cautiously counsels. "We'll keep it close. We'll watch our backs and yours. But, I'm afraid," he smiles tenderly, "you'll have no luck convincing any of us to let you walk it alone. Johnny, Carter, Zia, me, we all love you. You need to remember that."

Evan's grave nod kicks off a quiet silence, broken only by the clink of her fork chasing the remnants of her eggs.

And then she looks at him, looks at him with a measure of the young woman he remembers from the beginning. "You know this wouldn't be so bad except... I just know that something's happening. I feel it in me." She looks down at her stomach. "And I... I see it in my dreams. I see these places, these people... and..." She licks her lips nervously, "there's this part of me that says I should be freaking out right now, more than I am. And I think about it and it's right; I should be freaking out. But every time I'm on the brink of just losing it, there's this feeling like something's... happening, like I'm sitting at the center of..." She's too embarrassed to finish, throwing her hands up in frustration.

It's beginning. He cannot let on how ill that makes him.

Needing something to occupy her, Evan stands and clears the plates, setting them both on the black, granite countertop. She watches a greedy squirrel make a run at the garden's bird feeder. "I've been having dreams, like I said. And in one of them, I'm on the old clock tower and I'm staring at this amazing view of the city and how it's set against the ocean and the sky... it's beautiful! Anyway, I'm taking this all in when something catches my eye, in Little Harbor... this black dot, like something was missing, like the whole thing was a painting and the artist forgot this one spot. I could feel it. I could feel that it didn't belong. But I don't know how, or why, or whether it's my brain telling me I have a tumor." She shivers. "But I knew when I saw. I didn't know what it was, but I knew that... I'm in the middle of a storm, Francis, and I have no control!"

Numb, Francis follows her to the sink, handing her the untouched orange juice. "Drink. We've all day to work this out."

Soberly, she accepts, drinking as he scrapes the remains on his plate into the trash.

"You took all this pretty well." She's looking down at him, watching him.

"It's... a lot. But I care about you and I trust you. And I know that you will find a way to do the right thing, no matter what. Because that's what you do, no matter what comes your way. Sometimes, it takes you awhile to get there, but you get there. And that's an admirable quality in a person."

"You sound like a priest," she laughs uncomfortably. "Thank you," she says, hiding shyness behind another swig of juice. "Well, I've laid it all out for you. What do you think? Am I crazy? Too much RLTV?"

"No. Evan, I know you. If you were prone to insanity," he smiles slightly, "you'd be in a padded room by now. No, I could wish that you'd have come to me sooner, but we need to know Morgan's part in this. Until you know more, she's the only link we have. And, for all we know, she's running her own game." He rinses their plates.

She nods.

"Then, you need to get comfortable with the idea that you're not alone in this. You need help, Evan. We can't assume anything and the more people you have in support of you, the better I'll feel. We've been through some tight scrapes. We're gonna get through this one too. You've my guarantee on that."

Francis tries to project a confidence he does not feel. Watching her these years, she's become family, this beautiful, stubborn face that yet holds that old vulnerability. He dries his hands, to squeeze hers, whether to give or receive comfort he does not know.

"You believe me, don't you... you really believe me..."

"I always have... I always will." He believes in her. He must.

Morning gives way to afternoon and Evan has donned her freshly-laundered clothes by the time she finds Francis reading in his living room.

As the social center of his home, considerable thought and expense had gone into its decoration. A few pieces of modest art enliven the eggshell white of the walls. A sturdy couch upholstered in patterned shades of gray sits behind a substantial wooden coffee table with cabinets for modest storage. His entertainment center resides in an elegant, black console perched atop the coffee table, its projection screen dormant.

Her battered slate, never far from hand, is clutched before her as she walks onto the plush beige carpet. Francis marks his place and closes the book and sets it aside as he rises to meet her. With a shower and clean clothes, she is markedly improved.

"Hey." Her smile is sheepish. "Fat Bernie just messaged me. A few of Saturday's crew called in sick. He's willing to go double pay. Sounded desperate and I probably owe him a turn. What the hell is that?" She points to a vivid, green toad perched on a corner table.

"Oh, it's just something I picked up at a crafts thing." He plucks the creature out from where it had migrated under a reading lamp.

"Kind of creepy looking, but then, you are a pretty weird guy."

"That I am. But you should stay, at least until we have more information. It's not safe, that much we know. And there are calls to make about your apartment and people we..."

"I need something to do," she shakes her head. "Keep my mind occupied." She crosses the carpet, fond lips finding his smooth cheek. "Besides," her tone is rueful, "I don't think I'm getting my security deposit back."

Her humor is returning. Should he be glad of it? Accepting this rare slice of physical affection as calmly as he can, Francis nods. "Watch your back, okay?"

"I will. You keep trying to grow that beard. Maybe when you hit 40, you'll finally need a razor," Evan grins, turns, and is soon heard pulling her bike from where he'd roped it to the back of his car.

Only when he's alone does he allow himself a caress of where her lips had marked him. He takes a slow breath, holds it, and then finds his phone.

"Zia," he catches her on the third ring.

"Francis? Hey, what's up?" The sounds of the great city threaten to drown out her voice.

"I need you to do me a favor. It's Evan." Francis returns to his couch, contemplating his kitschy toad. "There've been some developments." Of the calls he must make, this is the easiest.

.

9

It is a resplendent Saturday afternoon as Francis says goodbye. Moments ago, Zia might've appreciated how the sun's reflection off the monoliths shimmer these crowded streets, but the call has changed all that.

Abandoning her coffee, she darts across the busy market to retrieve her bike. And, as she flies from the square, she snags a bio-pulp newspaper from a convenient vendor. When she finds that stupid girl... "Hi, Silvi. It's Zia. I need Evan's deliveries for this afternoon. Right. Thanks." And, ending the call, she bolts west.

Barry Towers is an 80-story corporate building that casts one of the most imposing shadows of the city's many constructs. Sun shines off tinted floor-to-ceiling windows of undivided glass which sheathe the building. On this day, with nary a cloud in the sky, what a view it must be from those highest floors...

Somewhere up there, Charlotte Barry, the inventor of sotton and a self-made textile baroness and one of Zia's role models, is overlooking her sprawling empire. Does she too have crazy friends? Must she endure their madness? How does she tolerate it?

Spotting the Yager out front, Zia rolls to a stop, dismounts, and has to wait only a few moments for her so-called friend to emerge from the vast, marble lobby. When she comes, it's warily, peering left and right as she makes for her bike. For all her efforts, she does not spot Zia, or the newspaper missile flying for her head.

"What the hell!" The Saturday edition catches Evan flush on the cheek. An arm raised late in defense intercepts only a corner, tumbling the disordered mess to the ground. Zia marches up, one black boot crushing the sports section.

"Are you stupid? Really, Evan, did aliens steal your brain? Because I'm at a bit of a loss with this." Zia had withheld one panel of the paper which she now thrusts into the girl's face. "Recognize this??"

'Bomb Suspected in Apartment Fire,' the headline proclaims. Beneath it, a detailed spread of the third-floor conflagration consumes half the page. The vivid still had been taken from above, capturing the undulating tongues of flame that shot through windows already blown out by the explosion.

"Why didn't you tell us?! You sat there, you drank your shit, and you told us it would keep! Savior, Evan!" Before the stupid girl can do more than blink, Zia tosses the paper aside to embrace her addled friend. "You stupid sipio." Her whisper holds tears. "I'm so glad you're okay."

When they disengage, Zia finds her fellow courier smiling. "You threw a newspaper at my head." They both bend to dispose of the trampled daily.

"C'mon," Zia insists. "Let's get a burrito."

Of the city's five town squares, the Watermark is the largest and the most scenic. Its proximity to the commercial harbor and the city's financial district means that suits and fashion plates outnumber everyone else four and five to one. These classy shops are nothing like the street stalls of the poorer boroughs. A cup of coffee here sets you back ten bucks minimum and it takes just as long in minutes to order it.

The friends stop at Amigos, a hole-in-the-wall tortilla shop squeezed to the square's fringes by the newer, glitzier joints Zia'd sooner die than patronize. Amigos pumps out the best wraps in the city. Veggie for Zia; double chicken for Evan, the scent of which sets Zia's stomach to churning.

They eat at the Seacliff, a multi-laned pedestrian throughway that runs along the water's edge. Fifty feet below, waves smash eternal over rocks smoothed by time. There is nothing of beach here, nothing of softness in the sea's distant thunder.

Joggers and dog-walkers mingle amidst countless couples who, hand in hand, revel in the concrete romance. The local birds also have a fondness for this spot for the waterfront boasts the city's finest dining for pigeons as well as humans.

Perched on the cliff wall behind them is a greedy cormorant. Dark, its eyes gleam at the prospect of a feed, its feathers rippling in the faint wind. It dares not go near them, its fear of reprisal edging out its lust for sustenance.

"So that we're on the level," Zia opens as they settle on the wall, "Francis called me. He ran down what you'd told him. Why you'd go to Francis..." She shakes her head, tonguing sauce from her lip.

"I wasn't just going to announce it to God and bar," Evan replies around a mouthful of meat. "I couldn't... I didn't..."

"Well, you could have pulled me aside. Whatever, it's done now... I assume this makes the leather mama who's been dogging you public enemy number one. No coincidence she shows up and something like this happens. I mean, Evan your..." Zia controls herself. Somehow, the girl seems almost calm when her hair ought to be on fire. Johnny will be so disappointed.

"I don't know that yet." Evan picks out a sliver of chicken and tosses it to a greedy gull that has landed on the wall to feast. "Oh, fine," and she throws another to the cormorant. "Go, git!" But only the gull obeys, leaving his dark brother behind to watch. "It'd be a lot easier if I knew how she played into this mess."

"Where is she now?"

Evan's thin smile is humorless. "Lost her, I guess. She doesn't like that."

"Well, hitting the Adelsons the way you did makes sense now... I'm sorry about the newspaper. It's just, Francis told me and then I saw it there and I lost it."

"Look, it... it doesn't have anything to do with you guys. It's not because I don't trust you. I'm just... I'm questioning a lot of things in my world, Zia, and I didn't want everyone to get all crazy. Everything's bug-eyed as it is."

"I hear you." She keeps a brave face for Evan's sake, but the enormity of all this gives her gooseflesh. What has the fool girl stumbled into? Her appetite gone, she wraps up what remains of her lunch. "You got some on your chin."

Evan wipes before swallowing her last bite. The girl eats as though her food might suddenly disappear from her clutches.

"You know that one word to Molly at the bar and leather mama won't be able to take a step inside that place." Zia shifts on the wall to face her friend. "I just wish you'd gone to the police. Shit, they aren't angels, but this Morgan... that's some ugly business. I know we been down some dark rabbit holes, but not like this."

"I know," Evan scrubs her hands along her jean-clad thighs as she stares out to sea. "I just need a little time. I need to know a little more." The battered gaze returns to her. "Just be careful, please? Keep an eye out for anything funky. And, if you see it, you go. I mean, you get clear and you don't look back."

"Okay," she promises hollowly, hopping off the wall. "You got deliveries. I'll ride with you awhile. I've missed that."

"Yeah? You missed it, huh?" Evan leaps at the chance to change the subject. "You know I lied about that."

"About what?"

"About why we couldn't ride together."

"Bernard was putting you on some different runs, you said."

"I know what I said, Zia. I said I lied about it."

"Why?!"

"Because I couldn't take the 'an object is not the same when different people look at it' crap anymore," Evan grins as they thread through the crowd on their way back to their bikes.

"I can't believe you. Seriously?! I'm hurt." Zia feigns a stumble, a hand going over her wounded heart.

Evan laughs.

"But why? Ross is a great philosopher. You shouldn't knock him."

"Oh, come on, Zia; an object is not the same when two people look at it?"

"It's true! If two people are looking at the same object, there's no observational way to prove that they are looking at the same object. Their eyes might perceive the colors differently, or the difference in the lighting based on where they are standing might skew their perceptions. They might come from different cultures which view the object in a different context and that alone would make it a different object for them. Yes, both observers might identify the object as, say, a table, but unless you can record how each of them sees the table, you can't know that they see it the exact same way."

"Oh, Savior," Evan groans. "See, this is why! Why does any of that even matter?! Because I'm telling you, right now, I have never been in a situation where how I and someone else looked at a table was in doubt."

"Because these are the kinds of questions that get at the very heart of reality, Evan! They get at the essence of how we experience the world and whether or not the way we experience the world has any bearing on how other people experience it. It forces us to ask other hard questions like whether or not what we perceive as the world is just some kind of shared hallucination where every person carries around their own reality and, when we interact, those realities overlap and mesh together. It asks questions about the nature of God and whether or not everything that isn't alive, like the table, is present in some kind of master reality in which you and I exist, like kids on the playground. You're gonna tell me none of that has any bearing on how we live?"

They are back at their bikes now and Evan is unshouldering her rucksack and fixing it to her machine. "And believe it or not," she tells the air around them, "that's an improvement on the 'plight of poor, tortured animals' stuff."

"Oh, that's right. Keep poking the bear! Let's see how *that* works out for you. You know," Zia glares, "I was all set to tell you that only the movers and shakers in our world, the leading lights, the visionaries, get bombed and shot at. Hell, Johnny has never been bombed or shot at. I was all set to anoint you as a superhero, but now you've pissed me off."

"Ha!" They are riding now, pulling away from the Seacliff and heading back into the city's shadows. "Superheroes have nicer thighs." With a burst of speed, Evan noses ahead, lifting her right hand in a dismissive, backhanded salute. "You're almost as slow as Morgan!"

"You're almost as fat as Bernard!"

"Oh, it's on, lupa!"

Zia has often wondered how she would respond to serious peril, the likes of which Evan faces now. The job they share has its harrowing moments, deliveries to bad parts of town where crimes you don't come back from are commonplace. But they take precautions. And anyway, that sort of potential danger is hardly as present as the risk of working construction, toiling 20 stories in the air with only a couple of ropes providing a lifeline from a fatal fall.

But then this isn't a matter of work, is it? This is personal. Zia can feel it. If this had been work, the disgruntled party would have wanted Evan to know why she was being punished. No, this is a deeper game; one that Zia comprehends about as well as Evan understands the philosophy of Ross.

The day is winding down and they are both near the end of their respective runs which, save for a few divergent deliveries, have kept them within a block or two of each other. That's well within the range of their slates to ping messages back and forth without the Cloud's aid. Though she's dying to know more, Zia's been careful not to pry too much, to let the day and the sense of camaraderie lead the conversation where they will. And, though Evan's given away little, Zia at least has the sense that her weary friend needs to think of something else for awhile.

And so thoughts of bombs and bullets are quick to depart when Evan powers up out of the Watermark, a broad smile cutting across her pale face of dark troubles as she pulls up alongside.

"What's up?"

Evan holds up a little tan booklet, opening it to flash a set of four black and white tickets at her. "Got 'em from a scalper. Cost me a fortune, but I don't care. Tomorrow, I'm a sipio. Tonight... Tonight, we are going to Infinitas."

Zia nearly tumbles from her bike into the street. "What?! Evan, girl, you don't have that kind of cash!"

"Don't care." Evan slips one precious ticket from the booklet and presents it, a slice of paradise pinned between fingers stretched out in offering.

Zia can't say no, she can't! She takes the ticket which seems to glow in her hand. Afraid of dropping it, she stows it in her wallet, then stows that against her skin. She is not losing that ticket. This is when it truly hits her...

"We are going to Infinitas!"

Evan calls Carter, and Zia rings Johnny and, once the men are over their astonishment, they agree to meet downtown, at the stadium. "I guess Francis is the low man out," Zia realizes as they end their calls.

"That's alright. He doesn't like Infinitas anyway."

"But mainly you could only get four tickets, right?"

"Guilty as charged."

From a mile off, the stadium is intimidating in its immensity, a thing of dark steel reaching up to cradle the horizon. Not even the setting sun is safe from its hunger as, for a moment their star hangs, burning, on its Conplast lip before, yes, it too is consumed, swallowed out of sight. And yet the stadium does not truly dwarf them until they are next to it, well within its worldwide shadow.

"This had to have cost a fortune," Evan breathes up at the waterfront edifice, its black facade brightened by holographic ads, a schedule of upcoming events, even a video feed of the interior which looks like nothing short of an ocean of humanity. How, in all this, they will find Carter and Johnny...

"Yeah, about as much as those tickets," Zia smiles, checking for her wallet for the umpteenth time.

But they do find their friends, out in front of gate three. "You won't believe how far away I had to park," Carter pants as the four unite with grins and hugs.

"So, Ev, this is your doing?" Johnny's trying to play it cool, to be the man pop culture cannot touch.

"Don't believe this guy," Carter smiles. "He's been all about this since you called."

"I was just asking a question! Hey, It's Infinitas. I *am* all about this. Let's get inside."

The security check is onerous, particularly for Johnny who rolls his eyes and promises to catch up with the rest of them later as guards take him to one side. Once they're clear, the vast, breezy concourse beckons them on with promises of fresh delights. "Gotta be a league to walk this whole thing," Carter blinks his amazement. "I knew a couple of guys who worked on part of this here, but I didn't know it was like this. Imagine just the sheer tonnage of material that went into this sucker?"

The concourse is a band about the main bowl of the stadium in which too many banks of seats to count stretch from the grass field below all the way up to the top of the structure where, surely, vertigo must assault the senses. But it isn't all bad for the nose-bleeders, the majority of whom would have a primo view of the nearby sea.

"Where are we sitting?" Johnny ahead, next to Evan, who hits the stairs and starts down into the bowl. "Really? You're kidding. We're not going up?" Smiling, Evan continues her descent, only stopping when they are a mere twenty rows above the field over which videos of the band play against a bed of shimmering light. "Oh, this is incredible. Lohner is gonna kill me for seeing this."

"Nah, you are gonna hold it over her," Zia corrects as they slide into their row and take their seats.

"This really is incredible, Ev." Carter is trying to find a comfortable configuration for his long legs. "This had to set you back a fortune!"

"Not too bad." But the girl sitting next to Zia is unwilling to say more on the subject as the bowl quickly fills and the lights die, plunging the entire stadium into darkness save for the fireflies of slate lights that glitter like stars in the black.

"Oh, wow. We're here," Zia realizes. "We're actually here."

Birthed from the smoldering ashes of Postpop, Infinitas had taken Eurowa by storm. As a four-piece supergroup, they inevitably drew comparisons to the other collaborative efforts to have ruled the musical roost in the last century. However, such comparisons are, to Zia's mind, nothing more than an overwhelmed media's feeble attempts to categorize a band whose raw, symphonic intensity blows all other contenders right off the stage. There is, in Infinitas, a well of talent so deep that no one can fritter it away.

Any conversation about Infinitas necessarily touches upon their abiding mystery. Despite living in the most media-saturated period in human history, the four members have successfully obfuscated their lives from millions of rabid fans and thousands of lusting journalists. Their enigma fuels their fame, a siren's song keeping the throngs forever wanting. Their sound shames simple classification: part opera, part rock, part electronica, all power.

The band is fronted equally by Time and Space. The former is a beautiful man in his late twenties with wavy, uncut silver hair spilling wildly around his perfect, glabrous face. Dressed in white and silver, it's impossible to miss the charismatic boyishness that prostrates his female fans. His preternaturally white eyes are a construct of contacts - a universe of time swirling within.

Space plays the darkness to Time's light; a gloriously dark-skinned creature in her mid-twenties with long, flowing hair dyed a shimmering onyx. Her midnight-black dress clings with enviable perfection to a body only the divine can craft, its flowing waves seeming to swallow parts of her whole. Shadow-born...

Surely every fan in this stadium knows it's coming, has seen footage of the performance before. And yet the mind-cracking thunder of the big bang reverberating through the chests of a hundred thousand standing souls is no less powerful. And out of that darkness, out of that thunder, light so brilliant, so consumptive, that it burns away all illusions, until only truth remains, truth and Time and Space appearing in the heart of a star poised over the centermost point of the stadium. They are mere flecks of humanity until they begin to rise to the surface, swimming through starstuff, untouched by that unimaginable heat.

They erupt to stand upon the apex of that star, the essence from which all life flows. They smile. And the crowd roars, loud enough for even the deafened to hear. It is a sound of rapture that explodes from all of them, an acknowledgment of their peerless skill. How they pulled that off Zia does not know and she would loathe the man who told her. There are some wonders best left to the theater of the unknown.

As the opening strains of "This is the Beginning" wash over them, and as the band floats gently to the stage of light hovering over the grass field, Zia turns to her best friend and hugs her. "Thank you," she has to shout into Evan's ear. "Thank you!"

"Thank you," Evan shouts back, but for what Zia may never know, though, she can guess. She takes up Evan's hand and holds it as their gazes meet. What shall come to pass? Can anyone say?

And then the music is upon them and there is no longer any time for the thoughts of the mundane.

***

Flat on her back, Morgan sees the knife streaking for her throat, its velocity so great she has already slammed her boot into the Zealot's knee and caused his killing blow to go wide before her brain has even registered a threat. If the girl had given her even a little warning!

But no! Morgan had spent the entire afternoon failing to keep up with a girl who seemed to know every shortcut, every detour, every hole-in-the-wall alley, and every workaround imaginable in this whole city! Five times, she'd been forced to resort to her tracker to re-acquire Evan, only to lose her mere moments later. Infuriated, she had been determined to set up ahead of the girl and give her a piece of her mind when the tracker brought her down to this waterfront colossus of a stadium which, by simply standing, seemed to hold the laws of physics in complete contempt.

Nothing like it where she comes from, though she does remember a kill in Brandenburg's football park, a silenced shot, quick and clean, as he entered an empty elevator. But she hadn't lingered to watch the game, much less to have her skull shattered by music and mercenaries.

Finding a ticket had been agony. After wandering around like an idiot, anxiety mounting with each passing second that Evan had been in that unsecured sea of people, she finally threw every bit of cash she had on her at the nearest scalper, promising that his evening would not end well at all if he refused to take up her offer. The man had wisely complied which had gotten her inside, into this place of a million unknown threats. And her charge blind to all of them. The stupid sipio!

At least she'd found the four of them, setting up on the concourse above their seats to keep a close eye. How desperate are they, this enemy of hers, of Evan's? Enough to take a shot in the open or would they wait for a more discreet opportunity? Do they even have such thoughts, or are they so drawn to her charge that their need to end her is stronger than their desire to survive?

She'd seen her kill coming a mile away. He'd been uncomfortable in the crowd. Why? Surely they'd trained him for it. They'd been the same eyes holding the same fire, and was that a knife he kept checking for in his jacket? The apartment and now here... How do they find her?

She'd let her prey know he'd been made, watched as his agoraphobia gave way to training as he slipped into combat time. He'd tried to become one with the crowd, lose her in this city all its own, but she'd had none of it. It'd been a risk to pull off Evan, but she'd wanted that kill. And besides, they've never worked in teams before.

Thanks to a moment of carelessness and the concussive force of a bathroom door being hammered into her skull, everything from after she began the stalk is hazy, fragmented. There'd been the sensation of falling onto this cold, filthy floor and then having a few punitive kicks thrown into her already battered ribs. Amateurish... and then he'd tried for the coup de grace with the knife from which only reflex born of experience had saved her.

And now she's in the heat of it, the liquid motion of combat time, of instinct, lubricating her every limb. Her stab-kick had knocked her kill down for one precious second. She's on her knees and hurling herself on top of him before he can pick himself up. Where's that goddamn...

His hand whips up at her, knife driving in towards her right ear, forcing a last second duck and earning herself a long, shallow slash across the back of her neck. Fire flares along severed skin, but that doesn't matter now. She gathers up the zealot's hair in one hand and crashes the back of his skull off the filthy tiles of the bathroom floor. "What be enough for you people? Huh? What be enough?" Is she screaming? She can't be screaming. She does not scream.

He tries the knife again, but this time she gets her forearm in the way, forcing his swinging stab to go wild. And now there's enough time to...

She has his head in hand and is slamming it off the tiles! Again! Again! Again! And now he's spasming beneath her, a seizure brought on by her anger. She does not care. "How many?!" But he will not answer. He will never answer.

Eventually, Morgan returns to herself atop a dead man, or an unconscious one at least. She struggles to her feet, panting, and pulls the body into the last stall, passing on her way the discarded knife that nearly ended her. It's an easy thing to position him on the toilet, to make sure he dies in a place and a pose no one will question for hours. "How many more," she asks him. "How many?" And when his eyes only roll, she makes sure of him with one last blow. The sickening sucking sound of his caved-in skull as it bounces off the toilet tank tells her she's done enough.

Shakily, Morgan washes her face in the sink, contemplating her dripping reflection in the mirror. Gods, but the world is blurry. And she's pretty sure that door loosened a canine. Two more stims will solve for that and her throbbing head, but for how long? She puts them in her mouth, swallowing them with water straight from the faucet. And then she's trying her best to walk back out into the concourse. The stims do what they can to clamp down on the noise, the light, and the chaos, but she's still staggering a little. That's not good, is it?

Morgan leans her shoulder against the welcoming pillar behind Evan's seats, watching them watch the world. And at times it feels like that's all she does, that and soak her hands in blood. She looks down at them, knowing they are clean, but knowing the lie of it too. This damn job...

***

For Zia, there's nothing like the exhilaration of a concert. The energies of a hundred thousand spirits in synergy, in union, is an experience that cannot be matched. Exultant, they spill out into crowded streets darkened by night. They have been transformed by a spectacular none of them will forget.

"That second encore," Johnny sways on his feet. "I think I'm ready to die now. Yep, pretty sure I'm happy enough for that."

"Hey guys, Johnny's completely lost it. Hey bud, where's your epic cool now?!" Carter slaps his friend on the shoulder. "Alright, alright, I'm with you. I'm a faithful man who intends to make an honest woman of the girl I love, but Space..."

"Oh yeah..." Johnny nods slowly, dreamily. "Ohhhhhh... Hey Evan, why you nodding too? You want her too?"

"I wasn't nodding!"

"You were totally nodding!" Zia giggles.

"I wasn't! Hey, I wasn't!"

There's no way any of them can just go home, so they bail to the Iguana for the comedown, piling into the bar to find their table held down by the two women their two men know best.

"Looks like you did some good business," Zia walks up to Molly, having to lean over the bar to hug her.

"Hey, you went?" The bartender smiles. "I guess I can't yell at you for not showin' up then."

"It was incredible. We need drinks and keep them coming. I think we'll be awhile."

"You got it. Hey, how's Evan?"

Zia throws a look back at her friend who's pulling off her pea coat and pouring herself into her chair, laughing. "Well, things look pretty good right now. Check back with me in five minutes and I might have a different answer for you."

Molly laughs. "Go on. I got you covered."

Zia drops into her seat next to Evan, warmly greeting Anna and Lohner, who've been summoned here by their boys, Lohner fresh from her plane into town, Anna from her sister's. Neither seems to know quite what's hit them, but then they have not witnessed god tonight. They have not been uplifted by a faith that must be experienced to be understood.

For the notoriously fickle Johnny, Lohner has impressively outlasted his recent relationships. Punk girl, animal rights girl, and environmentalist girl are a few Zia can dimly remember. All have fallen away, supplanted by this sweet creature that stands no more than 5' 3". The hip clothes, the pink slate, and the stylishly-tended dirty-blonde hair all speak to a flighty spirit, but these soulful blue eyes intimate something more. A mesh top of an emerald green flatter her modest breasts which bracket the back of Johnny's head as she stands behind him, arms on his shoulders, elfin chin atop his disordered curls.

That Johnny chases after hot and eager activists is no more a surprise than Carter's weakness for homespun women of the hearth. At 24, Anna is three years Lohner's senior. Her coloring is all central Eurowan: the long, fine, auburn hair flowing freely about gentle jaw and supple shoulder; deep-set eyes of aquamarine that glimmer with warmth and humor; the healthy skin on a face immune to wrinkles. Even her blue sotton top, modest as it is, draws covetous eyes from the elegant slope of her throat down to her prodigious breasts which will never need the restorative kiss of a surgeon's hand. If she wasn't in possession of the kindest of spirits, Zia would have had no choice but to writhe in jealousy.

"You should've just bought it. You have the money," Carter tells Johnny, amused and annoyed. "No need to turn to a life of crime."

"It is simply not stealing." On the Johnny scale of rage against the world's injustices, he is positively mellow. "They are robbing us. Everyone, from the CEOs down to the retailers, is a happy pig at the great trough of money that is the sale of Flats or Minidiscs. Everyone gets their payday and we get shafted."

"What are we talking about?" Zia asks. "I leave you guys for five seconds..."

"Oh, Johnny's just pissed because he says the Minidisk for Infinitas' latest album was $20 at those concourse kiosks."

"Oh, come on, Johnny. Was that what you were paying attention to tonight?"

"Okay, let me just say this, alright? The soul of the average human being has a decent nature. If you treat him with respect, he'll return that kindness. But that person also knows when he's being robbed by greedy, corporate pigs. Which is why, given the opportunity, he's happy to exact a little revenge by downloading it off the Cloud for free."

"Theft! Right there, theft..." Carter grins.

"Okay, but all I'm doing is balancing out the account here. They are being greedy; I'm being stingy. It equals out. And please, does it look like Infinitas is hurting for cash? I am not contributing to the destruction of my civilization. I'm tired of getting raked over the coals here. So maybe, you know, a little revenge..."

"Alright, tell you what. I'll play the game with you." Carter laces his hand with Anna's. "A homeless guy, we'll call him Hank, comes to my job site and tries to steal some of my copper pipe. Because Hank ain't exactly sober, or smart, he bungles it and we catch his sorry behind. He apologizes and tells me that he needs the pipe to sell so that he can buy blankets and so on. I bought the pipe, I had a purpose for the pipe, it's my pipe. He walked onto my site and tried to steal it. There ain't no arguing that. So talk all you want that the poor man should take every opportunity to get over on the big man, that's fine. It doesn't light my world on fire much either when I'm busting my hump for a living and the guy who owns the company I work for is off gettin' the private treatment by three stacked blondes in some tropical paradise somewhere. But at least have the decency to own that it's theft. Color it however you want. You stole. End of story."

"No, I'm correcting an injustice!"

"Big, fat, hairy stealer! You..."

"Oh, Savior," Johnny mock-realizes, "you want to be them, don't you? You want to be a soulless, 'working for the man,' 'foot on the throat of the lower class,' 'living in your 14 million dollar mansion' money-grubbing stooge!" He waves an accusatory finger in Carter's face, smiling all the while. "You want the three stacked blondes."

"Beats a dockside apartment with leaky pipes and a temperamental water heater you 'blinded by classroom idealism,' 'thinking he can change the world,' activist ass."

"Oh, that's definitely going on my tombstone!" Johnny laughs.

"Will you teach me how to be a money-grubbing stooge?" Zia asks the burly foreman, grinning.

"Anytime," Carter reclines in his chair, arm going around Anna's shoulders.

"Don't forget the fourteen million dollar house," Anna pokes her man in the ribs. "I'm going to remember that."

They talk then for awhile, luxuriating in the presence of friends, and the comedown. Only when Evan, silent throughout, stands for a refill does the table collectively remember her, remember the newspaper, and remember perhaps why she bought those tickets in the first place.

"What," she asks the staring faces. "Oh, you guys too? I've already been through this with Zia. I'm fine. I'm sure it was whatever it usually is: an oven left on, or faulty wiring, or whatever. I'm okay. Anyway, how do you even know? You don't exactly read the paper every day, Johnny. I thought it was, wait a minute, journalistically unfit to more than serve as toilet paper."

"Zia told us." And at her incredulous look. "Hey, she wanted us to find out from a friend, you know, not from a newspaper."

"And we didn't want to dump all over the concert," Carter agrees.

Johnny nods. "We would've found out anyway! It's a bomb, Ev, come on. It isn't nothing."

"C'mon, Johnny. You know how this goes," Evan flushes. "That headline is just to sell papers. Give it a week. It'll be some old lady who forgot to turn the oven off. I'm telling you."

"Where are you staying," Anna asks, eyes concerned. "We've got room if you..."

"Francis put me up," Evan nods her thanks before taking a deep breath of air made warm and smoky from bodies and herbal cigarettes. "It'll sort itself out."

"That sucks about your place, but everything does sort itself out eventually," Lohner agrees. She's sitting on Johnny's lap now. "Life just works that way."

Everything will sort itself out is a platitude for the weak-minded, Zia thinks, a way for people to take comfort from a world that is fundamentally unfair. There is no divine monitor of justice; it just is what it is. It's random and hard and it has to be grappled with in hopes of finding some kind of even. That or it beats the tar out of you.

Concerned, her eyes find a pensive Evan who clearly wants nothing more than to change the subject. What are they going to do? The lies have already begun.

***

Evan's burning as she makes her way to the bar with orders for another round for the table. They act like she went to the concert to escape it all, like she cannot handle life's blown notes.

Or can't she... An old lady who forgot to turn the oven off. Boomboom playing with volatile chemistry to get a better high. Boomboom, the Bickersons...are they gone? They must be gone.

"Evan?" Molly asks. "You okay?"

"Yeah. Yeah, I'm all right. Oh, umm, another round, but Johnny wants a Red River this time."

"Okay."

In the bathroom, Evan digests her haggard reflection through the smears on the vanity's mirror. Maybe she can't handle it. Maybe she'll never be able to handle it, to come back to herself from where she's been trying to hide.

Behind her, a toilet flushes, a door opens, a tall shadow in leather walks to the sink to wash her hands.

Where her nerves come from, Evan cannot say. But as she turns to Morgan, as she meets those sunken eyes, that sometimes bullish and sometimes sullen strength, they flutter a whirlwind in her stomach. "I..."

Morgan grants her a glance, an inclination of dark brows. Which is when Evan clocks the goose egg contorting the skin above her stalker's right eye. The mass has already purpled, angry enough to explode with the merest touch. "Gods, what is that?"

Morgan stares at her with those feline eyes that give away nothing, a twitch in her cheek the only aberration in her rock-like self-control.

"Looks like you ran into a wall, or a truck."

"Close," her shadow whispers.

"Which, the wall or the truck?"

Silence...

"Well, I'm... I just wanted to say... Are you gonna have that looked at? Zia knows first aid. Maybe you should let her look at..."

"No..."

"Okay." She must remember that this is the face of her enemy, the face of what has overturned her life. Its stern plains have denied her free will while its full mouth has withheld vital truths. The eyes though... the eyes that should testify to the madness clearly within this creature, this stalker... they only stare at her, stare at her with a pity not even Morgan can hide. Why? Is she brave enough to ask?

They stare at each other.

"Did you do it?" Evan whispers.

"No." Not a flicker, not even a hint...

"I don't believe you."

"Okay."

"You don't care that I don't believe you?"

"It doesn't matter."

"You don't care that I lost you today?"

"Of course I do."

"Then why aren't you mad?"

Silence...

"It wasn't on purpose. I guess I... I wanted to forget. That's why I took that shift. I guess maybe that's why I bought those tickets. I just... I don't want you to be mad. I don't know why, but I don't. I... I just know that, when I go to sleep tonight, I'm gonna see it. I just know. I'm scared of that. I'm scared of that and... I'm scared that you're not lying to me. How did you get... that bump?"

Silence...

"Fine," she breathes and turns to walk out. Her hand is on the door, pushing...

"It could be anyone, at any time, in any place, even in a crowd. It could be anyone. Don't be skipping out on me again, Evan. For the love of all you be holding dear, don't..."

Shivers chase their way up her spine, along her skin as she escapes out into the bar. She'll sleep tonight knowing she's safe but not knowing how, not knowing why, not knowing what from. Knowing only that she is. She'll sleep tonight and she will see things she cannot name, and she will see broken glass and a fire raging out of control.

Will she ever be alone again, with herself, with her life? Or have they always been there, watching, waiting, wanting...

DAY FIVE

10

The smoke plumes.

The harmless white-green fog wafts from his cigarette's burning tip, undulating into the air from where, abed, Carter enjoys this post-coital delight. The sheets beneath them are hopelessly tangled and drenched in their sweat. True, summer has refused to go gracefully, unwilling to lift her feverish hold over the world, but their bedroom's unseasonable humidity is hardly the cause of their perspiration.

Anna's ample chest flattens against his right arm as, naked, she snuggles close, a leg limply flung across his bare, scarred knees. So fixed is he on the lazy blues and reds of his bedroom's patterned ceiling that he's missed her head finding a home upon his muscled chest. A wonderful night, an epic night: concert, drink, friends. Then, Anna. Sluggish, his mouth forms a smile as he lingers on this last, these new memories, awash in afterglow's warm liquidity.

Hearing about the apartment fire from Zia had proven to be the evening's only discordant note. Evan can downplay the headline all she likes, but her eyes, shadowed bruises, make her a liar. She's stuck ten stories up, with no help and no rope, no way to get back down to normal.

This is reason enough to take two long, thoughtful drags from the herbal, holding the smoke, letting it work in him. Why had she been so quick to shut them down? Is she embarrassed, confused, scared? What, who, is making her scared? He is not a man for unanswered questions.

Everything has its place. That's the key to a smooth operation. Order is paramount. If you aren't on your suppliers, your materials will never be delivered on time; if you're never on your men, they'll take two hour lunches and come back sloshed; and if you have no head, or time, for organization, you'll spend your damn day chasing your own tail. Structure... order.

"Where are you?"

"Hmmm?"

"Where did you go just then?" Anna's purr holds a smile.

"Evan." His careless answer lifts her auburn head, turns it so that she might fix him with her cool eyes and raised brows.

He laughs. "Not like that. Tonight, at the bar... you saw..." Carter rolls, stubs out his light, and returns to his back to reclaim his lovely girl. "Something isn't sitting right."

A job site had staged their first encounter. Years ago now, though, he can't remember how many. He'd been a foreman for sure, new to it he thinks, still adjusting to his added responsibilities when this girl, all of twenty, had rolled onto his site looking for a job. The hair had been fading from pink, her natural chestnut slowly reasserting from the last dye job. Sad, he remembers thinking, eyes darkened by wounds. Pea coat and the ripped jeans is hardly his type, but the intrigue factor had been off the scale.

Just a few weeks, she'd said. He hadn't hesitated. It's customary for a crew to be supplemented by temporary labor. Guys showing up for a few shifts, earning the necessary for booze, women, or rent. Then, buggering off, most never to be seen again. The boys had had a pool going, betting on how long she'd last.

Though he had started her on the simplest of tasks, it soon became clear she had an aptitude for fundamental mechanics that far outstripped his expectations. It hadn't hurt, either, that she'd been damn strong for a girl.

Despite his crew's distrust of women in their midst, Evan had fit. An unassuming attitude, coupled with a willingness to take and dish large helpings of shit, ate away at their skepticism. One day, she had been just part of the team, regularly joining them for beers at the nearest watering hole. Two weeks later, gone...

She'd landed a gig with one of the city's courier outfits: better hours, better pay. No one could fault her. Still, they had been sad to see her go. Carter particularly. He'd seen something in the hard girl, an untold story. Broken, but not beyond salvage...

Like childhood friends, they'd exchanged numbers and promises to call, but neither of them had believed it. They'd been ships passing in the night. Maybe in the next life... Then, out of the black, she had contacted him, inviting him to some new joint in the city's harbor district. Clear as day, he can recollect standing outside the bizarrely modified bar, with this big ugly lizard over the door and him wondering why the hell he was there.

As a reader of women, Carter is far from an expert. He can oversee the intricacies of building a thirty-story office tower from heaps of wood and steel, but chicks... Had she wanted to give it a go? She'd brought Zia and he'd brought Johnny, so maybe. He laughs now, silently, remembering his wingman drooling over Zia's tattoos. Of course, the idiot had been speechless while they'd been there, and then he hadn't shut up about them, neither girls nor tats, on their way home.

They'd never looked back.

"There you go again," Anna prods. "You're making me jealous..."

"Just thinking about the first time at the bar."

"Ah, the bar. That was a good call, wasn't it?" She smiles.

For a pregnant moment, her meaning evades him. "Uh, yeah. Of course."

"You met me there, ass." Annoyed, she lifts from him, subjecting both his cheeks to her palm's stinging caress. "I gotta train you better, boy. My mother always told me 'you have to train them to love them' and here I was thinking not." Those aquamarines glitter. "Next, it'll be anniversaries, birthdays you're forgetting..."

"Ahh, damn! You didn't have to hit me," he feigns pain by rubbing at his imaginary wounds. And then he's attacking, forcing a squeal from her as he yanks her down, atop him, chests fusing in the dark. "Give it a rest. Anniversaries... pfft. Your mom ain't got nothing on me."

"Hope not..."

"That's it!" He rolls atop her, bedeviled hands seeking the prime spots for tickling. Oh, she tries to return fire, but such arrogance only redoubles his efforts to force a yield from his yelping partner.

"You like her, don't you?"

The storm has past, leaving sated lovers on their sides, but inches between their faces.

"Evan?"

She nods.

"Yeah. There's something..."

"I like that about you."

"That I like other women? I'm luckier than I thought..."

"No, oaf. I like that you want to protect her."

Is that all? There's no denying the girl has been marked for something. He isn't one for auras and destinies and that mumbo jumbo. But, Evan... "I don't know what it is."

"You're just a big softie, that's all." Anna stares sweetly into his eyes, kissing him as she frees the wrinkled sheets. "I love you."

"Mmm, love you too."

Casting the thin top sheet over their tangled bodies, she cuddles up to him. Sleep won't be long.

The morning dawns clear and crisp. Carter rises quietly, kisses his sleeping girl, gathers his work clothes and sneaks into the cramped master bathroom. He closes the door, sets his slate on the vanity, flips it to the news, and then methodically goes about his ablutions.

It adds a good fifteen minutes to his routine, but Carter loves an old-fashioned shave. Not everything has to be fast or four-bladed. He trusts his steady hand more than he does any machine.

The news offers its typical depressing fare: fires are burning up north thanks to this unusual heat wave which, experts say, might be the result of a changing climate, of course; another spike in housing costs, that's helpful; a steep hike to an already prohibitive gas tax to force motorists off the roads, like they aren't already taxed to death; the kings lost their eighth game in a row. Bums...

His ears perk when the news reader throws to a government official announcing the commissioning of a fleet of high altitude surveillance drones to be deployed at sea and along the country borders by the end of next year. Drones, flying machines in the sky, capable of snapping photos of objects as small as a slate from 5,000 feet up. Savior, he's living in a bloody science fiction novel.

As he rinses his face, he's reminded of a quote, something about trading liberty for security. His foggy mind fails him as he steps into the shower. He'll have to ask Johnny. Or not... Drones in the sky... The boy will be in fine, doomsdayer form today. Oh well, for now, his world is warm water and soothing steam.

Washed and dressed, Carter finds a robed Anna awake and blending in their small, linoleum kitchen. Approaching from behind, he fingers the robe from her elegant neck, kissing her there, tasting her sweet skin.

Outside their cramped one-bedroom bungalow, the din of morning traffic penetrates. The neighborhood's only a step or two up from bachelor row. Raising children in this urban clatter is out of the question. But this thought alone makes him think of the ring just waiting to be slid onto her loveliest finger. He hasn't time to get lost in that thought trap now.

"You off?" She turns, hands him a fruit-powered energy drink fresh from the blender. His manipulation of her collar has revealed a hint of breast beneath the gentlest of throats; fleshly treats infinitely more interesting than this blue-green concoction of half-frozen fruit. What the hell is the green stuff?

Hiding a grimace, he accepts, takes a sip. Bananas, because that makes sense, and something tart. A man of continental tastes or not, it's a far cry from bacon and eggs.

"Yeah. Sorry about today. Half day, I promise. It's just Fuck'le'roy..."

"What is it this time?"

"The glass guys. Special order... the little lord wants it done yesterday and he's willing to pay."

"I'm surprised you could get so many of the guys together on a Sunday."

"They moaned, but money spends, doesn't it?" A second sip... He turns for the door to hide his distaste. "You can go through some of those decorating books. I talked to the guy at the bank yesterday. He said Kenzington's shaping up to close on the 32nd. It'll be rough at first, but we'll get the crew over on the weekends to help fix it up. They'll do us a good turn."

"You did talk to him! Oh, that's great!" The warmth in her smile is belief in him. "I can't wait to get out of here, get into a place that's ours, that's really ours, where we can be a family. But the books'll wait. I'm taking your mother to church."

That brings him around, sharp, disquiet in him building. "You don't have to do that... I was going to cancel. It's just one Sunday."

"It's important." Anna is unaffected by his discomfort. "Someone should take her." Her smooth hands rub at a pretty face still half asleep. "And you're working." Guilt now? "And, anyways, you know how she is with us. It's an easy way to score points."

"It's not as bad as all that," Carter shifts his feet. "She's old-fashioned. You know how that goes. Her world isn't our world."

"That's how it is until our *status* changes... Anyways, it's half a law that mothers don't get along with the lovers of their sons. I'll make it work." But there's a certain look in her eye, of expectation, of waiting for promise to be fulfilled.

"You're sure..." This will come back to bite him; he's convinced of that much.

"I know the game. I'll wear white; I'll be a good girl. I'll even be nice while she grills me on the apocalyptic topic of our sex life. Now, get gone before you're late and all your boys run off for lack of good handling."

"You know my kind too well," he chuckles. It seems he cannot move her from this mission of hers, leaving only goodbye, well, and prayer. "Love you, babe," he kisses her again and is out the door and moving quickly down to his waiting truck. He'll go up the street a spell before dumping out the shake. Someone at the site will have hit Greasy Gino's, thank Savior. Now, if his mother could avoid destroying his relationship... Then again, if he's caught dumping out the shake, he won't need his mother's help in that regard.

The arboretum sprouts from land Carter used to visit as a youth. The whole family would pile into dad's old wagon, Carter and his sister fighting like dogs in the back, and they'd venture north to the city's oldest amusement park. They'd called it the Bob, though he can't remember why.

Unable to compete with newer, glitzier developments, the Bob had turned off its lights. Dated roller coasters, nickel and dime arcades and shoot-for-a-bear booths just couldn't compete with a VR trip to Mars. Everything has to be shock and awe now. There's no more room for class, for tradition.

The Bob had been sold to a developer who had stripped the old girl down to a vast and empty lot. Can memories be stored in pavement, in bedrock, or had they been scrapped along with the rides and the tents? The developer had intended to flip the acreage, but ten years on found the land still naked dirt.

Maybe the memories are carried inside those, like him, who remember the Bob, remember what it was, what it meant. He's not against business, against development. Business requires growth and growth necessitates change. But the harsh realities of life are no protection against nostalgia's bittersweet caress which hollows him every time he visits this old lot. His first kiss had been at the Bob, behind shooting galleries, where no one would think to look. Andrea... Andrea Goodman? Truman? No, Goodman... Andrea Goodman.

Now, Raphael 'Raphi' Merryweather has planted his flag. An environmentalist, he'd gotten his start by banging out some whizbang accounting software of some kind. A few shrewd investments in real estate later and he'd landed himself the Bob's old footprint which, thanks to urban sprawl, is now at the heart of a working class neighborhood and not, as it once had been, beyond the city's limits.

As anti-development as Commie Johnny can be, even he had been appeased by Raphi's nightmare - the city's first interactive arboreal conservatory. The diminutive local had provided him detailed specifications, down to the type of screw he wanted in the bloody light fixtures. Unused to such micromanagement, Carter had

had dreams about sticking screws in Raphi, but money talks, loudly. The firm is being paid far too well to permit his objections to derail this latest fancy of the stupidly rich and marginally famous.

His crew has been here for months. Ten years of debris had to be cleared before the conservatory's intricate skeleton could be erected. The frame is experimental Conplast that, in the lab, had proven sturdier than its predecessors. Then the second floor which, at Raphi's insistence, had to be an atrium to permit the proper flow of light in from the would-be glassed ceiling. Fifty delicate lamps had been installed throughout, while a ventilation system with global coverage is bunkered in the basement.

The glass they've been ordered to install is unlike anything Carter's seen: as durable as Conplast, as heavy as a steel beam, and easily six inches thick. Each pane has been specially commissioned, coated thrice in some protective substance and then flown in from Estria, of all places. It doesn't look like glass, more misty silver, more mirror than window. It is, Raphi claims, capable of withstanding small arms fire and direct hits from explosive devices. And he's going to use it for an arboretum...?

Parking his truck in the open, to give the solar on the roof maximum coverage, Carter gets out and approaches a fretting Raphi whose gesticulations only confuse the workers he seeks to direct. Carter's crew is unloading the remaining sixteen panes of glass that comprise the ceiling.

His minions dispatched, Raphi turns and nearly runs into Carter's chest. A generous judge would put Lord Fuck'le'roy six inches his inferior which is maybe why his lordship is so quick to avoid a collision. "Morning, Mr. Merryweather," he forces a smile. "Even on Sundays, you're on the job..."

"Absolutely, absolutely." The small, pale face peers wildly about, watching anxiously as the panes of glass are individually loaded onto a small platform where the crane will begin lifting them into position.

"Careful, careful," Raphi worries.

"It'll get done, Mr. Merryweather. It's just unusual work."

"Well, it's an unusual project," Raphi whips his balding head around to stare up at Carter. "What we do here might save the planet one day."

That snags the foreman's attention. He usually ignores the little guy's boastings. "How do you figure, Mr. Merryweather?"

Raphi jabs a finger at two large trucks around which the dozen minions had gathered. "Inside the conservatory will be placed every last species of plant we can manage, purified samples mind, no genetically-modified, environmentally-contaminated samples. Most will be placed into storage, here and elsewhere, but some will be planted, grown and shared with the community. This will be a sanctuary for mother nature: no diseases, no chemicals, and no interference."

"And you figure that, what, others will follow your lead?"

Irritated, Raphi scowls. "The best calculations say that the ozone layer will, in twenty years, be so thin that the most fundamental building blocks of life on this planet will be irradiated by the worst elements of our sun. Everything will experience unhealthy mutation: humans, crops, animals, the earth itself. And, as I'm sure you know," he continues pompously, "you cannot predict what those mutations will do. If steps are not taken to guard ourselves from this greatest threat, we may all be extinct in fifty years. It's simply a reality. It is our generation's greatest challenge."

Raphi extends a pair of pale hands that have never met a callous. Under the strong, morning sun, they shimmer faintly. "New blend of sunblock, keeps out the entire spectrum. Vitamin D I take as a supplement. I will not allow myself to be contaminated along with the rest of our doomed planet."

Carter flails for a way out of this ridiculous and depressing conversation. Doomsdayers... "Well, it's good of you to think ahead..."

"Yes, well, none of it would be possible without the glass your men are so cavalierly handling," Raphi natters. "It is the vision of protection, from all things natural and unnatural. Its filtration system is exquisitely sophisticated, allowing through only the harmless elements of our star, which, of course, is why we require the internal illumination. The Eden Conservatory will teach the world how we have tortured our planet and those it teaches will go out from this place and they will instruct others that it is not right to do as they have done before, that it is not right to destroy what we did not create. Mr. Carter, we have despoiled a world that we were made stewards of. It was not given to us to rape. Something must be done, a sanctuary maintained, knowledge kept. I'm sure you understand."

"Absolutely, absolutely," Carter tries to keep a straight face as he steps towards his men. "We'll be out of your hair by the end of the week, Mr. Merryweather. You've my word on it."

"See to it," Raphi shouts after him. "And handle that glass with care, mind! It completes God's paradise!"

He has never been so grateful to be back among the sane.

His slate thrums. Carter retreats to a safe distance before pulling it out. Johnny. Figures... He answers as he watches his boys fire up the crane. "Yellowbrick Construction, this is Carter."

"Yeah, this is Billy Bob Tumbleweed on Pink Swallow Lane. I need my floors waxed. Do you wax your floors, sir?"

"I don't do nothing to my drapes or my floors, Johnny, not that it's any of your business. But go on, keep it up. I'll wax your dome if you're not careful." Laughing, he leans against the cooling hood of his truck. "How you doing, pal?"

"Good. Anna said you were working. Tell me something. How well do the Sunday ladies tip their male strippers? Does church impact your overhead?"

"You whine so much that I'm stunned no one's put you in a kennel."

Johnny laughs. "You've seen my place. I'm already there."

"Fair enough. So what's up?"

"That concert, man. Oh, I still can't believe it! Incredible... But Evan, you know? Just dropping those tickets on us and that fire... that's at the heart of this, don't you think?"

"Yeah." The first pane of glass is safely hoisted aloft. He has a good crew. "Has she told you anything?"

"No, but she's talking to Zia. She told me about Morgan, that leather queen from the other night. She did for someone, maybe several someones, maybe to do with Evan."

"Did for? You mean..."

"Iced, axed, did for. Put out of business... never to trouble the world evermore."

Carter lets out a low whistle, until he realizes. "Evan?... She's got her claws into Evan? Why? What in God's name would anyone want with Evan? If there's a girl who keeps her head down and does her bloody job, it's her. She steal something maybe? I mean, I know those girls play it loose sometimes..." The first pane crests the second story wall and is shifted into position. "Morgan, huh..."

"I have no idea. But yeah, Morgan. I've asked some guys I know to look into her, gave them her particulars, not that we know much."

"That's something." Musing, Carter pulls a pair of sunglasses from his pocket, slips them on. "Truth be told, I feel more than a little useless. She's not letting us in. Why keep us on the outside? She'll tell Zia, but not us?"

Johnny grunts. "I'm still waiting to meet the first person Evan trusts, I mean, the first person she really lets inside. That girl... you pretty much have to redefine the term baggage, you know?"

"Well, let me know how that search goes. I mean, a shady character like this Morgan doesn't just start hanging around a couple days before everything you own goes up in smoke. That's not a coincidence. Can't be. And man, but... she was playing it awfully suspicious last night, trying to act like it's nothing. If this had all happened to me, I'd be pissed. Do we know if it was actually her unit?"

"No, keep you in the loop though." Carter can feel Johnny's grimace through their connection. "So, did you have to talk to Raphi?"

He groans.

"I take it that's a yes."

"He's the poster child for legalizing selective breeding; tell you that much." The big man sighs, feeling the sudden urge to play crash-test dummy with his slate.

"We are brothers, Raphi and I."

"In what, my wanting to put my boot up you?"

"As a destroyer of the environment, you'd never understand. It requires, you know, a conscience."

"Kiss my ass, Johnny. I got the solar put on my truck. What else do you want? Kiss my ass!"

"Don't tease, bitch! You got no idea what I'm capable of. But alright, I'll give you the truck, only..."

"Oh, what now?"

"Well, it took carbon to make the truck, you know. That has a footprint too."

"I'm giving up. I am. I just can't win with you people."

Johnny laughs. "Before I go, I was reading the paper this morning and..."

"I know, I know: surveillance drones, crumbling civil liberties, destruction of the world as we know it, blah blah blah. It's too early in the morning for your scary sci-fi, Johnny."

"I've been telling you. Haven't I been saying?"

Yes, Kerrilia."

"Oh, nice. Thank you for that. Oh, hey, I better let you get back to stripping. I just heard them summoning Crystal to the main stage. I'm assuming that's you."

"Oh, for the love of the Lord." Carter can't help his laughter. "Seriously, hit me again if you learn anything about this Morgan."

"If I come up zeroes, maybe I'll pull the woman aside and just ask her directly. I can be pretty persuasive."

"She doesn't seem the type to fall for your dubious charms, my friend. Besides, you and what army?"

"Well, I was counting on you coming to the rescue, as you always do."

"Yeah, right because I live for saving your ass. Bye Johnny. Gotta go." The second pane is ascending crookedly.

"Maintain the rage..." It is as much a blessing as will ever pass the imp's lips.

The rest of the half day goes well enough. The conservatory's employees begin installing some of their displays even as his crew rolls back the rooftop tarp to finish the northwestern segment of the ceiling. They'll try to finish the other three sections by Thursday. It's difficult work, but Carter finds a comforting simplicity in physical labor. The mind can just leave the body to that age-old dance of muscle and bone.

There's peace in simplicity.

11

It really is a scorcher.

The sun scalds the earth through a brilliant, cloudless sky. By mid-afternoon, Carter and his sweaty crew are too dehydrated to continue, even if they wished to.

Johnny had called again, reporting no progress with Morgan. However, the wingnut had contacted Evan and arranged for the three to grab a drink. "An intervention?" he'd asked incredulously. But the man had a point. Secrets are burdens and when they are not shared, neither is the burden. And even if, in the telling, Evan breaks faith with whoever might have sworn her to secrecy, confiding in trusted friends is a lesser sin than silence.

The day gas had hit $9 a gallon, Carter had succumbed to the will of the crazies. A man saving for a house can't afford to bend over for the oil companies. An electric had been the only choice, but its price had been high both in cash and in sentiment. It meant the sacrifice of his beloved gas guzzler upon which both he and his father had toiled and tweaked. He can almost hear Johnny's voice in his head, telling him that times are changing and that's fair enough; they can't just ignore the next 50 years of innovation out of a desire for tradition, for nostalgia, but does everything have to change so fast? He's not even sure he can fix half the things in an electric's engine if need strikes. How does ignorance help anyone?

But if having to squeeze every ounce of power out of this thrice-damned electric motor is the lowlight of his journey home, then turning up to find his girl in a beautiful, simple white dress is the highlight. The church frock is a soft white with splashes of blue about wrists and neck. And while its modest cut hid what a man loves most, it left no doubt that those firm treasures existed. Modesty is the sexiest of all virtues.

Carter glimpses her through the picture window. Regally composed, even while alone, she reads: lovely face cleaned of makeup save a hint of maroon upon the lips, smooth shoulders caressed by a spill of auburn hair, eyes like twin, soundless oceans. He'll never find better. And yet...

"You return to me unbroken," Anna jokes as he comes in from the heat. A half smile graces her lips. She closes her book.

"Back bowed with well-earned gold for m'lady," he agrees, grinning. "How was my mother? Did she torture you?"

A passing grimace as they move into the kitchen. "Could have been worse. She didn't declare me the devil in front of the congregation or anything. I'm considering it a success."

"True enough." Carter tosses his keys onto the table, kisses her. "I've got a little bit... Meeting Johnny later." He ignores the flash of her irritation as he washes his hands in the kitchen sink.

"Don't do that," she chides, "your bathroom. Your bathroom, remember? Your dirt, your bathroom."

Sheepishly, he nods, trying to take a towel for his hands.

"Not that one!" Anna grumbles, tossing him an identical towel. "Use this. This," she grabs away the one already in hand and returns it to the oven door, "is the good towel."

The girl's an angel, but there are times... They argue little save over Johnny. He still remembers the accusation she'd once hurled at him. "The way it is with the two of you, it's like he's a silent partner in this relationship. I don't know, Carter, should I look nice for him too? Dress up for him too, spread my..." She'd wisely stopped there, but then she'd made her point.

Yes, the Johnny look. These years on, he knows it well: the faintest of eye-rolls, the tiniest twist of a mouth soured. Whenever he goes out with his friend, that look. It's a wonder she hasn't patented it. And of course, she never talks to Johnny about it.

Damn, he's burned himself. The bathroom mirror reveals nose, cheeks, and forehead marred by swaths of angry red, sensitive to the touch. Stupid Sunguard...

Anna cooks an early dinner, quiet as they eat. She searches in him for a reaction when she announces plans to see a girlfriend while he's out with Johnny. She finds only a smile.

He's being unfair. She'd been so good about Infinitas, then meeting them afterward to drive the truck home... It's just a towel, right? It's just Johnny? Everyone has quirks, buttons. So looking up, he offers an olive branch.

"Ideas for Kenzington," Carter asks, using his fork to indicate the pile of books splayed between them. The fork returns to his plate to find more spaghetti. So good, made the way he likes it with all the melted cheese.

"Wedding stuff." Her reply is as casual as the elegant way she sips at her glass of wine. She claims not to be hungry. "My sister..."

From the coat closet, nestled in the pocket of his jacket, the ring scalds him with a heat to shame his sunburn. "That's... good. Getting inspiration, huh?"

"No, patience..."

He knows when to shut up.

For a month, Carter has sought out that perfect moment. Anna loves waterfalls, so his first thought had been to take her up to Elizabeth Crest and propose there. Of course, the next morning's paper had a nice, colorful spread detailing a couple that had done exactly that. There's clean and simple, the front hall of their new house, but is that special enough? Does that mean enough? Will she be disappointed? So many schemes, so many notions. Eventually, the flaws in each plan allowed him to put it off, to excuse away the choice behind all the plans. Except that, now, the more he puts it off, the less perfect any of it seems.

Needing to think and finding only uncomfortable silence at home, he goes out, driving past the site on his way to the ballpark.

He slows, stops, looks in at the arboretum, at the conservatory, at this Eden. He doesn't have much time for lord Fuck'le'roy, for any of them that stand on Johnny's side of the isle. Believers, who think they can change the world if they just try hard enough. Dreamers who don't realize that they'll never win, that it'll never be enough, that their enthusiasm will eventually fade and the vultures will be right there, circling, eager to wrest back control from the idealists.

And yet Raphael will leave his mark on the world. This will be his legacy. It will outlast him, barring some catastrophe. And that means something, legacy, memory... God has a plan for him; he believes that, but there's a freedom to move inside that plan. Legacies... choices... moments in time that change everything.

He's working all this through as he parks outside the Iguana, realizing, as he walks inside, that it's only a couple hours to midnight. Where's the time gone? Apparently, time flies when you're contemplating the future.

Last night's Infinitas blowout has resulted in so many casualties, the joint is three-quarters empty. And anyway, it's the last measure of the weekend for those luckier than him, a final, brief stretch of time to get done all the little things they've been putting off. But not for them...

"Hey Molly." The woman is rocking a maroon tank top tonight. He has to force his eyes away.

The bartender smiles at him, nods. "Ale?"

"Coffee, thanks. Something of an intervention tonight."

"You're an alcoholic," she says, grinning.

"If only." He moves to their table where Johnny has been keeping himself company with his favorite dark beer. "She show yet?"

"Bathroom." Johnny indicates the pea coat slung over the back of Evan's usual chair. His blonde hair's all mussed. He can't use a comb?

"You look a little," Johnny wiggles his fingers.

"What you goin' for there?"

"Not sure, actually," Johnny laughs. "Iffy I guess. You look a little iffy. What's up, cowboy?"

"I'm cursed by perfection," Carter strips off his coat and sits down in his familiar chair.

"Really. Perfection? And you're still not happy? That's quite a feat there, my friend. You really got to want to be unhappy to pull that one off."

"I mean Anna, you ass."

"Still haven't proposed, huh." Johnny's eyes twinkle. "Never pegged you for a man fearing commitment. What's tripping you up?"

"Beautiful, sweet, elegant, smart..." He sighs, a hand rubbing at tired eyes.

"Fruitful loins," the imp adds.

"Idiot..."

"I'm kidding. You should take the plunge," Johnny sobers. "You're good together."

"No 'there are other fishes in the sea' speech tonight? Thanks, Molly." Carter accepts his coffee, milking its black midst.

"I'm very misunderstood." Johnny lays a hand over his heart. "It's my cross to bear. Yours is being dependable, someone who doesn't cut out on a girl because he's feeling a little..." He wiggles his fingers same as before.

Evan's return to the table saves him from having to react to an actual compliment from his friend. Is that who he is? Dependable? Dependable people can pull the trigger, can't they?

He looks up at Evan and doubletakes. Pulling no punches tonight, their Evan, heating up the room with a devilishly thin silver blouse, its mesh loose enough to hint at the skin beneath. Its sleeves blow about her well-defined arms, across underrated breasts, and over a belly as taut as a drum. She can pull the dead from their graves.

"Is that new?" It's out of him before he can think better of it.

Evan fixes those gray eyes on him, cool clouds, as she sits. "Yeah. Why not?"

"Why not indeed," Johnny grins.

Evan's suspicious, studying them as she sips her water and perfectly unwilling to take Johnny's bait. "So... what's goin' on?"

"It's come to our attention that the woman that's been dogging you isn't exactly..." Carter opens as gently as he can.

"Zia told you," Evan rolls her eyes. "Fuck..."

"Yeah, no more games, Ev. No more distractions. She told us..." Johnny leans forward, all business. "Maybe you want to think that fire was some old lady messing around with her oven, but we all know it isn't that. If that's all it was, you wouldn't have your own personal shadow, would you? Morgan, right? Morgan wouldn't be hanging around, doing whatever she's doing, holding over you whatever she's holding."

"Easy, easy," Carter tries to pull Johnny back.

"But see it's worse than that," Johnny barrels on. "You knew what was going on. Oh, maybe you didn't know the whole bit, but you've had an idea. And instead of letting us in on it, us, your friends, you kept it to yourself which you may think brave. Who knows? I just think it's stupid."

"Johnny!" But not even Carter's hand on the man's shoulder will stop him, much less the anger flushing Evan's face.

"Oh, you think it's stupid," she hisses.

"I do. Because it hurts you and it hurts us. It leaves us out in the cold which means we can't protect you and we definitely can't protect ourselves. Lose-lose..."

"Fuck you, Johnny..." The glass of water goes whistling past Johnny's blonde head, missing him by three inches as it hammers itself to a thousand tiny pieces against the wall behind him. She's shocked, Johnny's shocked. The bar is staring at them as Evan, recovering the quickest, gets to her feet and leans over the table to put herself in Johnny's face. "You don't think I've thought about that?! You don't think I've spent half my waking moments wondering what the hell is going on and how it affects my friends?" Her voice is quivering. "I lost everything, Johnny, except for you guys, everything! Yeah, and I didn't want it to blow back on anyone else which is why I tried to keep this low profile. And if you think that was selfish, if you think I put you in danger, then fine. Walk the fuck away, right now. You know as much as I know. Walk away..." Have any of them ever seen her cry? The tears dance in her eyes.

Slowly, quietly... "That's not what I..."

Her rage is swift to cool to something more like pleading. "You guys have no idea... what this is like, what I've seen. And I know that's my fault for keeping it back, I do. I know you asked, but I couldn't... If I said anything, it'd be..." She bites her lip, hands on the table for support now, not for rage. "It'd be like saying it was real, all of it. Don't make me make it real, Johnny, please. I'm not ready for that yet, okay?"

Johnny and Carter exchange glances, neither man knowing what to say. It's Molly who, in the coming over to soak and sweep up the water and glass, gives them time to reset.

"I'm sorry, Molly," Evan whispers, back in her seat again, shivering.

"That's alright, honey. All in a day's work. S'alright..."

But even after the bartender's gone, they don't know how to move ahead. Clearly they don't know the whole story, but how to press it now? Carter gathers himself and looks at this girl who has been, for so long, their enigmatic friend, their private treasure. "We care about you, Evan. We hang, we talk, we argue, and we drink too much. Some might call us degenerates. But me... it's a bond not everyone has. It's a bond that... means something to me and I think means something to you too."

Their girl nods.

"I hear why you pulled back; it was the act of a friend. Johnny knows that too, much as sometimes he can't say it right. But this, whatever this is, that's happening to you? It's bigger than that. It's bigger than a good deed. You've got to trust us, Evan." He braces himself. "You've got no one else."

A few of those tears might have slipped free but for her turning away from them, to peruse the Sunday night crowd as an excuse to wipe at her eyes. When she looks back, she's solemn, and sad.

"Tomorrow night, midnight." It's but a guilty whisper.

"What of it," Johnny presses.

Carter steadies himself with a sip of coffee.

"I meet her guy," she clears her throat, staring at her water. "Her contact. She said he'd fill in the blanks."

"What blanks?"

"Why she's here... why she says she... has to protect me."

"We're going." Johnny's adamant. "That's the end of it. That's non-negotiable."

"We're with you," Carter seconds. "I'll talk to my boys. Some of them will want to back you up too."

A flash of gratitude before a slight relaxing of the shoulders as of tension lifted. "Just you guys, I think. Just you guys. I..." She nervously licks her lips. "I think..." But then she's shaking off this half-formed thought. "Just you guys..."

"You're scared," Johnny murmurs. "You're scared. Of course you're scared. If it was me, you'd see a big puddle between my shoes right now. I know from scared. Scared's good. Scared keeps you on your toes. So let me say this: from what I know of the world, and situations like this, everyone's running game, Ev. Everyone's got an angle. What we need to do is to figure out what those angles are. What is it about you? What do they want? And who knows. Maybe it's something stupid. Maybe tomorrow will put an end to it."

"Maybe." She's trying not to smile. "Who knows? Maybe."

What must it feel like to be chased, hunted? Carter reaches out, takes her hand, squeezes it, feeling her tremble. It's beyond belief. Evan, of all people. And for what?

"It's gonna be okay. We're gonna make it okay." But as much as he tries to reassure her, little of it seems to register. He is so used to staring into those eyes and seeing wounds there. Only now does he realize that seeing fear is worse than pain.

It's near on midnight by the time they split up. They walk Evan to her Yager and watch her ride into the black. It's Johnny who scopes Morgan.

"Look..."

Across the street, perfect eyeball on the Iguana's front door: the black coat, the hard face swathed in shadow. Astride that bike, she is the hunter, kicking the machine alive and following their girl without a single backward glance. They make for his truck.

"I don't like this." Johnny flings himself into the passenger's seat. "You look at her sometimes and you see a sixteen-year-old girl, you know?"

"You would know." Carter joins his friend in the cab. The electric motor coming to life as the turning of his key lit the display.

"Hey, I look, but I've never crossed the line! And if I'm not supposed to look, then maybe they shouldn't splash those girls all over the covers of magazines and the Cloud and..."

"Look, never mind that," Carter cuts him off, eyes on where that motorcycle had vanished. "Think we can follow?" But his mind is already supplying the answer: too dark, too late. "Damn..."

"There's nothing we can do, man. We said our bit and we make sure we show up in force tomorrow."

"I hate feeling..."

"Helpless?"

"Something like that," Carter grunts and makes for Little Harbor.

Each man keeps to his own thoughts during the ten minute ride to Johnny's dock-adjacent rattrap. It's only when Carter rolls the truck to the curb that he looks over. "Give Lohner my love."

"I will," Johnny cracks his door, steps onto the battered sidewalk. Thoughtful blue eyes glint as he leans back in, the dome light splashing off his sharp features. "I envy you, you know."

Carter blinks.

"About before... You got a girl who loves you and wants to be with you." He grimaces. "Look, you hit the jackpot. Don't blow it by overthinking it. Don't blow it because you're scared or confused. It looks good on you, the family thing. It's you and it's her and it works..." Straight forward, honest. This is not their language.

Then Johnny's pulling back and slamming the door before, touched, Carter can muster more than a soft "thanks." His eyes stay fondly on his friend's receding back. And then he's gone.

DAY SIX

12

The brick townhouse is like any other on Gibson.

Morgan makes the house by the familiar Pedarius parked neatly in its drive. For executive cars, it's modest, entry level. Francis' hazel eyes dance before her, taunting her. They are not the eyes of an entry level man.

Save for their brief exchange at the concert, Evan has turned being uncommunicative into an art form. Before the fire, the girl seemed to treat losing her tail as a kind of game, an amusement to brighten her day. But since that night of ash and smoke, there's been a crueler edge to this play between them, a whiff of humiliation that accompanies each of Evan's victories.

Evan seems to be capable of disappearing at whim. Alleys, parking lots, buildings... She can make a shortcut out of anything, forcing Morgan, each time, to go to her tracker, to find her with these cheating eyes. But not even technology can save her when she turns up at a toy store and follows her tracker's signal inside, down aisles populated by children bemused by her leathers... Finally reaching a display topped by a stuffed bear, the ULS locator torn from Evan's bike pasted on its nose.

Staring at that bear, she'd wanted so much to scream, to throw back her head and roar it out, to all those oblivious souls, the truth of what's at stake. She'd thought to run outside, after the girl, to find her in this impossible city and roar it at her too, her contact be damned. But the notion that the girl might've been in the store, at that moment, watching her, laughing at her, had cooled her rage. She'd not give her such an easy win.

But her admirable self-control had lasted only hours. The final straw had snapped when she'd gone into the Iguana, to ask the bartender if she knew Evan's location, and then come out to find her bike gone. She'd found her Roady up the street, a sign on it reading, 'See what it feels like?'

And so, when they had next come together, huntress and hunter, they each had screamed, hurling all their tired threats until Evan finally played the one card she knew Morgan could not resist, her safety.

"You tell me when I can see him, right now, or we're through. I will shut you out of everything. I will go to the cops and I will be free of you and your nonsense. And you'll be sitting in a cell somewhere, stewing, trying to figure out if they've killed me yet. That's where you'll be, rotting and not knowing if I'm alive. Maybe you'll find out about it in the paper, hmm? Maybe you'll see me chalked out, knowing you weren't there to keep the bullet from blowing out my..."

No need for the girl to finish her threat. Morgan had no choice but to yield, to give her time and place. "Yes," she had promised, "he'll be there," having no idea if he would, having nothing else to say. Later, she'd made the call to her contact's emergency number, told him how it had gone so wrong, but she's still to hear back from him. If he lets her down...

Where they stand now, Morgan can only judge by how hard Evan tries to lose her. That the ride back to Francis' house had been uneventful offered some hope for a truce, but nothing about this job has been normal, so she might as well flip a coin on what tomorrow will bring.

Resolved to pass this stakeout in digs more comfortable than that cold alley opposite Evan's now rubbled apartment, Morgan now squats in a house within visual range of her charge's bedroom window. Her perusal of the various mailboxes, under the cover of evening's shadow, had revealed that the Michaels, owners of the home kitty-corner to Francis', had not touched their correspondence in at least five days. Very sloppy...

With a professional's grace, she'd disabled the house's alarm, easily forced the rear window, and then crawled head-first into the laundry room. There'd been nothing beneath her to break her fall, so she'd tucked her head and hoped for the best, landing hard, shoulders first, on the tiled floor.

Had any of the nosy neighbors heard? She'd held a tense breath, listened... Nothing...

The Michaels will know of their home's violation, but Morgan has little time for such worries. The laws, and the conventions they uphold, have never applied to her. The home is viable, that's all that matters, affording her an excellent view of the target house, of the street that grants access to it, and of the locals who will be crossing paths with the girl boarding up in it. Necessities all...

Closed curtains conceal her from the street and allow her to observe her target from a crouch near the family room's picture window. Six days of this... six days!

Fatigue looms. The leading edges of its numbing storm reach for her even as Morgan pops another stim between her teeth. Though her foggy mind cannot remember how many of the pills she's taken, it records in great detail its burning passage down her dry throat; but she'll pay that price, won't she, for the clarity that blooms in her mind, a light that thrusts back the darkness. Her limbs fill with liquid heat, banishing her aches and pains. Migrating now, down, to pool in her abdomen, to quicken the core of her. She smiles as her revitalized vision tracks back to the target, watching.

Not her first long stretch without sleep, she knows how to power through when the job requires it. She's never gone this long before; though why not seems to have momentarily escaped her. Why can't she keep going? She can go forever...

Stims... Their benefits are many when taken moderately. Their extended abuse, however, exacts a toll few are willing to pay: hallucinations, recklessness, a temper quick to loose its shackles. But she's not there yet. No, she'll know when she's there and then she'll stop. After all, there's a lot at stake, including her own reputation. Sleep will wait.

The man at the concert had been number 18. He emerges, now, from Francis' carefully tended garden, allowing her to see him as she'd left him, poised on a toilet, his eyes empty of his particular venom. His number glows from his forehead; an accusation? They come quicker now, her enemy, as if spat out at her by some angry factory.

Why are they becoming more desperate, more willing to take chances? What's the point of speculating? She knows so little of them. She knows nothing of them, truth be told. She knows nothing of the men whose throats she cuts.

That should bother her; she senses that it should. As if professionalism demands that not so much be taken on faith. But then she thinks of the photograph and she decides that she does not care. She knows that face so well now that, with eyes closed, she can recall every exquisite detail. It sucks her down that soulful well, into a world where they are not what they are.

Back home, there'll be snow on the ground now, a dose of purity that might, for a time, wash clean the dirty streets she pulled herself out of all those years ago. She hasn't been back in so long, so many years, so many deeds. Even so, it's as if she can see her childhood home, as if it's yesterday, reflected in Francis' front window: the broken countertops, the overturned chairs, her mother's tears. No, nothing good ever came from that house. Nothing good ever came from those streets. She knows that now. Maybe she always has. Maybe that's why she allows herself to be pulled into her contact's schemes. She looks down at her gloved hands, and tries to think of the throats they've squeezed. But then they outnumber the stims, don't they?

This is how she spends the hours 'til dawn, thinking of the past until it becomes her present.

At three in the morning, it's not uncommon for cars to use Gibson: couples returning late from a party, kids exulting in the freedom of new wheels. But from the dark green sedan's first tentative approach, Morgan knows it is different. Its driver noses his nondescript ride slowly up the street, cruising past both the target and then her squat before it disappears into darkness up the street. Gone...

Morgan has just begun to relax from her alert clench when the car returns, now gliding back the way it had come slower this time. Checking addresses? Her hackles rise.

She's up and snaring her gun from the coffee table. Seven steps and she's at the front door, her gloved palm gripping the doorknob, twisting. The warm fall night washes in on her from the three-inch gap between door and jamb. Yes, the sedan pauses in front of the target, before continuing onto the intersection. And now an illegal turn, starting back up the road one final time. Her trigger finger itches.

The vehicle coasts to a stop three doors down from where her charge sleeps. Two souls, men by their size and her experience, alight and move purposefully up the street. Her heart pounds in her chest as she silently opens the door enough for her to slip through, her boots finding the front stoop. She's floating, no longer chained by anything as simple as gravity, much less the failings of the human form. No light can claim her as she keeps to the night's gloom.

Two doors down... they are both dressed in dark clothes. Making out their faces is impossible at this distance. Tall, though, and striding forth with familiar, regimented grace. The faces of the zealots who've come before writhe in the shadows. The Huntress finds a clip in her jacket, swaps it into the gun steady in her left hand. The click as it snaps home... she's always known that sound.

One door down... Hands reach for coats, finding weapons. The far one has what looks like a crowbar, the near one a gun. They are learning, or perhaps these have been in town longer than the others. She powers herself from the stoop and in a crouch towards the three foot hedge that frames the end of the Michaels' driveway. The landscaped bush's inadequate cover merely means she'll have to be that much better. She drops to a knee behind the hedge and takes careful aim. No mistakes...

Crowbar turns to check the street as they start up the driveway to 2311 Gibson. She allows those zealot's eyes to find her. Let him see her smile... He has time for a widening of his eyes before she passes sentence.

Old Faithful coughs, its discharge blowing through Crowbar's chest. The mouth gapes to emit a soundless scream, as he executes a backwards swan onto the driveway. Her second kill, at his friend's fall, spins round and lifts his gun to attack.

Another cough and the hammerblow destroys the gunman's shoulder. His weapon flies on to Francis' lawn as its now former owner executes a flailing pirouette, to fall face first to the sidewalk's hard embrace.

Silence. Two coughs, two quiet grunts... The Huntress eyeballs Gibson, left and right. Nothing... not yet...

Adrenaline sails her across the street and up the sidewalk to the gunman she's downed. He's alive, for now. "No speeches," she whispers in the night. A third cough, death through the back of his neck...

She finds the keys still in the car, the engine firing even as she performs a second street check: no second car, no third enemy assigned to take the back. With luck, she has a couple of minutes until a civilian happens by, but she won't need that long.

Pulling the car alongside her kills, she jumps clear and yanks open the door behind the driver's. Across the backseat, she muscles the body of the gunman. Crowbar follows suit, pitching into his dead friend's lap. The tools of their trade she collects from the ground, throwing them onto the passenger's seat as she slides back into the driver's and gets out of there, not bothering to close her door until she's well up the road.

Five blocks from Francis', she slings the sedan into a vacant alley. A check for witnesses as she kills the engine. No one she can see... Popping the glove, looking for registration. Unless one of these two princes is Gina Witherspoon, this is a stolen car.

Her boots crunch over god only knows as she gets out and opens the back door, hands searching jackets and pants for anything of use, but only incidentals and $80 in cash falls to her. "Sipios," she curses them. "Better luck next time."

She tries to feel remorse, guilt, but only anger cooks in her chest as she walks from that alley, leaving the grisly find for a bum on the prowl. Back to Gibson, unsatisfied. How dare they... how dare they challenge her, she whom gravity cannot claim.

The street is still as she mounts the sidewalk where the deed had been done. In the darkness, there are no signs of the brief struggle, but they will be there come the morning, short of rainfall. She crosses to re-enter her squat, checking Old Faithful as she settles in to wait out the dawn. Only then does her name return to her, unbidden, her name and her world.

***

Standing in the smoking ruin of what had once been the Iguana, Evan tries to process what she's seeing. Is that a length of charred table leg? A plank of the bar? Her boots crunch through smoldering debris, the heat a distant, unfelt force against her frozen bones as she crouches, hands digging into ashes to uncover the bar's namesake. Ian's face has been smashed in, its glass eyes long since blown out. Guilt snakes through her. She's never liked the creature much and here it is, in pieces. Isn't that how it is now?

She does not know how she came to be here, who called her or why. She knows only that the world is beginning to unravel, the familiar swirling down the drain of the unknown. Is there no one else to see this? No one else to absorb this cosmic damage?

Someone's back turned to her, blackened, wisps of smoke curling up off of ashed fabric. Evan kneels in popping glass and tries, with her hand on its shoulder, to turn the poor soul over, but only the arm moves, flesh and bone and muscle oozing free of the body and coming away in her hand. *Ohhhhh,* Savior!

Some force of nature propels Molly round to look up at her, eyes cooked, mouth open, skin crisped. She should be well gone, onto whatever comes after this, but the chest still weakly rises and falls with the last sputterings of life, as if she has been holding on for just this moment.

And so, in the ruins of what had once been hers, eyeless Molly looks up at Evan, looks right at her with those unseeing eyes and her mouth forms the question it is beyond her inflamed body to speak but which Evan somehow hears: "Why didn't you listen?"

Evan staggers out into the street, to collapse to her knees and to heave her lunch onto the broken ground. She is cradling herself, arms protectively about her middle as she rocks back and forth, trying to find something, anything, to put between her mind and these images barreling towards her. They seek to crush her, to embed themselves in her, to make it so that she will never forget.

To her feet now, stumbling forward, trying to call out for help, for the fire crews who ought to have come by now, but Collins Street is a ghosted block of abandoned shops and shuttered bars. Anyone who might heed her has fled. So why is she here?

She's walked through her own vomit, but Evan's too focused on scrabbling for her slate to care. "Network Unavailable," the device blinks mournfully. The Cloud, offline? She tries messaging Zia, Johnny, anyone... she tries emergency services... "Network Unavailable..," final and forever.

Her Yager is gone, so Evan runs up to the corner and stands, looking up at the sky. She can feel activity somewhere, in another part of the city, shouts and sirens blending into a panicked cacophony, but her eyes are only for the sky.

It's there, as she knew it would be, fingering the horizon with its corroding caress. A pestilent flower, it blooms across the near sky, stealing from them not just the glow of the sun but the light of their world. In some incomprehensible way, it is aware of her, aware of her attention, her eyes upon its oily skin. It writhes, knowing she is powerless to stop it.

Evan can't watch! She can't watch this anymore! She turns and runs into the dark.

The windrider wakes to the stink of people packed too tightly for too long. Where?

And then it floods back to her, the storm smashing down on the habitat, breaching the western wall and forcing them all to run like hell for the Underground, to pack themselves down into an enclosure of dirt and pray that they'll have something of theirs to return to. No wonder she has been dreaming of destruction.

A Force Five... They endure these once every few weeks. Not routine, but nor are they cause for rack and ruin. It's the breach... The careless leaving a seal unsmoothed, a flap unstuck, a tear unmended. One small mistake for the storm to exploit, to rip, to tear, until one small weakness has become a hole through which all the vicious wind can roar. It fights a war of attrition that puts them always in defense. How can you attack the wind?

Troy is gone. She looked for him, a familiar face under the shelter's piercing emergency lights. She found only his girl, a suit monkey for windriders, a girl who must have sealed her into a shift suit more times than either of them can count. The dirt on her face has not been smeared by any tears for the man no longer beside her.

She said she last saw him headed towards the rally point. He must have been caught in an exposed hallway. The habitat's defenses would have sealed the doors once it sensed the local breach. He would've had to beat at those doors, beat on the hardest material known to man, pleading to be delivered from this gruesome death. But the protocol cannot be violated, not for him, not for any of them. They are expendable; the habitat is not.

She turns away from the girl, thinking of Troy. The anger that rises in her is perhaps the closest thing he will ever have to a eulogy. The habitat must be preserved; the habitat must be protected; the habitat must go on; fabrics and pumps and Bibles; tables and chairs and scraps of paper... these are the things the Core has convinced them to value over their own lives. And though she understands why, that the power they provide goes to further the Project and sustain what remains, her outrage still smolders. So much is given and they hear but one word in thanks, "More..."

They, the storm-born refugees, eat their gruel and sit in their filth, and sweat themselves to sleep in the cocoon of the earth. And when the Force Five has spent its fury upon them, they ascend to sift amongst what remains. Dust and debris fill the air as they walk like wraiths through savaged corridors, their walls blasted clear of propaganda. But the power is offline, maybe never to return. The report comes back quick from the first windrider to go outside... 3,000 tethers ripped free of their winches, their precious wind cradles ejected into the infinite sky. No one winched them down. Not quick enough; not smart enough.

And now there is no reason to stay, no purpose for their being. They will have to retreat to the Core for re-assignment; it'll be years before the cradles are replaced, before this outpost is back online. She will never walk these sands again.

Evan wakes, thrashing in an ocean of sweat. She tries to open her blinded eyes, but a flood of tears have glued them shut. Again... again! Her only night of dreamless peace had come two nights ago, when her binge of Adelsons had rubbed out the world. She will be a drunk before whatever this is has finished with her.

Flinging herself from bed, Evan can't find the shower fast enough. Only its scalding spray can unwind the darkness from her bones. But while water can revitalize her body, it cannot touch the memory of filth, the filth that sees, the filth that wants.

And what of that other girl in that other dream, buried in dirt, entombed by a wasteland of sand and storm... She will forget these things, won't she? They will pass from her as dreams are meant to do, eventually, right?

Dressing quickly, Evan steals an apple from Francis' kitchen and then creeps her way out of his townhouse. It's only six bells, but she's determined to put in a full day of distracting work. If she lingers any longer on her nightmares, on where and to whom Morgan has promised to take her tonight, she will go mad.

But she gets no farther than Francis' driveway before this new world of hers reminds her of its ugliness. A stain, some ten feet beyond the Pedarius, has dried overnight, fading into an indeterminate rusted brown. Evan leans her Yager against the side of the car so she can have both hands free as she crouches down, touching her fingertips to the spoiled patch. Blood, and worse, a pool about a foot in diameter, not counting the other puddles, two of them, one on the sidewalk and one on Francis' lawn. While she'd slept... Her fingertips come away sticky with human grit.

Morgan... Evan looks up, feeling naked as she scans the empty street. Good people, normal people, are just now pulling themselves from their warm beds, lingering over their morning coffees and their news and their children. They've yet to join her, out here, in a changed world. Shaking, she retrieves the garden hose coiled at the side of the house. Its excoriating stream washes away most of the evidence, but she'll remember. A warning, some statement of prowess? She feels eyes on her.

Morgan, passing a parked car as she strolls up the opposite sidewalk. Their eyes heatedly connect.

"You?"

Her shadow stops directly opposite, leather coat an intimidating black against the gray of the pre-dawn sky. This creature does not belong to the light, to the world that Evan knows.

She nods... the hint of a smirk, for her, or for those she's snuffed?

Will death ever leave her? What if tonight is not the end? What if it only continues this...chaos? What then? She re-coils the hose. The job she's done on the three crimson stains will have to do because she can't stay here another moment.

Mounting her bike, Evan casts Morgan a final glare. Is that sympathy? It's a little late. "Well, at least it'll be over soon and I'll be rid of you and yours. That's something anyway." And then she's lowering her Yager's front bars into racing position. And, with a frustrated grunt, she launches herself out of that place, her overturned world reduced to her burning thighs and the thunder of her heart pounding in her ears. If she finds peace, it will be in motion.

The weather service has promised today's rains will break the unseasonable heat, but Evan doesn't see it, not in a mostly clear sky just now beginning to brighten under the sun's waking blaze. A few clouds, but they are of the fluffy sort, glistening a rich white against the rosy dawn. Another scorcher then and already the weathermen talk of broken records and incomprehensible fronts. Why not? Everything else is going to hell... She almost smiles.

It takes Evan five minutes to download her morning's run and fill her rucksack with the appropriate parcels. And when she ducks out of the loading area, the Roady is there, waiting, rumbling. What if, someday, that seems normal to her? What if she loses the ability to remember that normal people don't have stalkers? Tonight can't come quick enough.

Excluding a run-in with an effusive woman of 50, to whom Evan's delivery had occasioned a rain of kisses, her morning proceeds without incident, so much so she starts to wonder if tonight will go as smoothly. What will she learn at this meeting? Surely a great deal. She will finally know if Morgan has been telling the truth, as she knows it. She will finally be able to tell someone important that they've got the wrong girl, and Morgan's contact will confirm this and everything will be sorted out with apologies all round. Right? Right...

"Are you asking Francis along?"

Zia has joined her for lunch. The Seacliff is rife with the usual flock of hungry birds, many of whom prefer potato curls to the fare beached by the tide's latest ebb. A few crabs scrabble amidst other feebled creatures soon to die. She has never seen the tide out so far, exposing a stretch of alien beach.

"No. And thanks for telling Carter and Johnny by the way." She glares. "That really helped..."

"You thought I'd let you walk into the breach without someone to watch your back? Not a chance. You're playing with fire, Evan, whatever the truth of this. I wasn't going to let you get burned on your own."

"Yeah, well, I'm keeping Francis out of this one. He's already putting a roof over my head. I can keep him out of this mess, Zia, whatever it is. I owe him that..." A red crab claws weakly at the sand, seeking purchase. "Man, is the moon going to explode or something?"

"What??"

"The tide. Why's it out so far?"

"I don't know. Someone will blame us though. Have you noticed lately that everything seems to be our fault?"

"What are you talking about?"

"If it's hot out when it's not supposed to be, then we've gone carbon crazy. If some people get sick, it's because of something we dumped in their water. If some country's workforce gets exploited, it's because we buy their products. Can't some things just be what they are? Not everything has to have guilty strings attached to it somehow."

"Whoa, what got into you? I thought I was the one having the crisis here. And anyway, who are you going to blame a changing climate on, bunnies?"

"Why not? They eat carrots. Presumably that affects the environment somehow."

Evan laughs. But for a few bites of her wrap she couldn't taste, she's thrown the rest of her lunch to the greedy birds which cluster in on her now, knowing a good mark when they see one. "I'm so sure, Zia." She turns to retrieve her bike, ready for the roasting afternoon. "So you're saying that nothing is our fault..."

"No. Just that I don't like being blamed for things. So many people try so hard to convince us that everything we do, every little act, has this massive impact on the world. Do you know how many people actually have a massive impact on anything? Not very many. Maybe presidents or captains of industry, but it's not us, you know? And yet look at what's sold to us: too much oil, too many chemicals, too much waste... Everything around us is dying. Well, hey, everything dies, right? Eventually, the sun will puff up into a huge, red ball of fire and cook us all into oblivion. So if everything ends, then why does *how* it ends have to matter so much?"

"Okay, 'Johnny'. I can't believe you. You're Ms. Vegetarian philosopher, Ms. 'you've got to read Ross' and now you're giving me this, today? Everything dies so why does it matter?"

"I know. Please don't tell me to be logical. I will hit you."

Evan plays with her bike's security chain, more than a little disturbed to be hearing this on this of all days. "Seriously, Zia, what's goin' on? Are you worried about tonight?"

"Yes. I'm worried about tonight. I'm worried about you. I'm worried about everything. But I've also spent my whole life worried about things. And you get to a point where you just get sick of having people, important people, organizations, governments, whatever, telling you it has to be a certain way and guilting you into having you do it their way. 'If you don't do this, such and such will die.' 'If you don't do that, life as we know it will cease to be.' I guess maybe, for once, it'd be nice to be doing the telling, not the receiving. 'You do what I say.' It sucks to be a pawn."

Evan is staring at her.

"What?"

"You feel like a pawn..."

"Yeah, to corporate interests, you know..."

"You feel like a pawn..."

It's coming. It's past noon now. She's putting a lot of faith into a meeting, a lot of hope for resolution. If she finds out this has all been for nothing... Evan stares at the smoldering sky, sunglasses shielding her eyes. If all the worry and the fear has been for nothing... but wouldn't that be the better way, to know that she is clean and safely unimportant?

"So, when and where?" Zia intrudes.

"Ten, at the bar." Evan blinks back to the here and now. "I guess we'll take Carter's truck. It has the room."

"Nervous?"

"What do you think?"

"Good. You should be. This is insane."

"Well, at least I'm not alone."

Zia snickers. "How you gonna kill the time 'til then? We can only work so long."

"I'll figure something out. I just..." The sea hisses as Evan discards her lunch and faces her friend. "It's like I'm back at school, in, like, a production of *The Master* and someone hasn't given me the last ten pages of the script. So I don't know how it ends and I don't know my lines and... I'm messing up, but I want to see it through, you know? If I can just figure it out..."

"Oh, come on, you don't remember how *The Master* ends? Were you raised by wolves, babe? That thing's been around for 500 years."

"Yeah, yeah. Never mind. Hey, listen, when this is over, tonight, you and me are gonna have a talk about your big mouth. You getting Carter and Johnny in on this? It could be dangerous. I don't want that on me."

Zia's staring at her.

"What?"

"Sometimes I love you is all," her friend smiles.

"Get out of here!"

"Some secrets ain't worth keeping, Evan. Some battles aren't worth fighting alone. C'mon, let's move. Be cooler with the wind on us."

13

The sky has blessedly clouded.

Six bells after noon and Evan finds herself adrift. Her last delivery had taken her down to the waterfront where, fearful of what she might find, she'd looked in on Little Harbor and its beggar's trade. The dreams have been so vivid that her eyes know precisely where to look for the blight that haunts her. Nothing, not even a hint, but still she shivers in the punishing heat.

Both aimless and anxious, she turns into the Watermark's metroplex, a sprawling cinemall comprised of restaurants, arcades, and gaming shops emanating out from the mall's theatrical heart. Thirty giant screens running 24/7 with this year's biggest mo-shows.

Chaining the Yager in a cavernous lot, she joins the sweaty press of flesh filling the lobby. The bombarded eye cannot avoid staring at the kids, the teenagers, the parents, and the couples: buying food, pestering their companions, forming wildly disfigured queues before a dozen ticket windows. Mo-show posters, in all their three-dimensional glory, hang in the air, while sounds of epic struggles spill from hidden speakers. The uninitiated and the epileptic be damned...

Evan queues behind two girls, both 16, both sporting identical outfits: skintight mesh tops of a glittering black, slinky skirts hewn from skeins of undulating silver no lower than their bared knees. These are all the rage. After all, a long stride or a mild breeze will part the flowing strands and reveal the treasures their male counterparts so long to see. The fashion twins glance at her, giggle...

She feels the presence behind her. A quick glance confirms it. A quiet couple in their thirties is all that buffers Evan from her stalker, those green eyes scanning the sea of faces, the airborne promotionals, with such intensity that she seems like a half-crazed animal which, here, makes her almost normal.

The twins opt for a slasher flick, the poster for which is little more than an explosion of blood and broken bones. "Color me stunned," Evan breathes before stepping to the window. "One for Aether Bellum."

The numbed thing behind the window accepts her $15 and stamps the back of Evan's hand. Seconds later, the Mo-show's logo is coalescing upon her skin. The brand will last until the film ends. After all, tickets can be forged.

Dinner is a barely recognizable hot dog, the synthetic bun hiding any hint of meat within. Flashing her tattooed hand at a guard, she's nodded into her theater where she slips into a leather-covered seat near the back that has seen better days. Blessed silence is her only companion as she eats this mush of uncertain origins.

Then a figure slides into the seat next to her, ending her moment of solitude. Evan doesn't have to look up. "Mo-show 101: no talking, no slates, and management tend to frown when you take out the paying customers."

"I not be caring about the film." Morgan's voice is a whisper, her body wire taut in her creaky seat. There are fifty souls in this staggered theater which can accommodate ten times as many. Evan wonders if her shadow could close her eyes, right now, and draw each face, such is her focus upon them. "If you needed to kill time, I can think of better ways than a crowd of people."

"You think I'm going to get knifed at the movies," Evan asks, her mouth full of ersatz hot dog.

"If you can be hiding in a crowd, then so can..."

"So can the other guy... You're a walking cliche."

Oh, that did it. Snarling, her shadow leans close. "I be having no sleep in six days for keeping you whole." Chapped lips move against her ear. "Do you really wanna be doin' this here, hmm? Do you really wanna be pushin' me?"

Six days! Has she really never seen the woman sleep? But her outrage has little time for amazement. "Hey," Evan hisses back. "I never had to hose blood off my front lawn until you came along."

Advertising blooms on the big screen, bathing Morgan's pale face in unnatural light. "I had a choice, blood on the sidewalk, or blood spilling out of you. Want I should go back in time and do it all different?"

Evan's mouth opens to continue, but what's the point? Tired, frustrated, and sad all at once, she slaps her half-eaten dog into Morgan's lap. "Here... I'm not hungry anymore."

The theater descends into a comforting black. Here, she's just another face.

"He better have some answers."

"As long as it's 'yes, Morgan, you can go home,' I be happy."

"That'd be two of us."

Thunder puts an end to them.

Aether Bellum had likely begun life as a morality play of good versus evil. The finished product is little more than an action orgy. Greed for supreme authority has split a once whole family, dividing loyalties and friendships, drawing lines in heavenly sand. Their war shatters the universe, light against dark, white against black. And when it's over, death and sorrow and regret with the white light the victor. Typical...

This should be her stalker's kind of mo-show, all violence and death. But when she glances over, during one of the countless chest-vibrating explosions and finds her shadow still vigilant, something inside her shifts. Morgan may be about as subtle as Aether Bellum, but she is dogged and faithful in ways a psychotic isn't capable. This is what Evan tells herself, that Morgan's commitment to her job, to her word, must be a sign of truth, not of the dark deception Evan's worried over these last five nights.

The second the lights go up, Evan beats the wave of humanity out to the parking lot. The night beckons as she lopes for her bike, Morgan on her heels. The film has served its purpose.

"We're meeting at the bar on Collins." She unchains her unmolested Yager. "Don't be late. We leave at 10."

Showtime... Night has broken the heat of the day, its cool dampness entwining with the weight of the world's secrets to press down into her bones, to settle inside her in a place she cannot touch. It's here...

The three have been waiting.

Zia, Johnny, and Carter stand about the hood of the foreman's truck as Evan pulls up. A full moon they'd promised, but a clouded night's sky makes that something of a hidden treasure. The world's luminescence has been left in the harsh hands of streetlight.

All conversation stops as she stows her bike in the back of the four-door electric. The Yager will keep Carter's gym bag and toolbox company. She turns to her silent companions, who now number four with Morgan's dark arrival.

"I don't know what this is. So... last outs," she offers, her voice cracking.

Silent resolve staring back from each face.

"Alright... let's go."

Aboard her Roady, Morgan leads them into the future. The girls ride the electric's back seat while Carter drives. Johnny has shotgun, his nervous hands drumming denimed knees. Evan had told the foreman to cut his boys loose. Whatever this is, it is meant for her. A crowd will only muddle the issue. A dead man's knife has been wrapped in cloth and stowed within her donned pea coat. If push comes to shove...

Of the five major suburban boroughs, Wakefield is the sleepiest, home to many of the city's middle-class families. Countless townhouse developments are interrupted only by parks and rec centers, schools and corner stores.

"What the hell," Johnny speaks for all of them.

Morgan pulls up at an abandoned athletic park, the motor dying as she dismounts and waves them ahead.

"Here?" Carter squints at the empty diamond. "This got the right look to you?"

"I'll take a false alarm over thugs wanting to turn out our pockets." Johnny pops his door and joins Morgan on the sidewalk, Evan and Zia following. Carter's last as he parks the truck in a visitor's slot.

"He won't want these three here." Evan's shadow scans the diamond. The face is alert and calm, but Evan sees, now that she knows to look, a fatigue in these drawn features, in green eyes that shine in the night.

"Tough." Evan passes her friends, her hands thrust into the pockets of her navy-blue pea coat. She rounds one of the player benches and the wire fence to stand on one of the diamond's thin white lines. A quiet breeze rustles the tall trees that border this peaceful place.

She turns to admire her friends. Ever the maverick, Johnny has come to back her up in one of those patterned sotton tops whose design periodically cycles through a range of programmed images. Just now, a tiger lounges, its orange fur stark against midnight. The eyes are open, blinking.

Pragmatic Carter sports a woolen coat of a hunter green, jeans, and cowboy boots. The big man has come prepared, handing to Johnny one of the two aluminum bats he's pulled from his truck. The one he keeps looks tiny in his beefy hands.

Zia styles one of the mesh tops the twins in the movie queue had worn, hers a glittering emerald. Her anxious face is pale in the lengthening night. It is not dark enough to obscure the interwoven thorns tattooed on her friend's left cheek. Something squat and black occupies her left hand. Its muzzle, square and blunt, aimed at the ground.

The three have come out of fidelity to her, fidelity that, while she's not sure she's earned it, she understands and admires. Morgan has come for reasons Evan hopes now to discover. Her eyes find her solemn stranger, a readiness there, an eagerness, as though tonight might see a way through to union.

Evan faces the field with her life at a crossroads. Recent times have seen her lose a great deal, what made her warm, what made her good. She could not have replaced those losses with truer souls than those who stand behind her. "C'mon," she whispers into the black.

Shifting shadows along the left field's line reveal a man's approach. The look Evan shoots Morgan's way finds a nod of confirmation. Though the darkness refuses to reveal specifics, in her gut she knows it's him. Purposeful, he steps onto the diamond and stops some 30 feet from her and examines her companions. With her friends, he is neutral; with Morgan, he is disappointed.

"You were to come alone." The Contact's voice is cultured, firm. The lips hardly move, the eyes rarely if ever blink. "You were to be told..."

"Like I said to your little friend, tough..." Her feet volunteer her forward to meet the handsome if nondescript man upon whom her future rides. She hears someone try to join her, to get close, but they are stopped. There is no room for a third.

They come together in the diamond's heart, surrounded by wind and shadow. A steady hand extends from the sleeve of a steel-gray pullover. She declines.

"Are you responsible for what's happened to me?" To the exclusion of everything else in the last week, she has anticipated this moment. Now, she can think of nothing but the fire, the devouring of all she held dear. Her hands free themselves of her jacket, palms scrubbing at her thighs. "Did you destroy my home?"

"No." He is but two feet from her, his familiar eyes drinking her in with satisfaction he does not bother to hide. "My purpose is not destruction. My purpose is preservation. Upon you that hangs. That is why you have been hunted. That is why you have been protected... that is why you have been chosen."

There's truth in this face, truth and power. And now that she sees the man, and hears his words, and has an answer, she wishes he had lied. His truth makes her skin crawl.

"If it was something I delivered... something I said, please... tell them that I don't know anything. Tell them whatever they think I've done, I haven't done it."

Sympathy ripples. "They would not listen, Evan." Her name is something more when it is spoken by him. "Their desire is too great." His unnerving stare marks Evan's four who remain, with varying degrees of discomfort, on the sidelines. "I am permitted to give you enough for what you must do, but it is to you alone. Others may aid you, but they cannot know why. This is paramount. Future events cannot be polluted by what they should not know. Ignore me and you will end those you love. I'll have your promise before we proceed."

She tries again; she must. "Listen, okay? Listen... this is nothing I did. This isn't my fault. This isn't my fight. This isn't my problem. I did nothing, okay? You have the wrong girl. I did nothing."

The Contact shakes his head, his jaw set.

"Then tell me what the *fuck* I've got to do with it?!" On the sea of guilt she's been harboring for days, her anger is a spill of black oil set fire to and allowed to rage. None of this has been preventable, none of it her fault. Her balled hands lift, poised to strike.

"You must make the promise." The man does not waver in the face of her violence.

"No more orders," Evan growls, putting her nose to his. "I watch my home burn, I watch people die, get killed, in front of my eyes... I'm pushed to my ever-living limits! And you... you want promises?!"

"If we are to continue..." A narrowing of those intense eyes is the only sign that her fury has touched him. "We must proceed with your promise." He all-but pleads, "For the betterment of you, those you love, and those you do not know."

The sky is pitch black as she gazes up at it, light and warmth having fled in the hours since sunset. What light does belong to the night has been stolen away by thick clouds which deny her the coldly glittering stars. Somewhere, a heavy moon shines, though it's beyond her sight. How can she promise him anything? She wants to scream.

Heart thundering, Evan faces her adversary, anger still aflame. "I promise..."

The Contact's tension eases. He even manages a smile, the sight of which makes her knuckles itch to knock it from his superior face.

"You have been having the dreams," he begins, chilling her. "In these dreams, there is a dark place where the rules do not apply, a thing that does not belong. Every time you see it, it grows."

She shivers in the memory of filth on her skin.

"It is your beacon." The voice is meant for her ears only. "It is your mind's interpretation of a thing it cannot understand but knows does not belong. It is a flaw that must be corrected."

"What kind of flaw?" She's so deep in the memory, she forgets to ask him how he knows of her dreams, her most secret thoughts. Does he know of the other girl in the other place, the land of waste and storm?

The Contact takes a breath. "Ever since the species crawled out of the oceans, humans have born, lived, and died having experienced life through only their senses: tasting food, touching trees, seeing the ocean, hearing the birds. What you perceive is what is real to you. This field is real, I am real. The sky is real. This is your world. But what you sense is only the surface of a reality so complex that it defies understanding by those less than gods. That you cannot see a thing does not mean it is not there. Do you understand?"

"There are things that exist that I can't sense," she nods. "Germs, diseases, bacteria. What does that have to do with the price of fish?" Does he think her an idiot?

"Well, as vast as this universe is, it has just as many versions of itself. This," he spreads his arms to encompass the world, "is but one of a billion reflections. In the beginning, all were mirrors of one another. But, as time passed, and chaos had its say, they diverged. There are reflections where the sun never formed; where the earth was obliterated by asteroids; where your atmosphere never coalesced, preventing life from flourishing. This is as true here as it is for every other part of the universe."

Caught between fear and disbelief, Evan recoils. "How do you... how do you know this?" He cannot know it. He only states a theory, a suspicion, in an attempt to frighten her. "And what the hell does it have to do with me?"

This face stares back at her, his burden visible in his lined brow. Without changing expressions, he dismisses her questions. It is enough that he knows. "There are regions... where these reflections, rather than naturally diverge from one another, have traveled a similar path. These hotspots, these clustered reflections are not ordinarily dangerous unless intelligent life is omnipresent across the like reflections. This," he nods at the world, "is part of a hotspot."

The Contact turns, points to the lights of the great city which glimmer distantly against the dark sky. "Power attracts power and there is an inherent power to intelligent life. Given time, that life progresses, uses its limited resources, builds its civilizing machines, and consumes its available energy. All the while, that life begets more life which leads to more consumption, more need, more desire for the same resources that now must be spread among the many. The needs of the now trump the welfare of the future. It is a circuit of hunger that, sometimes, is not broken until the last resources are plundered. From where you stand, it must seem foolish. In their moment however, the need is blinding."

"You're talking about us, about fuel," Evan tries to follow. "You're talking about how we use up our resources..."

"It is a phase of development most intelligent life experiences," he acknowledges. "But you are not the threat." The Man kneels, his fine hair blowing in the night wind as his hands gather a few pieces of stone that have been kicked onto the infield dirt. "Each one of these is a reflection," he intones, looking up at her with the rocks in his palm. "If there is little or no activity, they are like this." He drops the rocks in a wide circle, not one within six inches of the others. "However, when there is a great deal of activity, they attract." His hands collect the stones, placing them in a tight circle, their rough edges nearly touching. "Their nearness creates stress and disharmony." He picks up two of the stones and bashes them together, little flecks of dirt and debris cascading from them. "They rub against one another, creating friction and... opportunity. Earth," he concludes, "is like this." He finds more stones and heaps them together with the first lot until he has made a mound of them.

"And this is what I see in my dreams?" She has told no one of that torment save Francis. Without this mysterious knowledge to his credit, she'd have been out of here long ago.

"Partly." The Contact looks down at his demonstration. "The energy density created by intelligent life and all its industry attracts reflections, grinding them together. That friction weakens each reflection's natural barrier, allowing for a bridge to be created. Some of these other worlds, they have grasped the science to make these bridges. They have known about the reflections for some time and they will exploit them." He straightens to fix her with his fiercest look. "Having plumbed the last of their world, they will do the necessary to find newer, fresher wells. You, this... is a fresh well. They will build their bridge, and they will cross with their machines, and they will strip from you every last resource in the furtherance of their own demands. They do not care about you. They do not care if you die, if you suffer... they do not know you. They know only their need."

Stones, reflections, bridges... Evan steps back from this fruit loop. "Like I said - what does any of this have to do with me? I can tell you right now, I have no idea what you're talking about. Pebbles in the sand, what... I deliver packages for a living..."

"You." The Contact's smile chills. "You are the key."

Dirt churns under his boot as he heads back out to left field, forcing his momentary disciple to pursue. They pace from infield dirt to outfield grass, where dandelions and other small flowers wave impetuously from countless blades of green.

"They try to end you because they know you can stop them." The brown-haired mystery man halts twenty feet from the field's fence, pivoting to face her. "They know you have it within you to stop them. That knowledge creates fear and from fear comes a need to eliminate the threat. They are not wrong to fear you. You have it in you to keep them from your world."

Evan can almost feel the last straw snapping. "You're a lunatic," she hisses, grabbing at his coat, yanking the fool close. "I don't know who you are, or how you know about my dreams, but, as of this very second, I officially don't care. You see those guys back there, my friends? Between the four of us, I'm pretty sure we can find a nice little ditch for you to die in." The words are coming fast, cresting on her panic. She prays none of it reaches her face. "It was you, wasn't it? You took everything... you started that fire and now you're trying to cover it up with some mumbo jumbo about destinies and reflections and rocks and meetings in the middle of the night. Well, I'm here. Take your best shot, creep. C'mon." A fever is in her chest, her vision blurring.

"The lasagna's in the freezer." The quiet words pass the lips of a man who shows not a hint of fear at her outburst. He stares with a tranquility that disturbs her more now than his stupid story did before.

"What? What now... more babble?"

"No. The last words she ever spoke to you."

Evan is unaware of having released the man's jacket, much less stumbling away from him. A great and cold wind sweeps everything else aside. A phone call, on that day... She'd been in class, had let it go to voicemail. Later, she'd played the message, her mother's voice telling her that she'd made lasagna, put it in the freezer at the house. Evan could pick it up whenever she wanted. An hour later...

"How do you know that?" Her voice is a little girl's quaver. "Who told you that??" Shock springs tears to her eyes.

He just stares, a quiet, forceful confidence that defies her to deny him. She cannot look away.

"When you were eight, a man cornered you at a carnival and tried to touch you. You threw your purple soda on him and ran into a crowd so he couldn't follow you. When you were eleven, you got tired of your best friend raving on and on about her new bicycle, so you slashed the tires, blamed it on a boy, and felt guilty about it for years after. At fifteen, you lost your virginity to Mike Todd, a senior at your high school, for no other reason than you were the last of your friends to do it. At sixteen, you were wrongly accused of cheating on a math test; a friend had copied your answers. You chose suspension and the loss of privileges over turning in your friend. When your father died, you resented him for being weak because he'd succumbed to his illness. Though many surround you, you are alone and you wonder if it has always been that way."

She has no defense against his words, or to the tears that spill down her frozen face.

"I am your best and only advocate, Evan. I've risked much to help you. In the beginning, it was not permitted to interfere with the natural course of events, but no one foresaw the interlinking of reflections and the devastation they would cause. Faced with disorder on an inconceivable scale, it was decided that one could be chosen to decide the fate of a world under a crossing's threat." His solemnity is terrifying.

"You are more than what you believe. Your loss gives you strength, courage, conviction. What chaos stole from you, you have replaced with the warmth of your friends. You will pave the way to your world's future. You will do what is needed."

Overwhelmed, Evan tries, fails, to speak, to plead. Her hands shake from the knowledge that this man knows things he should not. "How will I... how will I know what to do??" In search of a place to hide, her mind rushes towards oblivion.

"You will know." His hand extends, his fingers warm on her pale cheek. "We know you well. We chose well. Remember that when doubt finds you." And with that, he turns and disappears into the black, leaving her with the impossible.

Her knees threatening to give way, Evan faces her distant friends, all of whom wait eagerly. The hundred feet separating her from their fidelity seems an infinite chasm as the world she knew, the world she believed in, the world she understood, collapses. She will never be able to go back.

DAY SEVEN

14

Her eyes are troubled.

Johnny watches from the bench behind the wire fence as their girl returns to them. They'd all tried for a good visual of her mystery man, but the gloom, and the light rain which had kicked up a few minutes earlier, had ruled out specifics. His presence though... Johnny knows from presence, and this shadowy scrot has it in spades. About the only good thing in this whole affair is the marine mist, a splash of damp that breaks the unseasonable heat.

As Evan quits the field, her bootfalls ghosting over wet grass, they are there to greet her. They all have questions for which her fear has no answers. The four exchange silent glances. Even the birds, few as they are, have nothing to say.

"Well, let's go get a drink, talk it out," Johnny breaks the spell. "It can't have been too bad. I don't see you short any fingers. Toes? Did he ask for toes?" But no one laughs.

"She's tired," Zia shoots him a dirty look. "C'mon, Ev. Let's get you home."

"No." Evan's gaze never leaves the face of the darkest among them. "Morgan and me... we have some things to discuss." Her unblinking eyes are frozen, overwhelmed. They are all, in this moment, strangers to her.

Not a one of them likes it, least of all Zia. But then, when it comes to sharing confidences, girls rarely take rejection well. Carter looks ready to overrule their girl, bundle her under one of his massive arms and carry her to safety. He opts against it, but not without fixing an impassive Morgan with a hard look that vows retribution should she prove unworthy of Evan's trust.

"Alright..." Johnny is first to step up and clasp hands with Evan. "Be safe, huh?" He searches her bewildered face, finding there a stiffness that tries to cover fresh wounds. "Maintain the rage," he says, which earns him a tiny smile.

Johnny leaves for the parking lot as Carter says his goodbyes with a shake of hands, and Zia says hers with a bear hug that might have claimed a rib. And then the three are back at Carter's truck, its owner fishing for his keys as he stares back the way they'd come.

"Damn..." The foreman is tensed up. "What is goin' on?"

Zia fixes Johnny with a baleful glare. "Maybe if you hadn't been so quick to give up, she'd have come with us, you know, opened up. But no, you had to get home for your precious rally."

"Right, it's my fault she's confiding in a perfect stranger." Grimacing, Johnny hands off his bat, fishes for his herbals, and lights up, much to Zia's disgust. He takes a deep drag, offering one to Carter who is too focused on Evan and Morgan to accept. "It's her call, Zia. It's always been her call. We've been on the outside lookin' in this whole time. All we can do is step in when it all falls apart. The rest of it's on her."

"The Lord help her." Carter shakes his head.

They all take a last look at Evan who, he sees now, is in a heated conversation with Morgan.

"We could've said something," Zia moans. "This is bad. I can feel it."

"Then stay," he grunts. "Me, I've got a big day tomorrow." He checks his watch, smiles ruefully. "Today..."

"You want a lift?" Carter finds his keys, having to visibly force himself to look away from the silent confrontation. "You're on my way."

"You're going to leave, just like that, like this never happened." Zia is disgusted with both of them now.

"She said go..."

"No, she said she wanted some privacy. She never said screw off." Zia plants herself on the curb dividing parking lot from park. "I'm staying. I don't trust this lupa, Morgan."

"Alright, well, you do that. Let me know how it works out for you. I'm gonna walk, clear my head. Maintain the rage, kids." The men slap hands, Zia ignores his nod of farewell, and he's hoofing it out of there. He deserves no less than this muddle for venturing into suburbia.

Evan had always been an interesting case. Carter had introduced him to their gray-eyed girl three years ago. In the time since, she'd matured from a raw, angry adolescent into a young woman willing to adapt with the times. As Johnny strides these quiet residential streets, aiming for the great city's distant, throbbing heart, he realizes he envies her. Sure, she has a few screws loose - who doesn't? That does not alter the grace with which she's embraced her anchorless life.

He laughs as he tilts his face to the slow, refreshing drizzle. Evan, Zia, Carter; they cultivate their happiness by keeping their heads down, working hard and ignoring what lies beyond their control. Would that he could taste this emotional nirvana...

Wakefield, he discovers, has been built exclusively upon a long, sloping hill, the decline of which returns visitors to the city proper. Cutting against the grain, he jogs to the nearest, highest point, puffing as he makes the crest.

It is as beautiful as he imagined, the lights of his massive city firing one of the darkest nights he can recall. The sabled sky grudgingly allows the metropolis' multi-hued brilliance to stand in for the underwhelming stars. He'll never leave this place.

He lights a second herbal. There was a time he had flirted with laying down his burdens, becoming more like his friends who are content to let life's disappointments slide into the past. Except that he finds that he's incapable of detaching himself from the world's woes. Others can read the news and live without processing the tragedies around them. Meanwhile, he reads the same news and he finds sleeping impossible as he's slowly consumed by the deterioration of goodness in the world.

Why is it that those aware of the world's pain are the only ones who suffer for it? The blissfully ignorant go about their days happily, cheerily. Meanwhile, it falls to people like him, the tormented few, to warn of diminishing liberties and distant atrocities. And how are the vigilant rewarded? Indigestion, insomnia, and a slow death from stress-activated cancer.

"Lord, Johnny, you're gonna kill yourself behind all this," Carter has so often warned him from the depths of his rigid, traditionalist soul. Maybe so. But does it not mean something to oppose a world gone stagnant and dark? Does the principle of opposition not mean something? Everyone is so ready to embrace the status quo, even those he loves.

If there is a god, some star-surfing omnipotence who created this world, then the scrot has a twisted sense of humor. It's fine that anything worth anything is costly to the soul. If things weren't difficult to achieve, they wouldn't have meaning. But need the ignorant and the small, need the unawakened, seem so content with achieving nothing at all? Annoyed, he rubs out his herbal, tugs at his damp shirt, and starts down the hill to catch a ride.

Existence is without heavenly diktat. This is the only answer that makes life logical. Some have tried to convince him that life is a test. Nonsense this, the comforting conceits of old, white men who have no more insight into life's mysteries than he does. It is simple math, math that any open mind should comprehend. They are all alone. But as to whether or not that warms or chills him...

A ten minute ride on a dingy bus, with three to keep him company, deposits Johnny at a crowded public station dwarfed by a cluster of sky-stretched towers enclosing it. The trip down to the waterfront on the busy Underground costs him 30 minutes of his life spent pressed against sweat-soaked men and women. The four bells to midnight shift is headed home. He feels as tired as they look. The train had been deathly silent save for the jumbled leakage from headphones stuffed deeply into every ear. Oh, how near they are to a nation of oblivious zombies.

Twenty years ago, flush with business-sector bribes, the government had greenlighted a culling of the waterfront's desolate, industrial districts. Warehouses had been demolished in favor of high-end residential and commercial properties which, even now, gracefully flank the descent to the public harbor where restaurants, marinas, and nightclubs are omnipresent. There is no longer any sign of the factory in which Johnny's mother toiled for fifteen years before "re-zoning" had shuttered its doors and kicked her out into the winter chill of unemployment.

Two leagues southwest of this now-glam destination is the commercial harbor. The city's goods are shipped and received from four primary wharves that have not seen change in fifty years. The last economic downturn had given businessmen an opportunity to sacrifice yet more idle warehouses and replace them with low-end apartment buildings designed to meet the needs of the wharves' poorly paid laborers. Of course, developers had gone with only the most modest of housing. Savior forbid anyone grant more than a subsistence wage to the wharf rats upon whom the city's ten million residents are almost completely reliant for the supply of goods that stock the shelves of their favorite shops.

In the ten months since a dispute with his last landlord had put him on the street, Johnny has leased on the fourth floor of a five-story building on the edge of the Warehouse district. That is its given name, but it is not uncommon to hear it derogatorily referred to as the Warren. For those who value their teeth, or would prefer to not get dragged into an alley and rolled for all they are worth, Little Harbor will do.

There is no need for a key to the building's front door. Every resident knows the lock has long since given up the ghost. Johnny endures the faint scent of ancient cigarettes as he takes the stairs up to the fourth floor where a long hallway yields access to eight apartments, evenly distributed between the northern and southern walls. His key is already out as his shoes cross shit-colored carpet to 402. A twist of his wrist defeats the deadbolt and he's inside.

Before Lohner, a succession of women had failed to imprint themselves upon the 800 square feet Johnny can call his own. He'd torn out the puke-hued carpet and had chipped in as Carter and a couple guys from his crew laid down some nice hardwood floors. A minimalist kitchen to the right as he enters, a coat closet to the left. The main living area he'd converted into as much of an artist's loft as possible, splashing the walls with a quiet white before enlivening them with his art. Framed photographs of famous events hung in places of honor: Jefferson Parker receiving the gold for the long jump, the horror of the Garshon Concentration Camp, an aerial shot of Juno after the bomb, the first moon landing. These and more greet him every time he looks up, always reminding him.

Softening the cold floors are two auburn throw rugs positioned at the feet of two aged, black cloth couches set perpendicular to one another. Three overburdened bookcases are necessary to contain his treasured literature, two opposite the half square of the couches, and the third beneath his array of photographs. Almost 80 prized works are locked under glass. Even if they are dog-eared, spine-bent paperbacks. Their wisdom is in their words, not their medium.

In the living room's corner their planet dangles, done in greens, blues, and browns. Its slow undulations are performed at the terminus of a delicate chain anchored in the ceiling. All the near infinite assembly of life that inhabits that brown land, those blue seas...

By day, the sliding glass door grants a splendid view of the laws of commerce in motion, mercantile vessels nestled against the wharves as they take on fresh loads while their brothers, out in the harbor, wait to offload theirs. At one bell, there's little more than a canvas of black sky that hides the world and all its feverish activity.

A soft pink bag has been tossed on the coffee table, Lohner's. He smiles and makes for the bedroom.

If his living room is warm and organized, his bedroom follows a darker, more disordered philosophy. A thick pile of black carpet and walls painted a muted blue combine to absorb light, ambient and otherwise. But this is what he wants, a place to sleep and think in darkness. Two cushioned chairs are surrogate laundry baskets, draped in a week's worth of clothing. Meanwhile, a queen-sized bed, an old wooden dresser, a battered nightstand and an overtaxed closet leave behind little of unclaimed territory.

Stripping out of a shirt soiled by rain and sweat, Johnny adds this to his chair's chaos. Gingerly, he steps for the bed, where a figure, swathed in sotton sheets, slumbers. He sits next to her, caresses dirty-blonde hair as it spills over her perfumed pillow. She stirs, turning her face to his palm.

"You're home..."

"Yeah."

"Is the world safe?"

"Almost," he smiles. It's their joke. "Go back to sleep."

His hand moves from Lohner's smooth face to free her neck of tangled sheets. His efforts expose an expanse of tanned shoulder and firm breast which, even after all these months, tantalize. His blood warming, Johnny slides his palm along supple flesh smoothed by youth. Resisting her requires a strength he's never had.

"I thought you wanted me to go to sleep."

"Couldn't help myself. How could any mortal." He kisses her, tasting familiar skin. "I'll be in soon." The thought that had bloomed on the train must be committed to a place more reliable than the forgetful mind.

"You're always working. You gotta relax for five minutes, Johnny, sometime."

"I will, believe me," he smiles. "Don't go anywhere," he whispers into the sweet whorl of her ear. "I will be back to claim my reward."

He stays with her until she sinks back into sleep's warm sea. Only then can he rise and return to the living room, casting one last look at a girl he should love more than he does.

Opening the sliding glass door allows ocean-chilled air to buffet his naked chest. It restores him, sends him to retrieve his vice from a half-hollowed bible. He appreciates irony.

Out on his small balcony now and he's introducing his ass to the rainswept deck. He feeds his legs through the lesser of the two guardrails, glimpsing street, wharf, and water beyond his off-white runners suspended in the night. Cracking the baggie's seal, he frees the necessary: the papers, the powder. He rolls the special cigarette.

Unlike the ubiquitous herbals, this is decidedly illegal, cannabis liberally laced with Dust. The weed's depressant moderates the euphoria of the narcotic. His lighter's thin flame shimmers in the mist as he fires the end of the ready cigarette. The first drag is bliss unfiltered.

There's always a risk with Dust. Johnny doesn't care, not when the universe lights like this. An ethereal white luminescence rushes in to mantle the world, dilapidated warehouses shining like temples while the four scarred wharves transform themselves into the four fingers of god splayed upon the world's canvas. And the sky... Now white on black, it blazes, the random formations of its purple clouds holding answers to the universe's evanescent equations.

As he stares at that strobing sky, lights exploding behind eyes that see all realities, the face of the limitless universe comes to him. How is it that a soul can feel so insignificant against the vastness of space between stars, yet be simultaneously connected to everything, the thread of his existence woven into a tapestry of infinite, organic proportions? Only those clouds can answer him.

Tearfully enlightened, he rises unsteadily, joint half smoked and pinned in his fingers, he abandons his stash to return to his living room, retrieving his private slate from another hollowed book. Setting it upon the hardwood floor, he joins it, cross-legged, taking another deep drag as he waits for the machine to boot.

As the display flowers with his data, the lightboard unfolds onto the floor before him. The keys burn a soft, autumnal blue, ready for his use. His thumb opens a new document, the blank page asking for the hazy math he'd seen in that preternatural sky.

He rises long enough to douse and flush his joint. Then, before the enjoined glow of display and board, he finds answers.

The world is code.

Throughout their history, humans have tried to solve the mysteries of their world. After all, a world without mysteries can be considered understood, conquered. But while many answers have been found, many more of life's secrets have remained elusive. Instead of considering any of these mysteries problems to be explored, they have allowed god to be cited as the decider. It's an easy conclusion for a mind indifferent to the pursuit of knowledge.

Imagine it... What being of ultimate power would choose to be the shepherd of a flock of comparatively witless simpletons? The need for dominion over others is a construct of the mortal man. It is he who is powerless without his tools, not the omnipotent. What need has god of dominion when no one can challenge his power? It is the absence of power that brings on its lust.

No. The universe resulted from a great cataclysm of energies at the center of things. And from that flowed truth and the energy to make stars, the engines of life. And within that population of countless stars, there is at least one star system which lucked into the proper configuration to support carbon life. And on that living world, one species had reached a critical mass of intelligence that allowed him to pull back the curtain.

The universe is a code of unfathomable complexity, shaping stars, planets, elements, laws of physics. Man is an extension of that code, an offshoot of the main equation. He is a code, with biochemical chains governing his every action. He is like all matter, structure formed from cosmic numbers, machines differentiated only by consciousness.

The theory is exquisitely simple. If everything is a complicated code, it can be fixed when broken, improved upon when found flawed, condemned when irretrievable. There is no evil, just broken code, broken machines in need of repair. A thing that hurts, kills, is a thing in need of mending, not an example of some terrible evil. Evil has become the boogeyman, the threat of the punitive stick to the backside of a disobedient child.

Johnny tastes his dry mouth and shivers in the comedown's sudden cold. He has expended himself in a manifesto of unsupportable theories, but they are theories of truths, truths that should be spoken. He saves it and, shaking, shuts the slate. A quick check of his watch reveals that it's five bells. Four hours have disappeared on the whimsical wind. He closes his sliding glass door, pausing to admire the earliest fingers of perfect, rosy dawn.

If everything is code, he muses as he climbs in next to a sleeping Lohner, then his girlfriend is the recipient of an inviolate string. He wakes her with a kiss.

Those lovely blue eyes open, quietly knowing of him, of the world. She welcomes him with a moan as Johnny, his fading high still lapping at the edge of things, tops her, seeking in her a warmth found in no other part of life. He feels her gasp and arch, her arms drawing him in as he kisses her breasts. Her skin has imbibed the warmth of sheltered sleep. He is not alone.

15

Later, as it's light, Johnny can't recall sleeping, nor can he remember having a single thought in hours gone. He becomes aware in bed, twisted sheets imprisoning him. Lohner appears naked from the bathroom, fresh from the shower.

"You're going to have to roll out soon, sleepyhead." Her impish smile lights her elfin face. "Meet you at the rally later?"

"Mmmm?" If his mind is sand, his mouth is a desert.

"The rally? The thing you've been planning for, like, two months now?" She theatrically spreads her arms, bra in one hand, sock in the other. "Freedom! Throw off the government shackles, stand and let them know that blah blah blah, security crackdowns, blah blah..." She grins as she dresses. "If you blow it off, I won't forgive you, not after having to listen to you practice it 873 times."

"Why do I need to go?" He smiles. "You've got it nailed."

"Charm, Johnny, and *you* have so very much of it." Her sarcasm can fill an ocean.

"I'll be there. I just... there's something..."

"What? Whatever you were working on last night while every other sane person on the planet slept?" Her smile has an edge to it this time.

"Yeah. I feel like, I don't know. I feel like there's something here." His head has been stuffed with cotton. "Anyway, how do you know I wasn't sleeping all night?"

"Saw you," Lohner pulls on an ocean-blue mesh top over a black jean skirt. In need of a mirror, her delicate feet weave a path through the floor's disorder, returning her to the safety of the bathroom. "Heard you typing away... talked in your sleep too..."

He kicks away the mangled sheets and swings himself into a seated position on his side of the bed. "Wasn't the first time... won't be the last either."

She rejoins him, faint makeup now applied. She is such a creature of the day, yearning for sunlight's first kiss. She steps close, slides her tongue along his lips. "Don't be late. You know how riled up they get when daddy isn't around to keep things civil."

"I will," he strokes her cheek. "Don't work too hard, okay?"

"Like you care." Her smile stays with him after she disappears out his door.

Showered and dressed, Johnny seeks out his drug-addled musings of the night before. 'Manifesto.doc,' he'd called it. The arrogance... Soon, though, he finds himself correcting the document, losing himself in the screen's artificial glow. The day straddles and then passes noon. Only the persistent beep of an incoming call rouses him.

"Hey, Johnny." Zia's voice. He saves the document and answers the call on his slate. "Was hoping to catch you before you left. Big day, huh?"

"Yeah." He can't believe the time. "Actually, I need to get going. But what's up?"

"Look, about last night, I'm sorry I snapped at you. It's just..." Traffic cuts across her weary voice. "I'm just worried."

"Yeah, it's all pretty hard to imagine. Don't worry about it..." He's rushing around the apartment as he talks, throwing on a coat. "Clandestine meetings in abandoned parks, fires, murders... all that's missing is the big bomb we have to disarm before it blows the whole city."

She snorts. "Yeah. I just... I wish she'd let us..."

"Yeah." He stands by the locked window, staring down at the harbor, slate in hand, thinking. "I have a few irons in the fire on Morgan. She's the key to this thing. You can see that much."

Since he'd spoken to Carter two days ago, an I.D. search has been running on their enigmatic stranger. He'd used a picture captured on his slate while she'd been at the bar. Profile shot which put the face annoyingly in shadow. She hadn't noticed which, Johnny knows, is important if he wishes to remain whole. But the search has yet to turn up anything of note. "Maybe if we ask her nicely..."

"Right..."

"Yeah, well, we'll see. Carter and I... we thought we might try to put her in a position where she was forced to give us some answers. Maybe, if there was something on the line for her..."

"If you do that, Johnny, you say when and where," Zia growls. "Don't leave me on the outside looking in on this one, or I'm going to get very grumpy. Do you understand?" For Zia, grumpy is a euphemism for incandescent rage. "If that lupa goes down, I want to be there."

"I'll keep you in the loop, I promise." He's smiling. "Listen, I gotta go. I'm late."

"Good luck, Johnny, and don't forget me!"

"I won't. Maintain the rage..."

Closing the slate, he slips it into his jacket pocket before locking up. When you live in Little Harbor, you learn to take with you what you value most.

Thirty minutes later, he's running out of the Underground and on to one of the city's major arterial roadways where hundreds of lunching citizens are lethargically returning to work.

The overcast sky threatens rain, the air muggy and charged with electricity. A storm is gathering. Weather's the one variable in the equation that can turn this day to death: news crews off chasing vehicular pileups, concerned citizens passing by instead of stopping to pitch in. Shit... Offering half-hearted apologies, Johnny thrusts himself through the press and into the park opposite city hall where they'd agreed to assemble.

His gathering group averages out at 21 or 22 years old. Of the 300 already here, three quarters carry signs, all of them having honored the call to wear the country's colors. He'd been the one to suggest the display of patriotism. It will make the government's effort to vilify them all the harder when they are wrapped in the flag. This has to be a peaceful demonstration of patriots, fighting a pigheaded government policy. No one sympathizes with an angry mob.

He greets as many as he can: slapping hands, encouraging nods, the right words. These faces are familiar to him, the core of his movement. They understand that government will, when the people are quiet, invite itself to the dinner table of authoritarianism where it shall ask for a plateful of tyranny, cooked rare, so you can see the blood inside. When the people are silent, their freedoms disappear because government is, by nature, hungry for power. So these are his heralds, his screamers, his dinner party crashers. Later, his ranks will be swelled by men and women who have a specific beef with the security crackdowns. A demonstration, rebuking the government for its underhanded deportation of minorities should have no shortage of support from this quarter. And he's grateful for it, but they are not his people.

Juliana embraces him at the center of the gathering crowd. His co-conspirator has done most of the planning, having a head for minutiae he lacks. Every inch of her toned, 5' 5" frame oozes zest for the cause. Hair, dyed an eccentric silver, caresses a dark, Afjan face that, more than once, has been his downfall. Her lips meet his cheek in friendship as her hands pass him a sign. They are ready.

"We're here today for a purpose, aren't we?" Juliana's hands shoot into the sky, earning cheers from the gathered. "We don't like having our every action monitored, judged, curtailed, do we?" The assembly hollers back a no as Johnny, shoulder to shoulder with Juliana, feels the crowd's energy surge. This is better than sex.

The media is here. Good. He sees the lights on their cameras, their recordings. He will be seen by his country tonight. He will be counted.

"Men and women come to this country seeking a better life." The crowd hushes as he lifts his sign, focusing their attention upon him. Their eyes are conduits of electricity that connect him to the Code. "For centuries, we've been, for the world, a beacon of hope. We've said to the rest, this is where it is better, this is where it is safe, this is where you can prosper. Our families have fought for this ground! Generations of our ancestors sacrificed so that we might stand here today! Well, in the name of those who shaped this country, I am here to tell the world that this beacon lives on! No more deportations in the name of anti-terrorism! No more fear! No more cowering under our beds! The people own this country. *We* are the government!"

The crowd roars its approval, flowing across the street to take up its post upon the steps of city hall. Five and six deep, they begin to exercise their rights, their freedoms. And as they scream out their demands, as they give voice to injustice, Johnny closes his eyes and joins his voice to theirs, thinking of what he has done and where it will end.

The police close in. The well-warned media are here, with their news truck and their cameras, as much the protest's shield as anything can be. The prospect of nationally embarrassing themselves on 24/7 news stations is what keeps the riot cops, the head-knockers, from descending upon them and teaching them a lesson.

The counter-protesters may only number 20 or 30, but they are hardened and would love nothing more than a fight. They make sure they are heard... "Fuckin' nutjobs!" The yells cut across the organized din. "Those people take money out of my pockets, food off of my table! Why don't you go with them if you love them so much! Go back to the desert and take the scum with you!"

If he returns fire, it'll only encourage them. "Let's keep it together guys, keep it constructive," Johnny yells to his people. "We're not sinking that low!"

They always forewarn the youngest protesters about the vitriol that spews from the mouths of the opposition. But no amount of advice, no cautionary tale, can buttress their neophytes from the hatred flowing out of the mouths of otherwise reasonable men and women. It is a crucible, a painful experience none of them will forget. They will be veterans after this day, his veterans.

Within hours, the protest has surged to 2,000, a show of support that, given the now intermittent rains, has exceeded his best hopes. The wary-eyed police keep hands to batons, ready to leap into action at the slightest provocation.

'No more deportations', 'liberty', 'no security without freedom'. Their many signs wave enthusiastically at those trying to enter and exit city hall. The protest is not permitted to completely block the access. Still, it takes courage to walk through them and many choose to wait another day. Many of the ralliers have taken turns pontificating on the steps of the great city's governmental headquarters. Done properly, and with dignity, a protest can change the world. He feels that power as he takes his turn on that concrete pulpit.

It's from this vantage that Johnny's sweeping gaze picks out the bicycle courier hopelessly navigating the chaos. If the short, chestnut tresses hadn't given her away, then the pea coat surely would have. Waving for the crowd to part, he steps down to greet Evan as the chants momentarily abate.

"Thanks, Johnny," she smiles gratefully as she wriggles her way free of the crowd. She has a white-knuckled grip on rucksack and bike both. "I'm on the clock with this one. They told me city hall and like an idiot I forgot about..." She nods to the crowd.

"Don't mention it." He takes in the hollow cheeks, the dark circles under the eyes, the nervous teeth chewing at her cheek. Their eyes meet in silent communication, he evincing concern, she acknowledging and glancing away. He leads her through the parting crowd and up those hallowed steps.

"Heavy, last night." Even here, he can't let that pass unremarked. "I wish you could tell me," he shouts over the din.

They reach the doors of city hall where Evan turns to face him, sunken eyes swirling with mysteries she may never unwind for him. "If I tell you, one of two things will happen, you won't believe me and think me completely off my rocker; or, you will somehow believe me and then it's really real, and I can't deny it. Either way, Johnny, I lose."

"I'm a scrot for even bringing it up." Remorseful, he offers his hand for a slap which Evan gives him. "Go make your drop."

Evan nods, hesitating in the entranceway so she can stare out at his people spilled along the sidewalks, the steps, and drink in their passion. When she looks back at him, a small smile dims the darkness in her face. "Let me throw this off and then... you got a sign for me?"

He laughs, stunned. "Sure, sure I do!"

On his smile, she disappears inside, package in one hand, bike in the other. Every time you count on having figured her out, she makes you feel the fool. "Jules, you got any more signs?"

For two more hours, the multi-ethnic crowd work city hall. Are there 5,000 souls now, or is he simply wanting to see what he wishes to see in the faces of the humanity that take their turns on the steps, tell their stories of co-workers, friends, relatives, loved ones, banished to distant shores. The pea coat is tied around Evan's waist when next Johnny spots her; the courier I.D. no doubt concealed in a pocket so as to avoid finding herself in the unemployment line. Lohner had used one of her breaks to stop by and pass out sandwiches. His place tonight, she tells him. He is to be there too, so long as he wishes her to continue in his miserable life.

It isn't the ominous police or the threatening skinheads who put an end to their proceedings. That honor goes to Mother Nature who, after their hours of standing and shouting, drives them from their slickened steps by a steady drizzle from a slate sky. So, garbage is bagged, signs disposed of, and hands shaken. Before long, he and Evan stand alone on these hallowed steps, both searching in banks of dark clouds for a glimmer of sun. The rain is warm on their faces.

"Dinner?" Johnny descends to the sidewalk, Evan behind. Passing cars kick up plumes of dirty water neither of them are lucky enough to avoid.

"Sure. Seafood place up the way here that I like." The pea coat is back around Evan's shoulders, the wet blackening its navy blue.

"Show me the way to heaven."

Fifteen minutes later, they are taking their fish out on to the abandoned patio of Sarah's. The restaurant's interior is packed, so they've come outside. They aren't afraid of a little rain; their table's umbrella will service them just fine. Peace and quiet is more important than staying dry.

For ten minutes, they eat in silence. The food is excellent, every bite carrying him farther from the fatigue of the day. The only things happier than his stomach are his aching feet, but the day's success would soothe all his wounds.

"It's big, Johnny." Evan has ravenously cleared her plate, sipping now at a dark beer as she eyes the life around them: a middle-class Korasian couple walking their two kids home, a passing Abbot Navigator displacing half of the street's accumulation of water, two shrieking women running to their car in a vain attempt to flee the cloudburst. The nearest living soul is inside the restaurant, behind solid glass.

"Yeah?" He tries for noncommittal, sensing the moment's fragility.

"If it's true..." Suddenly, her palm is smashing down onto the table as her jaw grinds in frustration, lips pulling back nearly into a snarl. "Fuck..."

Chilled, he waits for the storm to pass.

"If it's true, it's huge, Johnny. It's bigger than any of the bullshit things we care about: bigger than that rally, I'm sorry to say, bigger than my apartment, bigger than any of it." A hand sweeps her drawn face. "But how do you know? How do you know if a thing is true when you've no proof? How do you..."

"Instinct." Shoving aside his hurt, trying his best to ignore the gooseflesh her declaration has stirred, he leans forward, elbows gracing the table between them. "You and me, Ev, we don't have faith, like most. Find a hundred people anywhere in the first-world and ask them if they believe in god. Sixty of them are going to come back with yes, thirty are going to say maybe, and the other ten will find the fortitude to say no. See, the sixty say yes because their families said yes and because it comforts them to say yes. The thirty who say maybe just don't care enough to go either way, so they hedge their bets and occupy the middle. But our ten? Why do they say no? They don't have any evidence. They don't have any proof. All they have is their gut telling them that the math doesn't add up. We're built to believe, we want to believe, but instinct is strong enough in the ten to say no."

"Yeah? Instinct, huh? I don't know, Johnny. I'd just rather someone come along and tell me I'm dreaming."

"Yeah, but see, that's the easy way, isn't it?" Johnny stares at her past the metal stem of the umbrella skewering the table's heart. Her damp face is blank as her eyes fix on a place somewhere beyond his shoulder. "I love Carter like my own brother. Not another soul on this planet who I'd rather have at my back. But the boy has this fixed sense of how the world works. He's got it in his head that the world was created by God to be some big jigsaw puzzle and once you figure out where your piece goes..."

"You're happy..."

"Yeah, you're happy. We're not like that, Ev. Our pieces? They're always in the pile that never gets placed, the 'I need something more' pile, if you will. We can't... make ourselves fit." He looks to the rain-swept street, thinking of Lohner. "When you never fit anywhere, you trust your instincts, your conscience, the math, and you assemble whatever comes closest to making sense and you roll with it. It's weird, but it's incredibly liberating."

"Yeah?" Evan focuses those gray clouds on him, her smile hinting at her doubts. "In this puzzle, are we part of the horizon, or the castle wall?"

He grins. "Something incongruous, like some pastoral farm scene. Of course, in this case, your piece is definitely the cow."

"Scrot." Snorting, Evan scoops condiments of soy and flings the lot at his head. One or two sneak through his hands raised in defense, catching him high on the cheek and nose.

"Hey! Hey!"

"What are you? A pig is way too easy."

"I'm something small, fast, and furry." He retrieves her spent missiles.

"Oh, really? Is that what you put in your personal ads?"

"Oh, you're asking for it," and then he's returning fire with her own soys. Napkins follow, then bits of food. People from inside the restaurant are staring incredulously.

"Hey, you almost hit my eye!"

"You started this war! I'm gonna finish it!"

"Gonna finish it under my boot!"

By the time they pay the bill, the rain has slackened to a mild patter. Their bellies are full of the sea's bounty as they amble off the patio. Evan retrieves her bike, and they are walking to the nearest Underground. It's going on to nine bells now and the clouds, having done their damage, are peeling away to reveal a modest sunset. There will be, somewhere out there, some spectacular stargazing tonight.

"It's a neat little world, isn't it?" Evan slides to the walkway's far side to clear out for an onrushing girl of seven. Her sedate grandparents are failing to keep up with the energy of youth.

Rejoining her at the intersection, across from the entrance to their station, Johnny can finally reply. "It really is..." His hand goes to the slate in his jacket as they take in the press of life around them: the dozens of cars stopped at the blue traffic light, the men and women of all ages out for a night's entertainment, the distant shouts from one of the city's open-air markets. Everywhere, a smile, a frown, a laugh, a cry...

He measures his friend as they await the light. Her thoughtful expression has a hint of tortured wonderment about it that brings back his earlier chills. Big, she'd said, but how big?

"Quit staring at me. People'll think I'm your girlfriend." The light turns and she is striding out with her bike at a pace that forces Johnny to a jog.

"Would that be so horrible?"

"The end of the damn world," she smiles.

Fifteen minutes on the Underground discharges them into the Watermark, not five blocks from their bar. Carter is waiting for them, smoking on the front walk.

"Hey," Evan leaves her bike to hug the foreman, much to his discomfort. Carter's blinking at Johnny in confusion over their girl's head before she goes to chain up her bike.

"Last night?" Johnny mouths, shrugging. What does he know?

"Well, hey to you too," Carter finally smiles before he focuses on his chief friend and antagonist. "You made the news with your little lesson in civil disobedience."

"Well, you know that's what I live for. Screw helping people, it's the news coverage that matters..."

"The blond-haired golden boy activist, championing the less fortunate and the ethnic minorities... They love you." Carter rolls his eyes. "You camera-loving activists disgust me."

"Hey, I use what I can. And, anyway, back up the bus. Like you've never been Mr. December in some construction guy calendar," he punches Carter's shoulder. "Like your massive biceps weren't used to heat the cockles of a housewife's frigid heart. Were you Saint Marcus, or one of the elves?"

Evan is trying not to laugh as Carter glowers. "Oh, you just... shut up."

The three make for the front door as the foreman puts out his herbal. "What's on for tonight?"

"Who wears the pants in the Carter household?" Johnny grins as he pushes into the busy interior.

"What? Was there ever any doubt?"

"Absolutely..."

Finding Morgan in the crowd isn't difficult. Johnny's putting in an order with Molly when he clocks her leaning against the bar's far wall. For a sobering second, their eyes meet, blue sparking with green through dozens of damp bodies. With more than a hint of the feral in that face, it is going to be a long time before his gut falls silent in the matter of Evan against the world.

"What have you done to her?" he asks of the creature who cannot hear him. "What will you do to us all?"

DAY EIGHT

16

The sky goes on forever.

Evan admires the heavens from a gritty street corner that, at two bells after midnight, is all but devoid of life. She's read that the light from a star can be thousands of years old, something to do with the time it takes for it to cross the intervening void and reach her sky. It's an idea she can barely comprehend, but that must mean that, whenever she looks up at these glorious stars, she is staring into the past. How many events, epics, have flared and died up there, unnoticed?

Francis had reluctantly agreed to take her bike home. The need to just walk, clear her head, had overpowered her better judgment. Twenty-six hours since meeting Morgan's disturbing little friend, since being informed that the world is not as she believed. No wonder then that sleep's become a fond memory, leaving it to coffee and adrenaline to fuel her body which is long past tired. And anyway, drugs, artificially tweaked or otherwise, won't help her to sort through this jumble of emotions.

Even though it's had time to sink in, she's no closer to figuring out how to respond to the revelation that she stands between her world and its end. She has two options, as she sees them. She can accept the Contact's words as truth. Yes, she'd risk looking the fool if he, as part of some incomprehensible game, is only having her on. But might it not be worth being made to look the fool on the chance that he is right? At least then, in that one-in-a-million shot, she stands ready to face that dark day. Or she can dismiss the madman's talk as just that, talk, the ravings of the sick of mind. She can walk away, right now. No risk of being a fool then, unless it all does come crashing down. Gods...

The light changes. Evan crosses the intersection and begins her journey down the last commercial block of shut shops and silent alleys. Her boots quietly scuff against pavement strewn with the day's detritus, her eyes using the glass storefronts to mark her shadow's pursuit. Twenty feet behind, the creature stands out starkly against the smattering of souls pushing to home in this lamplit hour. Why isn't Morgan their chosen? She's physically stronger and they must know she can kill without remorse. Evan can't do that. She can't pull a trigger.

What price will she have to pay in this secret war? Surely, she'll lose something in the bargain: her friends, her sanity, her job, her innocence, such as it is. The good guy never walks away unscathed, not in the stories. But those are tales, told to the young and the bored. Turns out, the real world has a lot more gray in it. There's a thin line between a savior and a sinner.

Not many will mourn her if she does die behind this: her father gone in high school, her mother her first year in college, no brothers or sisters, no extended family with whom she's ever nurtured a connection. Years beyond the deaths, resentment at being left alone is still an enduring flame. It doesn't matter to her that others have it worse. Her pain is her pain. It's more real to her than the pain of others. Years it's taken, for her to find a grave for even a measure of the bitterness and self-pity inside her. And now it's clamoring to be dug up and set free.

Her friends are a different tale. She hadn't set out with a plan, with intentions to reach out, to connect. And yet the circle had formed and endured: fights, breakups, new jobs, new responsibilities. All have taken swings and here they still are, loyal. If she's remembered for anything, she hopes it's for her part in that. Which draws her back to the Contact's hazel eyes and his penetrating words and his demands for action. If her friends are hurt...

Her morose study has carried her to another intersection. She has no concept of time's passing, but she must've been standing here for awhile, long enough to be mistaken for a hooker. A classy, black Auriga cruises up to her corner, its mid-40s businessman driver giving her the philanderer's stare, the anticipatory nod. Her mouth hanging open, Evan checks herself: the now dry navy-blue pea coat, scuffed jeans, tanned boots. Her murderous gaze lifts and blazes into the luxury car.

She's preparing a scathing rebuke when, out of nowhere, her shadow's hand seizes her arm and yanks her back from the corner. The scent of leather and rain is in the air as her erstwhile protector leans into the open window, breathes a few fateful words, and pulls back to watch the car screech away. It's only then that Evan clocks the gun in Morgan's left hand.

"You can't," Morgan starts, but Evan's already crossing the street and jogging up the next block.

Yes, that too is new; not the stalking, but rather the skin-prickling sense of exposure, of danger, that dogs her every step. Morgan seems to find enemies in every empty shadow, in every mild threat. No longer is a scrot in a car just a scrot in a car. Is this her life now, moments snatched between fear and worry? Heart thumping, Evan faces her shadow at the next intersection, nodding her ahead.

"How much did he tell you?" They aren't far from Gibson now. But as welcoming as her bed there may be, she's only going to thrash herself into madness anyway. Might as well have this out. It's been a long time in coming.

"Enough..."

"Do you believe him?" She imagines her questions like bullets, ripping through Morgan's leather armor.

"Yes. He's never lied to me before."

"That you know of."

"That I know of."

"I hate him, you know. I've hated him since the first moment you mentioned him in my apartment. I've hated that you gave him so much control over my life, that you made me believe, just a little, that he'd have some answers for me, that he'd put an end to this."

"That wasn't him," Morgan murmurs in the dark. "That be you."

"How do you figure?"

"You thought he be making a mistake, they be making mistakes, putting you at the center of something that wasn't about you. But it was. It's always been. You just be trying to find a way to grip it is all."

"Grip it, huh? Grip the end of the world? Do you know how insane that sounds? Reflections?" They can hear her disgust down in the Core. "Reflections, Morgan. He's holding rocks in his hands, trying to convince me that life attracts life, no, better, that there are a billion reflections of our world. 'Course, he's got no proof he's willing to show me."

"Did you ask for any?"

"What?"

"Proof..."

Evan flushes.

"Maybe next time you ask." Morgan lights one of her herbals, once she's scanned the street for threats. The cigarette is a flash of red light in the starlit dark. "Not the point, I know." Her shadow inhales. "Maybe you don't think about the specifics, the logistics. Maybe... you just be doing what needs doing and you be leaving the rest to him."

"Maybe that works for you, but I don't follow the orders of people I barely know. You don't even know his name!" That much Morgan had been forced to confess at the field, when Evan had processed her shock with some questions her shadow had only halfway answered. "Do not think I am gonna forget that you told me to trust a man whose name you don't even know..."

"You wouldn't understand." Those cat's eyes bore into her. "You've never trusted anyone in your life." She snorts away Evan's attempt at an objection. "Don't even be trying to say it be otherwise, girl. I be knowin' you. We be closer to kind than you think."

"Me, like you? Slim chance of that..."

"I not be sayin' that I believe... in the reflections, in everything. I not be sayin' that he shouldn't have done all this different. I be saying that you and me can't wrap ourselves around whatever it is he be tapped into. And he be tapped into something. I know that much. You don't need a name when you got faith. Where be your faith, Evan?"

"I guess it burned down with my apartment." She smiles as that one hits home, square. "Well, he is what he is. The question is, what do I do about it? In all your travels, you ever been asked to step into the breach?" Gallows humor... and through it she senses something she never expected to feel, not with this creature. Enjoyment of the back and forth, of having someone there in the dark.

"Yes."

"But not like me."

"No. Don't be imagining many have..."

"Been asked to..." No, she still can't say it. "Been asked to help people..."

"Mmhmm. I should be the last you look to for help there. But, well... there be a lot of dirt that goes along with what I've been and done. But sometimes, you find a moment." History swirls in Morgan's face, twitches at her pale cheek. "Sometimes, you be told to do a thing to someone who... someone who has done things to other people, lots of people."

"What are you talking about?"

"Carmaho."

"The dictator? You killed the..!" Will all her conversations with this infuriating creature wind up with her screaming?

Morgan's mouth works in something like a smile.

"That's... damn... why haven't you told Johnny? You'd be his hero!"

Morgan snorts.

"I guess that doesn't matter to you, huh."

"No. If it did, I wouldn't be here."

"So why are you here? Why are you protecting me?"

"I told you. Faith."

"Because he's never lied to you."

"He's never lied to me."

"And because he told you I was the one for... for whatever this is."

Morgan nods, a strand of dark hair slicked against her brow. A gust of wind fills Evan's nose with the scent of her leather jacket mixed with the grime of city streets.

Evan senses in the stillness of Morgan's demeanor that there'll be time for more questions. Her shadow has never seemed more willing to talk. Do the stims loosen her tongue?

She softens. "Has anyone...tried to kill you before? I guess that's a stupid question."

Morgan smiles.

"And I guess, given that you're standing here, they failed."

A nod.

"Have they ever been close?"

Wordlessly, Morgan grinds out her herbal and then rolls up her left pant leg, over her knee now. Save us... Evan leans in to get a good look at the crisscrossing maze of scars that consume the flesh there. Pink and white, they writhe, animated by an absence of good light and the fullness of her imagination.

"Did someone hit you with a hammer over and over and over again?"

"Something like that. Through the kneecap. Had to go in a few times, put it back together." The pant leg is returned to its normal length. "We should be getting gone now, inside, where it's safe."

Evan nods. She wants to know what sort of weapon makes such a hash of the human form, but now doesn't seem to be the time for that. "Thank you for actually answering me this time. We've never talked like this. I don't... I don't mind it. It's tiring, being mad at you."

"More moving, less talking."

"Oh, great. You're gonna be her again."

They are on a residential block now, capitalism reluctantly yielding to a galaxy of townhouses of all shapes and sizes.

"I wish faith was easier for me. I was talking to Johnny yesterday about it, and he thinks there are people who just aren't wired to believe. He says we're like puzzle pieces that don't fit. I've never fit. Is this why? This thing... is it why I've never fit?"

"I don't know." Evan is expecting nothing more from her shadow when, quietly, "We be in a sandbox, Evan, with things we don't understand, people we don't understand. It be making sense, to me, for their plans to have been in place long before this."

"So you think... they've interfered with... with me, that they've done things, that they knew..."

"I don't be knowing that. I cant' be knowing that." Morgan's voice ripples with disgust. "If I be knowing that, I be telling you. I don't be knowing that."

"I wonder if this has ever happened before, if it's real..."

"What, the end of the world?" Morgan's tone is dangerously flippant. "We been there more than you think. The only difference be that this time's about you."

"I don't know how you can be so bloody calm. I don't. It has to be tied to what you've been through, what you've done with your life, but... I still don't get it. You have to live in the world too, just like me, just like Zia and Carter and them. How can you be so..."

"That be easy. One way or the other, you've made up your mind. You be believing him or you don't; you be doing it or you won't. Doesn't help me to be worrying at it."

"We are so different, you and me."

On Gibson, Evan eyes Francis' home from the intersection ten doors down. The mere sight of it knots her stomach. Her gaze skitters to the abandoned street. Everyone has long since given themselves to dreams. Orphaned leaves skip past her boots in the mildest of breezes.

She does not want any part of that house, not tonight. Maybe if the front window had been dark with sleep, but a light she knows all too well leaks through those curtains. He is surely awake beyond them, awake to look at her with eyes that chill her bones.

"Do you... do you have somewhere... I can stay? Francis has enough problems without me putting him in the crosshairs." She's always lied well.

Morgan inclines her head in what Evan initially takes for thoughtful calculation. In fact, her shadow is indicating a modest house across the way. She carefully clocks the peaceful street before leading Evan past a thick hedge and up a short driveway, to the front door that yields to the press of her palm.

"Of course," Evan has to laugh. "You needed somewhere for the bodies, didn't you? Are they in the basement?"

"Vacation," Morgan misinterprets, referring perhaps to the family whose portraits ride the soft-pink walls. The front door behind her shuts solidly, reassuringly, putting a wall between her and destiny.

The silent, shadowed interior has more allure, just now, than a million dollars. "Couch in the living room," Morgan tells her, the scent of leather and leaves from her mixing with the fusion of wood and paint, dust and fabric, unique to every private home. "I'll take a chair."

Awkwardly, they stand in the simple foyer, more accustomed to acrimony than this soft truce. The unfamiliar desire to thank this creature for her protection rises in Evan. No, not yet, not until certainty overtakes doubt.

The living room couch is a comfortable step up from the one Evan had once owned. She strips to bra and panties, folds her clothes upon the nearby coffee table, and stretches out upon that cushioned nirvana, a heavy blanket shielding her from the world. Her last thoughts are reminders. She has no other clothes than these. Oh, she owes someone for her home's flaming ruin. When she finds that piece of filth...

Oblivion...

Perhaps, to them, these are simply accommodations, an average room for an average soul. But to her this is a hotel, a room with a view of a world she hasn't seen since she was sixteen. It's the Core, the hub of all their activity, the heart whose beats keep alive the meager tendrils of life that spiral out from it. And yet, even though they are half a mile beneath the surface, even though every conceivable element has been anticipated, adopted into the formula of existence here, clouds of dust still blow down the streets of this artificial town. It's not dust of course, at least not of the kind that is a part of the world. This is atomized debris, the machined remnants of things the filters cannot catch, clustering together like locusts without a bite.

The room is well-appointed: a bed, a closet for her clothes, a vid screen on the wall, a place for her food. The mattress yields to her in a way no military cot ever has. And yet it's empty in here, sterile. Or...

Maybe she left something, some essential component of herself out there, in her windrider station. Maybe the Force Five blew it away, that or losing Troy has affected her more than she expected. The boy had been nothing but a nuisance while alive and now, dead, he plagues her. She'd spent most of the evacuation to the Core pressed into the back of a supply train, bathed in green emergency lights that penetrate even her closed eyelids. Not a word had been spoken on that whole journey, not that she heard, but then none of them are expecting rewards for their failure. Someone missed a tear, someone or something. Maybe that's why the Core looks so lifeless to her, dimmed by the power she and her kind caused them to lose.

Marching, from outside. She rises to look out... blue-helmeted soldiers in spotless uniforms, staying sharp for what? For an insurrection that will never come? For an invasion they lack the energy to implement? Why do they bother? She's too far away to look in their eyes, to find answers there, but it's easy to imagine what she cannot see. She has only to recall Gary's face to know how important the discipline is to them, the readiness, the honor of the Selection...

A knock at her door. She's been waiting for this, so she's up and deciding whether or not to call her visitor inside or move to the door when it opens, her lock defeated by his clearance. Black boots on brown carpet. And then a man, his general's uniform, green with the blue world on his chest... She stares into a face cratered by all of life's trials, a face the regenerative treatments have done nothing for.

"Sir," she salutes.

"Do not mock me." The door behind the man slides shut. "We both know you don't mean it. Now, you got anything to drink in this place?"

Something that passes for beer and which is unfortunately, for her, just that wrong shade of brown to remind her of the storm that has put her here in this place she fled from so long ago. She hands it to him, careful not to touch him. The bottle will be their only connection.

A grunt of amused resignation. "Suppose I couldn't have expected anything else."

"I'm not sure why. You probably gave the order for the restrictions."

"I probably did." They stare at each other; she does not know what to do with her hands. She hates being aware of her discomfort.

"Are you ready?"

So that is why he's come; she should've known. Foolish to have hoped otherwise. "For what?"

"For what... for Selection..."

"Why?"

"Why what?" the general growls, already losing patience.

"Why me?"

"I can find others to fill the role if you're not up to it."

"I didn't say that, did I?"

"Why? Honor... to make up for what you didn't do before."

That stings. "Shouldn't I be going to the crèches instead?" She lashes out at him. "Isn't that the Council's wishes, for women to fulfill the necessary, to keep up the body count?"

"That was never you and I'm not a fool. Why bring the headache upon myself when I'll lose the battle? You ran away once, and for less."

She wants out of this conversation before she encourages him out her window, head first. "Fine. I'll do it. There's nothing else."

"Do not placate me." The general's face has darkened. He forgets his drink; he'd rather stalk over to her, to loom over her, to tell her how it should be. Seven years since he's been able to do that and yet, here she is again. Staring up into his face of stone and steel, she's sixteen again.

"There's nothing else? There's honor." He spits it at her. He's always wanted to smother her in his faith. "Honor... but I suppose I shouldn't be surprised that we can't get even that from you."

"Oh, please. Honor? Who told the priest to watch me, huh? Out of everyone there, he snoops on me? Who gave me this nice room? A company man was here last. I can still smell his cologne. Guilt and shame... working me because you've never figured me out. You got Garry, but you didn't get me."

"I never figured you out? Is that how you think it is? You left; you abandoned your responsibilities, your obligations. And what happened? You were punished. You were punished and we were punished."

"You're blaming me... for the storm? You're blaming me for a Force Five?"

"Disobedience..."

"Disobedience... that's convenient, isn't it? 'Do what I tell you because it needs doing, because it's your duty, because I want you to do it.' I'm sorry, did I miss the memo? Are you God now?"

He wants to hit her. She never smiled when his menace threatened such before, but she smiles now, a kind of reckless, thrilling freedom in saying no, in choosing.

"You broke faith. You broke with him and you broke with me by dishonoring your family. Windriding... it's beneath you. You know that now. You've been told."

"Who told me?"

"Do not be obstinate with me; the storm told you. And now I am telling you. The priests will tell you. You have upset the order of things. It's been 20 years since we lost a whole cradle station and you just happen to be at the one we lose?"

"This is about your ego. This isn't about me, or my failings, or the ways I've disappointed you. This, this pestering me, this guilting me... you want me to go so that the one, tiny stain on your record is wiped clean, that little dishonor... which is fine. It's all you ever cared about anyway. Just don't try to tell me it's about anything else."

He stares at her coldly. "I suppose... you'd go back to windriding, back to oblivion, back to where your name means nothing, even with the future of our people riding on the line..."

"If it means nothing, sir, maybe we should just shut down all the Windriding stations. I wonder how your project would go then."

Her head rocks backward; the world spins; and there's blood in her mouth. He has always loved to hit her. Not Garry... her... the creature he couldn't control. For a man of his elevation, is there anything but control?

"You have no respect for the sacrifices we've made. For the time, the science, the energy, the will."

"Did we get to vote on that? I don't recall getting to vote on that."

"It was necessary! It is all necessary!"

"That's as may be," she licks blood from her lip, "but I didn't get a choice. How can I have respect for something I got no say in?"

"Your brother? Over there, doing God's work. And you, unwilling even to step for a moment into his shoes, to do a man's work. Isn't that what you always wanted? To not be your mother..."

"I didn't want to be mother, burdened with your babies. Worse to be your slave though." Her knife isn't far and he's weighed down by 30 years of seniority. Manipulating her with her brother's name... She turns away from him. "Anyway, I told you I'd go. Now leave me alone."

This time, the blow doesn't fall. "I expect you down at the barracks at midnight. You ship out in three days. We'll be at apogee then. Complete the circle..."

When he's gone, she goes to the window. She will do what he wishes. No, not what he wishes. She's been set on this course since the evacuation to the Core, since the supply train's emergency lights. Maybe it's for Garry, for Troy, and the poor soul who missed the tear. Maybe it's for herself. Selection... For the soldier boys coming back round again, to fill the street below, it's an honor. For her? Release...

She collapses onto her bed and falls almost instantly asleep.

The cancerous mass has grown.

The flower of black blight that had begun to corrode the horizon has blossomed since she's been away. A half dozen city blocks have been conquered by a kind of domed structure of opaque sable that leeches light and life from the city it invades. Long barbs of undulating shadow ripple out from the construct at nightmarish intervals, tentacles that set nearby buildings awash in flame with a caress. And even this, this heat, this energy, it devours. At this ravenous rate, all of Little Harbor will be swallowed in a matter of days.

She watches her home consumed, from a distance. Has the clock tower fallen too? That perch is gone anyway, exchanged for one out to sea. Is she floating in the air?! Has it come to that?! A glance down reveals naked, wet feet blessedly anchored to and spread wide upon the salt-stained deck of a harbor-bound mercantile which bucks uncertainly on the broad back of an angry sea. Around her, men and women scream frantic instructions in a vain attempt to turn their ungainly vessel. They'll never manage it in time.

In need of bearings, she numbly approaches the ship's bow where she's out of the way of the careening crew. She still has her pea coat, stained as it is with salt, but her pants have been raggedly hacked off at the knees and her boots are nowhere to be seen. What has happened to her?

Empty hands lift to hold her face as a violent pulsation from the thing eating her city expands it, drops its bulk upon another city block. Its growth is exponential now, its hunger a force that drives it ever onward. Ships ahead of them try to flee the harbor, but fires have broken out everywhere, hellishly illuminating pitched battles on the decks of most of those cargoed craft. Mutinies, or worse...

While the bodies of the flailing wounded are hurled into the churning waters, the harbor district's main promenade thunders with open war. The flashbangs of gunfire pepper the air as her ship attempts a ponderous turn. How can they fight that? How can anyone fight that? It feeds on their energy, strengthened by what they throw at it. But perhaps the lack of any other option has pushed the resisters past caring about such unkind logic.

The captain throws his wiry frame this way and that in the hope he'll see his men through. He's clearly screaming as loud as he is able, but her ears are deaf to the commands spraying from his frantic mouth. They are not going to make it.

More agile pleasure craft appear from nowhere, many steering themselves alongside larger vessels. Gunfire from these attacking boats provides cover for darkly uniformed men, who swiftly board the ships and commandeer them by killing their crews. Madness!

Ruined by what she's witnessed, she averts her eyes from chaos incarnate. Why is she here? Why isn't she in the city, dying with everything else she knows? Panting, she kneels for cover and has a thought for her friends.

Her turn now... Evan feels the ship rock under the impact of a boarding. Shouts, screams, and she's forcing herself to look. Men, dark, menacing, spilling over the rails. Ten of them, armed with guns that seem cut from fiery shadow. Where their faces should be, there is nothing but two points of blue light which burn like stars. Twisted things, only halfway in this world. Searching...

The captain is the first to fall. He bravely rushes the nightmares, armed only with a metal pole, but their fire cuts him down less than halfway there. The rest of the addled crew panic and scatter. Some are coldly butchered even as they attempt to abandon the ship. Only seconds, and the ten intruders carry the day. The deck vibrates now, stressed by their bootfalls as they fan out and seek for what they must have.

Whimpering, she, the hunted, slithers towards an inviting lifeboat attached to the side of the ship. It will get her out of this doomed place. If need be, though, she'll jump for the roiling water. Any fate is better than the one behind her, hungering for her.

As she crawls, she notices that the world is changing, quieting, muting the distant detonations to events in another world. Colors too, fading into an indistinguishable smear of shapes and forms. It's as if some force is tearing at the world's dimensions, perverting them to its unknown need.

She feels them behind her, searching. Almost to some kind of safety now. Her hands are out for balance, one gliding along a guardrail, the other along the blood-spattered deck as she forces herself into a tighter crouch. Not a sound...

They have no faces, no souls, but still she hears their unintelligible shouts as she reaches her objective. One of many starboard dinghies sits empty, waiting to save a now-dead crew. Relief rips through her as she stretches to deploy it.

The impact punches her face-first on the deck as the shell crashes through her left shoulder. Her mouth emits a silent scream as a booted foot kicks her on to her back.

She stares up into a face like the void between stars. Nothingness, and yet she senses satisfaction from him, pleasure and relief. His gloved hand lifts his dark weapon as the sea growls. She cannot move.

The muzzle takes aim, its black maw merciless. The first shot kills her other shoulder, burning through skin, muscle, bone. Her flailing feet try to kick him away, but some force, some fear, keeps her still for the final moments. No air, everything packed in too close, too warm! A third shot takes her in the belly, a fourth in the chest, a fifth in the cheek, and still pain has yet to greet her. The impacts cause her dying body to bounce off the deck, but she is no longer in it. The tether has been cut. She is outside, floating, watching, and quailing.

The only sound comes from the thunder of her own panting breaths. And, as they end her, she sees past their looming shadows and to clouds that swirl madly in a sky as red and tumultuous as the burning city. Slowly, as the world fades, they form a five.

17

The light of a lovely morning blazes through the curtained windows as Evan throws herself awake. Air! She gulps desperate lungfuls before registering a suspicious wetness on her cheeks. Crying in her sleep now? Panting, she swings her feet from the couch and sits up, head throbbing. Her wounds! Panicked hands search stomach, arms, face... It hadn't been real. Not real...

Where is she? A whimper escapes her as she scans the unfamiliar living room. Too many days with this, too many nightmares, too many different places. One thing remains a constant, her statue seated on the floor by the front window. Morgan's emerald eyes are unreadable pools, set to only receive the external world.

Her shadow doesn't need to ask. They both know she has dreamed the dreams. Rubbing at eyes caked with sleep, Evan stumbles into the bathroom to examine a face ravaged by a succession of these nights. Lives she's never lived and now she's dying in them too? Every joint in her body feels stiff and swollen, her mouth a desert into which something has crawled to die.

How has all of this happened? How is she here, now, when a week ago life had been ordinary, if not normal? She cranks open the sink's cold water and she sends her head under its spray. The bitter chill stings her skin, but at least now the numbness is thanks to cold, not death.

There is something inside her... Evan strips, less to wash than to look at herself, at what this is costing her. From soft breasts to corded thighs, her critical gaze finds, in the vanity's mirror, only past wounds scarring pale, supple skin. Most are newer, work-related falls, but the faded lines scoring the inside of both wrists are older, evidence of a darker time. Her hands move of their own will, drifting over her belly's mild curve. Lower... Her navel, her gut... There! Deep within, an itch she can't possibly scratch... a kind of throbbing pull as if there's something sucking at her, eating at her, from the inside. It demands that she heed it, that she follow where it leads.

"Shut up," she whispers. "Shut up."

By the time she's completed a lethargic shower and returned to the kitchen, dressed in yesterday's rumpled blouse and pants, Morgan has put on a pot of coffee, the scent of which stops Evan dead. With the kitchen window's curtain tweaked back, her shadow is examining the street. Fingers of restorative sunlight sneak in around the creamy cloth, lending a shine to Morgan's black hair and life to her pale flesh.

"Pegged you for the homewrecker, not the homemaker." Evan pulls out one of the kitchen's cloth-covered chairs and lets herself fall into its cushion. Sunlight is kind to the home they've hijacked.

Morgan makes no reply as she rescues the finished coffee. With a steady hand, she delivers the steaming brew into two cups: milk for hers, two packaged rations of cream for Evan's. They are the kind found on the breakfast tables of diners. This killer has stolen cream. Her laugh is brittle.

"Sugar?" And sure enough, her shadow has those too.

They sit, then, in silence, each waiting for their liquid breakfast to cool. Too much has passed between them to tolerate idle chatter.

"Will they come after my friends?" Evan takes a sip, welcoming the burn.

"If they have to be going through them, probably, yeah. If your people be staying out of the line of fire, maybe it go okay for them... In the end, you're the one they be wanting. You're the one they be needing."

Evan flashes back to the woman in the hotel, the General in his uniform. "Who told you that, your little friend?"

"No. I asked one of them."

That needs no explanation. A chill walks her spine.

That is as much as they have to say to each other. There are more questions, more revelations, but Evan is too tired to endure new truths. The silence stretches.

"I'm going out. Need to clear my head." She swallows all but the dregs of her coffee, automatically rising to rinse out the smeared mug.

"Work?"

"No." Evan's laugh is quietly bitter. "Why would I do that? No point, right?"

Morgan nods and ducks into the bathroom before they depart. Evan wastes no time, snatching up her jacket and booking out the back. She must outrun dreams and fate both, a tall order for a rider without an engine.

Evan jogs across the street to Francis', unable to even look at the brick house. From there, it's a simple matter to retrieve her Yager which he'd left, as promised, against the side of his house, a splash of silver against hardened brick. She wheels it into the street, swings aboard and is gone.

Life in all its bizarre glory engulfs her as she enters the city's great heart, one amidst many. Reflexively, her eyes find Little Harbor unchanged, whole. She has to struggle to beat back tears of instinctive relief. But then she's having to stop, holding her belly as that deep-down pull, that pull she cannot touch, draws her towards that innocent cluster of warehouses. "I mean it," she whispers, "Shut up..."

High noon finds the world pulsing with life. Colorful pedestrians stroll the Watermark, taking advantage of what feels like the last sunny day for a great long while. On the roads beyond, slick cars cruise, some on business, more on pleasure. It is one of those spectacular fall days, in a city that sees too few.

The next intersection finds her locking eyes with an overwhelmed mother in her early 20s. Her baby has been harnessed to her chest, her arms in support as she waits for any of two dozen cars to yield and allow her across the busy street.

Beckoning the mother forward, Evan runs interference by fearlessly cutting in front of the plodding traffic, slowing to a stop and forcing them to do the same. They blare their horns and shout out their windows, but Evan does not heed them. She's shepherding the nervous woman to safety. By the time the mother turns to offer gratitude, the rider is already gone.

From a cloudless blue sky, the sun sets the sea awash in color. How pain of any sort can live in a place so beautiful... She parks and chains her Yager a few feet up from a homeless soldier wearing a jacket with patches that proclaim him a veteran of some forgotten war. She ignores the weariness that lives in his scarred face, the lifetime of sweat that's bedded down in the fibers of his tattered clothes, to smile at him, into his single, blue eye. Too many of them. Far too many. Into the donations box next to him she drops every coin she has before she moves on.

Life is so strange. While working, she never paid much attention to the faces around her as she blazed past. They have a tendency to blur into one, indistinct mask. But, afoot and drifting, she finds in the eyes of passersby such a variety of soul: the coed jogger, the slickly-suited lawyer, the pixie-cute mother. They are the millions she'll never know. They are the millions she's been asked to save.

Have they earned it? In all this normality, this aimless living, have they earned it? And how do you define earning to live? Is it a kind act to a stranger? Is it a life lived in service to others? These are noble things, kind things, but they are just traditions, ethics handed down from the times before. They are not universal truths. Who deserves what and why? And why has she been asked to judge?

Shoulders hunched, Evan enters the vast, air-cooled cinemall with a tolerable Wednesday crowd. She uses her slate to send her message before swerving left to face the wall of light and sound that is Astrocade.

Gaming centers have been a part of modern culture for 40 years, but never have they reached such sophisticated heights.

Explosions deafen unprotected ears while strobing lights from half a hundred consoles batter the eyes. This is no place for those weak of sensorium. It is exactly the place to be lost.

Animated movie and gaming posters occupy every inch of wall, while the ceiling, spared such adverts, is devoted to an array of countless stars gleaming against a field of endless black. Ten bucks gets you through the door, but then it's $5 more for each game you wish to play.

Evan pays her fee and makes for the rear, her journey forcing her to ooze through a nuclear explosion's soupy fallout. The next great war will be fought by robots, armed with nukes, commanded by two frenzied nerds. Sweat-stained ballcaps are pulled so low on shaved heads that the backward brims kiss their bony shoulderblades. Navigating the toxic cloud pitches Evan into an unsuspecting teenager who looks on with a sexual intensity as her boyfriend coldly vaporizes enemy spacecraft. "What the hell!" The girl screeches as their shoulders bump. "Watch where you're going, lupa!"

It takes Francis 30 minutes to arrive. Evan watches him bravely soldier through the deafening detonations and the bewildering fallout until he finds her in the back wall's relative gloom. He always comes through when she needs him, always.

His mouth opens to ask her something -- where she slept last night? -- but the wall of synthetic sound defeats him. Smiling thinly, she passes him a headset from her chosen console, gesturing for him to follow her lead. The leather-bound headset consists of the standard enveloping earpads for audio, the arched band that keeps the unit on the user's head, and two additional metal bands which fit delicately across forehead and mouth. Evan slips the smoke-scented assemblage into place, muting the external din to a distant hiss. Her breaths mist the cool metal.

"You stick out like a sore thumb, old man." Her voice echoes back to her in stereo. Francis has worn black and gray business casual to an establishment where chains sprouting from eyebrows are considered conservative

"Your idea, not mine."

Racing Mars' screen comes to life as Evan finds its wireless on her slate and grants it a one game withdrawal from her account.

Two high-performance vehicles fight to be first to transit a treacherous, Martian raceway. Evan selects a Charger from the list of ten retro cars qualified to operate on the fictional terrain. A bemused Francis opts for an ancient piece of crap that Evan doesn't even recognize.

While the game is largely played via the traditional console of joystick and buttons, the biofeedback headsets vault play to another level. The devices recognize the player's mental state, measuring focus, agitation, excitement, etc. A lapse in concentration can find one's car tumbling down the side of Valles Marinaris, while the focused player squeezes every bit of performance from their four-wheeled hellion.

The degree of interactivity is startling to no one more than Francis. Three seconds out of the red-rock starting box, his yellow wagon goes spinning into a cratered gully. Laughing, she charitably hits reset.

"Nice. I can see your training wheels from here."

"If I had time to study..."

"No one gets a chance to study."

The race begins anew. Plumes of tawny dust churn in the wake of the two rocketing cars which, neck and neck, roar along the lip of a vast, dusty canyon, its yawning maw so vividly rendered as to invite vertigo. Her Charger has inside position and is unafraid to use it, shoulder-bumping Francis' spidery motor at every opportunity.

For a brief, joyful moment, she loses herself in the competition, in the fantasy. Morgan, the Contact, the dreams... what she must do when this race is over. It all falls away from this simple fiction. She laughs.

Surprised, Francis glances at her.

"*Ohhh*, big mistake, old man." His momentary lapse causes his bucket of aged bolts to fishtail its clumsy way on to the track's rocky shoulder. Seeing her chance, Evan gives her Charger its head and watches it storm across the finish line. Kaleidoscopic fireworks explode into the red sky as bikinied girls swarm her steaming vehicle to celebrate her victory. She snorts.

"You tricked me!" The headset filters none of his playfulness.

"Nah, you just lost your nerve. Can't do that when the rubber hits the road, can you?"

"I did forget to study that at college. How negligent of me..." His laughter is easy, familiar, which only makes her hate him the more.

Evan opens her mouth to ask him, to get the answer she's wanted ever since the contact in the park, when she saw those hazel eyes so much like the ones here, with her, even now. She wants to know why: what he knows, when he knew it, how he could've kept it from her. How long has he watched her, waited for her? Those times that he advised her, nursed her, supported her... Had it been for this? Had all of it been for this?

Francis sees the question in her face, but if he senses the direction of her thinking he doesn't let on, waiting for her to speak the words that will change them forever, a dear friend become something else.

But she could be wrong. It could be nothing more than an uncanny resemblance. All those nights of talking her through the worst of it, all those days of encouraging her to stick through, teaching her how to feel after the deaths that soured her to life. Is he protecting her, even now?

She stares into those wise, hazel eyes and then looks away. Not him too. Not another lie... "Let's play again. Maybe you'll do better this time."

They race. And this time, Francis is the victor, the fictional girls draping themselves all over his character's triumphant form. "That just looks... so wrong," Evan snarks.

"Oh, I don't know. He seems pretty lucky to me."

"There's something I have to do," she tells him, reaching up for her headphones. "Thanks for coming."

"Wasn't there something you wanted to tell me? Your message sounded urgent."

Yes, urgent. And how quickly he came... "It's nothing. I was just lonely."

"Well, I'm here. You know that. I'm always here."

"I know." And then she's pulling the headset free of sweat-slicked hair, discarding it upon the console. A small smile of farewell and she gets 'round him, into the crowd. Nuclear war continues overhead as she pushes her way out of this sensory nightmare, ignoring the unexplained man in her wake. There is only one place she dares to find answers.

As if sensing her determination, the clouded sky has darkened.

The rundown factory squats near the end of an industrial wasteland of boarded warehouses and abandoned lots, a desolate stretch of Little Harbor populated by the homeless and the hopeless. She'll be in good company then, for she is both. But this does not stop her. Her home, her work, and her spirit have all been victims of these last seven days. She will not give up her sanity too.

The knife, for which she'd stopped to buy a sheath, hangs between her breasts from a bit of leather cord looped about her neck. Her pea coat, unbuttoned to her navel, is no impediment to her hand finding and gripping the weapon's hilt. She does so often while her tires silently grace these dead streets. A citywork's crew hasn't been this way in decades, leaving her and the occasional car to find grimy potholes, broken sidewalk, and shattered glass.

She's given into the pull which has been a more-than-willing guide, drawing her to the ass end of nowhere. She'd chosen the most circuitous route to avoid being followed by anyone, least of all her shadow who would have surely stopped her. Losing Morgan had been cause for a few pangs of guilt, and she's certain the woman would be comforting to have at her back in this, her city's grimmest neighborhood, but this is her journey, her choice, her need. This is where the blight began, the source of its power. Even now, she can feel that oil on her skin, see the darkness in this sky, but she presses on. They are just dreams.

Morgan's man had talked of the world, its fate, and her role in its future. More than that, he'd talked of enemies, of forces, that threatened their safety. But while her dreams had backed him, her wary gaze finds, now, only sagging chainlink, fluttering bits of newspaper, and empty-eyed windows devoid of glass. Does anything live here? This place where the Blight began? As far as she can see, it is a patient without a pulse.

Bumping onto an intersection north of the factory, which seems to be the pull's destination, Evan begins to cross the street when she sees the first movement. High up, in one of the deserted warehouses, a flicker of shadow. Ignoring the chill that demands her to accelerate, to get clear, Evan pulls her heavy knife, and holds it at her thigh as she slows, searching.

A tense, three-minute pause in the nearest alley brings her no further sign of life. A rat's scurry for food? A forgotten curtain disturbed by a sudden breeze? These are two of the explanations she's come up with for the phantom movement. Time to be a big girl now... She nudges the Yager back into the world and turns for the factory's dirty brick facade some two blocks down.

The moment the car materializes ahead of her, she knows. The aged four-door is an anonymous, dirty blue with no plates and the left front light long since smashed, but it's more than the car's condition that sends her skin prickling. That's thanks to the driver who comes straight for her. Evening's full on, but she can make their faces behind a dusty windshield, their workman's fashion, and their zealot's eyes. Her knuckles go white on the blade.

A robbery, a rape, a random act of violence? What do they want? The eyes put paid to her doubts. They know her; they see her; they burn for her. She sheathes the knife and lowers the bars for speed as her adrenaline spikes. And now there are running footfalls behind her! Gaining on her! Is she about to die? She moves faster than her fear, off the road and up onto the sidewalk, to make herself a harder target for the driver and to lend her the cloak of the buildings' shadows.

But on the old car comes, unafraid, roaring for her, forcing her head down, her body flattening out to knife into the wind. Speed! Her pumping legs launch her forward with a fury that blurs the sidewalk beneath her. The car, swerving! Her legs, driving! The tires hopping the curb! The grill coming straight for her!

And then she's past the screeching car which crashes into the abandoned storefront behind her. A fraction of a second slower and she's crushed between... Flashing down the sidewalk, another intersection, yells from behind her, but she's not listening now. A wild laugh bubbles free as rain begins to fall.

She's flying now, not even feeling the burn. The hounds on her heels are confirmation of so many things, the banishers of so many doubts. It's real and its realness has unlocked some well of strength inside her. Hearing the sedan reverse, turn, and launch a pursuit, she pushes on, hurling past the factory, past more of them running towards the commotion, past the rubbled lot beyond it all. Away!

The car thunders after her, devouring her lead in a matter of seconds. It's still accelerating even as she feels its steely menace looming behind her. They'll not bother with an interrogation, with last words. This is it... She braces herself for a desperate, last-second turn, when gunshots fire the night.

The power goes out of Evan's legs as she flinches, bracing herself for the impact. Her dreams have schooled her well in the feel of a bullet's icy burn. Nothing...

"Go!"

It's reflex that turns her head round to find the screamer, a leathered rider a block behind her. A gloved hand is raised to the level of her shadowed face. From that hand death flies.

Glass and fire explode from the sedan which swerves from its pursuit and hurtles into an expanse of chainlink. The fencing crumples without a fight. The car skews to a stop, the driver's body thrown upon the steering wheel, the back of his head gone along with half of the dash before him. The smell of fired rubber...

She finds the two that had been running after her in the middle of the street, bodies sprawled as if swatted by the hand of god. The explosive rounds have done things to both men that has Evan gagging, but then their killer is upon her.

A gloved hand wraps around Evan's arm and physically yanks her from the Yager. "No time!" Her shadow's pitiless stare vows retribution if she doesn't instantly obey, yield to what is now their only hope of getting out of here alive.

Evan gives the burning car one last look. Blood and flames... that is how it seems to end now. Only this time, it is the enemy that hurts, not she. Shaking with adrenaline, Evan swings aboard the Roady. The instant her arms have secured themselves around her shadow's waist, the throttle opens, blasting them into the black.

"Do you have any idea how goddamn stupid that was?!"

Morgan had refused to stop for so much as a light until they'd hit the crowded safety of the Watermark. Evening beautifully mantles the fashionable pedestrians who flow past, deeming the two women below their interest. The Roady has been parked in a nearby lot, leaving them afoot amidst the night's bustling trade. Evan stops for an apple, paying once she's checked it for worms.

"Ignoring me now. That be great. That be great, Evan." Her frustration is near incandescent. "The one thing I figured I could count on was you not being an idiot. The end of everything, Evan. The end of everything... and you be walking into..."

The apple's sweetness fills Evan's mouth as she watches the couples on their dates, not a one of them the wiser. Their world is being overturned and no one sees.

"I'm sorry. I had to know. I couldn't..." A little boy runs by in pursuit of his older sister. "I couldn't go on thinking that it was all just some..."

"What, some joke? Some prank?" Her shadow steps close so that her voice can lower and still have its intensity felt. "Do I look like a joke, to you? Do I be looking like someone who be falling for tall tales out of long nights?"

"No..."

"Damn right, no..." Morgan peels off her gloves, hitches them in her belt so she can run sweaty fingers through sweatier hair." And what exactly did you be learning that you didn't already be knowing, huh? And now they be having your bike, and your bike's computer, which means they be knowing exactly where you've been and where you'll be, not to mention that they be knowing you're aware of them now. Oh, I be never doing this again, no matter how much that bastard be begging me!"

Evan laughs.

"What?!"

But she cannot find the words to explain the kind of euphoria sweeping in on her. She's not insane. People want to kill her. And this makes her happy, for somehow this is better than the lie. Tomorrow, she'll deal with the enormity of it all, wonder at what she must do. Tonight is for the relief of the living. She lifts her hand, touching her calloused fingers to Morgan's suddenly unstoppable lips. "Thank you... for everything."

Her honesty is water upon the flames of Morgan's anger.

Evan turns to the market, soaking in the sights and sounds of innocence. "I get it now. I believe," she tells Morgan. "Come on," she smiles, a vitality returning to her bones, "let's walk a bit. We have a little time. Let's walk, and you can tell me about your world."

DAY NINE

18

"You can't say that!" Carter chokes on his beer.

The crew, minus Evan and Francis, had assembled a little after nine bells. A Wednesday, which meant *The Executioner*. He'd backed Gordon for the noose again, and this time, the stand-in for his uncle had not disappointed, flailing his way into the trees, his pleas for mercy swallowed by the dark. Finally! The only shame had been the meagerness of the pot, with only Zia and Johnny willing to ante up.

As the night had deepened, the girls had packed it in. Anna had gone first, having to be up early to help her sister with a fitting. Then Zia, who'd spent the whole night tensely waiting for Evan to show, cycling between worried and resentful, had chased midnight out the door. That had left Lohner napping in a chair next to her boyfriend, her head resting on his shoulder.

"Alright, then you tell me what I can say, Mr. Right." Johnny can't help a grin.

Carter leans forward, elbows on the table. "Y'can't junk thousands of years of belief, of prayer, of history just to fit the square peg of your crazy idea into the round hole of human knowledge. Do you think that, down through history, the billions of people who've believed in my lord were, to a man, completely off their bleeding rockers?"

"I will dismiss the billions, I will dismiss the dogma, and I will dismiss the prayers. No offense, okay? But let's face it. We're talking about an omnipotent being here. We're talking about a being who has unlimited power, unlimited knowledge, and easily a few billion souls to care for, right? And this being, who could do anything he wanted, is going to give a flying fig about you and me and our petty little problems? That drives me up a wall. No one is going to save any of us. We are thinking machines. We get up in the morning, we do what we can to inject some meaning into our lives, and then we go back to bed. Lather, rinse, repeat about 40,000 times until one day you never wake up. That's life. That's all there is. God exists because we are afraid of acknowledging what we are. Code..."

"That's so empty!"

"No, it's not. It's freedom. Look, I'll give religion this much... the threat of a divine willing to hand down ultimate justice kick-started civilization. Without that force of fairness, without that arbiter of right and wrong, we're ruled by the strongman, the scrot with a gun. Your divine gave our society time to develop an idea of fairness. So I give it credit for that. But see, there comes a point when lawlessness and chaos fade, where civilization does form and it does follow a code of ethics, and the light of knowledge and truth is allowed to shine. But when that happened, instead of relinquishing power to the intellectuals, instead of gracefully acknowledging that someone else might have another point of view, these preachers, these men who claimed to be above us, better than us... these men who claimed to touch a power higher than us... they, like any good group of dictators, clung to power. They demanded fealty, obedience. They demanded that people follow their interpretation, their slant. Men, humans, who got used to being the center of the old world, nothing more, to these men we gave our faith and our trust. These men, who devote their lives to following the teachings of a book, rewritten and redistributed so many times that no one even knows who wrote the damn thing! Does any of this sound sane to you?"

"Are you finished?"

"Yes, I'm finished."

"Good, because you're nuts." The foreman polishes off his drink. "Living without believing in something bigger is basically the definition of depression. If you don't believe in anything beyond this, then what's the point of anything, of life? Why have a society? Why help anyone other than yourself? Sure, maybe they'll remember you for the five seconds after you carried their groceries across the street. Past that, they'd never give a damn. Living without true belief just reduces your life to zero, Johnny.

"And okay," Carter concludes, "belief is hard and it's confusing with the 47 million faiths and the 47,000 factions within each. But that's how it works when everyone tries to find their path to some kind of happy. I believe that a great man died for us all. I believe that every day should be lived in the spirit of his legacy. I mean, what do you think of me, Johnny? Am I a fool because I'm so backward as to think that a greater power might look at my life, see that I've lived it honestly, and perhaps cut me a bit of slack when my kids are born, or when their father is earning a living 15 stories off the ground?"

Johnny shakes his head. "Happiness doesn't offset the wars, Carter, the death, the divisiveness, the rancor. It doesn't make up for how these faiths have degraded women. I give you credit, Anna is your queen. We all see how much you love her. But for as many of you that have come out of their indoctrination as happy citizens of the world, we've also got the guy who beats his woman because he thinks he's the head of the household, or the man who straps explosives to his chest in the name of divine retribution, or the gay guy who gets his ass beat because he loves someone he supposedly shouldn't. And in all those cases, God knew exactly how it would go down. All-powerful, all-knowing, right? He knew how it all would play and yet he let it ride. I've got a name for that, but out of respect..."

"Those are our failings, not his." Carter's solemn in his earnestness. "In order for anything to have meaning, in order for people to grow, it has to hurt somewhere along the way. And I won't deny that some of the ugliness that has flowed from faith scares me. But the alternative is to have God control everything, to give up our free will so he can make sure we have a painless life. As much as it hurts, at least we earned it. At least we figured it out on our own. It's proof of our worth."

"So everything he does that hurts us is for our own good and everything we do that hurts us is just our own ignorance. That's great. That's just a perfect little accommodation, isn't it?" Johnny sits back, a hand rubbing at tired eyes. "I give up. How are we even friends?"

"Because I believe in helping the ignorant," Carter smiles.

"Oh, that's rich! Well, it's not like we haven't argued about this a thousand times before. If you haven't come over to my side already..."

"Never gonna happen," Carter grins. "See, this is what makes us different. I know there's justice. You don't, and so you go through life trying to get corrupt people to act honorably when that is never gonna happen. You should come over to my side. You'd be a lot happier."

"Equally never gonna happen," Johnny smiles. "I'll go with the devil I know."

"Ha ha..."

"Well, I'm gonna let you do your good deed for the day and get the drinks. Hey, sleepy." Johnny nudges Lohner awake. "C'mon, time to go home."

"Finally!" Lohner stands groggily. "I need the girl's room."

"Of course you do, honey. We'll be outside."

One bell... Closing time is nigh as they make their way out from under Ian the Iguana and into the quiet street. Decent folk have long since gone to bed, leaving the drunken dredges to muddle their way to wherever they lay their heads.

"Anna," Carter imparts to his friend as they hang a right and head for the parking lot, "is going to have my balls."

"Sorry to say, my friend, but you lost those precious jewels long ago."

"Maybe I did, but at least I have the sense to grab hold of a good thing when it comes along. You, on the other hand, are going to wake one morning to find yourself on the wrinkled side of sixty. And, after you've finished your eighteenth pee of the night, you're going to stop and wonder where all the hot women went."

"Oh, you wound me so," Johnny scuffs his way to a halt, a hand theatrically lying over his heart. "The problem with your logic, buddy, pal, is that I'll have the memory of sleeping with thousands of hot women while you and Anna are lounging in your rocking chairs, reading *The Art of Making Love: Senior Citizen Style*. Tell me something. Think it'll have tips on how to get your thirty-years-wedded wife to put a little swing back into your stick?"

"Oh, shut up," he laughs. "It's all moot anyway. Lohner has you wrapped around her little finger. 'Johnny, it's cold, will you warm up the car?' 'Thanks for buying me this necklace, Johnny.' 'Johnny, can you wash my back?'"

"Hey, I know how to treat a lady right. You give a little here, give a little there, and suddenly it's kids' day at the fair."

"You... treat a lady right?!"

"I do!"

"I think a few calls to a few past loves might unearth just a little disagreement on that. I'm not so sure telling that animal lover's cat you'd skin it if it bit you again was exactly your smoothest moment."

"Hey, now! I explained that. She had, like, a dozen of the small, furry bastards. You couldn't sit down without squishing one of them. And the cat hair? I think I was within my rights to... file a complaint."

"File a complaint?"

"Well, yeah. I offered a felony, but that was only to force a plea down to a misdemeanor. You know, a day or two for the fleabag at the bottom of a dumpster?"

"And you don't know why she threw you out."

"I didn't have to offer the plea." Johnny's trying to hold a straight face.

"You keep believing that, brother. If that's what gets you to sleep at night."

The bar's parking lot is on the brink of total desertion. Security lights flicker weakly over their heads, dull against the waning moon now well into the night sky. In the twenty or so spots, Carter's dirty truck is kept company by a few sporty imports no doubt owned by patrons who'll be cabbing it home. Anna'd be pissed enough with him turning up at quarter past one. Doing so while drunkenly falling out of a cab... The couch would be his mistress for a week.

"So, anything on Morgan?" Carter sucks in a few steadying breaths as he searches his pockets for a couple of mints. He can't imagine they'll take any of the drink stink off of him, but it's worth a try.

"Not really, but there are crumbs." Johnny sobers with the turn in their conversation. "Lots of aliases... trying to attach the rumors and the maybes to someone real, you know?"

"If we had a security database where everyone was catalogued and..."

"Alright, alright, smart ass," Johnny snorts. "That's enough from you on that."

"I'm just sayin'." Just one mint. Oh well, Carter pops it into his mouth. "Well, it's somethin' I guess."

"Yeah. I do think it's time for us to talk with her though. Savior only knows what she's telling Evan. It doesn't help us much if it takes us weeks to figure out who this lupa is and, in the meantime, she's got her claws into our girl."

"She don't seem like that type to me. More like the type that does her thing and moves on. Not really vengeful, you know? More like... I dunno... she's more like something out of the mo-shows, the dark drifter, you know?"

Johnny laughs.

"What?"

"You like her."

"Oh, shut it... Anyway, right. Let's talk tomorrow. We'll make our move. At least then we'll know something about this mess."

"I believe her, you know."

"What on..."

"That it's big. You ever known Evan to blow something up when it was just all hot air?"

"No, but I've never dealt with the Syndicate before either."

"The Syndi? You serious? You think this is organized crime?"

"Parcels? Deliveries? It's my best guess. What else could it be? I mean, Evan's just Evan, right?"

"Yeah. I dunno. If you're right, she's screwed, so I'm kinda hoping you're wrong. Those scrots don't screw around."

"No kidding." Carter munches his mint. "Anyway, what's Lohner doin' in there, callin' the queen? I wanna get home before noon tomorrow."

"You know how girls are. The bathroom is a sacred place, a shrine to the goddess of beauty and proper deportment."

"Hey, you made a few pit stops tonight too, my friend. Let's not get too sexist." Carter fishes for his keys as his eyes wander the nearly lifeless lot. That dirty crew cab pickup parked down the way... and he thought his truck needed a wash. That poor mule hasn't seen the kinder side of a garden hose in at least six months.

"So, Anna likes the new house?"

"Damn well hope so... I'm getting a good deal, but I'm stretching myself thin on the mortgage. It's gonna eat at me that I won't own every bit of where I lay my head at night. Bloody banks... bloody economy..."

"Yeah, well, just don't put any crazy ideas into Lohner's head. I've had that conversation more times than I can count with girls. I have never won."

"If it isn't my favorite little twosome," says a gruff voice, from behind them.

Carter throws an annoyed look at Johnny before he comes round for a look at the stocky man disturbing them.

"Evening, boys. Out for a little lover's stroll?" The grimy face breaks into a drunken smile.

Dirty blonde hair is matted to a skull that has been so forcefully slammed upon the man's thick shoulders that there's almost no neck to speak of. A flattened nose and a sweaty face that seems wider than it is long, sleeveless army jacket that may have once been a firm fit but is now unable to contain his expanding bulk. But even if the man won't be winning any races afoot, there's still danger here. Belligerence in his stance, with poorly-tattooed black serpents oozing down his hairy arms.

Fifteen feet arrears, three men provide an audience for this nonsense. A wiry fellow giggles from between two meaty oafs. The gruff one on the left sports a biker jacket, but his fatigued expression suggests he'll only mix in if pushed to it. The fat man on the right looks ready to keel over, his prodigious belly completely obscuring the waist and crotch of his dirty trousers. None of the men are on the better side of thirty. Tough guy's crew? Carter's getting too old for this.

Johnny takes a confrontational step forward, glaring at the thug who would be king of this drunken band. Something in his voice, or his smell, registers as familiar, but Carter dismisses it. Half the men in every bar in the country wear that same boozy perfume.

"Don't remember me, huh? Guess I shouldn't be surprised. I'm the poor bastard who has the criminal goddamn misfortune of having to sit at the next table over from you two tongue-wagging freaks. Yeah, I have to listen to you make love to each other every damn night. It's disgusting what you two do."

"Oh, go to hell," Johnny sneers. "No one's forcing you to sit there. Switch tables or find another joint. I'm sure there's a mental hospital around here with a few openings."

"Johnny..." Poking the drunken bear is not the smartest move, but there's still time to turn and walk away. "Let it go, man..."

"Listen to your boyfriend, Johnny," the leader mocks, "better let it go. Wouldn't want either of you queens to break a fingernail."

What is this idiot on about? He can tear this thug's squashed head from his shoulders! Carter steps on his anger right quick. He's seen too many of his crew, here and gone, bleeding out at some hospital because someone pulled a knife.

"Not worth it," he grits to his friend, forcing himself to take a step back. They have women and their lives to go home to.

"Not worth it. Right." Johnny is hot, his whipcord body coiled and ready to spring. "Go pound another beer. Maybe then, you won't care that the closest thing to a girlfriend you'll ever have is the nearest lamppost."

Not helping!

"Oh, it's worth it," the leader snarls. "It's big time worth it. See, a man should be able to go into a joint, have a few and not have to listen to chumps like you going on about your stupid, little *issues*. Every time with you two and your 'better than the rest of us' attitude, yammering on about how you'd fix the world. It's all just shit. So let 'me' make it clear. We don't want your yammering. We don't want you. We don't want none of it. Don't want your blasphemy."

"Our what?" Johnny's almost laughing. "Your what?"

The three backing the leader's play haven't moved since the approach which Carter interprets as a sign of reasonableness. So he turns his back on the idiot showing off to his friends. Anna is surely already pissed that he's out so late. He disarms the truck's alarm.

"C'mon, Johnny. It ain't important. Come on."

"Oh, walking away," the greaseball taunts. "That's brave. That's very brave. Walk away. That's it. Walk home to mommy. Make sure she tucks you into your little bed like a good little girl. That's it... Walk away, lupas..."

"Oh, shut up," Johnny snickers. "And find a dictionary, okay? It helps."

Frustrated, Carter has to turn back. Alone, the boy is not going to heed his better angels. "C'mon, Johnny. They're drunk. Leave it be, man."

"Oh, I may be drunk," the greaseball laughs. "But you're screwed." The handgun's cold, metallic barrel gleams meanly as it's pulled from within his dirty jacket. Both of its targets freeze, captive to the wide, dark muzzle.

"You scared of these bums, huh? Rollo, yo, Jonesy, you peed yourself yet?" The gunman's words are for his motionless crew who appear as startled at the pistol's appearance as the men it's aimed at. "You're nothing special, are you? They're nothing much. They talk big. Oh, they love to talk. I bet they argue while they bugger each other in a field somewhere. Can't tell the wifey, *nooo*. All them words, all them stupid arguments don't mean nothin'. This," the gunman flashes the pistol's barrel at both of them. "This brings you down. This makes you small. You should feel small, thinking you're better, thinking your shit don't smell like ours do. Me shut up?" The gun's muzzle settles on a spot high up on Johnny's quivering chest. "You shut up. Yeah. Who's mouthy now, huh?"

For a moment, upon which time has no grip, no one moves a muscle. Stragglers exiting the bar stop and stare for half a heartbeat before running back inside.

When the gun pulls off, Johnny releases a long, shuddering sigh.

"You talk so big," the gunman slurs, "ain't nothing sacred with you two." His gun hand trembles. "Talkin' bout God like you do. You need to learn a little respect."

Carter has only once suffered the indignity of having a gun thrust in his face. On that occasion, his pants hadn't fared so well. This time, he's ready. He'll not stoop to this scum's level. "Johnny... come on." There'll be no begging.

And he turns for his truck's safety. Ten feet of soiled concrete is all the ground he needs to cover and this mess will be over. This will not improve Anna's mood one bit.

"Fine," the gunman's inebriated voice wafts on the wind.

He never hears the bang.

Where is he? Oh, his face and hands hurt! And there's a burning in his chest. Screams from the bar and the street echo as, bewildered, Carter stares at a partial reflection of his stunned eyes in the passenger side window of his truck. How'd he get here so fast? His legs... they are water. His panicked hand tries, fails, to soothe the burning in his chest. Why is it wet? Why is his hand wet?!

"No!!!"

Carter tries to gather himself. Then a shot... Another...! Another...! Their reports merge, thundering. "Am I shot?" he asks God as he risks a look down at his chest which oozes a fluid the night turns black.

And then the pain is on him, a burning poker spearing his ribs. He shouts, he screams! But he can only summon a whisper. Is this a dream? Is he lying next to Anna, her sweet skin within reach of his hungry hand? He smells smoke and metal as he slumps to the dirty pavement. He has to face them. He has to see. He rolls...

His blurring vision has not yet failed so much that he can't recognize the three who'd backed the greaseball scattering to the wind. The gunman stands at the heart of what he's done, a stupidity in his eyes. The weapon smolders at his side as he stares down at, what...

It exhausts him to turn his head, but when he finally manages... "No... No!" Panic comes down on the pain like a hammer as he finds his crumpled friend.

A liquid darkness pumps from between Johnny's frantic fingers as they try to dam the ugly wound in his throat. In agony, blonde hair spilling over his ashen face, he writhes, fighting for a breath, for a word.

Snarling, Carter commands his body to stand, but a great dizziness collapses him to his knees. That knifing pain ruins his trembling hands, but it doesn't claim his eyes which fix the gunman with his own god's fury. The scum, every muscle quaking, loses the gun from out of nerveless fingers. And then he's turning and running for his life.

"You better run," Carter gasps. "You run! Wherever you go, I will find you."

A dark more grim than the night around him creeps in on Carter's vision now, narrowing it, but he can still see Johnny. That's all that matters.

"Hang on, pal." He flops forward, crawling for his friend, but he only manages five feet of gritty pavement on his hands and knees before a pressure, building in his head, defeats him. This is the worst headache he's ever known. Sounds swamped out by the pounding of his racing heart, trying to keep his watering eyes on his friend through fragmenting vision. "Johnny, where are you, man?" A cough sends something wet onto the pavement. "Man, I can't see you. Say something..."

Time to try again. Another foot, another... He reaches out, finds a bucking thigh. "There you are. Damn! Johnny, it's me. You're gonna be okay. "Another cough, but this one won't stop. Over the sounds of his painful hacking, he can hear someone gagging. Is it that bad? He can't remember.

Blank.

"Johnny!!"

A scream... Carter blinks to focus vision shattered by a thousand lights. Had he been away? He has no memory of the previous moment. More hacking seizes him as he sluggishly recognizes that voice. Oh, Lohner. Shit. "Lohner," he tries to call her name. But now it's a siren silencing him, a siren that carries him away.

The last thing the body feels is the roughness of Johnny's jacket before a light whites out the world. It's warm, wherever he's gone, warm and...

***

The ringing is endless.

Has it thundered all night, Zia wonders sleepily as she slowly comes awake, finding herself alone atop tangled, sweaty sheets. Night's shroud still engulfs her tiny bedroom as she becomes aware of her arm mindlessly fumbling for the phone. Something small clatters to the floor as she clutches the bedside's old-school cordless. "What?" But she hasn't turned it on. There... What time is it?

"Zia!"

The scream bolts her up from bed, groping automatically for clothes carelessly discarded the evening before. "Lohner?" She'd expected Evan.

"Zia! You have to come! Please." It is Lohner. And the fear in that voice convulses the world.

"Honey, calm down. What is it? Is it Evan?"

"It's Johnny..!" Even the bad connection cannot blunt the girl's torment.

"What's happened?" Zia's stomach flips as she bends for her jeans, slotting home one foot on the first attempt, the other on her fourth. There isn't time for underwear.

"I can't get anyone to talk to me," Lohner gasps. "We're at Memorial North! I'm outside... He's been hurt really bad. Carter... Carter's hurt too. They shot him, Zia!"

What?! Zia struggles to follow. Memorial North Hospital. That isn't far, quickest by cab. The practicalities focus her mind, but her heart is racing with darkness. "How...bad is it?"

"He wasn't breathing!" Lohner sobs. "Johnny... there was so much..." The attempt to speak the unthinkable sends the girl into a wordless cry.

"I'll be there as soon as I can," Zia whispers, numbly killing the connection.

"No," she admonishes her wobbling knees. "Not now. Not now!" One second of weakness, one moment's indulgence, and the floor will claim her for hours. She stabs three for Evan.

Johnny gone? Even with eyes squeezed shut, she cannot escape that horror; her stomach is a tsunami. The phone rings, and rings, and rings. "Answer the phone, Evan. Answer the phone, Evan... Answer the goddamn phone, Evan!" Hands shaking wildly, she ends the call.

"Hello?" Francis' sleepless voice floats to her after three interminable rings.

"Francis, it's Zia." There's a rock in her throat. "Johnny's been shot. Lohner's at the hospital. Carter's been hurt too, don't know how badly. Can you tell Evan? I'm going to the hospital now, Memorial North." Where are her damn keys? Her shoulder painfully catches the frame of her bedroom door as she stumbles through the darkness and into the living room. Keys, keys? Coffee table. She plucks them from atop back issues of forgotten magazines.

Silence falling down the line for several seconds before, terrifyingly calm, Francis acknowledges. "Yes, I'll find her." Then, too late, "How b..."

But she's already moving on. There's no time for status reports. "Rip it off like a band-aid, like a band-aid... Oh Savior..."

"Hello?" Anna's sleepy voice holds a measure of irritation and confusion. "Who the hell is..."

"Anna, it's Zia." Three bracing breaths are no help. "Carter... he's been hurt. Memorial North. Lohner called me. Johnny's..."

"Memorial North," Anna shakily inhales. "I understand." And the line goes dead.

Zia stares at her now useless phone, watches it drop from dead fingers. For a time, the only sound in her universe is of her anxious, panting breaths. And then her lip is quivering and the already dark world is going misty and she's getting out of there before she completely falls apart.

19

Morgan opens the door.

Francis has already sensed the bodyguard's displeasure, but one look at her eyes confirms it, green tempests. Dismissing her irritation, he steps forward, daring her to impede him. Wisely, she yields.

He'd known the night Evan stayed with him, that her guardian would find a place in the neighborhood from which to spy. The Michaels aren't due back from the subcontinent for another week; the bodyguard's chosen well. His damp shoes squeak softly on the foyer floor. "I need to see her."

"She's sleeping," Morgan murmurs, composed in the face of his demands. "No more than an hour ago." But as her mouth opens to insist he wait for morning, she's struck by the steel in his gaze. She blinks. "What is it?"

"Her friends," Francis replies, pushing on through without her permission.

The living room is, like the rest of the home, devoid of any light. Splayed upon a patterned couch, Evan softly snores from under a powder-blue blanket. He burns a precious moment to watch the play of shadows across her peaceful face.

The second he imparts his ugly knowledge, those gray eyes will flash with familiar pain. She'll straightway assume the shooting is connected and he will have the pleasure of watching another bit of her battered soul blacken and drift away like ash on the wind. All his hard work, to preserve, to protect... Words have such power.

Bracing himself, he puts his hand firmly to her shoulder.

The eyes slowly open, focus. And, at not finding Morgan looming, she shoots upright and fully awake. "Oh! Damn, Francis. You scared me." A little smile inclines the corners of her mouth before she realizes the ominousness of the hour.

There it is. He watches the cloak of grim anticipation settle over her slumped shoulders as the reality of his presence makes its mark. Her lovely eyes a shade of pain, she stands to put distance and her back to him. "What is it?"

As he tells her, a sickness ripples through him. Every flinch of those hunched shoulders, every dip of those unsteady knees, every kernel of disquiet filling her frame takes her farther from the girl he'd cherished, the girl he'd coached. He watches her trudge for the bathroom as if each leg weighs a million pounds. His gaze meets Morgan's, both of them worried as they register the sounds of her retching.

It's ten minutes before Evan reemerges, ghostly and shaking with thinly-shackled emotion. "Let's go," she orders them. "I want to see them." A blankness has claimed her eyes. They'll have to be vigilant tonight.

***

The desolation threatened to sweep her away.

Evan stands in Memorial North's chaotic emergency room, her fried eyes digesting the crying, the bleeding, and the numbed. Nowhere among the pained can she see Anna or Lohner. Morgan sticks close while Francis peels away to ask of the overtaxed nurse where they can find two gunshot victims.

Gunshot victims... It's a minor miracle that she's not still over the Michaels' toilet. That this could have happened because of her brings on a need to scream until her voice dies out. Is this a message? Is it punishment? Had her need to see the enemy invited this nightmare? Answers are seeds on the wind.

The harried nurse directs them to a quiet waiting area apart where they find Lohner, her reddened eyes swollen with stanchless tears. Words aren't necessary. Johnny is gone...

Evan clutches at her head. Less than two days between now and seeing him at the rally, so impassioned, so proud. Even hours ago, he must have laughed, smiled, and cared, as he always had, for a world he could not save. Now, there'll be only silence...

Francis stays with Morgan at the waiting room's entranceway while Evan falls into the battered chair next to a widow, putting a heavy arm round her thin shoulders. She has no words.

At full flight, Anna bursts into the small, sterile lounge, nearly bowling Morgan over in the process. Zia is hard on her heels.

Carter's girl has held it together, but while no tears have escaped, her control is moment-to-moment judging from her trembling hands which cycle between fist and flight. Lohner's bereft expression is a gut punch that jerks her forward. "Oh Savior..."

"They're trying with Carter," Lohner gets out, hands rending at her pants, fabric snared within small, pale fists. "They took him in for something... 20 minutes ago." A shudder ripples through her as Anna sits down gravely on Lohner's other side.

"What... were they saying?"

"I don't know. I couldn't..." A whimper lapses her into her own mangled thoughts.

The longest hours of Evan's life unfold in a funereal quiet that claims all of them. Someone asks if they need anything. The world... Francis fetches coffee, but no one but Morgan has the heart to drink it. Her shadow sips the brew while eying the hazel-eyed man with something less than friendship. And so, when the exhausted doctor finally arrives, it's an end to purgatory.

He's in his early 30s, ruggedly attractive but for the gravity in his black eyes. The reaper's messenger. He'd taken the time to wash before meeting them. There's a protocol to these things.

"Carter Patrick's family?"

Quietly composed, Anna stands to greet the weary physician, mouth thin against their worst fears. "I'm his... fiancée."

Receding brown hair is combed back by the doctor's thick fingers as he nods. "I'm sorry. The bullet's angle of entry... caused damage to the heart and the left lung. The trauma was... too severe. We were unable to stop the bleeding."

Anna... frozen still for a long, impossible moment. "I... want to see him, please." And though polite, she has given him an order from behind the iron mask of her desperate control.

"I'm not sure that..." But, before the doctor can finish, Morgan is next to him, seizing his arm and guiding him off to the side for a private word.

Evan ignores the exchange in favor of Lohner. The tearful storm has passed and now her empty eyes gaze out at some infinite point far beyond these white walls. Is she replaying events, or attempting communion with something beyond the physical world? Evan can only think of the burning, broken car and its lifeless occupants as her own fears creep in on her. What has she done?

When the intimidated doctor returns, he refuses to look at Morgan as he gestures shakily for them to follow him down a quiet hall and into a prep room just off a now vacant operating theater. Carter... No, Carter's body is already there, his bulky frame laid out upon a wheeled gurney and beneath simple, white sheets. Evan holds Lohner's hand, ready to catch her should she fall. There is stability to be found in caring for another; a means of sidelining one's own pain.

The doctor has Johnny brought in on another gurney, giving them all five minutes to say their words. He leaves them orbiting the two motionless bodies. Anna is the first to approach, quietly tugging the sheet back from Carter's empty face and closed eyes. Her heavy, gulping breaths signal the coming storm as she slowly buries her face in his swathed and idle chest.

Lohner, still in her own world, focuses on the other body. She pulls from Evan and makes her numb approach. Her hands are nearly as white as the sheet that she draws from Johnny's slack face. Just the smallest whimper... Her fingers gathering in his curls. Kisses she gives him, his cool forehead and then his motionless lips. It's goodbye...

They all have their moment, even Morgan, whose touch to each man's shoulder bestows a warrior's respect. Her place among them is at best uncertain, but death trumps all temporal alliances. Evan is brief, holding Carter's hand, then mussing Johnny's hair as he'd so often done to her. Tighter than brothers with faith that lit the world. Who will shine that light now? Who is left?

When their time ends, the doctor returns to claim the bodies. Anna and Lohner are asked to remain to sign papers and collect personal items as the rest numbly file back out to the waiting area. Every speck of sensory data informs Evan that this is real, that she is awake. Still, she can barely believe it.

She had known what was at risk. She'd feared it a thousand times, endured the nightmare scenarios in her head a thousand times. Her family, exposing them to her madness... These strangers ask so much of her. Where had they been when Johnny and Carter had needed them most?! Where had they been when her family needed protecting?!

Her weakness galvanizes anger. And, as it sparks to a welcomed burn, she turns on Morgan. "I want to see him, now..." It's her turn for tears. "I want to see him now..."

Morgan blinks, slow to catch on. But when recognition strikes, her head shakes. Then Zia is adding her strength and fury to the mix, nothing of her reason or humor left as she confronts the strangest among them.

"If I ever find out... that you, or anyone you know, is behind this?" Zia whispers. "There won't be a blade of grass you can hide under, sister, not a blade of grass. I swear it, on all I hold dear."

Morgan has the wisdom to keep silent, only a flickering a look at Francis. "Evan, maybe," Francis starts before a shake of her head silences him.

"Where do we find him?" Evan's voice can cut glass.

Morgan hesitates, then, as gently as she can, she palms Zia back a step. "He contacts me, sets up a meet. The diamond... it's the only place he knows to look if something goes wrong."

"Then I'm going to the park," Evan locks down her grief, letting her anger burn. "And you're coming with me."

"I'll stay with the girls," Zia glares at Morgan. "Someone should..."

"I'm going," a grim-eyed Francis murmurs, resignation twisting his mouth.

Evan leads them from the hospital, quick-timing it to Francis' car which they'd used to get here. She takes shotgun, forcing Morgan to squeeze her height into the back. "Screw the lights," she commands Francis. The blaze of mid-morning splashes brilliantly across the windshield. Have they been inside so long? "I want to look him in the eye." She meets Morgan's worried stare through the rearview mirror. "I'm getting my answers."

Francis is true to her instructions.

The small park is devoid of all but a handful of men and women walking their dogs. A Thursday nearing noon finds few children out to play on any of the four diamonds. That will change once school lets out. School... how that simple time appeals to her just now. Her bootfalls flatten a strip of grass strewn with fallen, dried leaves.

It's one of life's crueler ironies that, as a child, the wish for adulthood is paramount. Despite all the parental warnings that growing up is not the prize it seems, the desire still burns. It's only when hitting the uncertainty of adolescence that one realizes innocence's loss and responsibility's burden. By then, the way back to simpler days is cut off forever, as unreachable as the sun.

Finding a discarded, scuffed ball nestled at the rusted foot of a field-side bench, Evan scoops it and uses her jeans leg to dust it off. The heft feels good in her palm, something like a weapon as she sits to wait out he who has destroyed her life.

Where did she go wrong? Last night? Her apartment? Fighting Morgan as long as she had? How had she exposed them to her... to this? If he, the Contact, knew of this, sensed it, anything...

Her impatience grows with every passing moment, but her resolve won't waver. If it takes sitting here until the dawn of the next millennium, then so be it. He will answer for his sins.

Noon comes and goes, then two, three, four. Francis has left thrice: once to buy them lunch from the nearest sandwich shop, once for a round of water, and once for a bathroom break. Still, she stays rooted to the spot, though she did accept a sandwich. As expected, the neighborhood kids had come out to toss the ball around, but a light rain had kicked up around three, forcing most indoors and into the seductive arms of their waiting video games. Probably where they prefer to be, anyway.

The once-lovely sky has slid towards the tempestuous, gravid clouds hanging low with dark promise. Only on the coast can a day change so drastically. They draw from Evan the only smile of her long, silent vigil. Perhaps she does have some greater influence over events. If so, she pities the great city's many homeless. If her mood is a bellwether, they'll be snowed under by morning.

"Do you remember the herbal flood?" She inclines her face to the arriving rain, letting the cool droplets dance across her lips.

Morgan's head turns, eyes quizzical. Francis snorts.

"Johnny loved tobacco. I mean, he loved smoking it, he loved smelling it. Boy was all about excesses. Then they ban it... Johnny's all over how unconstitutional it was. He's like, 'it is the right of an individual citizen to choose the means by which they kill themselves,' blah blah."

Evan closes her eyes. "He'd always said he wasn't addicted to anything, that he could control himself. What does he do, the very day herbals go public? He buys 20 cartons, 400 packs, 8,000 herbals, right? And these weren't cheap either. He says to us, 'hey, how do I know they won't ban these too?' Like a month later? There's a flood at his mom's place in the country. He'd been storing them in her basement because he was laying his head in this studio rattrap in Little Harbor, didn't have the room. So, the flood comes, two feet of standing water in Johnny's mama's basement, right? Of the, what, $1,200 of herbals he'd bought, he's got about twelve packs that haven't been ruined. Twelve packs. And even those were kinda off. Might as well have burned his damn money." She almost smiles. "Said he'd quit after that, but I never believed him. Not worth it for half the price, he said."

"I can top that." Francis stands off a pace, handling the scuffed ball she'd found. "The bumper sticker..."

Evan's nostalgic laugh draws Morgan's attention from the damp state of her battered leather jacket. Since the rain had started, her fastidious hands have been obsessively wiping at the treated skin. "What?"

"For days, the two of them were locked in this argument about inner-city ethnic minorities and how to de-ghettoize them. Carter wants to leave well enough alone."

"Our boy last stirred a pot around the time we invented fire," Evan tries to fight down tears.

"Johnny says, 'ghettos are sanctioned segregation,' promotes divisiveness and second classes. Carter sticks to, 'people will live where they want to live,' and it goes on like this until Johnny downloads a racist bumper sticker from the website of the national party. We're talking, 'all for a white nation, say I'. He slaps this onto Carter's truck and the poor guy doesn't notice until he's getting honked at all the time by people giving him the thumbs up. He tells his crew about the attention he's getting. His crew is like, 'well, with that bumper sticker, what do you expect?' The thing's been on there for three days."

"I thought for sure Johnny was dead," Evan snorts. "He was so pissed!"

"Brave boy." Morgan is impressed. "I would have killed him." She flinches a look at her charge. "Anyway, what did he do?"

"Oh, Carter got him good," Evan picks up the tale. "He printed up about a thousand of these 'free Oryan' flyers, signed Johnny's name to them, and papered them all over Johnny's neighborhood: cars, buildings, his front door, the whole bit."

"Oryan... the terrorist? Damn." Her shadow laughs. "That's payback alright."

"Johnny was in hiding for a week. They nearly broke up after that."

"They sound like they had a good thing going." Morgan tentatively joins Evan on the bench. "The flyers may have been a little much..."

"Yeah, for like two weeks, they wouldn't speak a word to each other. Neither one wanted to be first to back down. One of them would come into the bar and sit down with us. Then the other would come along, look at us as if we were butchering puppies, and walk out. It was awful."

"How'd they work it out?"

"They didn't." The meager sun sets behind the intensifying rain and growing clouds. "We borrowed the storeroom in the back, Molly gave us the key. Locked them in there until they'd made up..."

Recollecting her friends during happier times allows her a moment's forgetful peace, but in the end they've suffered because of meeting her. She'd trade anything to have them back, to have their deaths on another's hands. She'd give this wet world to have that peace of spirit. Her eyes find Francis, Francis who knows the stories, knows how to tell them, knows their lives... Francis who...

Day fades to night. The diamond has been saturated with hours of rain and now shadows join the quiet puddles. Evan's thumb clears moisture from her watch so she can see that it is now eight bells. Nine hours they've waited. As quick as that, the anger returns.

"He better show," she turns her heated gaze upon Morgan's resolute green eyes. The bitch will need a new jacket after this.

"If he knows how important it is to you, he'll show." Eight hours and that's the best her shadow can do?

"If he doesn't? It's on your head," she vows. "All of it, you and him. If he doesn't show, then I quit and you can all burn."

DAY TEN

20

When he finally appears, the day has gone to black.

Evan has waited, cold and wet, for fourteen hours, rising only for breaks in the nearby bathroom. Time enough to reflect upon their past and her future and how the two have intertwined. And, in this, she has found some measure of solace. What had Morgan's madman said? Billions of reflections? Maybe there's a world where Johnny and Carter are alive, where she is not responsible for their end. These thoughts and more billow through her, until the shadows come alive.

Having mantled them for hours, the otherwise capricious rain stops near to the minute of his arrival. Her hazel-eyed man, his resolute features partially cowled by the deployed hood of a gray-blue sweatshirt. He walks from the mist with a purposed dignity that, at another time, might've been regal.

Speeches have spun through her mind, scathing attacks that strip him down to nothing, that force him to beg for her forgiveness. But, at sight of him, at his confident, almost annoyed, approach, the world falls away, taking her ordered thoughts with it and leaving behind this pressure in her skull. Like she's pulled him from something important, something more important than this...

She flies for him, covering the 20 feet between them in a blink. And, before she knows herself, her fist is smashing into the Contact's face, flesh and bone giving way under rage and sadness.

Even as he spins to the ground, she's on him, snarling as her knee stabs his sternum and her right hand pounds his face. He's trying to get his trapped arms up, but he's far too late to mount an effective defense. Crack! Crack! She hits him, her mouth striking its own screaming blows.

The thing beneath her tries to roll away, causing a few of her raging punches to glance off, not that this has saved his nose or his teeth from her vengeance. But it's not enough. For them, it'll never be enough.

Hands are on her then, yanking her from her prey. Voices shout, but all her focus is on that pulped and bleeding face and what it's made of her life. But as she slowly returns to herself, she becomes aware of being imprisoned between Francis and Morgan, each of whom have an arm. Her right hand is a single, throbbing mess. She wants more!

Shaken, the Contact plucks himself from the ground as Francis shoots him a sympathetic grimace. How dare he! How dare he! The Contact's tentative hands lift to gingerly prospect the wounds she's given him, as if he's never felt pain before. He stares in wonderment at his fingers which come away red. And then he's cleaning them on pants soiled by grass and mud.

"You have my condolences for your loss."

Snarling, she tears her arm free of Francis' inadequate grip, eager for round two, but Morgan bests her. Evan can handle herself and, even so, her shadow swings her round into a tight clinch. "Let me go," she tries fighting Morgan off. "Let me..." Tears blur her vision. "Let me..."

No... no! Not yet. Not here. She will not lose it here!

"Get off of me!" Growling, she forces her way free of wet leather, coming round to face her battered enemy. "You told me they wanted me! Me! Not them... She told me they'd leave them alone!" A finger stabs at Morgan, as her eyes take in her enemy's pity, hating him for it. "What do you have to say to that, huh? Wrong again! The all-knowing one fucks up yet again!"

"She was not wrong," the Contact coughs, ruining his sleeve in an effort to clean his blood-smeared mouth. "This had nothing to do with your destiny, Evan. This was life."

"Life," she spits, storming back to the man she's just pummeled. Her accusatory finger is a hair from worsening his already crooked nose. "What do you know about it?! Two of my family are dead!" The final word echoes through this abandoned place, unimpeded by wind or rain.

The Contact takes a step back, a protective hand on his broken nose, the slightest pressure on which brings forth winces. "Life. The chaos of life. I told you this at our first meeting. We are not in the business of interfering beyond the matter of your task. To have changed the course of events would have required foreknowledge and a willingness to alter the outcome. I have... we have neither." He seems to make peace with his wounds, his posture straightening as a new forcefulness lends strength to his words.

"You should have stopped them... you should've protected them. If you wanted this from me, you should have stopped them!"

The man's eyes burn. "You seek to bargain with us? You do not see. You cannot... To interfere in the way you ask is to violate every rule we hold as truth. You are the exception. You are the allowable variable. The complexities of time and reality demand that we elsewise stand apart and let the future unfold as it will. This works no other way."

Silence between them, warriors gathering strength.

"Your friends," his voice softens. "This has always been their end. Their fates are tragic, but it is inviolate. They cannot return by my hand, or any other. But, you." An urgency is in him. "We have given you a choice to protect all that you know. Now, more than ever, you must remember that. You mustn't change..."

"No. All your fancy words, all your little clevernesses..." She puts her nose to his, lips pulled back in a snarl that silences his pleading. She can smell his blood. "You should have helped them." Her whisper cracks the world. "Fuck... your... destiny."

Evan doesn't wait for his denials, his protestations, his efforts to excuse her guilt. She shoves past her enemy, quitting the playing field and hurrying into the black beyond. She leaves all of them for the darkness in her heart.

***

The three who have been left behind watch Evan's bedraggled form dwindle. Silence has mastered them until Morgan breaks the spell.

"I'll..." The guardian inclines her head the way of her vanished charge. But, she has barely begun to depart when the Contact catches her elbow.

"Let her stew," the ageless man murmurs, resigned. "This will pass. It must pass."

In the next moment, he's flat on his back, his fall so swift that his hands hadn't even time to rise in defense. Over him Francis stands, his left hand reddening from its violence.

Morgan gawks as Francis crouches over the man he's suckered, hazel finally meeting hazel. The grim line of his mouth speaks with more eloquence than words ever can. His message sent, he stands, nods a farewell to Morgan, and runs after his friend.

"Damn..." Then, looking down at the Contact, "Aren't you supposed to be smarter than this glutton for punishment crap?" She kneels, wincing at her employer's state. She offers her hand.

"He has his role to play and he does it well." He closes his eyes, wavering, and then begins the agonizing journey back to his feet. "I will have to make her see." Careful fingers explore his jaw for breaks. A groan of pain.

"Yeah, I don't see her listening much." Morgan looks into the dark, then back to her contact, her... friend? "Listen... listen, if it comes to it," she says it quickly lest she lose her nerve, "I can fill in. I'll need danger pay," she forces a laugh, "but..."

"Oh, Morgan," he pants. "Faithful Morgan. I know you better than you give me credit for." A bloodied hand finds her cheek, stroking warmth into it, warmth that seems to roll back the tide of her fatigue. "It's only a few days more." It hurts for him to breathe. "Keep her safe and watch for me. As you say, I'll be in touch... In her state, we're all blind to the future." And that, to him, is unacceptable. "I need to think on this."

And then he too is departing, opting for the right field fence to avoid crossing paths with the one upon whom everything hangs. She shivers. He's never spoken her name. She's just watched her employer viciously beaten by the very girl he'd contracted Morgan to protect. She shakes her head. It's enough to boggle the most ordered mind.

***

Sodden trash sloughs along the ground as Evan, her thoughts muddled, halts at the park's street-side terminus. A thin strip of grass, heavy with rain, separates her from the paved sidewalk that borders the two lanes of empty road. It's hardly a notable obstacle to her escape, yet her legs refuse to complete another stride.

Toeing aside a small pile of mushy leaves, she crouches and soaks up the verdant grass, the swaying trees, the waterlogged dandelions, the life around her. Excluding the omnipresent human debris of paper and wrapper, it is clean, innocent, pure. When it can all be snatched away at any second, it's important to appreciate these things.

In the First Cosmic Bank of Karma, has she not made enough deposits to grant a respite from this hellish week? Have they not all earned reprieves? They pay taxes, honor their families, break only a few modest laws, and largely keep to themselves. Why hadn't that earned Carter and Johnny last minute clemency from the high court of divine fucking fairness? Sure, they've all blasphemed from time to time. "Is that your goddamn problem?"

She asks this, generally, of the irrigated earth and, in particular, of the clump of wet grass she's spitefully torn free. "You took my mother and my father. And yeah, I'm sure they did a thing or two along the way they weren't proud of. But did they deserve that? Did I? What did I ever do to you? What about my dreams? What about what I want?" Her wrist snaps, flinging the dead mass onto the nearest pile of leaves.

"When does some of this come back good on me, huh? When? Because I'm waiting and I'd love to hear your answer on that score. The count's up to four, scrot! How many more do you need before you're satisfied?" She welcomes the viciousness, fingers plucking at the tiny, defenseless flowers.

The wet should have prevented a silent approach, yet Francis manages. She looks up and finds him a few paces off, his hands in the pockets of his wool coat, eyes respectfully averted. How much had he heard? She should say something; if not now then when? But she's already lost too much tonight.

"I know I should do it, for Johnny, for Carter, for me, for... for everyone... I should do it, what they want of me."

He nods.

"But I'm so... I'm so angry, Francis. I just want to tell them to... let someone else do it. Let them pick someone else and leave me alone."

"Are they punishing me? Did I screw up one of their little tests? I can feel it tugging at me, Francis. I feel it, every damn morning and every damn night and every damn dream. It's guiding me to that... to that place, and I'm just a puppet."

"I'm sure it's not a test." Wisdom in those eyes. "In any event, it'll wait on sleep." Her Francis, practical down to the roots of his conditioned hair. "Things always look better in the morning."

"Better be one hell of a morning."

Evan turns and conquers that strip of grass, her boots quietly squelching as she reaches the sidewalk. A glance back at her friend, no, at Francis, reveals Morgan quick-timing it over to them. Something about her urgency brings on a smile.

Back at Francis' Pedarius, Evan reflexively goes to retrieve her bike before remembering when and how she'd lost it. She wants, needs, to be back where she belongs, feeling the strength in her legs, the freedom in her soul. Just let the wind take this last week and blow it into the beyond.

"Heading to a hotel," she informs both of them. "I'm not taking any more chances." Her determination silences all protests. "Follow, don't follow. I'm going to sleep. I'm too tired for destiny."

The seven-story hotel has been hit hard by ten years of rampant globalization. Greedy multi-nationals have consolidated most of what had once been locally owned accommodations, restaurants, and even some nightclubs. The centralization of operations, coupled with superior resources, has created a toxic environment for the independents just trying to earn a living and provide a personable product. For too many of them, it's sell out or be put out, of business that is. Soon, everything will be owned by someone somewhere else. One of Johnny's old saws...

Having refused to sell out, the Shanesberry hotel has been left without funds to protect it from time's corrosive caress. Wooden balconies droop, the brick veneer discolors, and creatures visibly nest in the untended crannies of the upper floors. Evan smiles. In all its tarnished glory, the place is perfect.

Two ten-minute jogs, sandwiched around a 20-minute bus ride, had landed her here. It is nearly two bells. Half dead, Evan pushes through manual double doors and into a drab lobby that, while meticulously clean, is surrendering to age. 'Cash only, no slates' reads a sign over reception. Good...

A thrice sounding of the antique bell at the intake desk summons a modest Afjan woman in her fifties who, in spite of the ungodly hour, smiles kindly. Selma Shanesberry offers an unwrinkled hand that Evan accepts, black skin cool to the touch. If she's roused this woman from her bed, it doesn't show up in her august bearing or her unrumpled dress.

The quaint pegboard, hanging on the wall behind the desk, sports keys for half the hotel's rooms. Seeing that the whole of the fifth floor is vacant, Evan engages 506, uses two weeks worth of tips to pay in cash for two nights, and signs the registry as 'Jane Ditherington'. The extra, a crumpled $20 she slides across the old wood desk, is for protection. "A heads up if anyone stays on my floor, yeah?"

Selma's amusement doesn't preclude her from making the bribe disappear. "I'm sure we can manage that," the old eyes twinkle as she surrenders the key.

The room is pleasant enough: white curtains closed against a window filled with night, a passable burgundy rug that muffles the sounds of her footfalls, an adequately-sized bed garnished in sky-blue sheets and bracketed by wooden dresser and aged nightstand. The key flies on to a round table near the door, her clothes into a heap at the bed's foot, and Evan is slithering under the cool linens.

For all of three minutes, her tired mind turns over the day's unbelievable events. That it's real, that she'll wake to a diminished tomorrow, frightens her into a ball. And, with her back to the door, as shielded as she can make herself, she falls down the rabbit hole.

The sky is empty of stars.

The window through which the Rebel views the world has been shattered, leaving behind a frame of exposed and chipped wood that, from afar, has the eerie configuration of an empty eye socket. They are only permitted quick peeks outside, lest they be marked for killing. She doesn't care. She wants to see.

Many of the city's noted monoliths still stand, their imposing bulk swaying at the edges of her line of sight. But a glance upward reveals an empty heaven: no glowing moon, no glittering stars. In their place stretches an expanse of forever-black that she knows all too well from prior dreams. The blight that had once been only a dot, a blemish on the canvas of Little Harbor, has now supplanted the sky. A man can be fought, a machine overcome. How can you win against a thing that separates you from the eyes of heaven?

The street fares no better. Fires squat in once-lush parks while bands of starving humans huddle behind Conplast barricades in a bid for a moment's shelter. The cratered road, victim to some past explosion, is worthless to wheeled transport. Had that been their doing? She shivers and looks away from scurrying children which remind her too much of overmatched rats in an impossible maze.

She's shocked to look down and find a gun in her hands, though it is a disservice to name it so simply. The bestial rifle is the biggest of an unkind breed. It seems designed to be fired from hip or shoulder, depending upon the needs of its master. Its scarred, metallic surface shows signs of great use which is cause enough for the thing to fall from her nerveless fingers.

The man next to her utters a quiet curse. Retrieving the weapon in one gnarled hand, the soldier returns it to her, his single eye asking if she's afraid. Her quivering lip answers him.

She stands on the third floor of what had once been an office tower, in a conference room now occupied by filthy rebels. They lack a consistent uniform, though the ones who'd been military before the Fall retain their torn combat fatigues. Half of their number is female. Chivalry is an unaffordable luxury in a war they've already lost.

"Nervous, rook?" It's the one-eyed soldier. His rugged mien suggests a factory worker, or a dock rat. Unsurprising, then, that he makes no effort to cover up the ruined hole where once his left eye had been.

"Yes," she trembles, glancing down to find that she wears camo-colored cargo pants and a surplus army jacket that is a poor fit on her slimmer torso. "I don't... I'm dead. I'm supposed to be dead, here."

"Well, that ain't new," One-Eye snorts a laugh.

"I have to die again?"

"Guess that's up to you, isn't it?"

"I don't even know how to... I've never even fired a..."

One-Eye smiles, his practiced hands lovingly caressing his own rifle. "Now there, you're in good company. None of us were ready, rook, but that don't matter any more. Now, it's a fight not to be made a bitch."

"It grew." She turns back to the window and points past the spires of nearby buildings still standing, to the darkness that cocoons them all.

"Solar," grunts One-Eye who, after finishing his massage of his scarred weapon, cradles it on his lap like a cherished child. "Ambient light and all that. Sucks it up like a sponge. Nothing can punch through it, not that we've seen. You think it would get cold, but it's like having two suns up in here. Does somethin' to the atmosphere too, heats it..."

"I have friends... I..." She shivers. "Have you lost...?"

"My kid." A hand produces a worn wallet, a bruised thumb prying free a dog-eared snap of a black-haired girl of thirteen. "Building collapsed. Couldn't get to her. So now as she's gone..." He lifts his rifle in readiness.

A nearby explosion sends her into One-Eye who catches her with one grizzled paw. He holds her upright while putting away his treasured wallet. The street urchins flee to ground, replaced by shadow-shrouded vehicles that buzz to the scene of the conflagration which rains flaming debris down upon the city's nearest sectors. A ragged cheer goes up as she frees herself from One-Eye and moves quickly to the window.

"Hey," he warns her back.

At the vet's sharp tone, the unit's diminutive commander comes round to face them. Tresses of matted blonde hair worm free of a sweat-stained ballcap while the calculating, hazel eyes of a once feminine creature immediately measure the situation. "Let her go," the feral woman orders, a delicate hand poised above a pistoled hip. That face knows her soul, knows her intent. "Let her go. She's already lost."

Effortlessly, the Rebel does a front tuck through the window and floats to the devastation below, landing on hands and knees on what had been the street's sidewalk. She stands, slowly, checking herself for wounds that aren't there. Her rifle! Gone, lost beyond her ability to find it. She looks back, to see from where she's come.

Stewart Tower's sculpted facade has been devoured by gunfire and worse. Exposed superstructure is visible through the gaping ruin of once whole walls. The steely sight chills her, as if she's staring into the inner workings of some once great machine brought low.

Distant strains of gunfire pepper the indefinite night as she starts up the rubbled street. She passes alleys packed with filthy children, abandoned cars from which only eyes peek, the desiccated bowl of a once proud fountain that now houses a handful of starved souls. Everywhere her eyes have the misfortune to track, something or someone is broken. They'd done themselves honor in their resistance, but the fight is now over table scraps. Defeat hangs in the air; it smells like dirt and Conplast.

Three blocks north of her origin, the humans dwindle out. Where once familiar faces had stared from alleys and streets, shadows now writhe to a soundless thrum. Zealous men and women, their faces blanked by the same darkness from last time, ignore her as they go about their business, uniformed in triumph.

A roadside stall that once sold fruit is now home to three combative snakes. She stops to gape at the snarl of powerful, lashing bodies as they spar violently over a few meager apples. Feeling naked without a weapon, she cringes and hurries on.

What drives her ahead, she cannot say. She knows only that some force compels her fearful legs onward and into the Warren's market.

It had never been the best the city had to offer, but this... this place of earthly commerce has been perverted into a playground for the devil's children. Stalls that had once fed, clothed, and entertained have been commandeered by things of inky shadow. Spidery legs crawl over what's left while a host of the same faceless assassins mill about, some watching, some in conversation, others in prayerful poses. This is no longer a place for her kind.

She turns to leave this hellish place when two of the faceless nearest to her arrest her eyes. Those burning blue points for eyes have her, pull her apart, recognize her. She freezes, trapped beneath the weight of their satisfaction.

From out of the infinite sky writhes things she cannot name, things both dead and alive. With a vicious grace, they wheel across the world's ceiling, winging for her and her alone. No, she cannot name them, but she does know their mass and their dark intent. She is now the thing that does not belong. She is now the alien.

The two who had first noticed her seem somehow to summon the attention of the other faceless in the square, so many turning to her, capturing her in those points of light, the only stars left to her world. And then, from nowhere and everywhere, a disembodied keening soars into the night, a united siren more kin to an insect's call than a cry of battle. For her they come. For her they yearn, mindless and all-knowing, both.

Run... run! She spins free of their light.

Shattered streets, devolving into an indistinct blur as she flies over the jagged earth. The pursuing swarm stretches forth their eager arms, grotesque fingers rippling chills down her spine. As hard as she tries to flee, as important as she knows it is, it's as if mud has claimed her feet.

Through the twisting alleys and bombed-out intersections they come, tireless as the wind. They'll never stop. Terrified, she turns onto a rubbled street and bolts for an abandoned factory. The Factory... Even through adrenaline's kick, she recognizes it, the whole structure fired by a blue light that burns away the world.

Once she's through the front doors, she can run no more, only turn and face the onrush of nightmares. All those points of light... they combine and glow and crash over her. Their hands tear at her, snatching her into their dark midst. She is devoured by their hunger. And, as she is sundered before their alienness, as her soul is ribboned by teeth that cut through flesh and bone with effortless lust, she knows failure, again.

When she wakes in the barracks, to the sound of the assembly siren, she knows it's her day. It ought to take time for her mind to warm up, to fetch the memories that define her, that tell her she's T minus six hours, but no. Instantly, the knowledge is there, imprinted on her very soul. As she sits up, in a dorm filled by 40 zealots, as she clears her eyes and drinks in the gray walls and the brown floors and the military cots and the machine-like precision of the project's harbingers, of her father's harbingers, she wonders about destiny. Is she meant to be here, fated to be here, at this moment, for this purpose? It feels that way. But then isn't fate just the mind's way of filling in the blank unknown with a human's limited logic?

In some measure, their lives have all been driven by the search for an ultimate authority, someone or something clean enough, wise enough, informed enough, to show them the right way, to teach them the right ethics. They have all lived with flawed governments, overthrown by their own discord. They've all watched unrest sweep the world while the last gram of energy is sucked from the old resources. They've all sought out answers from the authorities who claimed to have a handle on the rhyme and the reason for their collapsing world. In the end, it all boils down to a fundamental need to know where they went so wrong, knowing all the while that there's no one left to them capable of conceiving the whole picture.

No, each side blames the other. Then it splinters and a third side blames the sixth and the sixth blames the sixtieth and books are published and reputations defended and commissions established and inquiries held. And it's all just so much wasted energy, falling toward an imperfect truth. Dig deep enough, try hard enough, and eventually all the evidence will be found. But evidence alone proves nothing. It is how that evidence is interpreted that forms a conclusion. And no one short of God can give them a final answer. No wonder they are here, entrapped by absolutes.

She showers with a half dozen other project members, a mixture of men and women coming and going from their shifts. One of the engineers propositions her in a way that would have had her knee crushing his balls if they'd been back in the dunes, but here she simply walks away, dresses for the last time, and moves down the grim hallway to the mess, where they are serving steak.

Steak... from where?! How?! And then the first taste of it, the juice of it, the sheer meatiness of it, and she forgets all those irrelevancies. Four years... But her body has not forgotten its texture, glorying at every mouthful. She can almost feel the iron spilling into her system as she cleans the last morsel from her plate and returns it with a smile. The final briefing, a talk the other twenty soldiers packed in here might've heard a hundred times, a picture of the girl and nothing more, and none of them knowing into what they'll be dropping. Information doesn't flow both ways. They must simply march into the maw and pray they are not eaten in vain.

A thousand times she's asked herself why she is doing this. As the commander giving the briefing recognizes her, asks her to stand to receive the blessings of the others, she still has no answer. The right to do what it takes to perpetuate the species, is, to her thinking, dubious at best. Does it not sometimes come to pass that a people play out all their turns, coming to find that there are no more chances? That there are no more hopes? Or is survival an imperative that overthrows all the rules, a universally acknowledged understanding that to do anything less than persist until the end is to sin against all the generations who were born, lived, and died just to pass the species on to its next evolution? Is that the only truth? Is it the fundamental force that powers every action that denies suicide even when it seems the only palatable choice?

Surely, survival of the species is the only reason she is here, enduring this, the only reason she has not walked out into the storms and let them take her to whatever comes next. Maybe it's for Garry and Troy and for all those who hadn't known a way out. Maybe she just wants to be the one person to do it, to make them all look at her and hail her. She's glad there's no more time to wonder.

Each of the harbingers in the briefing approaches her, to touch her, to pass on some cosmic talisman of luck and fortune. And then the priests are anointing her, excusing away her sins with their pious murmurings. And then they are asking her to remove everything metal she has upon her person before she's stepping into a dark room from which she may never emerge, a room sealed from the world more thoroughly than any that's ever existed.

The door of her tomb thunders shut and she does not look back to see if the father overseeing all of this is there to watch her do this thing. The walls begin to spin. She must stand perfectly still while everything she knows dissolves and the light tears her apart.

Where she had been is gone. There is only where she is, blindness on the floor of some cold room.

She has come. She knows what she must do.

21

There is a sound from an unremembered place.

Shouting in pain, her eyes squeezed shut against that terrible light, the female hurls herself from a rumpled bed, nameless and frightened. Where is she? Who is she? The dreams take everything.

And then memory is crashing down on her: the Shanesberry Hotel, Selma at the desk, the Contact at the park, the hospital with... Loss churns Evan's stomach as she pries open her eyes to find that the light is of a wholly natural source. It streams in through unfamiliar patterned curtains that fail to keep out the glow of the mid-afternoon sun. This room isn't hers; this life isn't hers. Everything belongs to someone else.

And then she's registering that strange pull that's been with her for two days now. It doubles Evan over as she fishes her beeping slate from her heap of dirty clothes. Five missed calls. Her thumb silences the alarm that woke her. Urgent messages, five of them. She presses play as her bleary vision tracks from the floor's chaos to the bed's mess. It's as if the thrashed sheets have hosted a clowder of cats and not one, restless girl.

"Evan." Zia. Her failing knees deposit her upon the bed's unyielding foot. "I've been trying you for hours. I know you went to that park and I know there are some other things going on." Her tired voice rasps her irritation. "I've been up all night doing for these girls. And I'm looking around and I'm not seeing anyone else. The least you could do is answer me."

Evan eases the slate from her ear, staring at its unforthcoming display. The next message begins more softly.

"Evan, Zia. I'm... I'm at my wits end." This is, for Zia, an apology. "I had to call Johnny's mother. Lohner's still crying. Anna's trying to act like nothing's happened and we know that won't last." A soul-deep weariness is in her sigh. "I... wish you were here."

Numb, Evan scoops her silvery top off the floor with her foot, snares it with three fingers. These are the sum total of her earthly possessions, the sullied pile before her. Even her Yager is gone. That her life has been reduced to this is bad enough. That Zia thinks she prefers being elsewhere to helping with Anna and Lohner makes it worse.

"Listen. Anna wants to have a wake at the bar. I told her it was too soon and other people will want to come, but..." A deep breath... "The hospital... gave her Carter's things. There was... a ring in his pocket, an engagement ring..." Fighting tears, she forces herself on. "So that happened. And now she's saying Carter wanted it, the wake, claims he told her once, but... it doesn't matter now. Lohner... stopped staring at the wall long enough to back her up. So, eight bells, tonight. I've been making those calls too..."

Evan hits speaker and drops the device on the bed as she dresses in clothes she's only managed to wash once in too many days. Has it been a week since the fire? Long enough for them to smell of smoke, rain, and sweat. She has become a vagabond.

"So let me know how things went with you. Who knows, maybe you have good news. Otherwise, I'll see you tonight. Hopefully, you'll show." Maybe she'll show... If the crumpled $50 left in her pocket, the last one left to her name, had been enough to cover a new slate, she'd have hurled the damn device across the room.

Morgan must have spent the whole night squatting against the hallway's far wall. At least, it looks to Evan as though her shadow has not moved in many hours from her loose, alert crouch. These feline eyes disengage their scan of the hallway to find her, greet her, muscles in her shoulders and thighs flexing rhythmically in an attempt to stave off stiffness. This face looks as drained as Evan feels.

She lets the door lock behind her as she returns the stare from across a stretch of battered beige carpet. Pride insists she remain silent, but her dignity will hear none of it. "You have a place? Not the Michaels', an actual place. I need..." Her nightmares flash before her eyes, that killing light, her city torn apart, her friends entombed in sterile sheets... She has to force her encrusted eyes to close against the flood. "I need a shower, clothes..."

Francis must be sleeping nearby. This close to... whatever it is, he won't want to make any mistakes, will he? Perhaps they've taken turns watching her door, not that Morgan is the type to share. Uncoiling gracefully from her easy crouch, her guardian nods and leads her out into the world.

Afoot, they push down into Little Harbor. Morgan had chosen to stay by Evan's side rather than retrieve her Roady from the hospital lot. The bike's absence necessitates a ten-minute trip on the Underground which she spends trapped between a glassy-eyed businessman, who never once removes his dirty fingers from his greasy mouth, and a blonde man of Francis' age whose wheelchair she's forced to crowd. She can't find it within herself to care about the dirty look from Rollerboy, or the curious one from the auburn-haired woman accompanying him.

"You're supposed to give me room," Rollerboy educates her, his finger pointing out the lines on the floor marking his space.

Before Evan can unload on him, the companion intervenes, one lotioned hand resting reassuringly on Rollerboy's shoulder. The eyes, a fine brown, study Evan with interest.

"Tell someone who cares," she grunts, sparing the woman a little smile before settling in to ignore the world.

But in her seclusion, she cannot hide from her dreams. They are so vivid that, while she sleeps, she is convinced of their reality. As regular dreams, they'd have been chilling; as visions, to which the stench of destiny clings like cheap perfume, they steal her soul. That other woman... the hardness of her life, that deep-down desire to find something real, something worthwhile.

From the woman in her dream place, it is a simple thing for her tortured thoughts to flit to the ever-present threats closer to hand, threats to herself, to her friends, to her world; threats that scratch at her, claw at her, infect her with fevers that sap her spirit.

There is no peace. There is no peace and she wants to scream.

Who's to blame? The affliction arrived with Morgan, but the leather-clad creature next to her on this cramped train-car is hardly responsible. It's her boss. That hazel-eyed demon is capable of anything to get what he wants; of that she's certain. For someone who knows so much, is seemingly capable of so much, is it beyond him to frighten her until she's compelled to obey him? Well, if the dreams are lessons, she's ready to burn down the school.

But of all the riddles, this pull inside her is the worst of it. An ache that tethers her to her fate, it devotes every waking moment now to gnawing at her, demanding she comply and relinquish to it her freedom of will. Hell no. She let it lead her once and had been nearly crushed beneath the wheels of a two ton car for that foolishness.

This is a punishment, right? This and Carter and Johnny? Had she transgressed in prior lives? Had she been a murderer of men, a venom to the virtuous? She is not her own master and the knowing of it shrouds her in a helplessness she's not felt since her parents' funerals. She's never been one for faith, certainly not like Carter's. If only he could be here now, to teach her to surrender to his god. Anything would be better than where she stands now, in the gray twilight between faith and isolation.

Morgan's apartment is commendably plain, simple white walls and loud wooden floors. Evan follows her shadow's nod into the unadorned bathroom. Spotless, the whole place, but that owes more to how little it's been lived in than any effort at cleanliness on Morgan's part. Evan ceases to care the second she's stripped off her stiff clothes and thrown herself into the tiled shower. The spray of scalding water is her first brush with warmth in an era.

Where does she stand? Of the friends she can trust, she has Zia, who knows nothing, and Morgan who knows too much. To bring Zia in on this will force her to confess her suspicions about how Carter and Johnny were taken from them, which will leave her with only Morgan. Zia won't tolerate that, no way. She shoves aside Francis and the Contact, suspecting betrayal from the former and certain of it from the latter. So what then? What can she give a world relying upon her for so much? If she's meant to be the key to all this, what's she to do? Will the dreams tell her? Trusting in dreams now to guide her path...

Carter and Johnny... She shivers and lets her tears mix with the water.

Later, having seriously tested the building's boiler, Evan shuts the water and stands, bathed in a cloud of steam. Her clothes are gone and in their place are some of Morgan's things: a hooded black sweatshirt one size too big, a pair of worn jeans that make her feel like a girl trying on big sister's clothes. The brown belt keeps them on her waist and rolling up the hem keeps her from tripping over herself. It isn't her look, but then she hardly recognizes herself in the steamed vanity mirror. Her eyes are sunken and bagged, her cheeks hollow and colorless, her chin too sharp, her lips too pursed. Screw it. For her brittle bones that shower has restored years.

Morgan's made coffee. The reassuring scent floods the place as she thumps into the living room to find her shadow perched on the arm of her leather couch. Steam curls from Evan's mug which sits, waiting for her, on the coffee table. Grateful, Evan slumps into the couch, gathers up the mug and blows on it. Six bells. A little while yet.

"We're going to a wake tonight," she shares, her rough voice barely louder than the couch's crackling leather. "Anna's idea... says it's what they'd want. I guess... he was going to propose to her, had the ring..."

"I hear you be having some experience with that, wakes." Even in her own home, Morgan wears her battered jacket, her hands stuffed into its pockets when she isn't holding her coffee. There's respect in how she cuts her eyes away, giving Evan space.

"This is different."

"Worse."

"Worse. They meant... they didn't..." Frustrated, she roughly returns the mug to its coaster. "They never meant anyone any harm, no one. They talked about the world, Morgan. They talked about how to make it better. They didn't let the fact they didn't come at it from the same side bother them. They didn't let that get in the way of their friendship, or what they thought was true. Look what it got them? Look what I gave them? Tell me where the lesson is in that, where the good is."

Morgan doesn't answer right away, letting the gravity of Evan's words have its moment. But then she shifts to face her, jaw set. "We be living different lives, you and me, but that don't mean I don't be understanding how this be weighing on you. Some things be cutting across all lives... We all miss the ones who be gone, just like we be taking for granted the ones still here. That's just how we do. But there be a lesson in it."

"Believe it or not, I been in a few scrapes and I be knowin' from right and wrong them that I put in the ground, or them that I hurt, they might disagree, but we all be living by a code. And I've never put down someone who didn't be playin' dirty, who didn't be steppin' over the line, who didn't be having it coming. That be my code. What I'm saying is this." She takes a breath. "Everyone be throwing things at you, what you should be buying, what you should be having, who you should be with, what you should be doing, not doing... At the end of the day, the only thing that be mattering is how you be sleeping at night, how *you* be sleeping. The rest of this don't mean a damn thing if you ain't right with yourself. That's what they all be missin' when they be saying this be right and that be wrong. They be putting their own thing on you, when how you are be the only thing that be truly yours and no one else's. I be good with what I've done, from where I've come. I hope you be getting there too before all be said and done."

Evan looks away. "Thank you," she whispers. "That's a kindness." Then back to Morgan, to look her shadow in the eye. "But have you ever killed your friends? I might as well have pulled the trigger, Morgan. I might as well have had a gun and aimed it and pulled the trigger my..."

"We don't be knowing that. We don't be knowing that, Evan, and you know it."

"Yeah, well, I only have his word on it, don't I?"

"Well, then if you don't think his word be good on it, then you avenge it. If you be thinking that's the truth, then you avenge it, one way or the other."

Evan stares at her enigmatic companion. "Did you just tell me to... never mind. If you did, you're not going to say it."

The corner of Morgan's mouth turns up ever so slightly.

They are quiet awhile, neither of them looking away.

"Will you... will you sit with me awhile? I have to think... about what to say, for tonight, and... maybe you could."

"Not a thing would move me, Evan."

Evan really looks at her shadow, an imprint of a thing never quite in phase with the world. Even here, in this place that is ostensibly hers, she does not quite belong. What has she sacrificed? How far has she come to safeguard an ungrateful girl? As much as this world hurts, as much as she blames herself for that hurt, life is better than the cold, empty alternative. And, but for luck and Morgan's skill and fidelity, she'd have been consigned to that oblivion days ago.

"They, uh... they were brothers and I... I owed them..."

A hand calloused by dark deeds reaches out to seize hers, a leather sleeve whispering against her forearm. A squeeze, as her shadow nods.

The bar on Collins is packed.

They'd taken the Underground back to the hospital to retrieve the Roady which Evan now leaves Morgan to park while negotiating her way inside the bar. Anyone seeking entry has to pass the crime-scene tape which cordons the parking lot. It makes her ill to even think on what had happened there not 40 hours ago. 'Closed for regular business,' reads the makeshift sign over the door. It won't deter everyone, but the gesture means everything.

Evan's never seen the three flatscreens blanked before. The stillness has affected the sober crowd who number about a hundred spread over most of the Iguana's tables. Many of these faces are unfamiliar, and yet all pay their earnest respects by approaching Anna and Lohner, who already occupy their customary table, offering them a few kind words before withdrawing to allow others to do likewise. Zia guards the two grieving women, her understated, black pantsuit likely the only formal outfit she owns. She wears it well.

Behind the bar, Molly serves drinks, her eyes swollen with spent emotion. Catching her eye, Evan exchanges solemn nods with the silent partner in their time together. Molly's guilty look makes Evan shake her head in denial. She won't accept another's fault in this.

Some in the crowd have recognized her and now watch as she completes the long walk to where they've all shared so much. Anna and Lohner both sit next to empty chairs, each draped by a familiar jacket. Carter's brown leather coat, Johnny's royal-blue windbreaker... unearthed from closets, or taken from their backs, she doesn't know. Her memory of that night is fogged over by her own trials.

Will she remember them as they'd been in life, or as they'd been in that hospital, bodies destroyed by a weapon any coward can wield? She takes her seat.

They're silent. Lohner's teeth have permanently claimed her lower lip, her ravaged face broadcasting her distress. Anna, meanwhile, coolly greets and manages eye contact with all who approach her. Some will call her aloof, but they who've known her long enough will respect the public mask that hides the private storm.

The wait to complete the circle doesn't take long. Francis is escorted to the table by a quiet Morgan, his long legs folding him into his usual seat to Evan's right. For all that she may suspect, he belongs here too. Zia takes her seat to Evan's left, completing their diminished circle. They have no words.

Molly appears with drinks. Had the girls asked, or had the bartender presumed? To the sound of only scattered murmurings in the otherwise silent bar, she sets down a Roots at Johnny's place and an ale at Carter's. There are drinks for the rest of them too, but they are as ceremonial as those for their fallen friends. Then Molly withdraws to the safety of her mahogany bar. None of them touch their glasses.

"A toast," Zia asks, breaking the silence.

Do they sense her culpability in this? Eyes turn to the widows first, but it's not long before they fall on Evan. She stares at the two chilled glasses and takes a deep breath. "To absent friends. May they rest in peace." Evan feels her own cool glass come into her hand.

"Absent friends..."

They clink and sip, none of them managing more than that. It tastes like ashes.

The turn out is overwhelming. Zia must have been on her slate all day. Johnny's activist friends stand out in all their leftist nonconformity, while Carter's blue-collar crew drinks quietly at two nearby tables. Two disparate worlds briefly share an orbit. In this small way, their legacy lives.

After a moment to brace herself, Anna stands and immediately has the bar's silent attention. She's chosen a modest, white dress, cinched at her elegant waist by a pearl-studded belt. The open neck reveals a gold necklace none of them have seen before, its delicacy suggesting it's for more private moments than these. Her courage earns her the room's admiration, as does the ring on her finger, a band of faultless gold supporting a circular setting of glowing sapphires centered by a single, glittering diamond which reflects the bar's votive light. "Thank you all for coming." Her strong voice leaves no corner unsounded. "Many of you will think this is sudden, but it is what Carter wanted. And, for the love that he gave me while we were together, I owe him this." A hard swallow is the only sign of the moment's difficulty.

"You knew Carter Patrick as a principled man, a man who worked hard for what he earned. But our public faces are the easiest to wear. We can all fool strangers, friends, into believing the best of us. It's when you see the private face that you know a man. I say, to every one of you who knew him that I've never met another soul who was so very much in public what he was in private. He showed you everything. He gave you everything. And that... was the best of men." Rapt silence as Anna struggles to sustain her composure.

"I'm not so kind... I'm not so forgiving. I had the one I wanted forever. I had him next to me for the last three years. We talked about kids. A boy would be Timothy, after his father. The girl would be Helen, after my mother. Vacations, houses, retirements... It doesn't occur to you that someone... could come along and, in the blink of an eye, rob you of every last hope and dream." As Anna's breaths quicken, Evan stares at the table, unable to meet the woman's eyes.

"We all have our vices. We all need our place. And that's why I tried not to quibble too much when Carter wanted to be here and not in our bed. I knew that others had claims to him, that his friends meant as much to him in some ways, as I did." Tears now, glimmering in pools of wounded aquamarine. "But if I knew that it would be the death of him... if I knew that some piece of filth would take him from me for no reason at all? I'd have taken him from all of you."

Evan looks down.

"If that's what it took, then I'd have done it. Because to feel this, today? To stand here in front of God and all of you, knowing that my dreams and my life were shattered by a scrot with a gun?!" She chokes on her grief, tears now freely falling. "I could not wish it on anyone... I love him. I'll always love him. May his memory live on in all of us. And may the ones who did him harm always suffer for it." Her knees finally fail, dropping her into her chair. Not a pin drops.

They had all expected Anna to break in some private moment. That she lifts her face now, allowing them all to witness the grief running down it, touches them all.

"Amen," someone says, then a chorus as Zia passes Anna a napkin, leaving her hand resting supportively on the bereaved's forearm.

Lohner is next to stand. It's natural for her to speak for Johnny, but surely Evan hadn't been alone in wondering if Johnny's last blonde would be able to wrench herself from the infinity her unfocused eyes have been contemplating for days now. But here she is, back in the world with them. Johnny'd finally found someone worthy of him and he of her. That he won't be around to realize it...

Lohner's nervous hands toy at a gray jacket normally considered cute. Tonight, it fails to enliven her limp, dirty-blonde hair, or to lend any color to her gaunt visage. But for strokes of carefully applied makeup at eye and cheek, she might've been a ghost.

"Johnny, I'm... going to miss you." Only the crowd's respectful silence allows her words to travel. "You were a riot. You kept me guessing, every day. You were sweet. You were playful... You were passionate when things were good. But I saw the rest too, your fear and your doubt. I saw how... it cost you to try so hard. A smarter girl maybe walks away from that when she knows that she doesn't come first. But I... knew you were true." Crying, she stares through the crowd, seeing only one face.

"Thing is, I loved you most in those dark times because I had a part of you others didn't. I was the only one who got to see you hurting for everyone else, for the world you lived in. But that's when I knew that you needed me. That's when I could help you. You taught me... so much. You taught me that even champions can be scared and still... make it through." Shivering, Lohner looks down. But just as they start to consider her finished...

"You were wrong, you know. There *is* a world after this. And it's ahead of you. I hope... you hang around a few days and see that you're missed and loved. I know you think it's weak, but if believing a myth keeps you alive, somewhere, then that's how I'll live my days. I'll tell them, Johnny. I'll make sure the world doesn't..." Those blue, blue eyes blink, breaths coming hard and uneven now. "I'll make sure they never forget you, or what you wrote. I promise..."

It took every last ounce of will within her small body, but Lohner says her goodbyes. Zia's crying as Evan, shivering, turns her head to find even stoic Francis biting at his lip. And suddenly, she has to get out of there.

A whispered *excuse me* and she bolts for the bathrooms. The door to the ladies yields to her shoulder as she all but spills into the empty room. Three stalls squat opposite a long vanity, a sink for each stall. Each of the three smudged mirrors, spaced along the wall, catches a fragment of her reflection as Evan punches open the nearest stall's door and, inside, falls to her knees. Her stomach had been empty, but there's still plenty of water and acid to come bursting out of her throat.

For days, she's been dining on a cocktail of sullen anger and dogged depression. These emotions and more have been her friends, willing to snuggle up to her in the dark, offering their ulcerating comforts. Evade, ignore, deny... With these, she's manufactured a life. But not until now has she felt shame. Those two brave souls have done, with effortless grace, what she fears to do. It's one thing to come up with the words in the gloom of

Morgan's apartment; it's another to say them to people, to friends, to take responsibility for...

And so here she's run. Here it ends, fetched up against the grimy rim of a public toilet.

Her panting breaths thunder in Evan's ears as, shakily, she stands, flushes away her pain and stumbles to the nearest sink to rinse her mouth. Oh, the Contact and his band of merry morons have chosen so poorly. Her, to face what's coming? She hasn't Johnny's will, or Carter's strength, or Lohner's fidelity, or Anna's fierceness. Why? Why her?!

The bathroom door swings inward to admit a young pink-haired girl. Their eyes meet before the girl glances away shyly, moving about her business. One of Johnny's, no doubt. Evan almost smiles.

By the time she reemerges, Francis has left. She's not surprised, but this is not the night for that. Speaking now is one of Carter's crew, a mop of raven hair doing nothing to disguise haunted eyes. Then, a lovely Afjan woman is sweetly reminiscing of her time protesting with Johnny. Evan takes this in from her post near the bathroom, needing time to assure herself she won't be returning to a supplicant's pose.

When Juliana sits, Evan finds eyes seeking her out. Reluctance and guilt briefly war in her before pride snuffs them out. They had been her brothers. They deserve more than silence.

"It's hard to have the words." She comes to stand before the bar, Molly behind her. Her gaze sweeps the faces, finding familiar, foreign, and Morgan at the door. "I'm not a poet or a scholar... I'm not much of anything. For as long as I can remember, I've been about smashing into one disaster after the next and finding, in between all that, something to hold on to. I don't know about any of you, but for me life alone is like drowning, you know? We spend so much time underwater, flailing, caught up by the problems before us. The only time you ever get a break is when someone reaches down from above to grab you up so you can suck a moment's air. It's your friends pulling you up. Without Carter and Johnny, I would have drowned a long time ago."

She hardens. "We want to think there's a god because then our loved ones are sheltered in his glow. We want to believe in karma because the good get rewarded and the bad get punished. Where was god when those shots were fired? Where was karma? Where... was I?"

"If there was a god, if there was karma, our friends would be alive tonight and I'd be in their place. There's no karma. We all get dealt a hand: genes, parents, birthplaces. You get your cards and you play them and you hope you win before you lose. Carter, Johnny, you were two of a kind and you were taken. I'm sorry... If people live on in memory, then you'll never die. On that, I give you my vow. I won't forget you... I won't..."

Her face flushing, Evan makes her way to their table, seizes her drink of ashes, and hoists it high. "To the best of us."

"The best of us," they echo back.

And then she is sitting, drinking in the faces of those left behind. And, for one precious night, they drink and talk and commemorate, for they all know it will never be the same: their wounds too fresh, their dreams too varied, and her destiny yet to exact its price. But, for tonight, none of that matters. Tonight there is no tomorrow.

DAY ELEVEN

22

"Where am I?" she asks of the world.

Deja vu's unique disorientation suffuses the Dreamer as she becomes aware of her perch on the clock tower's roof. The blight, having devoured Little Harbor and the commercial wharves, now spreads its malignant fingers into her city's granite limbs. And not for a moment has the infection been checked by anything hurled against it.

Powerful explosions shatter the horizon, launching the tower beneath her into a dance of groaning stone. The fearful millions, who've been reduced by distance to scurrying ants, flee the devastation, their panic worsening the chaotic snarls that already clog the outbound roadways. Not that it matters now; no one still within the city's limits will escape the blight, or its growing dome, upon which she can now make out spitting spires that hum with foul electricity. It's at least 2,000 feet high, its black shoulders taking seconds to smash to rubble what it had taken her civilization a hundred years to plan and create.

The gloomy sky taunts her, challenging her to name the preternatural things that whip past her in the forever night. An impression of great wings, coming straight for her! Her hands rising to protect herself...

"Do you see?"

The voice is familiar to her, the hearing of it nearly causing her to fall from this high perch. She well remembers the ugly thing that threw her to her death the last time she occupied this spot, so, before she turns to confront him, she puts 30 feet of distance between them.

Gone are the casual jeans and sweaters, replaced by a white track suit which is nearly the brightest thing in this soupy darkness. She'd have put him in his late teens but for a trim beard that ages his boyish face. The body can change, but the Contact's hazel eyes will forever remain.

"Do you draw me here?" She's right at the edge now, her right foot flirting with the roof's pebbled cliff. She'll not be trapped, not again, no matter the cost to skin and bone.

"Tonight," her visitor acknowledges, folding his lanky legs to sit next to her upon the edge of the world. "The rest are yours, your mind's interpretation of the consequences of failure. We do not have much time."

"Failure." She returns her eyes to her warring city, marking the fiery flashes of distant gunfire, the burning ships in both ruined harbors. "It's cruel," she judges, her voice hardening. "This is your doing. This is your trick, your dream."

"I cannot be here long," the Visitor repeats, side-stepping her condemnation. "I have limits. With each visit I run the risk of violations. Coming to you in the park alone could have ended our partnership, but I knew the depth of your need. This," he nods at her crumbling reality, "is not something you can quit."

"I decide what I can quit," she whispers. "You have no say in that." He bears no sign of the beating she put on him. Can he even feel pain?

"Stubbornness... No one foresaw the situation with your friends." He grimaces.

"You should have..."

"We've no time for that! I have bought us moments. We must use them."

"What for?"

"You are angry. You have questions. Ask them." Is that desperation in the man's face?

"You'll answer them?"

He nods quickly.

"Okay" she smiles. "Who do you work for?"

At his flinch, she finds herself looming over him, panic forgotten. The hands that reach for him are claws, jerking him to his feet so their eyes can meet, so he can understand what it means to be helpless. For a fleeting instant, she considers shoving him into the black.

"It will change too much of how you will proceed!" Her prisoner pants, his long-fingered hands failing to keep her grip from his throat. "When I said I was your best advocate, I was not lying. This must be preserved... a line must be drawn. And you must draw it."

She feels the truth from him. It earns him a reprieve, for now. "Alright. Why am I drawn to that?" She releases him to point to the bulging blight.

"It is the origin of the crossing and a warning of what comes," he swallows, pained. "Their need is great. They will not stop at taking what is required. Their wells are drying and you are their oasis. When the time comes, you will know where to go and what to do."

"But they've crossed before. They must have. You knew they'd be coming after me. You knew enough to send Morgan. They've been here before."

"They have," he acknowledges, fighting for focus. "It is not... a simple thing to rend reality's curtain. Natural forces keep the reflections from contact. But, there are times when the attraction of energies wins out and a connection is made. Only then can a crossing be tried." His fretful tongue wets dry lips. She's never seen him uncomfortable before. It's oddly gratifying.

"Most of these windows... pass harmlessly. Either their need is insufficient, or the technology is inadequate." Blood appears on his upper lip. "But if someone is sent, well, then there were others, before you, who stood in harm's way and... made the sacrifice. And once the window passes, it is... awhile until orbits will again collide. This is, as you say, the good news."

"The bad?"

"A bridge requires enormous power. But, once it is established, it will be more than fed by that..." He flinches at the distant, black mass. "Allow them a foothold, allow the door to be cracked but an inch and there will be no return."

"So, I'm meant to stop that... from happening? If I'm there, at the right time, if I do what needs to be done, I stop this? I close the window?"

He nods.

"What about the ones who hunt me?" She's merciless. "How do they cross?"

"As a window nears, there are moments of synergy, when all is aligned. It is in these that, at great cost, the briefest of connections can be made. They last all of a few blinks of the eye, but it is enough for someone... to be sent."

"How many..."

The Visitor shakes his head, closes his eyes, his body set to a constant shiver.

"You should have told me this before!" She builds back to simmering anger. "You've left me to question everything I believed in. And all of that because you wouldn't open your damn mouth?!"

"It is not permitted." The voice is sad, the face sagging under some invisible effort. "We are sworn to stand aside. It is free will that is treasured and free will that you have. We... I risk all to contact you. I have no power to control you, to prevent you from telling anyone of these secrets. You can change your world's future with what you know, with what you can do. You could make this... a child's musings." His hand waves at the strife below them. "It is only here, in your mind, that I am free to speak without oversight."

That freedom has clearly come at a price.

"It was easier before," he continues with a groan. "There was a greater ignorance in your world. In the past, the Chosen had faith that we knew of what we spoke, of what we did. Your distrust blocks us from a simple outcome. The more you know, the more you question. I tried to warn him that you would buck, that you needed more. He disagreed, so I took a different road... I am from... I am of your world... I had to act." His face is tortured, muscles contorting under skin tugged taut.

"Are you insane?! There are billions here who believe in gods they have never seen. Why in the name of all that's holy did you pick me if all you needed was faith?"

"You are of... you are of my..." But deep gulps of air are no longer serving him; he raises his hands to cover his spasming face.

Rage and panic flash in her as she seizes her struggling visitor, separating his flailing feet from the ground with the smallest effort. "You're a liar!" Her scream tears the darkness. "You've been lying to me the whole time, telling me what I want to hear, twisting it to take away any fault you may have in this. This is you, your mistakes!"

"I haven't lied," he says with gritted teeth past quivering lips. "You have the strength I said you had." Blood is filling his mouth. "You are... their future."

"No! I won't be done by you any more." She brings the Visitor close, glaring into those pained eyes. "You take this back to your boss. You tell him to go to hell. And you... you can have a head start."

She hurls him into her city, watches his puppet's limbs flap as if he seeks to fly. And then he's gone, leaving her alone on this cold perch.

Destiny...

She's only had a few hours to explore, but already she knows this is a world so incredible, so complex, she will never understand it. The warehouse had been one thing, waking up alive and whole and surrounded by things familiar to her. That she can grasp. But out here, in the rain? In a green world not yet devoured by their unsustainable need? She has to stop every now and again just to gather herself, to let the miracle of it sink in.

If she'd paid attention to her lessons from long ago, perhaps she'd know how they are able to generate enough power to electrify all these monstrous buildings, the thousands of lights that give them life and the countless personal transports that ferry so many people to and from them! It is a hive of activity, a gestalt of personality and innovation, for which a thousand briefings could not have prepared her.

From where she's come, a crowd is fifty people huddled in some room somewhere, being droned at by a company man selling his company line. Standing on one street corner, of which there appear to be a million more like it, she can count fifty people in seconds. How many people live here?! And in just this one... city? How many more people are there, in places like this, exposed to the open sky, with no Force Fives to menace them?

She is no company man to know such things, but she imagines their number, the sum total of her society, to be no more than 50,000. Would they comprise a neighborhood here? Could they come here, settle here, integrate here? Might they even have something to offer? These computerized slates she sees everyone using are hopelessly out of date. In three seconds, she can do more with the implant in her left wrist than they can do in hours with those wastes of plastic they haul about. An exchange, an understanding... but this is not how generals think. And perhaps they'd be right.

She stops in one of the open squares, fishing in her pocket for some of the paper currency they gave her at the warehouse. She stares at the bills, at the stalls, at the entrepreneurial souls who man them. They will take this paper? Overwhelmed by the sheer number of people to navigate, to keep track of, she carefully approaches a stall selling red globes the size of her fist. "Can I have one?" she asks, indicating the reddest of the red.

The plump woman blinks at her uncomprehendingly before her mouth moves, issuing sounds she doesn't understand. Oh, they warned her of this. She is too new to know their tongue. She points to the fruit and the stall's owner puts it in her hand.

Payment now... She hands the woman the topmost bill, watches her eyes widen in shock, but she doesn't wait around to figure out if she's broken some societal more. She takes her fruit and departs, biting into it and discovering it far harder than it looks. But when that tart freshness fills her mouth? When the juice threatens to pour down her chin and over her jacket? She's stunned into weak-kneed stillness as a suspicious wetness stings her eyes. Not even the steak she had prior to leaving can compete with this... this slice of heaven. What kind of life has she lived never to have had this, never to have known such a thing existed?

She does her patrol, eyes sharp for the face she's recognized, the gray-blue eyes that blazed at her from the image they'd seen in the briefing, but she cares more about the fruit that has made her hand sticky. Not even this bothers her, wanting only more, only to go back to the square and buy more things, more treats and just sit down and try them all and decide which ones she loves most and rank them and forget about everything else. She has never been happy before, but this is how she imagines it to feel, as though the world still holds secrets that are worthy of discovery.

Secrets... a world big enough, dynamic enough, rich enough, for secrets. Will her people take these away along with everything else? She's beginning to feel sick, but they told her this might happen. She hurries to find somewhere to unburden her stomach, wondering if she can see this ocean of theirs, if anything can possibly be as large as the numbers claim. But she needn't see an ocean to make up her mind. She knows now what she must do.

The room at the Shanesberry is still dark as Evan bolts up in bed. Deep, gasping breaths are drawn into reluctant lungs as she scrambles from the thrashed sheets and straight into the tiny bathroom. A hand cranks the cold water tap, and sh puts her face in its sobering spray. "Gods..." Her heart thumps to beat the band. The horror mixed with... that woman, that soul as lost as she. So vivid...

They had all stayed at the bar long past midnight, finding security and comfort in a crowd. Before they could leave, a cop had approached their table with good news. They'd made two arrests, including the scum who had done the shootings. Real winners of society too, by the sound of it... And now she's here, coming down off four hours of sleep and no prospect for more and with dreams to digest.

Water drips from her chin as Evan snares a nearby towel. Thinking back to the clock tower, to the Contact, she experiences something like gratitude for the risks he took to tell her as much as he had. Assuming, of course, that these dreams are real and not the morbid musings of her mangled subconscious.

This pull inside her, this force she has to fight to keep from dragging her into Little Harbor, had the Contact told her its purpose? 'You will know where to go and what to do...' As though it senses her thoughts, its grip upon her tightens, spasming inside her, dropping her to her knees. And as she loses her stomach into the toilet, she can only hear its siren's song.

When the world rights itself, Evan heaves herself up and out of the bathroom, dressing in the bulky things she'd borrowed from Morgan. In the dramas, there are rewards for this sort of pain: cool cars, hot girls, some sort of superpower. And she's dressing in another person's clothes, down to the last few credits to her name and totally incapable of holding down anything more substantial than water thanks to this thing inside her. She wishes this was fiction... She nabs her keys from the nightstand, knowing somehow that she'll never return to this place. She doesn't stop for a last look.

Evan cracks the door in time to see her hazy shadow, crouched in the hallway, pop another of her blue disks. While the feline eyes still shine with life, the passage of a week has replaced her intense clarity with naked fatigue and numb emotion. Her pupils are pinpricks centered in orbs of an irritated red. Even as she watches, the drugs engage, relaxing her posture and easing the burden of what must be an immense fatigue. But at what cost? Evan isn't sure when she started to feel pity for this creature, but it's there now, a slow pulse of warmth amidst the pull and her hangover.

"Up and at 'em," she whispers. "Going to work today." Her smile must have in it something of madness because Morgan just crouches there, blinking, until Evan's down the hall and then she's forced to catch up before her charge disappears inside the neglected stairwell.

"The day of bloody reckoning be damn near nigh and you be going to work?" Her guardian's framed by the stairwell door as Evan thumps to the half floor landing. "What the hell you be thinking?"

"It can keep for a few hours." There's a kind of peace in surrendering to insanity. "My big bad wolf... C'mon, give me a ride to the depot."

After everything that's hit her in the last ten days, Evan never expected to feel free on this of all mornings. The storm's about to break over her and she feels like laughing. Has she gone over the edge, or is there simply nothing she can do but stay alive? Until the appointed hour, she has nowhere to be, nothing to do but live. And this is her life. She mounts the Roady behind Morgan, her arms wrapping round her driver as shafts of rosy light lance through heavy cloud. And though the penetration is enough to let them all know night is at an end, a light rain persists. Her throbbing face lifts to the drizzle as they rocket into the city.

"Where the hell have you been?"

Bernard's abundant jowls ripple with fury as Evan strolls into the busy warehouse. It's getting on to seven bells and about ten bleary-eyed employees are loading their morning runs, with their boss' boorishness encouraging them all to hurry. A few give her the cold shoulder, but she deserves it. A rider down, especially one down without explanation, leaves slack the rest must pick up.

"Miss me?" Impish, she crosses to her belligerent employer. The rest she ignores.

"Actually, no," Bernie glowers. "Not since I fired you three days ago." It's a cool morning, yet sweat still streams from his balding dome. Behind a closed mouth, his teeth chomp at his tongue. Of all the nervous tics, it's no surprise the fat man favors the oral.

"Sorry, Bernie. It's been a little..."

"I don't want to hear it," he chuffs. "Everyone else somehow manages to be at work on time. As you are talking, I see that you haven't lost the power of speech. I also see that you are also in possession of two unblemished hands, and two functioning legs. No excuses... Not one call! Not one! That is disrespect. That disrespects me, that disrespects my place, that disrespects everyone who works here. And I just won't stand for it!" His thick arms are crossed in judgment.

"You're right, Bernie. You're right. C'mon." She's smiling in the face of his anger. "This might be the last time we see each other. I'll ride wherever. Put me on the Black Run; I don't care. Don't pay me; I don't care. Just give me something. It's my last day, you know?"

"Your last day is right," Bernie growls. But then he hesitates, eyes narrowed in suspicion. "You're not going to jail, are you?"

"No, I'm not going to jail."

"Not in trouble with the law?"

"Not in trouble with the law..."

"Because you will be, I can tell. You've been trouble ever since I met you." Bernard's piggish nose has stopped flaring and the arms are slowly returning to his sides. "Alright. You're on probation though! And any more screw-ups and you will find my boot up your backside. And, from then on, this door will be closed to you. Am I understood?"

"You're a good man, Bernie." She does her best to hug his startled bulk before fishing out her slate and borrowing a Yager 19-02 from a handful of spares. Her boss is incredulous.

"Another bloody junkie..."

Evan has never been on the 15th floor of Barry Towers, but her morning's first delivery takes her into its plush environs. The floor's humming with corporate activity, employees at toil in their large, glass-walled offices. They're like perfumed drones buzzing through some plush and infinitely complex hive. A bit less death in her life and a bit more focus on school and she might be here, a cog in the great machine of industry, going home to a family, a mortgage, and an auto lease. The air's redolent of expensive coffee.

A grateful executive, blonde curls spilling about dressy shoulders, takes the delivery and eagerly tips Evan $20 before rushing off. She's left to stare at the bill in her hand. A lesser cynic would consider this a promising start to a profitable day. But with her luck?

Her second mission has her across the city, pitching up at the ruddy door of an upper-middle-class residence. The neighborhood's spacious lots are bordered by tall, elegant trees that cast long, discreet shadows. The only signs of disrepute are conspicuous piles of sodden leaves. The season's worth of accumulation makes it clear landscaping is not the owner's first love. She crests the three stone steps to the front door and lays her thumb on the bell.

It's answered by a glowering man who's clearly been burning with anger for some time now. Despite being on the wrong side of forty, he's kept himself fit, but his diligence is all but erased by the gunmetal-colored suit unpleasantly stretched over his stocky frame. His face red with annoyance, he snatches his precious package. "Where the hell have you been?! I ordered this delivered last night. I made arrangements to be here last night. This was to be here last night."

"I'm sorry. It says..."

"I don't care what it says. Why should I care what it says? I care where it was. I care when it arrives. I entered into a contractual relationship with your concern. Angel couriers," he snorts, "I should have known. Tell me, did they wait for you to get clean, or did they recruit you right from the Dust den? Wait here." Disgusted, he spins into his marble foyer, critically examining his property before gingerly setting it upon a waiting table.

Just another scrot, she tells herself as she goes for the thumb imprinter. She'll be gone from here in a moment.

"I think you've damaged it," the man yelps. "Yes..." He wheels back to the door, even more flushed than before. "Careless idiots," he snarls. "You've taught me a lesson, haven't you...? Who's your supervisor?" With spite in his eyes, he ignores the imprinter.

"Bernard Golden. Do what you need to do, sir."

"Are you being flip," he asks sharply. "Are you being flip with me after damaging my property?"

"Nope, wouldn't dare, sir."

"Oh, fine. Just give me the damn..." her peevish client growls and snatches for the thumb imprinter. "Here," he sneers, thrusting the device back at her. "Try flipping burgers. You might have more success."

The perpetually unpleasables... Their misery is the price of doing business. Walking away has always been the best policy. But today? Well, something inside her shifts and, before she knows what she's about, her foot shoots forward to block the scrot from shutting his door on her.

"What the! Get your fu...!"

"Let me give you some advice." Something in her dead eyes or her flat voice silences him. "I've pretty much had the worst week of my entire life. And, believe me, I don't say that lightly. Poking the stick in? Not the best idea when I've got nothing to lose, pal. I have a gun, you know." She smiles at him, almost sweetly. "Do you want me to use it?"

The man takes a step back, his lips wordlessly flapping and his eyes darting here and there. When was the last time anyone challenged him? Long enough ago that he feels entitled to this. She likes the look on his face, the fear, the discomfort.

"Tell you what, friend," her voice takes a sinister drop. "For being such a nice guy, I'll let you in on a little secret." Her boot kisses the door wide open so she can really lean in, really stare at him. "The world's going to end tomorrow. That's right... Word of advice? If you want to keep your testicles, such as they are? Go far, far away."

And then she's hopping down those stone steps and the door behind her is slamming closed with urgency. "And don't shoot your messenger next time! If there is a next time..."

It's quarter of noon when Evan finishes her morning run. Her last client is a lovely woman in her eighties to whom the many years have been kind, her wrinkled visage a map of laughter. Helen has been a frequent patron, owing to a love of all things garden.

"Oh, thank you dear," the well-groomed grandmother beams as Evan hands over the planter-shaped package. "Very kind of you."

"My pleasure," Evan smiles and follows her into her little two bedroom townhouse. They have the routine down. Helen goes for her purse as the courier ducks into her decades old kitchen to pull the old lady's garbage. Deft hands quickly tie the bag as Helen returns with the dollar tip, agreeably pressing her thumb to the imprinter. Evan lacks the heart to educate this creature on inflation.

"How's Timmy and the kids?"

"Oh, wonderful. His youngest is off to college now." The proud grandparent. "Let me try to find a picture."

"Oh, wow, look at that," Evan says when Helen returns with her photograph of a tall youth in his smartest clothes. There's innocence in his clear blue eyes, an absence of a negative. "He's cute. Tell him a girl said that. He'll like that."

"I will. Where are you off to next, honey?"

"I don't know. I really don't know."

"Well, then, thank you."

"You're welcome." Evan hesitates at the door, looking back at this woman who has lived a long, full life. "Good luck, Helen." And she's out the door, trash in hand, back in the world. The door closes behind her as her angry shadow marches up from the street.

23

"What part of this don't you be getting?!"

Morgan's snarl is something to behold, quivering lips drawn back to release gnashing teeth. "Never fitted you for stupid, but your inability to be following the simplest instructions got me wondering. You not be stupid, hmm?! Maybe your mama dropped you on your head when you was small? I want to be hearing the words." Raging, she blocks Evan's path to the road as her hands fly about, now pointing, and now fiddling with her jacket's zippers.

Evan startles backwards, hefting the bag of trash. Had she lost her tail? She'd been so grateful for even a moment's oblivious pleasure that she hadn't thought to check. "I didn't," she starts to apologize.

"I had to be calling Bernard! You didn't be noticing that I wasn't with you for the last hour?! You know, I figured this would be happening at the beginning, you jumping scared, but now?! No one else be knowing where you were! Do you be having any idea..." The eyes are wild with an inhuman rage and panic both. "Twenty-three... Twenty-three... How many killed, for you. Twenty-three, by my hand, for you, dead...all of them...for you."

Evan flinches back. "What are you talking..." and then surprise overwhelms horror, protecting her from this creature's dark deeds.

"Bernard told you where I was?"

"Told him I be a cop..."

"Oh, he'd buy that. He thinks I'm his A1 troublemaker." Unnerved by Morgan's fury, Evan sidesteps her shadow and moves quickly down to the garbage can which is already at the curb. She has the lift up and she's tossing Helen's trash as she feels Morgan coming from behind.

"He and me both."

Behind her, a growl, a scuff of boots... Evan comes round to find Morgan looming over her, only a foot away, burning even hotter than before. Gods! Evan retreats.

"We be so close to the end of this, for bad or good. And still you be yanking my chain! You win, okay? You win... I surrender, I give up. You be the top dog. What do you want me to say, huh? What?!"

"You need to calm down," Evan breathes up at her shadow.

"I don't need to be calming down! Do you be knowing what I done for you? Do you be having any idea what I done for you?!" Morgan's screaming now, spit dampening Evan's cheek.

Traffic is surprisingly brisk along a street zoned residential, but the cars, and their oblivious drivers, move along far too quickly to witness this. That burden falls to the few pedestrians out and about, a handful of elderly residents walking their equally ancient dogs. Morgan's Roady is only a few feet away, but Morgan is freaking Evan out so much right now she'd not have hopped aboard if it was the only way out of here.

"Look," Evan tries for conciliatory. "I wasn't trying to lose you. I just lost..."

"You just. You always just... You always be having a reason. You always be having something to say! Here's what I say. Just don't be doing it!"

"You are so out of control right now," Evan looks up into that pale, sweating face. "Do you even know where you are?" Pupils like pinpricks... And *she's* irresponsible?! Getting quickly around her shadow, she hustles up the drive to fetch her Yager. Her boot lashes up the kickstand as she swings round and wheels her substitute ride back down the driveway. Where does this junkie get off?

"Tell me something." Her worry is evaporating in the furnace of her anger. She's had enough today. "Where'd they find you, pill-popper? Was it the school of washed up mercs? They bring your sorry ass out of retirement? Broken down soldier fights for the few scraps left to her because the young took the rest? Don't you yell at me, you sad sack of shit!"

That does it. Her eyes incandescent, Morgan is ready for war, gloved fists cocked to fire. But Evan's tired of showing weakness, tired of holding back, tired of trying to do the right thing and it never working out. She glares Morgan on.

They simultaneously notice the Garibaldi.

It's the powerful engine's fevered pitch that does it, a fury that propels the wide-bodied luxury car ahead at speeds that laugh at residential limits. What begins as a blur of silver in Evan's peripheral vision rapidly resolves into two men, both up front, in a heavy car with only one intent, written into the pale features of its driver with his expression fixed in devout concentration. Forty-five hundred pounds of metal and rubber veers from the road, powering straight for her.

In the scant seconds from appearance to impact, her thoughts tumble. Is this how it had been for Carter and Johnny, a paralyzed observer in a moment of disbelief? Will her unkind words to Morgan be the last they'll ever share? From where she's come... to have it snatched away now...

And then she's flying! The world spins as she crashes to earth! Pain explodes through her back, lancing her chest as she slams down onto the sidewalk and bounces into the street. A moment of bright-white shock and then she's shaking, her hands scrabbling down her body, searching for... No mangled legs, no gushing wounds. Evan's frantic eyes lift from her split second examination to find answers.

The car has effortlessly bested the curb and has, in one try, mostly demolished Helen's hedgerow and the garden behind it. The machine screams as the driver tries hitting reverse, knowing his mission is incomplete.

Morgan! Her scrambled mind pulls together, remembering hands upon her, hands that hurled her clear! But at what cost?!

Morgan's powerful body crunches down on the Garibaldi's roof with enough force to halfway cave it in. And now the memory is bobbing up to Evan, the sound of the Garibaldi's grill catching Morgan flush, pinwheeling her into the air. A sacrifice...

Morgan's momentum is too great to keep her on the car's roof. It propels her into a half bouncing, half slithering, dismount onto the trunk where she seems to balance perfectly for one, frozen moment. And then down onto the sidewalk, hitting hard, and then rolling to her final resting place, with Evan, in the street.

"Morgan!"

Blood is everywhere, welling up through jeans shredded in countless places. Her leather jacket hides the damage done to her torso, but her face... The Garibaldi has made Morgan a malformed puppet, her strings cruelly slashed. Something builds within Evan then, a coalescing of emotion that bursts from her mouth in a scream she cannot hear.

Reverse has only spun the Garibaldi's tires uselessly, so the driver yanks the balking vehicle into drive and plows forward, obliterating what remains of Helen's garden. A running start at reverse is his only hope of getting clear.

And he's coming now, accelerating fast, spraying pulped plants into the air as the car launches itself backwards. He's bulling straight for Morgan with enough weight to crush her.

Evan has managed to roll over and is just now climbing to her feet as the shooting starts. Morgan's bloody hands clutch her strange, black weapon and, for a precious moment of sublime focus, they are rock steady. Despite the blood streaming from her shadow's face, Evan can see her lethal concentration, her feline eyes narrowed into slits of green ice.

Exploding glass razors the air as the back windshield shatters under the first two blows from her hammer. The third executes the driver who's thrown with such force upon the steering wheel that he sticks there, crucified while he burns. The passenger doesn't wait for the fourth shot, hitting the door release and flinging himself from the car-cum-deathtrap.

But the fat mouth of Morgan's gun is undeterred, tracking and finding the target... Firing!

Evan's crawled halfway to her fallen companion when the passenger's chest bursts, his scream all too brief. Gods! She doesn't hear herself whimpering as she fetches up next to Morgan, a wounded lioness who growls as she passes her gun into her right hand, her left feeling for injuries they both know will be there.

Crunched head on by a speeding car... her legs are surely broken. Ugly lacerations to shin and thigh leave Morgan wearing more blood than denim. Had the Garibaldi's roof been any kinder to her ribs than its grill has been to her legs? The memory of that careening, bouncing impact will haunt her.

"This isn't happening. This isn't..."

"Don't," Morgan spits blood from her mouth, her slippery hand grabbing Evan's wrist, yanking at it, yanking her back to the here and now. Her eyes are full with purpose and pain as sweat streams down into the blood rivers crisscrossing her face. "No time." Gusts of air escape her nose as her mouth hardens against the pain. "The car..."

"What?"

"The car!"

Understanding, Evan gets to her feet and hobbles to the driver's side and, bracing herself, hauls open the undamaged door. She gags at the gruesome interior, hot blood oozing onto her skin as she yanks the still-smoking body clear, tumbling it upon Helen's ruined lawn. She looks down at herself, at hands running red, and hears the pounding in her skull.

Cars have stopped and now frightened bystanders are emerging from what little cover they found in the chaos. No time!

Back for her wounded shadow, kneeling so Morgan can sling an arm about Evan's neck. Then up, thrusting hard, to their feet and shambling to the passenger's side door, every second a painful eternity.

Every step, every contracting muscle, should be cause for screams, but Morgan's stubborn jaw stays clenched. She refuses to yield to her body's weakness. Wedging her into the open door, down into the seat and... in!

Slamming the door, Evan hurriedly hops to the driver's side and collapses into a seat of melted leather. Have to get out! No time for their abandoned bikes. No time for prayers either. The Garibaldi's still in reverse, so she finishes what the dead driver started, lurching the car from grass to sidewalk and then bumping down onto blessedly solid road. Drive... She rams the bulky shifter forward as Morgan lets out her first groan. Evan slams the gas, and they are out of there, escaping into afternoon.

"Slow down..."

It's been years since Evan's been behind the wheel, but it's her speed, not her rusty driving, that worries her passenger. Alone, the battered Garibaldi would've drawn unwanted attention. But shooting through traffic at top speed? That'll definitely bring the law. As red flags go, it's right up there with daylight shootouts on residential streets!

"We need to ditch the car." Morgan needs both of her broken hands to fish out the pulverized pill bottle from her coat. When she finally gets the twisted top free, a single pill falls into her bloody hand. The rest is half powdered fragments awash in broken plastic. But Morgan doesn't even hesitate, the blue disc disappears between quivering lips, swallowed down by a dry and hungry throat. Only then does she bother to brush away the useless remains.

"What?!"

"Ditch the car! We need to ditch the car!"

"How?!"

"Pull over, in an alley somewhere. We'll walk."

"Walk? You want to walk?!" Tears sting Evan's eyes. "You can't even..."

"Slow down!"

"Fine." Evan complies as it begins to rain, windshield wipers coming on automatically as she reaches for her slate. Seemingly undamaged by the fracas, it beeps sluggishly to life. Thank the Savior! She punches for Zia.

"Evan?" Four rings have never taken so long.

"Zia! Bless you. I'm in a spot." Evan turns left, heading north for the nearest commercial district. The more people the better. "I need you, uh... I need you to pick me up. Is your car still insured?"

A weary silence travels down the invisible line. "Yeah... Evan..." A pause. "Not so much with the patience for this right now, so this better be good."

"This is no joke, Zia!"

"Okay, where do you need me?"

Two blocks south of the Wakefield market, Evan guides the disfigured Garibaldi into its new home. The cold, wet alley, which has already taken in a repellent dumpster, gang-tagged walls, and two wary bums, is as good a place as any to abandon a marked car. Killing the engine, Evan turns to check on Morgan, finding the mercenary performing a battlefield self-examination. The stim has numbed her enough that she can push her long fingers bravely through inches-long gashes at thigh, knee, and shin with little more than a flinch.

"Ohhh, I'm gonna throw up," Evan groans. She pops her door wide and thrusts her shaking body into the alley. Her clothes are marred by the blood of a man who'd done his best to kill her, but this means nothing to the two shabby urchins who slowly approach. Dust, and probably drugs far worse have done a number on both men. Neither seems even peripherally aware of the rain that washes down on them. They are moths drawn to the flame of an easy score.

"Keys are in the ignition," Evan declares, retreating to the rear bumper and skirting it to come up alongside Morgan's door which has already been opened. Her gun, seized by a stim-steadied hand, stays below the level of the dash, ready to lift and fire at the smallest twitch. "Give us a couple of minutes and she's all yours, guys, no charge." Evan gives a nervous smile...

The two junkies exchange glances. A moment passes and then they are nodding, withdrawing a few steps, neither taking their eyes from their windfall.

Just getting Morgan out of the car and onto her feet is enough to make Evan wince. Even through the painkiller, her shadow's face is a sweat-soaked mask of stress. If Evan looks down, will she see broken legs? No, don't... There's no way she can stomach the answer. Instead, she bends her knees, slipping Morgan's right arm around her shoulders. She straightens to take the wounded woman's weight and... damn!

But they don't have far to go, 20 feet to the mouth of the alley, charge supporting guardian this time while that gun remains ready and willing to defend her in a left hand of iron. As it's ever been...

The ten minutes they wait for Zia seems an eternity. Then the late-model, maroon Lustro is rolling silently up their street. Zia has only kept the four-door hatchback for the odd journey out of the city, or for those rare occasions a bike doesn't suit. Thank the Savior for that because Evan doubts she's ever seen anything so beautiful.

Sighting them, Zia's quickly out of the car, her blue eyes wide with concern. "What hap..." But it'll keep. She cracks the rear door, driver's side, and helps Evan gently maneuver Morgan across the backseat. "Save us," their rescuer gasps, staring at the carnage. "We need to get her to a hospital, Ev. This is..."

A mangled hand shoots out to snatch at Evan's forearm. "No hospitals," the broken thing snarls, eyes dull in spite of the fresh stim. She's so far gone even drugs fail to keep her battered body numb.

The two friends exchange worried looks. Evan's at a loss while Zia keeps glancing in at Morgan who, despite being prone, is just as resolute.

"Okay, my place then." Zia's magenta hair seems to blaze her agitation as she slams Morgan's door and slithers into the driver's seat. Evan quickly limps round to join her and they are off as silently as the car had come.

"We shouldn't stay."

Of all her friends' homes, Zia's has easily the best view. The westerly-exposed apartment is situated on the top floor of a ten-story building, its red brick facade showing nowhere near the age of buildings not a block away. Leonard Avenue delineates the profitable and glamorous waterfront from the shabby and industrial Little Harbor. This is where elegant steakhouses reluctantly shake hands with squalid diners, where $300-a-top clothing boutiques barely tolerate ratty department stores.

Zia has often expressed her love for this place, pointing out how perfectly positioned it is to observe the different socioeconomic strata of society. The girl is sitting on a nearly unobstructed view of the ocean, glimmering not a couple leagues distant, and she wants to look at how the gentry interact with the homeless? Screw strata...

No time for admiring the view now. Evan supports Morgan in through the building's rear entry. Then they're down the impossibly long hallway to the lobby, hooking a right into the elevator whose doors quickly close.

"I can walk," Morgan growls, but in truth she's managing to do little more than cling to Evan's neck. Frustration is mounting within the warrior, but none of them have time for pride now. No time for Evan's fear of elevators either.

And yet it jumps out of the dark to seize her the moment the cage lurches into motion. Evan keeps her eyes focused on her boots, her bloody boots, the brown carpet beneath them, Morgan needing her to stay upright, the Contact needing her to stay alive, anything to stave off the sense that any second now...

Out onto Zia's floor and quickly into her welcoming apartment, where the warm hues of wall and carpet and the spaciousness of simply-configured rooms are trappings for a theater of light. They both aid Morgan into the bathroom.

"We really need a doctor," Zia frowns, glancing between the stranger, stranded upon her lidded toilet, and the friend, who leans on the vanity to relieve her burning thighs.

"I can manage," Morgan grunts, taking a few preparatory breaths. "This ain't my first time at the dance..."

"Yeah?"

"You don't be having stims, do you?"

"What do you think?"

"Didn't be thinking so."

Painfully, the wounded soldier wriggles free of her dirty leather jacket, then the stained top beneath. The leather had spared most of her upper body from lacerations, but leather's no protection from the blunt laws of physics. Blotches of angry purple bruising have already begun their march up and down her right side, as though god's hand had tried to crush her. So Evan adds broken ribs to a list of fractures which include her right wrist and at least four fingers, three on the right hand. How in the world she'd held the gun for even a moment... And the way she's hunching her left shoulder? And none of this accounts for the legs which... Evan looks away.

"The old fashioned way then..." Zia cracks the medicine cabinet, ready to get to work.

It takes hours for them to put Morgan back together again. Pints of blood had temporarily glued the rent jeans to her legs, forcing them to scissor them off in stages. The ribs are wrapped, the finger bones set, and the lacerations cleaned and disinfected by an agonizing stay in the bathtub for which Morgan had needed the sleeve of her jacket to bite down on to stop from screaming. The left ankle is sprained; both feet are black and blue. And half her lower body will be covered in bandages for a month. And yet Evan's left wondering how it isn't worse...

And when the cleaning's done, they use up Zia's emergency first aid kit in the dressing up of all those cuts. Morgan growls through the pain as she stiffly stitches each prior to its being bandaged, a gruesome task her nurses haven't the will to watch.

"How you're not cut in half..." Evan shakes her head as they gently settle their patient on the living room couch. "You must have been in the air when the car hit you. If your feet had been planted on the ground." She winces. "If I had your luck, huh?"

"Not so much," Morgan grunts, worrying at her bothersome shoulder. "Good money be saying I led them right to you. I call Bernard, I track you down. Should have seen them. I should." Her head gives a slow, disgusted shake. "Be figuring on them following the old patterns. But they be smart too. They be adapting. Damn it. I... be better than that."

"You're exhausted. And you are better..." Evan stands just off the arm of the green cloth couch, fingers toying at the flowery, blue stitching. "Been about the eighteenth time you've saved my ass since you showed up. Planet's gonna have to get together and give you a medal or something." The angry, awful things she'd said...

"Evan." Zia hands Morgan a glass of amber fetched from the kitchen. "Drink that," she orders Morgan. "You, come with me." And her tattooed friend is dragging her into the guest bedroom's relative privacy.

In this cramped room, a double bed, sheeted in grays and blues sits upon the thick pile of a carpet so dark as to be black. A heavy wooden dresser and a small nightstand crowd the bed, their rustic hues visible against the stone-colored walls.

"What the hell is going on?" Zia doesn't take her eyes off Evan as she punches the door closed, her aggressive stance brooking no more evasions. "And don't give me some lame story either. This is more than today. This has been going on for a couple of weeks now: the fire, the guy in your place, that lupa out there that we know nothing about. And I see you... I see how it's swallowing you. We've known each other a long time, but I look at you, and I don't see who I used to see."

Evan perches on the foot of the bed, patterned blue stark against the dirty black of her borrowed sweatshirt. It's already been a long day and it isn't yet two-thirds done. Wearily, she takes her first deep breath in hours, arming herself for a conversation she can no longer put off. The distant sound of rain on the window...

"I get that it's rough," Zia softens. The mattress beneath Evan shifts, absorbing Zia's weight. "And I won't deny that I'm freaked out. Whatever happened today, it made mincemeat out of whoever's on my couch. And I didn't think getting hit by a bus would stop her, but..."

"There've been... there've been more attacks, on me."

"Damn it, Evan. How many more?"

"A few," Evan whispers. "I don't know. I wake up and I see blood sometimes. I think... Morgan has been protecting me without telling me about it. Then, today..."

"Evan, why didn't you go to the police?!" Zia interrupts, shaking her head angrily. "Go on, today?"

"A guy... two guys... they tried to run me down with a car. We were fighting, me and Morgan were fighting. I said some things to her and... she pushed me... she pushed me away. She took the hit." She stares at the wallpaper's stone canvas. "They won't stop. They won't stop until they have what they want." Her voice is a rasping whisper.

"Do you know why?"

Evan steadies herself within the sanctuary of this clean, dark room. She will regret this, her selfishness, but she has no choice now. The Pull is her only healthy ally and it can only tell her where and maybe how. It can't comfort her; it can't be there for her at the end. Swallowing hard, she meets Zia's eyes and lets it all go, confessing all of it, from that first night in the apartment, to the dreams, to the Contact, to the destiny, to the gut-twisting compulsion to get up from this bed and walk into Little Harbor. These are the ashes of a life.

It takes time for Zia to cycle through shock, disbelief, and denial. But when anger comes, it sparks her blue eyes and launches her to her feet. "Evan." She is pacing, mouth stretched into a thin, grim line. "Did... Tell me... Johnny and Carter... Tell me none of this... Evan, look me in the eye and tell me they weren't caught up in this, Evan. Tell me..."

Zia has her answer when Evan can't bring herself to look up from the carpet. When she does speak, her voice is a child's whisper. "He says no. He says it was... wrong place, wrong time. But I... I..."

"Evan, you... Look at me! You..."

"It didn't." They both startle, Evan looks up, and Zia spins round to find Morgan darkening the bedroom doorway, her good shoulder leaning against the frame as she fixes Zia with her conviction. "It didn't be having anything to do with Evan. Evan be nowhere around when it happened. And didn't your cop be saying they caught them? Lowlifes?" Pride is keeping her upright.

Zia grunts. "I don't know what to believe anymore." She whirls back to Evan now, ice in her eyes. "Except that... this. This, all of this, has been about you, somehow. I feel it. I knew it from the day this started. This has all been about you. Nobody gets the benefit of the doubt now, not from me. Our friends, Evan. Your family..." But as much as Evan wishes she would, Zia can't drive the knife fully home, managing only to lift her furious hands to rub at her face.

"You're right," Evan whispers. "You're right. I feel it too." She finally looks up, meeting Zia's dismay and Morgan's discomfort with shamed determination. Forcing herself to her feet, she stabs a finger into her gut. "I feel it right here, pulling on me, demanding... things of me. I don't know what it means, or what we'll have to do. But you're right. I... I owe it to Johnny's mom and to Anna and Lohner and you and... and Francis. I owe it to you."

The three stand quietly then, not knowing what else to say. An afflicted Morgan gazes at Evan with something like pride. Has she earned that? Speaking the words and backing them up with actions are galaxies apart.

With something between a growl and a sigh, Zia turns for the door. "I'm going for a walk." She barely gives Morgan time to swing herself out of the way before she's striding into the living room and sweeping on her jacket. "Be here when I get back. I need to clear my head." She shoots Evan a furious look, all sparks of blue lightning. "Who the fuck are you?" And then the front door is slamming in her wake.

For eleven days, she's struggled with that very question. Had some greater force intended this all along, or had she hit on all seven numbers of the interstellar lottery of bad fortune? If so, is it the body or the soul that's marked? She shivers as she helps a sweating Morgan back to the couch; sitting with her while the world darkens.

Not for a moment have the gray skies abated.

Zia will find no clarity out there, Evan decides as she artlessly slaps together two meager sandwiches. Had cooking been a requirement for this job of hers, she'd have surely been passed over. Bleu cheese and ham on some kind of no-carb bread constitutes dinner; that and some manner of pickle. She sets Morgan's down next to her before carrying hers to the French doors, looking out.

The pleasant morning is only a distant memory behind this driving cloudburst that grays out all but the grandest of the city's features. The ocean, what little of it she can see, is angry, its unrelenting chop lashing those foolish enough to enter its domain.

They've been quiet for awhile now, each to their own musings. Evan's tried to fix her mind to what's coming, but that only reminds her of the Pull which makes her want to throw up. So she releases her thoughts, watching as they wander right back to Helen's driveway, replaying all of it from the screaming Garibaldi to her broken protector cartwheeling through the air...

She's lost so much in the last few years, she figured herself immune to the hollow hurt it leaves inside, deep down, where it can't be filled up. But then she thinks of Morgan, and she thinks of the ring on Anna's finger and there it is, her old malignant friend, coring out her insides. She tries to shake it off.

"Are you ever going to tell me how you met him?"

Her injured shadow is managing well enough with dinner, but then it'd take more than broken fingers to make her ask for help from anyone.

"Probably not." Morgan's smile is the first in a long while. "Be ancient history."

"I'd like to know." Evan puts her back to the ugliness outside. "It creeps me out that he knows things no one else knows. I guess I haven't really wanted to look that in the eye. Afraid of the answer, you know?"

"He be good at that."

"What?"

"Making you afraid." Morgan awkwardly devours the last bit of her sandwich, and not a single complaint throughout for the meagerness of Evan's cooking. "He paid me to kill someone."

"What?"

"How I be meeting him... he paid me to kill someone."

Evan flinches.

"What? You expecting it to be another way?" Morgan smiles through the bandages. "Ten years ago now, one of the early continental summits. High level... allowing new member states, adoption of common currencies. It be that sorta thing. Water?"

Evan is more than happy to escape those merciless eyes, coming off the window and walking into Zia's kitchen to oblige.

"I be in a bar, waiting for a mark when he comes in. I don't be giving him much mind until he be sitting himself down next to me. He don't once look at me, not at first, but there be something about him, something that be making me think he lives in my world. 'You're waiting for someone.' And then he does look at me, with those eyes. 'That,' he says, 'is unimportant, petty.' And I be ready to leave my drink and walk away from this crazy when he pulling out an envelope and handing it to me, heavy. 'A down-payment,' he says, 'on our future.' And he be standing and walking away."

"How did you know...?" Curiosity gets the better of Evan as she returns from the kitchen. "How did you know what he wanted?"

"Note inside," Morgan chuckles, accepting the glass of water. "Instructions, directions, times, everything I be needing."

"Who was it?" Evan can't help herself.

"An ambassador, Carmaho's ambassador."

"What?! What was an ambassador for a dictator doing at a confederation meeting? That was half the reason for the Union of States, to protect against people like him!"

"Well, don't you be a student of history. Johnny be telling you that?"

Evan flushes.

"Mmm. Anyway, there be a year's wages in that envelope. So I did it. I found him and I did him."

Evan has to look away.

"As for the why, that got outed later. Blackmail, the ambassador on at least three of the representatives there. He only needed one more on board to vote Carmaho a seat at the negotiations."

"They would never have let him in. He could've talked 'til he was blue in the face. With his record? No way."

"Not the point. Sometimes, it be enough to seem acceptable, to seem reasonable, to talk your way into grace. It don't be mattering how you are; it be mattering what you be to other people."

Well, then... I guess you did a good thing, assuming you're telling me the truth."

"Maybe." Morgan finds two herbals left in a crumpled pack that somehow survived the crash when the bottle of stims did not. She stares at them mournfully. "But you see, each time you be doing something like that, each time you be taking a life, you be making a choice." Morgan looks up at her, the meditations of a reaper swirling in those green irises. "You be picking a winner and a loser. There be no good or bad, light or dark. There just be choices. Choices we make."

It's strange, but Evan is heartened by this confession, this acknowledgment of the difficulties of Morgan's world. Maybe she doesn't take it so lightly after all, all the death in the name of necessity and, before that, fortune.

"You were there, at the conference, to kill someone else right? Before you met..."

Morgan nods.

"How do you do it? How can you..." Evan blows out a breath. "I just... I can't imagine living a life like that, making those choices, deciding who gets to live and who gets to..." She trails off, chilled.

"Die? You will," Morgan smiles. "We all be called upon to do things at one point or another in the journey. Sometimes, you be lucky and those choices wait for you, down the line, when you be ready for them. For me, those choices were on me when I was... well... they be on me when I was young. And so it never bothered me much. You, those choices come to you late. And so you don't think that you deserve to be able to choose for others. You don't think it be fair. Nothing be fair."

"I guess you're right." Evan perches on the arm of the couch next to Morgan, staring down at the wounds earned in her defense. "I'm... sorry. I'm sorry you were... hurt. I mean, thank..."

"My turn," her shadow cuts her off, unable to tolerate sympathy. "Where you be meeting Francis?"

"That's out of nowhere," Evan blinks. "College, quad I think. Why?"

She shrugs and looks away. "Just be reminding me of someone is all."

"You know something about that, don't you?" Evan breathes.

But before she can get an answer to a question she'd rather remain a mystery, there's a sound at the door. Mangled hands or not, Morgan fumbles her gun out and into readiness, bracing it on her knee, as they both hear the turning of the lock. The door swinging inward... magenta hair poking out of a wet hood... Morgan relaxing...

Zia pulls off her windbreaker and hangs it up, saying nothing to her guests as she secures all three locks on her door. Little Harbor is only a block away. Water is dripping from her matted hair as she steps into her living room, taking in both expectant faces. She just looks at them, long enough for a little halo of water to accumulate around her feet.

"I don't know what your deal is, Evan, I don't. A story like yours," her head gives an incredulous toss, "I should kiss you and me goodbye and have you locked up. But, I do know you, don't I? Too many years, too many scrapes, too many nights on the other's couch..." She pauses, composing herself. "I've lost too much this week. We've all lost too much. I'm not losing you too..."

Zia paces to the window, staring out at the ugly wet that had so recently enshrouded her. "Those of us who... believe in something more, something divine, we should have it easy when it comes to matters of faith. After all, that is the essence of the thing, be we believers in just some force, like I am, or be we believers in a god like Carter's. We have faith. We believe that faith will be confirmed, at some undefined date in the future. Then you come along, and you tell your tale, your unbelievable tale, with everything riding on the balance, a test of faith if I've ever heard one. And what do I do? I question, I wonder, I doubt. I have no faith."

She turns back to them. "But that's the thing, isn't it? We don't believe in a divine we expect to meet tomorrow. We don't believe in a divine we expect to see around us. In fact, if we saw his work, we wouldn't believe it at all. Why? Because Miracles can be questioned. Miracles can be debated. Miracles can be doubted. Faith is belief in a thing that cannot be proven. But it's more than that. People have faith precisely because no one can ever take it away from them, from us. No one can ever disprove it. We believe in it because it is ours; it is inviolate.

"I realized that out there, you know why? Because 95 percent of me is saying, 'Zia, you have nearly 30 years of life experiences telling you that your best friend is nuts, or high.' That's my rational side. My other side? My faith side? All it's got, its five percent, is a feeling, a feeling that, somehow, I've always been expecting this. Since the first day I met you... I knew you were a runner: never accepted, never happy, never comfortable. Five percent, if that, and the rest of me saying 'you're a fool, Zia' but I don't care. If I don't stand with you now, then what's the point of any of it? What's the point of loyalty, of friendship? What's the point of faith? I love you like a sister, Ev. It's time to stop running."

And so they are three. Evan rises from the couch's arm and moves to her friend, embracing her hard. They are three and she is not alone. They know her secrets and she is not alone. Eventually, they pull back, Evan gazing into Zia's shining eyes.

"I checked the news on my way back," Zia sobers, forcing her voice to steady. "They're reporting your dust up, shots fired, two bodies. No descriptions, yet, but there were witnesses, cameras. They'll be wanting answers."

"The Shanesberry," Morgan insists as she begins to struggle to her feet. They'd replaced her ruined jeans with a pair of Zia's baggiest sweatpants as to not disturb the bandages. A sleek blue top, also pilfered, fits tightly beneath the passably cleaned leather jacket. Not even a car can separate Morgan from this, her most treasured possession, for more than an hour.

"The safest place," Evan agrees, pulling back from her friend. "There, I'm Jane Ditherington. No one cares about her."

Zia shakes her head. "It's ugly as sin out there and we need to do some planning, some talking. Stay here. People in this building are good about security. Besides, your friend there couldn't make it as far as the table if prime rib was waiting for her."

Morgan can't hide her wounded pride. "I'm fine," she growls as she uses both bandaged hands on the couch's arm to keep her weight off her battered legs. "I can make it..."

Zia snorts. "Morgan we'll put up in the guest room. Ev, seeing as how you've landed us in this mess, you get the couch." She fetches a blanket which, for tonight, will be Evan's duvet. "I'm going to bed. I only do Armageddon on a full night's sleep."

Together, they maneuver a stubborn Morgan into the guest room where, at her nod, Zia withdraws. Wounded pride or no, dignity demands she soldier on alone, no matter its cost to her in pain and damage. Evan lingers, watching her injured shadow fail to get comfortable upon an unfamiliar bed. Has she slept since they met?

"I be good," Morgan declares. "Just going to rest here a minute and... I be good. You can be going now."

Kicking the bedroom door with her heel, Evan pads to the bedside, looking down on this now familiar face: tensed, scraped, bruised. In these final hours, she has so many questions, questions that will never have answers. "You should sleep, not just rest," she whispers. "You've more than earned it."

"Never gone this long on stims before," Morgan acknowledges, shivering. "Wearin' off... gonna be needing more..."

"Forget the pills." Evan's knee presses into the mattress, her hand encircling one wrapped wrist.

"Can't be forgetting the pills. Keep you awake, dull down the pain. Let you focus..."

"Yeah? And what price do you pay when you come off them? What about that?"

Morgan grits her teeth, trying to pull her captured hand free of Evan's gentle grip. "It don't be mattering. And anyway, you've been hating me this far. Don't be starting in on the worry now. I'll be mending, pull my weight. I got a reputation to protect."

"Only superheroes heal that fast," Evan smiles through the tough talk. "Are you a superhero, Morgan?"

A chuckle is her only reward. Morgan looks away. "Superheroes don't get hit..."

"Look at me." Feeling herself opening up in ways she hasn't felt since before she was alone, Evan waits for her shadow's eyes to find her, feline, green, and loyal. Why does it take so long to realize such simple truths? "I know how I got here. I know who I owe for that. I know how much of a pain I've been. I'd be... grateful... if you'd chalk it up to a normal girl gone mad thanks to, well, you know. I'm sorry. Let me..."

Shutting the bedside lamp allows night to unfurl from the corners of the room. Evan reaches into the darkness to pull at her warrior's armor, deftly avoiding the wounded hands that try to keep her from the zippers, buttons, clasps. Tonight, no is not the answer to any question.

"Last night on Earth." Evan's whisper is a thread through the black as the leather jacket comes away, heavy with the bulk of many weapons: the gun, a knife, other things she can't possibly name in the dark. She drapes it over a chair.

Morgan's discomfort throbs between them as a rough hand catches Evan's wrist as she returns for her shadow's shirt. Those eyes, staring up from clean sheets, asking questions her mouth cannot form.

"It's okay," Evan says.

Morgan hesitates. And then her hand relents. Stripped of weapon and cape, she seems smaller somehow, softer, though there are still signs of war. Two long and ugly scars amidst a field of nicks undulate along her chest and belly, flesh a cruel and twisted pink where visible between the many, many bandages. Evan is staring at a canvas of battles fought and won, wars passed into memories. Her fingers hold the sweetness of a nurse's touch as they trace those old wounds.

Then it's Evan's turn to slough her second skin. The hoodie finds a home atop the leather coat, her sweatpants pooling in a corner. She slithers beneath that cool comforter, not much between them now but sweat. The simple, soothing warmth of another's nearness... She'd forgotten how amazing that could feel.

Their eyes exchange years in these quiet moments, two burdened souls searching out a piece of perfect in a world that gives them no control. Trembling with the beginnings of the comedown, a muscled arm slithers under Evan's neck, drawing her to a shoulder scored by circular scars.

"I was so harsh," she starts, smelling the balms she and Zia had used to clean all these cuts. "I said things I..."

An unbroken finger goes over her mouth, silencing her. "Shh. I know..."

"I shouldn't have..."

"Shhhh."

"I just wish..."

"I know. I know."

And then Morgan begins to shudder, her face turned away. The drugs, that perfect, painless crutch, are leaving her now and there's nothing for it but to hold on, to wrap her arms around her shadow and, in the shared darkness, remind her of what this is all for.

DAY TWELVE

24

Desolation.

From where the Chosen huddles next to an abandoned pickup truck, it's all she can see of the world. The sky she knew has been stolen, its replacement a canopy of infinite black that spoils her celestial memories.

Her city has fared no better. Lines of destructive force, radiating from the epicenters of countless explosions, have opened cavernous cracks in the earth, mouths that have sucked down sidewalks and lampposts, cars and storefronts, until even they can eat no more.

She comes to herself crouched behind one of the few abandoned cars that have been spared the chaos. From the clock tower, it had been so easy to distance herself from the horror. But down here, in the trenches, there's no escaping the fallout: gaping craters in the sides of blasted buildings, shadow-shrouded bodies spilling from the battlegrounds of alleys abandoned by light, the flotsam of daily life drifting on a sea of crippled Conplast.

Seeing no threat, the Chosen quits her shelter and, obeying some impulse she cannot name, pushes up towards the nearest intersection – '12th and Paradiso' reads the blackened, twisted street sign. Her feet turn her right, taking her down a familiar throughway.

She knows this street. The last time she'd been here, a million faceless demons cornered her and tore her apart at the threshold of...

Yes, coming up on it now, working her way through the rubble to... the factory, its filthy brick shoulders rise, untouched, out of the destruction surrounding it. This sepulchral place is the source of what draws her, its gravity slamming her down to hands and knees. Her palms scrape along the broken road, opening cuts she can neither prevent nor feel.

When she looks away from that place, the heaviness eases up on her bones. Why? Has she removed herself from its notice? Surely, they know she is here. She sees no one, yet she knows that, from every vacant window, every pile of debris, every haunted alley, she is being watched.

Fresh combat cracks the silence, sending her skittering for cover in an alley not twenty feet hence. Whatever dangers linger there, she'll risk. The alternative is being trampled by a ragtag group of fleeing soldiers who fly past her now, outnumbered and outpaced by a throng of faceless enemies on the hunt. She shivers, remembering.

It's so futile. From her hiding place, she snatches glimpses of human faces straining to survive. But though they are armed with gun and bullet, their fire is fruitless. A soldier will spin around and let off a burst into the enemy and perhaps he'll even have the satisfaction of watching one or two of them fall. But when other nightmares take their place, filling up the gaps as effortlessly as if they were ghosts? Then his hope is crushed and he can only run for his soul.

A hand catches her shoulder, yanking her deeper into the black. Her mouth opens for a reflexive scream which dies in her throat when she sees the hazel eyes, the unscarred face. The Visitor bears no sign of harm, not from the beating she put on him, not even from being thrown from the clock tower, to be sacrificed on her city's spires.

"You should not be here!"

The Chosen jerks herself free, escaping into a crouch against the alley's far wall. "I thought you brought me here..."

The Contact shakes his head, keeping his intent eyes fixed upon her. "You came of your own accord." That seems to both impress and annoy him. "You must go. It is not safe."

"There are things I have to know." She's resolute. "Tell me what you are. Tell me what I am. Tell me how to win."

He grimaces. "I have done all I can. To do more would be to risk the wrath of those who could stop you, stop me. Trust yourself. Trust what is inside you. Trust who I have sent to you." A nearby explosion rains debris upon them. "When the moment comes, do not hesitate. Now, go back. Go to your rest and leave this place!"

More evasions... more half-truths. A kind of reckless anger overtakes her then, swallowing her fear. She's staring up at a man who has manipulated so very much of her life. She burns to know what that factory holds. And so she assumes a defeated slouch.

And the instant he relaxes, she's past him, bolting for the factory that calls her. It seems to her that she flies, her feet striding but never finding purchase as her reckless dash brings her into a fresh darkness. But she knows where the walls will be and where the door will open. She has been here before.

The Contact is hard on her heels, his wordless voice demanding she stop, but she's already at the door to hell and is flinging it wide.

At the center of things, a blinding brightness pulses, a steady vibration around which yet more of the horde stand. They seem in prayer, their souls bent to a united desire. They and the world around them are bathed in that blue brilliance, its magnitude too grand for human eyes to witness. But that is not what fills her with awe. It is alive...

If this is her world, subject to the laws she knows, she does not need to fear any of this. But this isn't her world. She's touching something now, something that belongs to an elsewhere, to other rules. The faceless turn to her, hunger and anger warring in them. Entering will show her a world's fate. Entering will show her the mind of god. Entering will see her killed.

Nightmares chase her from that place, chase her out and down the rubbled road, their keening calls calling others to the hunt. She tries to fly over the earth, as she did before, but her earlier speed has vanished. The Pull, so near its source, its reason for being, slows her to an impotent crawl. *Go back,* it whispers at her, as the ruined street beckons. *Go back and finish it.*

It's an airborne demon that catches her, slamming viciously into her back and driving her into the pavement with the force to send her senseless. It rips at her, claws and teeth tearing, seeking to snuff out that spark of life which sustains every living thing.

She's defenseless, arms cast weakly upon the ground, legs limp and numb as the thing's claws pierce through flesh and bone, churning deeper with savage single-mindedness. All that's left to her is her scream.

She feels a rushing, as of a great wind. And then, someone is above her, smashing aside the soulstealer. She flops to her broken back, looking up... the Contact's resignation is swimming in her field of view.

"Go," he whispers to her soul, a great finality in him. "Go." And then he turns his back to her, confronting the wall of attacking nightmares.

She never sees the clash, sensing it only as a conflagration of forces that buffet her as she slithers for safety. He has given of himself that she might live and do what is within her to do. She calls out for freedom, straining for that other place she barely remembers, knowing it is her only hope of leaving this.

Seized by a piercing stiffness from her shoulder blades to her knees, Evan comes to in the guest room's only chair, uncushioned wicker which does absolutely nothing for the bruising she knows she'll find up and down her back. Or will it be claw marks? Is she bleeding out even now? No, the Garibaldi being thrown into the road...that is the culprit, not some silly dream.

She stirs from under her blanket. One breath and she knows it by its heavy scent: Morgan's leather coat, its reassuring bulk giving her the courage to force open sleep-caked eyes.

"Bad dreams." Morgan should be lying down; she should be in bed! That is, after all, why Evan crammed herself into this chair to sleep, so her thrashings wouldn't aggravate her shadow's injuries.

Instead, the stubborn lupa has dressed and is sitting up, a noteslate, confiscated from the nightstand, poised on her knee. Her bandaged left hand holds a laser pen, her thumb rhythmically clicking it on and off.

Evan's groan is apparently a signal for Morgan to show her the slate: 'No!' 'Factory,' 'Paradise,' 'So many!!!' 'Get off me!' 'No!!!' "Also something about a frog becoming king. I didn't be catching." Her slight smile is almost playful.

Words on a slate... They're like the casualties of a war observed from the safety of the living room. They aren't real, not unless they're being experienced first hand, seen through human eyes. Stiffly, Evan rises and stumbles to the room's small window. Her left foot is asleep and swollen while her ribs feel as though the Garibaldi had spent the night squatting on her chest. Anxious hands draw the curtains to reveal. "Oh, for the love of the Savior!"

Last night's deluge has continued into her day of judgment. The heavy sky, with its bloated clouds, lets through only faint skeins of sunshine, whispered promises of enlightenment denied by grayness. Rain sheets from the roofs of nearby buildings, plumes from passing cars, and soaks the bedraggled pedestrians hurrying through the morning gloom. She can't remember her last sunrise.

"Did I snore too?"

"You be all right. Heard worse."

"I'm happy I amuse you," Evan's hand sketches little designs on the window's moist glass, circles within circles, until she's reduced to just a single point. "It's today... It's really happening, one way or the other." She doesn't need confirmation; the Pull declares this truth. It's so strong now, separating her insides, demanding her compliance. No way she can rip it out now, not without lethal consequences. She is the lamb; she knows where the slaughter is.

She hears Morgan grunt, the floor creak as it takes her weight. Careful, painful steps coming toward her, and then she feels the weight of a warrior's hand on her back, slipping up to her shoulder, trying to squeeze. "Look at me," Morgan whispers, her face a map of hurt. "You have a job. And you will do it because you know it be right, because you know it be meaning something. Remember what you been through. Remember what got you here. And when the time be coming, when the moment hits, no flinching, no hesitating."

"That's what he said..." Evan shivers. "So you've never hesitated, huh? Never made a mistake?"

"Oh, I be making mistakes, many, many of those. Mistakes near got my leg blown off. I showed you. Benefit from my being stupid. The rehab be a bitch."

"Your knee," Evan tries to smile, but she can't savor the banter. The memory of helplessness before that demon, ripping at her soul, trying to numb her forever... "If we're going to do this," she whispers, "we have to be more than we are."

"We'll be finding a way. I been in worse scrapes than this."

Unlikely. But that Morgan had made the effort to reassure her meant a lot. Evan brings her hand up to find Morgan's on her shoulder, gripping her in common bond. Purpose settles over her like a cloak.

"Get dressed." Morgan is first to pull back, lifting a splinted finger to stroke across Evan's cheek before she turns away. "Francis turned up an hour ago."

"Thought you didn't like him."

"I don't have to be liking him to know he'll be doing what it takes. All that matters." Her shadow starts stiffly for the door, to grant Evan some privacy. She tries to hide it, but each step is painful enough to bring tremors to her hands.

"Are you going to be okay?"

Morgan pants as she reaches the door, turning back to look at her with bruises around her sunken green eyes. "When I be getting what I need..."

Stims. "Isn't that dangerous? You just came off them. I'm... I'm surprised you're awake at all."

"You don't be worrying about that," Morgan whispers. "You don't be worrying about that." And her scarred shadow backs out of the room.

Their war room is a couch and a coffee table. All of Zia's effort to create a warm and welcoming home go for naught on this, the grimmest of days. It's mid-morning now and night's pall still lingers, blanketing the windows and lingering in the living room's unlit corners.

Francis, carrying coffee in from the kitchen, stops at the sight of Evan. He frowns, unable now to hide his worry, the uncertainty of his footing here. But whatever questions she has for him, of their past, this present, and her future, will have to wait. Their eyes meet and she is first to look away.

Four steaming mugs and a handful of aging rolls plucked from Zia's cooler rest on the coffee table now. Four, not three.

The mistress of the house stands by the blurred window, drinking in the deluge as if its digestion might release hidden truths. Zia turns at Evan's arrival, watching as a hobbled Morgan painfully follows.

They're all looking at her now, looking to her, for guidance, for leadership. She is no general, no leader of men. She had hours to work herself up to speaking at the wake and even then it'd been shame of failure that got her up there. A speech, to convince her friends to pitch in on her destiny? She opens her mouth without the slightest idea of what will come forth.

"The where's 12th and Paradiso. It's an old factory. When's around midnight." She scans their determined faces. "It's gonna be ugly."

She sits, cradling her mug as she tells them of what she's seen, last night and in dreams past. That not one of them has so much as a blink for her at the revelation that she's been receiving instruction in her sleep tells her everything she needs to know about the insanity of these last twelve days. But then, for them, maybe it's all in the outcome. If tonight they find nothing, then tomorrow, there'll be four padded walls and a smooth-talking therapist waiting for her. But if reality matches her dreams...

As she brings them up to speed, Morgan staggers to the bathroom, returning with fresh bandages. Silently, she sits near the darkened window, gingerly pulls her loaned sweatpants down to her ankles and proceeds to immodestly change her bloody bandages, leaving Zia incredulous.

"What will we be up against?" Francis is on a couch opposite Evan, the coffee table between them. He's projecting his customary composure, but Evan sees through it now, sees the lie in those eyes.

"I'm not sure. I sure hope it isn't the things in my dreams." She has the urge to cross her fingers.

"Your mind is interpreting and giving life to your fears," Zia psychobabbles, unable to take her eyes from Morgan's grisly work. "It's not real. It's the embodiment of a threat."

"I hope you're right," Evan shudders. Not a single good look at the hissing, spitting nightmare, but she can still feel its claws, its alienness, its conviction. Loosing that upon the world... "We all better hope you're right."

"So, what do we do?" Francis asks, this time of Morgan.

Her shadow stares right back, something like anger or condescension flickering in her feline eyes, a flash, there and gone, her hands not pausing in their work. Those legs... Evan can barely look at them, mashed up like they've been some shark's chew toy. And Evan figured she knew from tough...

Francis waits her out.

"I was told there be a window of time," her shadow grunts. "From now 'til zero hour, at which point, if Evan not been and done what needs to be done, it be game over, for us anyway. So, tactically, being that they've failed every time they come after Evan, and being that the hour is close, you wanna be falling back, protecting home. That factory be ground zero for zero hour and they will be guarding it with all they got: on the roof, in the alleys, up the street, across the street. They be covering every approach." She swallows, applying a new bandage. "When we go in, we be going in hard and with heat."

"How do you mean hard?" Zia whispers.

"Well," Morgan smiles savagely, "other than a Conplast barricade, there be no defense against the wired car. Big. A cargo van, or a truck, something with horses. The look I got of that place? No upgrades I saw which tracks. Keeping a low profile, until the moment be coming and you be making your move."

"In the dream," Evan winces, "it wasn't much on the inside either, hollowed out and something..." She looks away.

"Well, Evan and I both have had run-ins with the shadier elements," Zia says, eying Morgan. "Private deliveries, after hours stuff, no questions asked, get paid triple the rate... I know where we can get some guns, but it's going to take me most of the day to track it down. And money will need to be on the table."

Zia had only been speculating, musing, but Morgan's immediately into one of her coat's many zipped pockets, coming out with a small brass key which she tosses between Zia's feet. "Storage locker, 1867. It be on Dogwood Street. You be finding it stuffed with boxes, books mostly. Box on the bottom left, under the dirty mags? $20,000, cash."

Zia had started down to fetch the key when the figure freezes her in place. A moment of perfect stillness and then, gingerly, as if it's the trigger for a bomb, she scoops the key, giving Morgan her best, hard stare. "Who the hell are you?"

"We be needing a distraction that be drawing their attention away from the van. Back door, something big... Low profile don't mean no profile. We be walking into the hive and there are gonna be surprises."

The enormity of it, what rides on a single night's adventure, is crushing to Evan and Zia who haven't lived lives hardened to the necessities of what must be done. But for stoic Francis and battle-hardened Morgan? There's only grim determination, not a moment's softness.

"I'll take care of the vehicle," Francis volunteers. "I'm sure I can rent something that'll suit us."

"A few things at my place we be needing," Morgan murmurs to Evan. Her grisly medical efforts are complete now, so up come the sweatpants, pulled up by hands shaking noticeably now. There's a hunger in Morgan's eyes, a need for a fix she can't afford to shake. Her lips quiver.

Evan nods, worried.

"So, it's done," Zia hisses out a breath through clenched teeth. "Can't go to the police because they'll lock us up; can't go public for all the chaos; can't go to the hills for fear of being wrong. Guess we're boxed in, huh... Meet at the bar when we're ready."

"Johnny would've loved this," Evan's mouth works its way into a nervous smile. "This is civil disobedience at its best."

"And Carter would've turned us all in," Zia smirks back.

Evan and Zia look at each other. To be two more than they are...

Evan slowly stands, taking a minute to stare at her friends. All of this, everything they plan to do, everything that will happen, everything... It rides on her say so, rides on her willingness. But she won't get it done without them. She knows it as surely as she knows the Pull will throw back up any food she's stupid enough to put down. She should have words for them, words of gratitude.

"Okay," she whispers. "Okay..."

25

The heat wave is a dim memory.

It had looked sufficiently grotesque from the shelter of Zia's apartment. To actually be in this foulness is quite another tale. Swollen clouds eject fat raindrops at such speed that the downpour has become a wall of gray. The wise find protection under ready umbrellas, leaving the surprised to suffer.

Evan has a brief, mournful thought for her Yager as she summons a cab. All the leagues, all the deliveries. That assemblage of titanium and rubber had been more loyal than a dog, and she'd left it to rot in the street. But sentiment doesn't keep you alive, does it? She helps Morgan into the waiting car.

At Morgan's masochistic request, their eastern Eurowan driver deposits them three blocks up from her apartment. "Always be coming at a place from a position of strength," she tells Evan as they disembark and watch the taillights disappear.

"Fuck that," Evan shouts over the roar of the rain. "You just like pain!"

Morgan smiles and hobbles ahead.

The apartment is as they'd left it. Evan immediately goes for the thermostat while her pained shadow, face set in rigid concentration, bangs into her tiny bathroom. The light winks on as Evan finds her old clothes washed and left on Morgan's unused bed. She changes into her last possessions on earth. The silver top and the slate pants won't make her invisible in the night to come, but maybe a black hoodie over top will help that some. If it comes to dying, she's not going in another woman's clothes.

"You need help?" The bathroom door is partially ajar and, as Evan moves to it she sees, reflected in the mirror, a sight that has her palm striking at the door, opening it the rest of the way.

Morgan had gone straight for the medicine cabinet to replace the stims she'd lost in the accident, and now the fresh bottle has been pitched into the wastebasket, its precious contents spilled, like a blue wave, across the vanity. So many pills that Morgan doesn't seem to care that a fair portion have slopped into the sink, filling the drain. No, there's only room for hungry relief in her eyes as she gazes upon her sea of blue nirvana, her worshipful hands gathering a small mountain of the disks and shoveling them into one of her jacket's many pockets.

"Morgan!"

Their eyes meet through the medium of the mirror, her fear clashing with swirling green pools in desperate need of a fix. The consequences of this abuse, longterm... She doesn't hesitate in the slightest, popping two, forcing them down with a gulp of water straight from the tap. And just as it had been on their first night together, back in an apartment that's now rubble, the reaction is chillingly swift. Her wounded eyes soften, her battered mouth loosens and her crippled posture turns fluid; liability to lethality in maybe a minute.

"C'mon," the mouth curls its way into a slow, dangerous smile. "Got something to show you."

It turns out to be the back of the bedroom closet. Evan shifts nervously behind the tall, drug-fueled creature tearing out a rack of meager clothes to find and free a cardboard box whose lid quickly thumps to the floor. Newspaper, underwear, and books are all tossed aside to find, nestled at the bottom, three lines of green-silver eggs, each the size of a human fist. A quick count makes 24 in total, in three groups of eight.

Tucked next to the serene grenades is an unmarked box wrapped in black cloth. Ceremoniously, Morgan sets this at her feet before retrieving one of the bandoliers and turning to give Evan its weight.

She has to sit down. Evan hardly feels the made bed beneath her as the bandolier splays across her lap. The only sound is her heavy breathing as the final piece of her new reality falls into place. Overwhelmed, she plucks one of the destructive fruit and gazes at it, slowly rotating it in her hands.

"Ever fired a gun?"

"No," she shivers.

"Well, we see what Zia be getting you, but I'd be sticking with those. Pull the pin... throw it where it be needing to go, duck and cover. Pull, throw, cover. Simple..."

"I'm going to need a bigger jacket..."

As Evan tries to return the bomb to its home, she bumps the bandolier which now starts to slither to the floor. A yelp and she's snatching for it, and forgetting that she holds one of the bombs in hand, dropping it instead.

Evan's heart is pounding louder than the thump the bomb makes when it hits the floor, sitting there, innocent, as if it isn't capable of annihilating both of them in a heartbeat.

"Oh, Savior," Evan pants.

And then the rich wave of Morgan's laughter is rolling over her, filling the bedroom.

"Don't... That wasn't funny!"

"Oh, I not be so sure. Your face..."

"Lupa..."

Later, Morgan has laid out an arsenal on her coffee table. Accompanying the grenades is an impressive collection of blades that her shadow intends to sheathe on her person, though there cannot be enough places for all twelve knives. And, in the middle of it all, the black cloth box which has been joined now by a like-wrapped friend. Morgan prowls from the kitchen with an ice-cold bottle in her hands.

"Been waiting to use this for awhile. Won't be getting us too far down the line, but..." She pours the near-clear liquid with careless skill. It seems, along with restoring some of her color, her high has steadied her hands, but for how long? "Tell me something," Morgan smiles, "Any regrets?"

"Are you kidding, I regret everything!" After her last bout with Adelsons, Evan's reluctant to indulge. But then her thoughts brush against what lies before her and she's accepting the proffered glass and putting its rim to her lips. The beautiful, ice-cold burn finds her throat. "At the first sign of trouble, I should have blown every cent to my name on... on something! I should have done something! Thrown a party, anything. And then run like hell. Instead, I... Well, I run around like a headless chicken, jumping at every shadow, worrying over every sound, wondering if I've lost my damn mind..."

Morgan snorts.

"But I mean, more broadly? About my life? I dunno. When you spend your days running, something funny happens. You never think about what you're doing, the time you're wasting. You're looking ahead to the next thing which means, of course, you're never looking to the now. And you know, mostly, I was happy. I wouldn't think about getting screwed by the universe, or god, or whatever." The second swallow goes down just as sweet.

"But then there'd be a night. It'd be raining and I'd be rolling home. And I'd get inside and it'd be so dark. I'd look at those photographs, my photographs, and I'd see it. I'd see all of it. Carter and Anna marrying and having two kids, living in some great house he built from the foundation. Johnny pounding that drum of his 'til it breaks him and sends him somewhere warm to settle and write about what all he's done, handing the burden of it onto the next ones. Zia getting her grad degree in psychobabble and teaching. And Francis would... well. Anyway, and there I'd be, sitting in that bar, wondering how I'd been left behind."

"And now?" Morgan sprawls at Evan's feet, a jaguar at rest, a glass in her hand.

"Aside from being mad as hell about the obvious?" Evan looks away. "I dunno. I wish I'd done more. I wish... I'd seen more of the world. I wish I had more time, but maybe that's what everyone thinks when they feel like they are staring at the end."

"But mostly? I keep thinking about people: the cabbie, the single mom crossing the street, the bum on the corner, the punk playing in Astrocade. I think about Bernard and the woman who runs the Shanesberry Hotel and even my scrot clients, my *unpleasables*, you know? I think about what might happen to them if I don't... I regret that it's me. I regret that it's happening at all. I regret that I couldn't do this for Carter and Johnny. I regret the thing in my gut that pulls me to that... place." She drains her glass.

"You know what's funny though? If I do this right? If we do this right? No one will ever know, right? I mean, life goes on as normal, everybody doing their thing. I mean, nobody will believe me if I tell the tale, right? Saving the world? I just said it and *I* think it sounds nuts. But if we screw up? If we don't get this right? Then I dunno, but I'm figuring that someone'll be sizing me up for some serious blame and life as everyone knows it goes to hell. Tell me where, exactly, the fair is in that."

For Evan's incredulity, Morgan has a smile. "There be no fair, not anywhere." Heedless of the stims, she polishes off her drink, setting the glass on the table. "I came out of a place where you had to be hard, you had to fight for everything. And I learned how... I be so good, I never doubted I be doing what I be doing. Could've gone army, could've done it straight, but it wasn't in me, never was. I seen war, I seen people fight and die for what they believe in, knowing their names'll never ring out. Yeah, a name'll be etched in a wall somewhere, but that be it: no news at six, no heroic sacrifice. Just gone, thrown away by a world gone stupid over glitz and glam. To be paying that price, that ultimate price, knowing that no one will ever sing songs about you, knowing no one will ever know your name? Time was, I thought that foolish, stupid... dying for someone else's war. But I was wrong. Looking at you, seeing you? No glory, no legacy, no parade... Your name will never be ringing out. Your name won't even be finding a wall somewhere. That don't be foolish. That don't be stupid. That be the purest act." The intensity in Morgan's face will not allow Evan to look away. "That be the purest sacrifice."

Gooseflesh riots along Evan's arms. "You got me in the ground, huh?" Her laugh is nervous. She has to numb the sting in her eyes and push down the emotion riding up her throat. "Well, if I do get this done? That goes to my family, Johnny, Carter... they've been my rock. What comes of me goes to them."

"Well, you be telling them, Zia at least. You never be knowing how nights like this play."

"Yeah." Evan needs to stop talking about this now. "Anyway, how about you? How you holding up, Morgan the Machine? If a car can't stop you, what can?"

Her shadow smiles, understanding. As for her fitness, the sleek way she flows to her feet leaves no doubt. Her grace may have been purchased at the expense of abusing pharmaceuticals, but that's tomorrow's problem. Tonight... Tonight...

***

The specter of another workweek looms over the Iguana.

These last few precious hours of weekend serenity find the bar at its lowest ebb, a circumstance only worsened by the downpour outside. Of those who are here, most are men, unlucky stragglers looking at a last shot at glory before the week turns over. Little chance of that. But for Evan and her crew, the only women here are serving the drinks.

The replay of a laconic motor race plays beneath the conversations and the clink of glasses that is the soundtrack of the Collins Street bar. The reality screen is fixed to a contest to find the next great porn star. Unsurprisingly, this draws far more interest than the news feed which has ghoulishly attached itself to some girl just liberated from some scrot's backyard bunker where he'd imprisoned her for the Savior only knows how long. Typical that the media has found the tortured faces of the girl's parents, cameras demanding comment. Evan shares a disgusted look with Morgan coming in behind her. And these are the ones she's been asked to save...?

Zia and Francis are already at their table, untouched waters before them. It's all so familiar, the way Evan pulls her coat off and slings it over the back of the chair, the feel of the polished wood under her hands, the smell of this place that's been the setting for so much.

Molly is here, murmuring something to Zia. She turns as Evan sits down. The bartender's been hollowed out by the deaths. Ugly bags under reddened eyes suggests she's slept less since that night than Morgan. Gazes, connecting for a quiet, reflective moment.

And then she's pulling back and away, letting them complete their new circle.

"How did it go?"

"The van's in the parking lot," Francis murmurs around a sip of water.

"And I had some luck as well." Zia's grim smile blends satisfaction and consternation as she hands Morgan the key to the storage locker. Her shadow taps Evan's shoulder and swiftly leaves the way they'd come.

Evan answers their confusion with a toothy smile. "We didn't want to show up to the party empty-handed. That'd be downright disrespectful."

"She doesn't have the van's key," Francis balks.

"And you think she needs one?"

By the time Morgan returns from her task, Evan has ordered them a round. She'd come with the intention of keeping her mind clear, but none of them, not even Morgan, has ever touched danger like this. A strange buzz is rippling through her, exhilaration. And as she tastes it, as she understands it, she begins to get the allure of the job, the street, the con. She feels almost alive as she lifts her glass.

"I was thinking 'to success', but that's not quite it." She meets their eyes, lingering longest on her shadow who sits now in what had once been Carter's chair. "We're nothing like perfect, us... our little planet out in the middle of nowhere. We make mistakes, we squander opportunities. Hell, we squander our lives, some of us, caught up in the endless going from here to there, never stopping in between. We don't... get to have any control over who wins and who loses, over who stays and who goes, over who lives and who dies, much as we'd want it to be otherwise. But in the end, this is what we have, this... This is what's ours, in all its flawed glory. And if we don't defend that..." Nerves choke her voice. "So, to the future, with its trials and its triumphs.

"The future..."

"Good speech, coach," Zia snorts, setting down her frosted glass. "Where'd you rip that from?"

Evan smiles.

They are quiet then, reflecting upon the past and speculating on what's ahead. It's one thing to make plans in the comfort of a living room; it's another to carry them out. Looks are exchanged as they endure this tense, difficult waiting, a waiting in which there's plenty of time for Evan to fixate on the Pull inside her, that now constant demand for action. But she's at least keeping the Roots down anyway. The minutes just crawling along and no one knowing what to say...

"This be about ten years ago, before I be getting smart and working out there be other ways of paying the bills," Morgan says as she shifts in her chair, eyes glinting. "I be sent east to extract this Eurowan asset who annoyed the local authorities who now be wanting him ditched. Must've cut a sweet deal with his Eurowan masters to get me on. I don't be coming cheap..."

"Not what I heard," Zia smirks.

"Alright," Morgan smiles, conceding the point. "I get tooled up: hair extended, skin darkened, eyes get contacts, the whole deal. I even be wearing the conservative dress. No one be looking twice, right?"

Evan chokes. "Now that, I cannot picture."

"Anyway, I contact him, code through the local paper he knows to be reading. He gets replies the next day with the location of the meet. Everything be fine, that is, 'til I be getting there. And this guy, big guy, 300 pounds, chins. Me and him... Like we having spotlights on our backs, that badly matched. But if that not be enough, this guy be having, no word of a lie, forty cats with him, forty! Nonsense about them being sacred... This asset be looking at a firing squad if I don't be extracting him and he be standing there, with his chins, telling me that he's not leaving without these cats of his."

They're smiling as Morgan pauses for a sip. "So, I be telling him, 'you can get other cats.' And he be shaking his head, telling me there be no way he be leaving without his anointed, sacred, 'breeding like rabbits' cats. And I be saying to him, 'how exactly am I supposed to be doing this with your little herd here? How am I to be doing that?' And you know what he be saying to me? He point at me and he be saying... 'no one stop you and you look like dog.'"

And all of them are laughing, even Francis. Evan tries to control her smile and fails. "Did that actually happen?"

"You be calling me a liar?"

"No, ma'am," Evan snaps a mocking salute. "You got him out?"

"Of course I did," Morgan is affronted. "I always be getting them out, Evan, always..."

"Well, that's... that's something I guess." Evan has to look away as she stands, kicking back her chair a pace. "Bathroom..."

'You look like dog...' For a second it'd felt like the old days. It's different; it'll always be different, but maybe that'll be okay at some point.

Business done and hands washed, Evan quits the bathroom, ready to finish her beer, when the closing of the bar's back door catches her eye. She stands in a carpeted hallway which sees most of its use from trips to the bathrooms and journeys into the alley for those in need of a private smoke. Not ten steps separate her from the quiet hum of the common room to her right; not fifteen steps between her and freedom to her left.

Some compulsion drives her left, boots pressing into carpet. Her palm cracks open the door.

The drenched alley stretches 20 feet to either side, the brick wall opposite tagged by nonsensical graffiti and forgotten flyers sodden beyond legibility. Somewhere, thunder rolls as she watches the rain spill along filthy pavement. A few neglected crates are her only company.

She gets it then, why she's here. No stretch of storm-swept, garbage-strewn alley has ever been more inviting. Torrid black clouds skid across a sky of tuneless gray, threatening to soak her at any second and still she feels temptation's kiss along her skin.

The dreams, the warnings, the Pull, the explanations, the layered reality... She knows so little of it, the big picture. And what little they'd granted her, she hadn't been ready for. They hadn't asked her. They hadn't sought out her permission. They decided; they demanded; they insisted, telling her how it would be. They frightened her with the cost of failure and never hinted at the sweetness of victory. They take everything, everything, in their need to set right something she barely understands and then they are furious at her for digging in her heels and asking questions and wondering at the fairness of it all.

Ten steps... ten steps, and the night's beckoning, willing to cloak her in its anonymity, in its generous gloom. Ten steps, willing to forget all of her big talk from earlier, all her resolve, willing to let it all burn on the...

"Evan?"

She jumps, spinning round and letting the alley door ponderously close behind her. Zia stands a few feet from the ladies' room, quizzical stare fixed on her. "What's goin' on?"

"Saw someone," she tries to smile. "Just...wanted to make sure it wasn't anything." Her hands sting with sudden sweat.

"Okay," Zia shrugs before palming her way into the bathroom.

26

It's time.

They had shared with each other, in these last few hours, memories, stories, and jokes told in the hopes of avoiding the stare of what lies before them. Time had, at least for Evan, momentarily lost its lease, stalling her in an endless moment. She'd glance up at the old clock over the bar and note the passage of mere seconds when it had felt more like hours. The wait had been a misery she'd wish on no one.

Now, it is half past eleven bells and her symptoms intensify. Anxiety doesn't just sweat her palms now; it is forcing her heart to a gallop. Nerves tear and churn her guts until she's once more bent over a toilet and watching her internals swirl away.

Then back out to the common room for one last look around the place: the old tables, the tropics on the walls, the screens behind Molly, faithful Molly. Evan gives the bewildered woman a hug.

After all that time... "Be good," she whispers into the bartender's ear. "It wasn't your fault."

And not for a second has that unrelenting Pull abated, not even when she's going. It yanks her from the bar, quickens her pace to the van where she finds the doors locked. Having to wait for Zia to make her own goodbyes, then Francis. And now they come, the doors unlocking, and she can scramble inside.

Francis takes the driver's seat, Morgan riding shotgun, Zia in back next to Evan who stares balefully at her shaking hands. No command on earth can get them to stop. She's really doing this.

Her crew isn't immune to the moment either. Morgan had swapped Zia's borrowed sweatpants for loose-fitting cargo pants which have an endless multitude of pockets stitched about the thighs. The professional among them is anxiously stuffing those pockets with knives, pills, a spare gun, and ammunition. And all the while, her green eyes are constantly quartering her surroundings, tensely seeking external threats.

Francis is, as always, an enigma. Why had he taken an interest? Why had he stuck with her? But she knows why, doesn't she? It's in his eyes. Does he regret it? Whatever he sacrificed for this? His face, which normally gives away very little, gives away even less now, fixed as it is in grim purpose. A jacket of a hunter-green wool atop a pair of brown slacks makes the man look more the fuddy-duddy professor than the man of action he's volunteered to be.

Zia forgoes nervousness for anger. A blue windbreaker keeps the rain from her lucky, black Infinitas hoodie. A pair of black jeans cover knees that bang against one another in irritation. Here sits her oldest friend, with whom she's shared dreams and rides, crappy days and crappier nights. Out of loyalty she is here. Loyalty... is there anything stronger?

What she's asking of them... when had it changed? When had she allowed them in? When had she stopped trying to zero the collateral damage? Johnny and Carter? Or are there just things too big to do on your own?

"Last outs..." She takes a last look at the Collins Street bar in all its waterlogged glory. Ian winks wisely from his perch over the door.

"I be in."

Francis nods gravely.

Zia glares out her window before turning inward. "I'm in," she snaps.

"Okay." Evan's deep breath fills the van. No more time... "Let's go."

***

They've traveled uneventfully into Little Harbor and are now, according to the filth-splashed street signs, only a couple minutes out. Zia turns in her seat to retrieve the goodies their combined efforts have collected. Evan hands up to Morgan the cloth-wrapped box the soldier had earlier so reverently handled. Then it's her turn to reach in and fill the pockets of her pea coat with three of the silvery ovals. A fourth she holds tightly in a left hand white with stress and purpose. Zia passes her a gun.

A grim gray, the pistol glows in the passing streetlight. It's cold in hand, heavy as if it knows what rides on its use. Evan starts to shake her head, but Zia is having none of it.

She's never held a gun before, but purposed fingers swiftly familiarize themselves with its lethal grace. Down through history, skill and strength have been prerequisites for killing, to heft a club, to dance with a sword, to fire a bow, all requiring years of training to forge an understanding between mind and muscle. None of that means a damn thing to the gun which needs only clear eyes and a steady hand to deal out death. No honor, no code...

And yet such is its power that, if her aim is true, if it helps her complete this task, the world will go on. Allow a moment's doubt, a hint of confusion, and her failure will spell their names in blood across a shadowed sky. She finds the safety, hesitates, and flicks it off.

Francis drives with his left hand, pocketing his own arsenal with his right. Then it's Zia's turn, taking the necessary and stuffing what's left into a cloth sack she'd brought for overflow. When she's done, the angry philosopher actually smiles, watching the streetlights pass through a haze of grime and wet.

"Alright." A general's quiet command in Morgan's voice. "You'll be dropping me one street up." She speaks to Francis while her eyes scan the road ahead. "Be giving me five minutes to set up and then you come hard. If I done my job, you'll be knowing it." With care, she hefts her black box. "You be hitting that door and you be hitting it hard and we don't stop until it be over. This gets done, no mistakes. We all be clear on the plan?"

Nods from Francis and Zia come as Evan stares at the woman who's not once voluntarily left her side since they'd met all those days ago. And now, she's going in alone. One bullet from one lucky lookout and down goes the best of them.

"No." The gun shakes in Evan's quivering hand. No, not alone.

Morgan is gentle as she twists around in her seat, reaching back to free the primed pistol from her charge's frightened grip, laying it on Evan's lap. "No arguments now," her voice quiet, her warrior's face kind at the last. "This not be the time to be getting soft on me, Evan. It be the way it is. It be the way it meant to be." She offers her calloused hand.

It isn't for mere mortals to know how much time they'll have with the strangers who enter their lives. Life is electrified by an ignorance to the chance encounters that might beget allies, friendships, loved ones. To be a god, for just one moment, to see how it will play, to assure herself that this won't be the last time she looks into these feline eyes to the battered soul behind them. So much time wasted on spite, and now there's no more time. She grips that scarred hand as hard as she can.

The Pull intensifies now, to the point of nausea, as Francis slows a few blocks up from Paradiso. Their hands slowly part. And her shadow is turning to their driver. "Five minutes," she tells him. "You be hitting that mark..."

"We'll be there." A gruff strength is in the man, a strength Evan's never seen in him before.

"Okay." Morgan scans the faces as if she worries on forgetting them. A hand, beginning to tremble, fished out four last pills, popping the overdose past pale lips. And then she's hitting the door release and slithering into the gray.

Five minutes, the most hellish of Evan's life. For so much to ride on the acts of so few and to not know all, see all... Her hand soothes her knotted stomach. She wants, needs, to throw up.

"She good enough?" Zia stares into the darkness as Francis tensely tracks the time. He'd stopped about two minutes out, the heavy engine rumbling at idle. "She said they were all falling back."

"Better," Evan vows, unable to control her panting breaths. "She's better than good enough." She looks ahead to Francis, calling his name, earning his stare. "Who are you?" No more time left for not knowing.

There's something inscrutable there, something powerful. He is silent.

"Are you... allowed to do this?"

"What the hell are you talking about?" Zia blinks, confused and angry.

Their driver stays silent as he returns his stare to the street. The non-answer is answer enough. Evan begins to cry.

And then there's no more time. Thirty seconds and Francis, his face rigid, hits the gas.

What she sees then, chills her. Minus the devastation, it is the intersection from her dreams. Twelfth and Paradiso, coming up on them hard, its battered hydrant, its drooping lamppost, its ravaged white lines like signposts to her destiny. It asks if she is enough.

Ten seconds. Francis slows, one eye on the approaching intersection, one eye on his watch. Five. Four. Three. Two. One.

"She's good enough," Evan whispers.

Everything blurs.

Francis cranks the wheel and they are screaming into the turn onto Paradiso. A vicious stomp on the accelerator sends the motor yelping and the van rocketing ahead: past derelict warehouses, past gaping alleys, past abandoned lots. Every last inch of dilapidated chain link is as familiar to the Chosen as if this had been the place of her birth. She'd look to reassure herself that the sky is still her own, but her eyes are squeezed shut against the speed of their commitment.

No explosion, nothing but the engine's roar. Had Morgan been caught? Had Evan's boasting of her shadow's skill brought a god's laughter?

Even protected by metal and glass, the sound deafens! The road bucks them a foot into the air, but a determined Francis keeps his foot to the floor as they slam back down to earth, spinning wheels finding traction and launching them onward, even through the shockwave which nearly blasts them off the road.

The Chosen's eyes fly open to find chaos has stirred the hornet's nest. Faces flash, rousted lookouts who turn and flinch at the detonation, weapons at the ready. No time to revel in triumph. The van is making another turn.

With a burst, they blast into the factory lot, leaving behind them all those who've been posted to warn. And there it is, the bricked building exactly as the Chosen remembers it. She can't breathe. She's here and, for now, the stars still shine.

It begins as a throbbing in the Chosen's skull, a sensation she hopes to control, to force down, by closing her eyes against it, but it does not pass. No, the throbbing becomes a pounding. And then the pounding becomes a keening. And the keening rises to a pitch she can no longer hear, just feel, inside, in her soul. It's as if some great force has found the crystalline frequency of her existence, hoping to shatter her into a million, useless pieces. Violently shaking, her hands drop the man-made things of war and fly to her temples, trying to hold herself together, to keep herself...

Dimly, she's aware of the concern of someone near, but the pain has swallowed her world and all the names with it. That sound, that soul-shattering sound, is beating at her from inside the factory, obliterating every thought, every memory. She doesn't hear her scream.

The thing in her skull insists she depart; the Pull at the core of her demands she continue to the factory which, somehow, she knows is on fire. Opposing powers, repelling each other, straining against each other, tearing at each other, and she caught in the middle, their instrument, their toy, their battleground. Faintly, she hears a sound in her scream, senses a shaping of her lips. "Go!!"

She forces her eyes open and sees, through a haze of red, a man looking back at her. Some tiny part of her recognizes his worry, his concern, so she screams the sound again! And this spins him forward, back to his task.

The world seems to burst as the metal missile transporting them hammers into a barricade. A thunderous sound! And then the door is yielding to them, to their charge.

They spill into an uprooted hive through which figures run in every direction, through smoke and fire, fetching weapons to defend themselves, diving for cover from a two-pronged onslaught. And in the center of it all, the bridge.

Her dream had made it a column of blue light that had told all futures. As the dead van grinds to a stop, there's time to find the truth of it. The factory has been hollowed of every unnecessary element to make room for things alien to her eye. A perfect circle of silver-black machinery dominates the cleared area, two dozen units in all, each the size of an oil drum, and spaced evenly and cabled together by black cords as thick as a man's wrist. An identical circle has been suspended from the factory's roof and is in perfect alignment with its brother on the floor. And at the heart of each circle, a disc of deepest obsidian, black menace swallowing the light that deigns to touch it. The heart of the machine, where the door will open and spill out its hell.

She hears cries from those with her, but from that shred of herself she's kept apart from the war tearing her body apart, she senses that it is not the technology that provokes their fear. It's the burning light pouring off the networked machines, a blue so deep they doubt they will ever see another color.

A great energy snaps along the network, vibrating the snaking cables connecting each device. Power, building to a peak. This is her klaxon! This is what sets her skull to clanging. This is what she has been made to end.

"Go," the Chosen calls above the chaos. "Go!"

And they are out from their mangled van, forsaking shelter for the battlefield, moving for those who have tried so hard to end her. They're falling back, regrouping around their creation, the thing that should not be. She ignores the bedlam, ignores the deafening roar of too many sounds. She concentrates only on the eggs in her hands.

Discarded pins fall at her feet as the Chosen hurls destruction into the smoke and the fire. These acolytes, these worshipers of the foreign... they do not belong here. They are a violation of rules so fundamental as to invite a collapse of infinity's house of cards. But it's more than that. These are those who took from her, stole from her, threatened her. They will pay now, for all of it. She will make them pay.

And then she's pushing ahead to that sacred circle as voices call across the thundering tumult: some shouting commands, others appealing for aid. And around her, her family, Francis ahead and Zia to her right, both of them opening up on any enemy they can mark. Francis and Zia... She has their names. She has their names and her own. She hurries before the forces inside her make her forget why she is here.

Seconds... and then lung-charring smoke zeroes visibility, cacophonous explosions tearing at the factory's foundations, launching people and material into the air. A curtain of debris yearns for her blood, but it won't keep her. She's thrusting through to journey's end now, unaware that her numbed hands are stretched out before her, having dropped her weapons of war as they reach. Just... a bit... more.

And then Francis is falling. The Pull screams at her to continue, but her knees have made up their own mind, collapsing her next to him. Blood seeps from his wool-covered chest, pain blazing across his straining face. He shakes his head, a liquid coming from between his lips. "Go," a god's demand in his divine voice.

The part of her that remembers she is Evan wails and beats at the walls of her prison, pleading for the Chosen to return to Francis' side, but her feet are moving, moving her away from the fallen and deeper, covering ground she has somehow always known. She's so focused on what lies ahead, she doesn't see Zia join the fallen.

The battle has occupied those who would've stood between her and her goal, and so there's no one to stop her from stepping over those snaking cables and into the heart of the machine. The instant her foot touches the other side, an alarm louder than the explosions cloaking her peals across the growing ruin. Two more steps and she is on that disc of onyx.

Twenty feet to the center and...

The ground shudders up to meet her as a thing slams into her back, crashing her face-first upon this field of depthless onyx. Her anchorless hands scrabble desperately at a galaxy of smooth, black floor while her attacker tears at her, punishing her. A knee seeks to crush her spine as the hands fetch a weapon to end her journey.

She pushes at the ground as, with every ounce of strength, she hurls herself up and away, pitching the thing free as she slams hard on her throbbing back. Her attacker recovers, pounces, his weapon spinning into smoke.

Recognition lights up the face of her enemy. "You..." His training ensures that there will only be one outcome, her defeat. And so he beats at her, his hands falling like hammers while his face blurs, loses its integrity, morphing into so many faces, so many lives, friends and enemies, from worlds that are and worlds that will never be. The barriers separating realities are falling and she is at the heart of it.

She fights him every way she knows: knee to the groin, hands to the eyes, jab to the throat. And though he's as weaponless as she, he's still stronger. Her nose shatters under a strike from his elbow, her ribs cave under the crashing of his relentless fists. Then, as her world begins to spin, those hands, now bloody, seize her head and smash it over and over into the unyielding disc beneath.

The world blurs beyond understanding as the arctic blue of machine emission shatters into a million sparkling sapphires. She isn't aware of her hands lifting to seize the attacker's throat. For, in that moment of concussed chaos, as the mind flails for who and what it is, the driver takes control. That animal force that had protected her in her grief, demanded she press on, live on, is in command now, driving her claws up and about his own throat, squeezing. She has a mission.

He abandons his effort to break her skull, hands flying to the defense of his own precious throat. Through vision shattered by blood-dappled brilliance, she tastes his desperation. With strength she should not have, her hands squeeze; the interferer shudders and her arms hurl him away. She is their future.

Twenty feet.

The world quakes. More explosions, sending the floor jumping up to meet her. She pitches upon hands and knees and crawls for the center. Webs of that gamma-blue energy form overhead, a process begun before they arrived, a process they cannot stop. The air is on fire.

Fifteen feet.

The bullet slams her face-first upon the onyx with such force that a mind past battered flirts with fainting. The pea coat's faithful wool is no diversion to the thing that pulverizes her back, setting her body ablaze with an agony that whites the world.

Ten feet.

Hands claw at the ground. It takes the Chosen a moment to realize they are hers. Her legs won't move, trapped or damaged she doesn't know which. Rivers of sweat and blood flow free across her face, filling her mouth and falling to the black beneath her. She is blind. Morgan. She'd known someone named Morgan and Francis, and Johnny and Carter and Zia. The names come to her slowly as the system starts to fail. A life... There had been a life.

Another bullet, felt not heard, crashing through her body. Where? She can't feel it above the white noise of her agony. She's pitched onto her back, looking out at a desperate soldier doing what he must, what he's trained to do. The black maw of his weapon, aiming...

And then someone is behind him, pulling his weapon down... the bright flash of a knife across his throat. And the man is falling, leaving a dream behind him, a dream with gray-blue eyes, a dream who nods at her in recognition. A face chiseled by storms stares at her, no joy left, no future left. She came for this, knowing this is how it must be. "Go," mouths the wind-cracked lips. "Go..."

Five feet.

The air sizzles with energy as the body moves on automatic now, crabbing backwards across that black. Something is happening. She blinks up through blood and worse to see, suspended between the black discs, a vortex of blue energy, forming, swirling. Yes... And at its coming, the force repelling her from this place goes silent, allowing thoughts to return and, with them, relentless waves of pain.

She is Evan. She delivers packages to old ladies. She has been chosen. Three souls believed in her enough to get her here. Three souls brought her to the crux of things.

No more. She cannot move an inch more. Beneath her, the onyx hums as the vortex accelerates, spinning faster and faster, burning her blind.

Her dying blood glues her to the disk beneath her, infusing her life into this foreign place. Her hair blows in the wind of one last explosion, touching the center of the gathering storm. Is this the end? Is this why she's lived?

The tumult of energies converge, flex, and begin to expand into a shape she can no longer see. It is happening. It is around her. It is ending.

She forms a thought, but there is no more time. The Pull seizes her, forces her flesh up to that crackling storm. Bathed in blood, she is delivered.

***

There is, Morgan senses, an instant of stillness.

From the cover of one of the strange, silvery units, she watched Evan inch towards that column of agitating energy. The mercenary has done everything to keep back the enemy, firing, at times blindly, into the eerily lit gloom. She's fired so often that Old Faithful's treated plastic had blistered under intense and constant heat. Neither of them are meant for such use.

The soupy fallout from countless concussive blasts fills the factory to its quivering roof. Not only does it set her lungs to screaming, it keeps her from targeting anything more specific than the impression of movement. With no way to tell friend from foe, she'd been forced to draw down on everything, no matter the cost.

But now that's over. The vortex, generated from this sprawl of unknowable equipment, writhes, burning off the smog. Weapons fall absently to sides, as enemy and ally alike watch the die cast. Spotlighted by the climaxing discharge of force, a body arches up and into that blue undulation, causing it to hiss, snap, and tear at the human daring to disrupt it. But it's too late. The world has already ended.

Annihilation...

Morgan is flying backwards and landing on and under collapsing debris as the detonation lifts the damaged roof clear off, sending it to spear the sky. The blast wave crushes the very machines that had generated it, hurling them into the smog where they too explode. Devastation...

Hellfire tears at the walls, at the debris, bringing it all down even as the now ungoverned, uncoordinated lightning rockets upward, limbs of corrugated energy lashing at the night with a violence that transforms the heavens into an electric cerulean storm.

Morgan looks on numbly as shuddering night is made day. The sunless stars glimmer behind a curtain of power that spends itself attacking the quiet clouds. The world is blue and purple and black as small pockets of sky detonate under the force of the expending of an energy no one should own.

Black...

Something had struck her. Morgan returns to herself to find her head throbbing and her mouth filled with blood. She has to get free of this dying place, but commanding her exhausted body to move again is a torture all its own. Not yet... Turning her head so that she might clear her mouth. Just a little more time.

She hadn't been gone long because the factory is still in the process of collapsing in on itself. The blue storm has flamed out quick, reduced to tiny arcs of energy in the burning gloom, yet it lives on in hungry fires that devour in a ravenous search for fuel.

Could Evan have survived... that? Morgan spits more blood before trying to get a fix on the factory's heart. Flame and smoke interfere, but she can peer through to where a shuddering sparking mound of shattered material sprawls out over where the disks once were. Even as she watches, the mountain of debris quivers and settles down into a crater of its own devising. Nothing can live in that. Now, more than smoke stings her beleaguered eyes.

Not a soul is afoot. Morgan has no idea how she'd not been crushed, burned, or dashed into the next life. There'll be time for that. Gathering herself, she thrusts free of the flotsam that had buried her, coughing as she gets her shaking legs beneath her. Her left ankle is done, but then it has good company; for, she'd taken a wicked ricochet in the left thigh during the battle and a straight shot to the right shoulder while mounting her initial assault. But these she ignores. There is one last duty to perform.

Dead lie strewn about her, some gnawed by flame, others crushed by fallen debris, still others cut down by blast or bullet. This will be their tomb. They will rest about her charge like the slain enemies of a great warrior's last stand. It should've been her in that vortex, her with the sins to atone.

She finds Francis. A dead enemy had shielded him from the worst. She slumps to the ground, the stims momentarily holding back the agony, and shakes him. The eyes open, bleary and bewildered. It is over, her voice soundless. But then he's looking about, seeing it for himself. The walls are coming down and there is nothing left.

Together, they find Zia. The blast had crumpled her against the side of a sputtering piece of machinery. They can't wake her and there's no time to consult for a pulse. Wordlessly, they lift her and limp out.

It's a shock to feel cold air. They stagger and collapse on broken sidewalk. The stims are failing and the random firings of overtaxed muscles are prompting spasms beyond her control to end. None of that matters now. The job is done and the bitterness of that thought settles over her like a shroud. Will she ever see her contact again? Will she be able to pay him back for what he's wrought?

On her back now, Morgan watches the dying throes of that factory as rain falls against her burning face. Voluntary movement is beyond her as Francis slumps next to her. Together, as the sirens near, they watch the final collapse, the flames now rising higher than what's left of the building. A pyre, a sight she'll remember for always. Green eyes meet hazel, acknowledging their victory and their secret. Her hand twitches, extends, is gripped.

And then she's falling down that infinite well, the world receding to a point far above her. She welcomes oblivion. It is a place where grief cannot grow.

EPILOGUE

Thoughts drift in the void.

She is someone; that much remains. Memories of faces float out of nothing. And, while she cannot name them, she can recall their import: a serious man with hazel eyes, a hard woman with a gun in her hand, a philosophical friend with a heart too big for her own good. These and more accompany her in this null place that is neither warm nor cold, bright nor black, full nor empty. She sails upon a sea of nothing as she finds her past.

Down a long, warm tunnel she travels, delivered into a world of searing light and jarring sound. Never before has she experienced her birth, never felt herself swaddled and given into her mother's arms, never tasted the happiness of those who had created her. Brought home to a room painted green, she is bathed in warmth and laid to rest beneath a slowly undulating assemblage of colored balls which always seem just beyond her immature reach. These faces... they are made mother and father by dint of a daily routine that brings them to her whenever she makes noises. They are hers. She belongs, safe in a world of primary colors.

Slowly, she grows, crawling then falling, walking, then running. As her skills develop, so does her world. Foreign places beyond the limits of her home are given names: school, park, car, street. She is to spend time playing with others of a size to match her own. She is to understand them, to befriend them. While some are open to her overtures, others shun her. She learns rejection.

As time passes, other problems assert themselves. At home, mother and father, the first and second in her universe, fight. This makes knots inside her belly she cannot undo.

At school, she is asked to learn a range of symbols. These, when strung together, make words and many words make thoughts. Are her thoughts words? There are numbers too.

At the park, she is told not to speak to strangers, which suits her well. She is much happier watching the birds. They can fly. She yearns to fly. If she could fly, she could leave behind the young man with the hazel eyes who always watches her. She tells mother as instructed, but mother never finds the man even though he is there, at the park, many times. Can he fly?

As the memories march on, she sees what became of her. She watches her adolescence unfold frame by frame, the whole knotted together by a grimly imperfect world. The minutiae of life, the petty alliances and betrayals, had obscured greater truths: the souls that had shaped her, the forces that had molded her, and the events that had put her in fate's firing line. Nothing is random; nothing is meaningless.

It's only now, as she revisits her ever-complicating world, that she understands life's test; for to live is to endure the world's endless assault on the flawless innocence of one newly born. The test is to preserve just enough purity in the hope that the unsullied soul can see its way clear to doing the right thing. A life is the management of a constant fall from absolute grace. How much will you lose? How fast will you lose it?

She knows not how the knowing has come, yet it is within her to conceive of what the Contact had told her: the countless reflected worlds, the infinity of reality and life. The tapestry of the universe unfolds before her and its majesty returns her to her final memories.

In that apocalyptic place, wreathed by hell's shadows, she embraces the storm. Its lightning savages her, firing every nerve, destroying every cell, inducing in her an instant of perfect agony. For all her days, something has been building in her, a charge that can no longer be leashed. With her death, it tears out of her, screaming into that vortex of energies, creating an untenable disruption!

An explosion... whiting out her world... rocketing her along connected lines of force. Where is she going? What is she meant for? All dimensions shiver in stress as her blood bears her in, to the root of things.

In a single moment of perfect clarity, she holds the totality of her world: tasting the lives of her eight billion brothers and sisters, feeling the weight and complexity of all of humanity's systems, seeing all the cities in their ceaseless grandeur. There had been other crossings, other violations, all throughout the history of her world. They are determined to have a victory she will turn to ashes. This... ends... now.

The enemy dares to dip its prying fingers into her realm? She breaks all of them, her rage slamming the door to her world. And then she's following the energies back to their source, spilling her into a vast chamber with the same networked circles that once entombed her flesh. Greeting her are strained faces of determined humans who gape at the sight of their own end. For she is now the lightning.

Terror is in them, their eyes widening at the sight of an effort gone spectacularly wrong. They are all in white lab coats smudged with sweat and stress, faces scored by hunger and centuries without sky. They are mice trying to flee the tempest of their own creation. They have touched what should not be, sought what is not theirs to take. They are punished...

Explosions fire the chamber with an inextinguishable burn that blackens and beats at sturdy glass walls, revealing this to be the insulated heart of some greater underground. And as those walls crumble, the souls who had thought themselves safe behind them perish. Under her lethal sweep of energy, desks are smashed into installations that pin the forsaken; papers are blown about in a storm of white, each winking alight for an instant of forgotten glory; powerful computers detonate under a lash of fury their hardened shells cannot withstand. Her inferno erases what should have never been.

On a distant wall hangs an arrangement of flags unfamiliar to her. Her destruction gnaws at the heraldry. The red maple leaf on a bed of white and red is first to fall, twisting away as though there's hope to escape oblivion. Next, the fifty white stars squared on blue, bars of red and white beneath, is torn into the storm, followed quickly by the topmost flag, a white world, encircled by branches, centered on an ocean of blue. They all fall. Into her rage, they fall.

She rises. Neither steel nor rock impede her ascendance into a world not her own. As she abuts the sky, she looks down and finds desolation. A globe once green with life and blue with water is now a desiccated, brown husk of wind-torn plains and sanded hills. But there is past glory here. And so she reaches back for it, rewinding her sight to earlier days, watching water return to the seabeds, watching planes return to the skies, watching cities rebuild themselves across the world.

The shapes of the continents are as she remembers them. But the names of these shining cities: London, New York, Tokyo, and Beijing? And there are more, many more... Her awareness glides up through thinning atmosphere and into near space where the metallic bodies of countless satellites gleam against a brilliant sun struggling to penetrate a polluted sky. It had been these, these before they'd been driven underground, these before desperation had seized them, these who had threatened everything she knew.

Bathed in uncounted stars, she expands. The limitations of the human mind no longer ceilings of her universe. She feels all worlds as a distant, constant throb of life and light. It is yet beyond her to reach to explore, but this will come. She'll savor their similarities and marvel at their differences, knowing she has preserved what had given her life.

"Do you see?"

A man materializes before her. A smooth countenance of tanned flesh enshrining ageless blue eyes. Black hair spills over a broad brow and along the nape of an elegant neck while a day's growth of hair roughens rugged cheeks; the lips part to reveal perfect teeth. A tangible creature in an incorporeal void, he stands upon what seems a cloud that had not been there before.

"Do I see what?" She knows not how she speaks.

"Do you see the pattern? Have you found meaning?"

She nears him, centering her focus upon this anomalous corner of reality. How can he have form and she feel as nothing but a chain of thoughts? "Your man, he did not lie..." She casts about for other anomalies, finding only her void. "I'm dead..."

"Yes. It is not for the living to possess your knowledge. This was always your fate."

"I had to die. From the beginning, I had to die..."

"For the rest..."

She agitates, narrowing her purview until the Man and his cloud are as giants to her, filling her new universe. "Explain yourself..."

The Man glances down at himself as if judging his own appearance. A hand, clean of age, plucks experimentally at the unfamiliar cloth covering his chest. He seems amused, unruffled. "We have never met, yet I know you well and those who came before you. You know my agent in matters temporal."

"The Contact..."

"The Contact... He is as a brother to you, now, having been long ago called to serve, just as you were."

"He was called? Another crossing, from before..."

"Yes, another threat from a very different reflection, as he calls them. He did as you have; he answered. He... will not be joining us, for he has disobeyed me."

"Disobeyed you..."

"He told you more than you should have known, gave you more aid than you ever should have had, and meddled incalculably in matters beyond his mandate." The Man is stern. "By influencing you, he irrevocably altered the futures of two worlds. To interfere on such a level is to violate the profoundest laws."

"Disobeyed you... It was you! It was you who controlled things. It was you who forced him to stay silent, to lead me on like a dog scenting shit. It was you..."

Fury gives her form; she coalesces before him, the pea coat draped about her shoulders, a platform of latticed steel flooring her world.

This development, like her words, displeases the Man. He frowns. "It was necessary. Pollution of the natural order is to be at all costs avoided. To correct the unforeseen, we allow controlled amounts of information to flow, enough to redress the balance. Beyond that, we cannot interfere."

"Why?!" Her hands find her hips. It is good to feel. "You've killed me. There's no reason to hide behind your coward's rules."

For an instant, the Man appears on the brink of dismissing her, but then patience carries the moment. "Many worlds follow a similar path of evolution, regardless of the species." Clouds of knowledge float within his eyes like oceans. "As intelligence reaches a critical mass, it begins to ask questions of its environment that it cannot answer. What does it do when it finds it cannot provide sound answers to its questions?"

She thinks for a moment, staring at that ageless face. "It believes in a greater power?"

"It *invents* a greater power... to which it then ascribes omnipotence and omniscience. For surely someone has the answers to their questions. Why not a being of infinite power and knowledge?" The Man is amused.

"You find that funny?" she asks harshly. "Making billions of people believe in you. You think that's funny?"

"No, I find it innocent." His smile fades. "If the universe were as simple as some intellects would have it, it would be of such insignificant importance as to not hold my interest for an instant of your time. And yet, such simplicity would have avoided the problem you were called to mend."

You're God," she concludes, frowning at his white skin.

"No. Idols given worship by temporal beings are gods. Gods do not seek the answers to their origins. I am not a god. Had I been a god, I would have foreseen the error."

Her arms cross, and her eyes narrow in the expectation of unpleasant revelations. She grits her teeth.

"Just after time's dawning, we lived," the Man murmurs. "When we awoke, there were no planets, no stars." The scale of him shrinks as he approaches her lattice. "The universe was molecular clouds of gases and elements, the building blocks of life strewn across an empty page. We woke knowing we were attached to the beginning. We could see the pattern, we knew of its glorious complexity, and we understood our place in it.

"We are the Gatekeepers. It is as much who we are as it is our destiny. By whose hand the universe was born, we do not know, but it was born incomplete. It was our task to finish the experiment, to build the frames of reality that you see about you now and to observe them in all their varied growth."

"Experiment," she snatches from the stream of his words. The latticework of steel beneath her sprouts spiked fortifications that shield her from the unseen. She feels vulnerable and here the defenses are. Wishes form the formless.

"We believe it so," the Man nods. "It is for every sentient being to believe what they will of what governs. Some of even my kind believe that our creator is, as you might call him, a god. Others feel otherwise. Regardless, we are the children who created reality as you perceive it and we watch events play out across the many reflections, each showing a different path to a different destination. The knowing, the watching, the experiencing, enriches us all. Each of my kind have laid claim to a region. I am responsible for the region from which you came. And that," he smiled thinly, "has kept me busy: many paths, many destinations."

"Your man said many of our reflections had grown life," she nods, gut-punched by the notion of being little more than a rat in a maze.

"Indeed. An incredible will to survive despite the many obstacles arrayed before them. Given enough time, they will adapt to hot or cold, air or water, desert or forest. It is a hunger few can claim. Unfortunately, it is within hunger to defeat reason. This drove your enemy to find a way into your world. They learned the science to cross dimensions, to harvest your energy so as to fuel their lives. Their need overwhelmed their reason."

"You sound like you admire them," she growls. "If you like them so much, why'd you let your little boy help me stop them?"

"It is within us to admire the will without condoning its actions," the Man chastises. "No amount of admiration would have precluded me from sending 'my boy'. We desire that the natural order of things be maintained."

"The natural order?" She closes the gap between them, her defenses disappearing so that she can step her boots upon his cloud. "You stand there, telling me how it is, calm as can be... You've ruined my life, and in the doing, you've changed the course of countless lives. We're all just mice to you, chasing after cheese... Yeah, talk to *me* about the natural order of things..."

"We are all servants. We all have our roles to play." The Man refuses to flinch from her. "If you are the experiment's end, then we are its means. We served our function in the time of creation and now we watch and from that we learn, we experience, we live, we protect, and we maintain."

"And not to interfere... that'd be another rule, right? Oh, but you can interfere to fix what you screwed up. I nearly forgot about that little exception." She will not yield. "How did you mess it up, huh? How did you take all of this power and wisdom and still wet the bed...? Do you have any idea, any idea, what you've done to me, to my friends, to my world?! I've lost everything... and this is *my* reward?! I'd hate to see how you're punishing your son. You've probably got him burning in hell, huh. This is *all* on you..."

"The flaws were unforeseen." The voice hardens. "The first crossing could not have been anticipated. It was never meant to be thus. To cross is to upset a balance so delicate as to shatter the mortal mind to conceive of it. When it first occurred, we, the architects, knew not what to do. There was a great gathering and it was decided that for each crossing one would be given the power to break the bridge. It was upon the Chosen to decide the fate of the crossing, not us."

"How brave of you," she scoffs. "How satisfied you all must have felt knowing that someone else was to clean up your mistake. Meanwhile, you, the one who causes this all to be, stands aside, watching... because that's fair..."

And that finally breaks him. Fierce, the Man comes for her, bringing blazing eyes near enough to block out the void. "For us to interfere, even in this, would be to invite upon you *unending* chaos. For among us, as among any group, there are dissenters who would use that exception to create *more* exceptions, to work for *more* interference, to sow *more* chaos, to be kings, to be gods. These forget that we, too, are servants and it is not for the servant to shine more brightly than that which he serves, for then he *is* a god."

She won't step back from him. "Instead," she whispers, "you let the fates of billions ride on the choices of a single person. You must see the suffering. You must see the countless who are born, hurt, and die, never to know happiness while you stand by. Are we no more than puzzle pieces to you? Are we just a curiosity? Does it give you that good little tickle inside, knowing that you could stop it and never bothering?"

His jaw works in irritation. "You seek justice from an authority that should never give it. To tamper in the way you wish of us would open the door to disaster. To shape reality as we saw fit? To fashion everything in our image? To force servitude and worship from those born of less? We would tear apart reality in a war to prove our predominance. And it would not be us who suffered for it, but you..." Breath huffs from the Man's nose. "We did what we needed to do. The rest is up to you, to them, to decide. It is their future, not ours. We fulfilled our function."

"But that's not quite true, is it?" She has nothing to lose. She is already dead. "You interfere. You just make sure the stink isn't on you. You just make sure it's justifiable to you and yours. No, you took the convenient way, the easy way... What you did with me? That was so you wouldn't feel guilty. Don't pretend it was *anything* else...Well, you got it. You got what you wanted. You maintained your precious balance. All it cost you was me and mine. I'll take that win and maybe, with time, I'll forgive myself, but not for you. I'm not playing your sick game. To have power and not to use it..." She allows her form to slip, letting herself quietly return from whence she'd awakened.

The Contact had asked for her belief, pleaded for her trust. In the end, she had given it in hopes of saving a world deserving of a second chance. And, in time, perhaps this will be enough to soothe her. But to find, at the end of the road, powers capable of righting wrongs, of easing suffering, of granting light to the darkness of ignorance... and to learn that they have, all along, refused to intervene? There are no words for her disappointment.

"You're not ready." The Gatekeeper had been stony through her tirade. Now, he's resigned. Despite her shapelessness, he finds her, follows her. "Not yet..." He lingers, thoughtful. "You will not pass into nothing. We give you knowledge for your service, for what you have proved to us. For as long as you wish, as far as you wish, you may travel. You may watch, you may learn. And perhaps, one day, you too will protect, you too will do your part for order. Watch your friends, see the birth of stars, know the answers to the questions you've long sought. If we have taken from you, then this is what we give back, membership amongst the stars and the knowledge of all the worlds. In time, you will learn."

Resentment still burns, but this is a gift, to go back to her world, to know how it ends.

The Gatekeeper does not wait for thanks. He nods, finding in her a compromise with which he can make peace. And then he is gone, out there, among the stars, willing to listen if she should need him.

The void welcomes her and waits for her commands. For she finds then that she can shape it, bend it that she might see great distances and into the lives of things she's never imagined. In that place, she yearns and the yearning bends the beyond.

Truth comes to her in flashes of moments gone. The first pitches her into the alien lab her fury ultimately destroyed. Amidst the thrum of organized activity, she finds the Contact's familiar face as it oversees the determined bustle. Why is he here? Adorned in the uniform of a military officer, he hands her photograph to a craggy general who studies the gift intensely. At every step, the enemy had dogged her, tormented her, and burned everything she loved.

Why? Why?! Sensing her proximity, the betrayer turns, his eyes searching for her. And when she allows him to find her, when their eyes connect, she drives down into him, finding the truth, his fear that she would not heed the danger if there was no genuine threat to her life. Knowing that, eventually, she would turn to Morgan; turn to him, when she had nowhere else to go. But there's more.

Flash!

The night is dark and the familiar park empty until two men meet near the diamond. Hazel eyes met hazel eyes as the Contact and her oldest friend exchange nods and words. How long had Francis known? How long had they planned for her coming? Had it been a lie from the beginning? Had she been but the means to their end? One to threaten her, one to nurture her, and one to guard her back, and all of it so that she might obey? As her traitors turn, she stares into Francis, ready to pull the truth from him, ready to know the depth of his lies. But then she throws herself from him, from them. No! Friendship is a fiction she will not relinquish.

Flash!

The cramped cell is only one of thousands in the dingy prison. A tiny sink, an un-flushed toilet, and an unfinished floor strewn with dirt are the trappings of a dead man's existence. On a mussed cot sits the vacant-eyed greaseball, an unread magazine splayed across his lap. What are those eyes seeing? Is he watching his purposeless future unfold before him? He deserves nothing less for the lives he snatched from her, from the world. Is he a pawn of the Contact? Another game inside a game? Or did he work on his own, just a coward with chrome in his hand? His punishment will never be enough.

The prisoner shivers, and looks up for the first time in hours.

Flash!

Anna and Lohner have engaged a table at Sarah's, the little seafood place at which Johnny had last dined. The loved ones left behind stare at one another past the umbrella skewering the table's heart, neither possessing the proper words. Their hands slowly meet in remembrance of those who have gone from them. A third joins them. The magenta hair had been allowed to fade, but Evan would recognize that face no matter how many scars it earns in fidelity to friendship. Zia apologizes for being late, offering a hug to each before she sits with them. They are moving on. Lohner looks up as the waitress approaches.

Flash!

Somewhere in the world, an apartment, cramped and cold. Winter happily penetrates French doors carelessly flung open, welcoming its numbing caress. Morgan sprawls on a leather couch, one of the living room's few spartan furnishings. This is a place of metal and stone. Her feline eyes are closed; a drink is clutched in a hand plagued by a permanent tremor... the price of a nervous system fried by stims. She sips from her amber tonic, eyes moving behind lids gone blue with chill. She refuses to shiver. She never shivers. She is alone until... Her beautiful eyes open, her head cocks. Does she hear a sound?

Darkness...

To see and yet to be apart is an ache only time can master. Perhaps, in awhile, she will visit them again, but not soon. She finds herself above her great city, it sprawling beneath her, mantled in morning fog off the water. She watches bio-pulp newspapers flop onto front stoops, taken inside by sleepy residents who glance down at the fiery cover: "Warehouse Explodes As Part Of Suspected Drug War; Mayor Promises Action Against Gangs And Dust." The blight is gone, the factory is rubble, and the lives of the oblivious millions go on as they always have. Her name will not burn across the sky, but she will be remembered by those who matter. That is enough.

And somewhere, down in that place, a woman from another world walks the streets, seeing sights she has never seen, watching lives lived as she never knew they could be lived. Evan hesitates. Then, smiling a little, she sends a thought down to that gray-eyed woman who has survived so much, an image of an apartment wreathed in frost and of a soul in need of healing as much as she.

The void returns. There are other places, other worlds, other secrets. Somewhere out there, those lost by death persist. She will find them now, to heal herself.

Meaning, like the countless stars, beckons.

ABOUT THE AUTHOR

Spencer McLean is an unsighted but insightful author living near Vancouver, British Columbia. He has written several short stories and is a prolific reviewer of books. Evan, published in December 2010, is his first novel. Gnaritas, his second novel, is to be published in 2011.

Made in the USA
Lexington, KY
22 March 2011